"See this? His paws are raw. He's worn the pads right off. The hot, rough asphalt acts like sandpaper on them. Poor thing...that has to really hurt."

Big blue eyes the color of a cloudless sky looked away from the dog and up at him. Eyes filled with sympathy and determination. "I'm going to call Dr. Marshall. Murphy will need some pain medication, and maybe some antibiotics."

As he listened to her make arrangements, he let himself look his fill. The concern on her face did nothing to detract from her beauty. Pale blue eyes were a stark contrast to the mass of ebony curls attempting to escape the clip she'd secured it with. Her skin was fair, her cheekbones prominent, and then there was that mouth, those perfectly pink lips that she pursed when she was concentrating. A man would have to be blind not to want to kiss those lips.

That doctor had better show up soon; if he was alone with the sexy vet tech much longer, he might end up panting as badly as the dog in front of him.

Katie Meyer is a Florida native with a firm belief in happy endings. A former veterinary technician and dog trainer, she now spends her days homeschooling her children, writing and snuggling with her pets. Her guilty pleasures include good chocolate, *Downton Abbey* and cheap champagne. Preferably all at once. She looks to her parents' whirlwind romance and her own happy marriage for her romantic inspiration.

Books by Katie Meyer

Harlequin Special Edition

Proposals in Paradise

A Wedding Worth Waiting For

Paradise Animal Clinic

Do You Take This Daddy?
A Valentine for the Veterinarian
The Puppy Proposal

Visit the Author Profile page
at Harlequin.com for more titles.

Girl's Best Friend

Katie Meyer

Previously published as *The Puppy Proposal*
and *A Valentine for the Veterinarian*

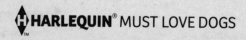

HARLEQUIN® MUST LOVE DOGS

ISBN-13: 978-1-335-69091-3

Girl's Best Friend

Copyright © 2019 by Harlequin Books S.A.

First published as The Puppy Proposal
by Harlequin Books in 2015 and
A Valentine for the Veterinarian by Harlequin Books in 2016.

The publisher acknowledges the copyright holder
of the individual works as follows:

The Puppy Proposal
Copyright © 2015 by Katie Meyer

A Valentine for the Veterinarian
Copyright © 2016 by Katie Meyer

Recycling programs
for this product may
not exist in your area.

Printed in U.S.A.

CONTENTS

THE PUPPY PROPOSAL

Dedicated to:

My parents for giving me a love of books, and my
husband for telling me to write my own already.

All the friends who supported me,
especially Jilda, Rebecca, Elizabeth,
the ladies of The Well Trained Mind
and the incredible women of Hearts on Paper.

All the wonderful veterinary professionals
I've worked with, especially Mary C. Fondren, DVM,
who supported me in countless ways
over the years.

And of course, my agent, Jill,
and the wonderful editorial team at Special Edition,
who took a chance on me.

Chapter 1

He'd almost missed it. Had the setting sun been just a bit lower, the light a bit dimmer, he would have missed it, *it* being the most pathetic-looking animal he had ever seen. The dog—if that was the right word for the wet, filth-encrusted beast limping along the side of the road—was obviously in trouble. There wasn't much traffic right now on this stretch of highway, but the Paradise Isle Bridge was just ahead, or so said the tinny voice of his rental car's GPS. Crossing a highway bridge on foot, or paw for that matter, seemed a dangerous proposition. Besides, it was limping.

But limping or not, it wasn't his dog. Wasn't his problem. He was in a suit. In a rental car. On vacation—well, sort of a vacation. A working vacation. So this grimy creature was definitely not his problem.

Surely it knew the way home or would be picked up by someone that actually lived around here. Not that he was exactly sure where here was, GPS or no. He hadn't passed a single town in over an hour, and the only brief glimpse of humanity had been a roadside stand selling gator jerky and boiled peanuts twenty miles back.

Nic Caruso tightened his grip on the steering wheel as he approached and then passed, telling himself the dog would be fine. But his gaze kept returning to the rearview mirror, where he watched the muddy stray as it slowly hobbled east. Then saw it flinch as a wave of dirty water thrown by a speeding car drenched it yet again.

"Damn it!"

Nic swung the small SUV to the shoulder, slammed to a stop and quickly located the emergency flashers on the unfamiliar dash. It might not be his problem or his responsibility, but he couldn't bring himself to just leave the dog there. Resigned, he undid his already loosened tie, carefully laying it on the suit jacket occupying the passenger's seat.

"Here, boy! Come here now." He used his most authoritative voice, the one that he relied on in boardrooms across the globe.

Nothing.

The darned dog just kept going. So much for doing this the easy way. Nic opened the passenger's door again and retrieved his tie. A quick slipknot and he had an impromptu leash. Great. Somehow, he didn't think Hermès would approve.

"Easy, boy. That's it. Eaaasy…" Nic inched his way across the muddy roadside toward the now cowering dog, careful not to spook him any closer to the highway.

A furry ear cocked in interest. The softer approach seemed to be working.

"Good boy. Come on, that's a good boy. How about I give you a ride wherever you're going, okay?"

A small tail wag was quickly followed by a cautious step forward. Hoping to appear less threatening, Nic crouched down, putting himself at eye level with the cautious canine. Brown eyes watched him warily, but the dog did keep moving in the right direction.

Only a foot away, cars sped by, but Nic kept his focus on the muddy beast in front of him, willing him to co-operate. Only a little bit farther and…

"Gotcha!"

Nic slid the improvised leash over the dog and held tight, just in case he bolted, but the bedraggled beast seemed to have lost his earlier apprehension. A happy, wriggling bundle, he licked and yipped in gratitude. The frenetic thank-you dance gave Nic an up-close study of what appeared to be a border collie—admittedly just a best guess with all the grime matting down his fur. He was a good size, maybe fifty pounds, but from the look of the large paws, he wasn't done growing yet.

"So what do we do now? Any ideas?"

An enthusiastic face-licking was hardly an appro-priate answer.

Nic stood and stretched while he thought of what to do. A week in the heart of Orlando on business, night-mare traffic on I-4, miles of desolate highway and now a muddy dog. When exactly had he completely lost control of his life? The only thing he could think to do was to keep heading for the island, and hope there was a shelter or veterinary hospital still open. Resolved, he started walking the dog along the shoulder of the road, only to be stopped by a soft whimper. Crap. Crouching again, he gathered the grubby canine to his chest and lifted him up. Carrying him to the car, Nic tried to ignore the ooze seeping through his shirt.

"Up you go." Nic held the door open with one hand, and the makeshift leash with the other. No more encouragement was needed; the dog bounded into the rear seat easily. Hopefully, that meant he wasn't badly injured.

Rounding the car, Nic brushed the worst of the dirt and fur off his clothes before sitting behind the wheel. He checked his mirrors and pulled carefully back onto the highway, then rolled down his windows as soon as he was up to speed, hoping to keep the wet-dog smell from permeating the upholstery. He doubted rental insurance covered that particular contingency.

That was a mistake.

Tempted by the open window, the dog nimbly hopped into the front seat and shoved his muzzle into the rushing air. Nic cast a grin at the happy animal's expression—then cursed when he saw the now ruined suit jacket under his muddy paws.

Nic mumbled uncharitable remarks about the pup's parentage until the top of the Paradise Isle Bridge, where he was seduced into silence. From the apex of its span, he could see fishing boats bobbing among the diamond topped crests of the Intracoastal, then the lush green of the island, and beyond that the Atlantic Ocean, where pink-and-purple clouds flamed on the horizon, caught in the last rays of the setting sun. In his rearview mirror the atmospheric show continued, a kaleidoscope of colors, constantly shifting as the orange orb of the sun slipped further toward the horizon. The sight of all that sea and sky managed to melt the last of his work-day tension, leaving him feeling, for the first time in a long time, almost free. Or he would be, once he figured out what to do with the dog.

"Yes, Mrs. Ellington, I can see how that would be upsetting." Veterinary technician Jillian Everett rubbed her temples with one hand while cradling the oversize phone receiver in the other. "But remember, Tinker Bell is only nine weeks old. It's perfectly normal for her to not be housebroken yet… Oh. Well, no, I'm afraid I don't know of any products that will get that kind of stain out of a leather handbag."

A loud snort of laughter betrayed Dr. Cassie Mar-shall's presence behind her.

"Yes, I agree, replacing it probably is the best idea. But, I really think you should consider waiting until Tinker Bell is older before carrying her in your purse for so long. When she's a bit bigger, she'll be better able to control where she, uh, leaves her presents. In the mean-time, just stick to the feeding and training guidelines we sent home and I think she'll be fine. If you have any other questions, I'm sure Dr. Marshall would be happy to answer them at your appointment next week." Jillian mouthed a "gotcha" at Cassie, who was holding up her hands in a "not me" gesture.

"Okay, Mrs. Ellington, we'll see you next week. Have a good night and kiss little Tinker Bell for us. Bye." Jillian hung up and glared at Cassie. "You set me up! You knew what that call was about, didn't you? Why is she calling the veterinary hospital for a poopy purse, anyway? Don't those fancy dog purse things have liners for this sort of situation? Or an emergency number to call?" Shaking her head at the absurdity of the situation, she made a notation in the file and stood to put it in the appropriate place.

"I didn't set you up…exactly. After all, helping with the call tonight was your idea. But yes, Mollie may have hinted at the situation before she left, and I may have made sure that particular chart ended up with the ones you so generously took off my hands." She smiled. "Perk of being the boss, sorry."

Jillian didn't think Cassie's wide grin looked the least bit contrite. But she *was* a great boss, and Jillian *had* volunteered. Cassie had a young daughter to get home to, so when Jillian saw the big stack of files requiring follow-up phone calls, she had offered to take the majority of them. She planned to give Mollie, the receptionist at Paradise Animal Clinic, a piece of her mind tomorrow for that final absurd call, but really, it wasn't as if she had anywhere else to be. No one was waiting at home for her tonight. Or any night. Most of the time, the animal clinic was more of a home to her than her tiny apartment was.

She didn't have any family. Both of her parents had been killed in a car accident, and she'd been too young to really remember them. The last in a long line of her foster families had lived on Paradise Isle, and she had found a sense of belonging here that had kept her on the island long after she'd aged out of the system. She had never been adopted, but the people of Paradise Isle had become a kind of surrogate family. Most of the time, that was enough. But on nights like tonight, when she had nothing better to do than stay late and file charts, she couldn't help but daydream about someday having a real family to go home to.

"I'll lock up on my way out. See you in the morning," Cassie called from halfway out the door, juggling her keys, briefcase and a stack of veterinary trade magazines. She might be leaving the office, but Jillian knew she'd spend a few more hours working after her daughter, Emma, was asleep. Cassie was a single mom, and had taken over the clinic from her father, after he was permanently injured in a car accident a few years ago. Now her parents watched Emma during the day, doting on their only granddaughter, freeing Cassie to focus on the veterinary hospital. It was an arrangement born of necessity, but it worked because of their strong love for each other, something Jillian couldn't help but envy.

As she filed, the only sounds were the bubbling of the fish tank and the hiss of an overworked air conditioner fighting the Florida heat. A full day of barking dogs, hissing cats and chatty clients had her appreciating the temporary quiet, only for it to be broken minutes later by a banging at the front door. For a second she considered staying out of sight, behind the tall wall of files. People often stopped by after hours to try to pick up last-minute items, and she really didn't want to deal with that tonight. But, as always, her sense of duty won out.

Pulling her unruly black curls into a mostly service-able ponytail, she forced a smile on her face, ready to

serve whatever tardy client was making such a ruckus.
Approaching the heavily tinted glass front door, she
could make out, dimly, a very large man holding what
appeared to be a squirming dog. Medical instincts
kicked in at the sight of the would-be patient, spurring
her to run the last few steps to unlock and open the
door. Standing behind it was a seemingly solid wall of
muscular man. Ignoring him, and her suddenly rapid
heartbeat, she focused instead on the very familiar-
looking dog.

"Oh, no, is that Murphy? What happened? Is he
hurt?" Her voice came out more forcefully than she'd
intended, but the shock of seeing her favorite patient
being carried in by a stranger had her protective instincts kicking into high gear. She tried to assess the
dog, but the man holding him was so tall it was hard
to get a good look.

"I have no idea who or what a Murphy is, but I found
this mongrel on the side of the highway as I was driving into town." He shifted the dog, holding him away
from what had once been a white dress shirt. "I don't
think he's hurt too badly, but he definitely needs a bath."

Jillian relaxed a bit, her mouth twitching up despite
her worry. The guy, whoever he was, made quite a picture holding the pathetic dog in his arms. He was tall,
over six feet, dark hair and eyes, with broad shoulders
that filled out his business clothes well. The bristly stubble starting to show only added to his masculine aura.
That he was carrying the nearly fully grown dog without visible signs of strain impressed her. That he had
stopped to rescue the dog at all impressed her even more.

"So…are you going to help him?" the man asked, eyebrows raised. He probably wondered why she was just standing there, staring up at him like a fool.

"Oh, um, yes. Let me take a look, see if I need to call the vet back in. Just bring him in here." Jillian snapped back into work mode, chiding herself for ogling when there was an animal that needed help. Motioning him into an exam room, she told herself she was a professional. And professionals were not supposed to check out the client's rear end, no matter how nice it was.

Chapter 2

Nic carried the dog into the small, spotlessly clean room, gently lowering him onto the slick exam table. Immediately the troublemaker tried to jump off into Jillian's arms. "Oh, no you don't. Stay," he said, grabbing the squirming dog before he could take flight.

"Good reflexes," she commented, smiling that pretty smile again.

"Years of wrestling with my younger brother," he answered. "You said you might need to call the vet. I thought you were the vet." Confused, he pointedly looked at her scrubs. Scrubs that did nothing to hide her feminine curves.

"Me? No, I'm the veterinary technician, Jillian Everett," she corrected. "Cassie—I mean, Dr. Marshall— already left. But let me take a look, and then I'll give her a call if there's anything wrong." She opened a drawer below the gleaming examining table and removed a small scanning device. "But first, let's see who this furry guy is. I'm pretty positive it's Murphy, Mrs.

Rosenberg's border collie, but a microchip would tell us for sure. Hopefully we'll luck out, and the scanner will be able to find one."

Upon hearing his name, the dog whimpered, wriggling in delight.

"I think you just got your answer as to who he is. And speaking of names, I'm Nic."

"You're probably right, Nic, but let's do this by the book, just in case." She held down a button and ran the scanner up and down the dog's neck, stroking his black-and-white fur with her other hand. Her affection for the dog was obvious. When the machine beeped, she wrote down a number that had popped up on the screen. "I've got Murphy's chip number recorded in his file. Let me get it and I'll be right back."

Left alone with the dog, Nic found himself hoping the veterinary tech would come back soon. He liked her smile, and the way her dark curls kept falling across her face. Liked the gentle way she stroked the dog without seeming to notice she was doing it. He wondered if those hands felt as soft as they looked. But mostly, he liked that she was focused on the dog, not him. Fawning women had become a huge turnoff.

"It's definitely Murphy," she said, striding back into the room. Murphy squirmed in glee, as if happy to be recognized. "All right, boy, I know you're happy to see me. I'm happy to see you, too. But I've got to make sure you're not hurt, okay, handsome?" She ran her hands along the dog's back and along his sides, feeling through the thick coat. "Murphy's a favorite of mine, smarter than most dogs, but as likely to get into trouble as his name implies."

"His name?" Nic looked down at the dog in his arms, confused.

"Murphy. As in Murphy's Law?" She picked up the front leg and continued to check him over for any obvious open wounds or signs of pain.

"Ah, I take it this isn't his first misadventure, then?" Nic could relate to that. He'd had his own stretch of mishaps growing up.

"Oh, no, Murphy makes trouble his hobby. It's really not his fault—he's just a smart, active dog without enough to keep him busy. Border collies are herding dogs—they need a job to do, some way to channel their energy. Mrs. Rosenberg is very nice, but she's in her seventies and just not up to giving him the kind of exercise and training he needs. So our boy here finds his own exercise. He's broken out of her apartment a few times before, but I've never known him to make it all the way over the bridge. That's quite a hike, even for an athletic dog like Murphy."

Annoyed by the owner's lack of forethought, he asked, "If she can't keep up with him, why did she get him in the first place?" His whole life was nothing but responsibilities; the idea of someone being so irresponsible, even with a pet, rankled him.

"She didn't, not exactly. Her son, who wouldn't know a collie from a cockatiel, gave him to her for a present. Said a dog would keep her company. As if she needed company—she's a member of every committee and social group in town. She tried to talk me into taking him, but my apartment building doesn't allow dogs." She paused, bent down to look at something more closely and then frowned. "Nic, can you hold him on his side for me, lying down? I want to get a better look at his paws. I think I know why he was limping."

Nic complied, concerned that she might have found something serious. Had he missed something? He hadn't stopped to check the dog over before getting back on the road. His only thought had been to find somewhere that would take the dog off his hands. When he saw the sign for the Paradise Animal Clinic just past the bridge, it had seemed a good bet. Second-guessing his handling of the situation, he gently but firmly turned the dog on his side, careful not to hurt or scare him. Then, while he held the dog in place, Jillian carefully checked each paw.

"See this? His paws are raw. He's worn the pads right off. The hot, rough asphalt acts like sandpaper on them. Poor thing...that has to really hurt." Big blue eyes the color of a cloudless sky looked away from the dog and up at him. Eyes filled with sympathy and determination. "I'm going to call Dr. Marshall. Murphy will need some pain medication, and maybe some antibiotics." She picked up a phone hung on the back wall of the small room and placed the call. "Hi, Cassie...yes, I'm still here. We've got a little problem. Murphy Rosenberg is here. Someone found him on the side of the road again. He seems to be in good shape for the most part, but he's really done a number on his paws this time. I think you'd better come take a look."

As he listened to her make arrangements, he let himself look his fill. The concern on her face did nothing to detract from her beauty. Pale blue eyes were a stark contrast to the mass of ebony curls attempting to escape the clip she'd secured it with. Her skin was fair, her cheekbones prominent, and then there was that mouth, those perfectly pink lips that she pursed when she was concentrating. A man would have to be blind not to want to kiss those lips.

That doctor had better show up soon; if he was alone with the sexy vet tech much longer, he might end up panting as badly as the dog in front of him.

Jillian hung up the phone, relieved that help was on the way. And not just for Murphy's sake. Being alone with his rescuer was making her a bit nervous. Not that she was afraid of him; she couldn't be afraid of someone willing to stop and help an injured animal the way he had. He just made her…uneasy. Especially when he looked at her with those intense brown eyes, as if he were examining her, looking inside her. Raising her chin, hoping she projected more confidence than she felt, she asked, "Can you carry him into the treatment room for me? We can clean him up a bit while we're waiting."

He easily lifted the dog, once again making the movement look effortless. "Just show me where."

Jillian held the rear exam room door open, allowing him to pass through into the heart of the veterinary hospital. She wondered how it appeared to him. To her the stretches of gleaming chrome and spotless countertops, the bank of cages filling the back wall, the tangy scent of disinfectant were all more familiar than her own apartment. However, she knew the microscopes, centrifuges and bright lights could be intimidating to the uninitiated. Some people actually got a bit queasy. But Nic, who was waiting patiently for her to indicate where to place the dog, seemed unaffected by the medical surroundings.

Pleased by his composure, she pointed to the long, shallow treatment basin covered by a steel grate. The six-foot-long sink was table height, and would allow her to bathe the dog carefully while checking for any other wounds she might have missed. He placed the dog on the grating, and Murphy, no stranger to a bath, behaved himself as she uncurled the spray handle from the end of the table, then rinsed and lathered.

Nic made an excellent assistant; he had rolled up his sleeves, exposing tanned, well-defined forearms that easily maneuvered the soapy canine according to her direction. Thankfully, she could lather and rinse the pleasant-smelling suds on autopilot, because those muscled arms were proving quite the distraction. Worried he might have noticed her staring, she bent down to retrieve a clean towel from the stacks kept below the sink. She tried to focus on toweling the dog off, rather than on the larger-than-life man across the table. But he wasn't making it easy.

"I hope you don't mind," Nic said, unbuttoning his shirt. "This thing smells like, well, wet dog." He shrugged out of the wet, muddy fabric with a grimace, leaving him standing in an almost as damp, but considerably cleaner, sleeveless undershirt and dress slacks.

Jillian nodded, eyes drawn to his broad, bare shoulders, then down to the impressive biceps that had restrained Murphy so easily. The revealed bronze skin spoke more of Mediterranean ancestry than hours in the sun. The tight undershirt did little to hide the chiseled chest underneath or the flat abdominals below. She might have continued to stare, basking in all that male beauty, if the sound of the front door hadn't snapped her back to reality.

"Jillian! Jillian! Where's the doggy? Is he hurt? Can I kiss his boo-boo? Who's that?" Emma Marshall, four years old and the spitting image of her mother, barreled into the room. Her strawberry-blond ponytail swished as she looked from Emma to Nic, blue eyes blinking rapidly.

"Emma, I told you that someone found a doggy and brought him here so I could help him." Cassie appeared in the doorway behind her rambunctious tyke. "Hi, I'm Dr. Marshall. Thank you for helping our Murphy here. I'm afraid he's a repeat offender, but we all love him, anyway."

"I'm Nic." Brushing away the compliment, he offered a tired smile and said, "He seems like a nice dog, now that he's cleaned up."

"Murphy was a mess when Nic brought him in, covered in mud and God knows what else. He helped me bathe him, but his shirt was a casualty," Jillian explained.

"My shirt, my tie and my suit jacket. But, hey, who's counting?" Nic shrugged his shoulders, and then returned his attention to the women in the room. "Can you do something for his paws? They look pretty awful."

Cassie moved to the table and gently examined each of the dog's feet. "They do look pretty bad, but they'll heal quickly. I'll give him an antibiotic injection to prevent infection, and he can have some anti-inflammatories to help with the pain. Beef-flavored tablets, he'll love them." Cassie drew up a syringe of milky-looking fluid. "You aren't squeamish around needles, are you?" she asked, cocking an eyebrow.

"Not at all." Nic eyed the syringe. "But shouldn't you be calling his owner? She's got to be missing him by now, right?" Nic looked first at Cassie, then at Jillian. "Shouldn't she have to approve treatment or something?"

"Normally, yes," Jillian answered. "But we have a standing permission for treatment in Murphy's chart. Remember, this isn't his first time getting away. Besides, Mrs. Rosenberg won't be home tonight. She's over near Orlando on an overnight trip with her seniors group. She mentioned it to me when she stopped in to buy dog food yesterday. Murphy will have to stay here tonight, I guess." She grimaced. "I hate leaving him. If he scratches at the cage door, he's going to make his paws worse, and after his big outing, I'd rather he have someone keeping an eye on him. But my apartment manager won't allow me to take him home, and Cassie—I mean, Dr. Marshall—is currently fostering a dog at her house that doesn't get along with others. He'd beat poor Murphy up. So he'll have to stay here until Mrs. Rosenberg gets home."

Nic's eyebrows narrowed. "You're going to just put him in a cage?"

Cassie responded matter-of-factly, "It's not ideal, but he'll be safe—a lot safer than he was a few hours ago, thanks to you. There really isn't any other option."

"Yes, there is." Nic was firm, arms crossed. "He can stay with me. The Sandpiper Inn is pet-friendly, and I can bring him back here in the morning or to wherever you say to take him. I'll keep an eye on him, give him his medication and make sure he's okay overnight." His eyes dared anyone to disagree. "I didn't go through all the trouble of rescuing him to abandon him in the end."

"I don't think that will work…we don't even know you. Mrs. Rosenberg doesn't know you…" Jillian floundered. In her wildest dreams, she would never have expected this man to offer to play nursemaid to a gimpy dog. Knights in shining armor might be the norm in storybooks, but that kind of thing didn't happen in real life. Saviors, she knew from personal experience, were few and far between.

Cassie stepped in. "Why don't I call Mrs. Rosenberg and see what she has to say? We'll let her decide." Turning to Nic, she continued, "I'll need your contact information, and you'll have to fill out some paperwork, if she agrees. Does that sound all right?"

Nic nodded in agreement, still standing stiffly, as if ready to defend his newly found canine friend physically, if need be.

While he and Cassie worked out the arrangements, Jillian clung to the soft dog. She had lost control of this situation somehow, not something she generally let happen. Watching the gorgeous man in front her, she wondered what kind of man did this, dropped everything and did whatever it took to save the day. As if sensing her bewilderment, Murphy squirmed in her arms.

Comforting herself as much as the dog, she buried her face in his fur. The dog turned his head, straining to keep Nic in view, something he had done since the minute they'd arrived. "I know how you feel," she whispered in the smitten animal's ear. "I know how you feel."

Nic pulled into the parking lot of the Sandpiper Inn and turned the key, content to sit for a few minutes before he had to wrangle the dog and luggage. He still couldn't quite believe he had acquired a pet, yet another responsibility, even if it was just for the night. But he couldn't have left him in a cage, scared and hurt, any more than he could have left him on the side of the road.

At some point, taking on responsibility, taking care of others, had become second nature. He had always been the one to get his kid brother out of trouble, even when it meant getting into trouble himself. Later, he had tutored his sister, taking it upon himself to make sure she passed the dreaded algebra class. Then, after graduation, it had been impossible to say no to a job working for his father, eventually ending up where he was now, Nic Caruso, Vice President of Property Acquisitions at Caruso Hotels. The internationally known chain had been his father's dream, not his, and he found no joy in traveling from city to city, scouting out properties and securing new locations for the ever-growing company. He often wondered what it would be like to settle down in one place, to meet someone that appreciated him for who he was, rather than what he could provide.

A soft woof from the passenger's seat brought him out of his daydreams and into the present. "Don't worry, I'm coming. I didn't forget about you." Grabbing his overnight bag, Nic set out with Murphy across the covered breezeway connecting the parking area to the main house. In front of him the inn rose out of the darkness, spotlighted by the moon against the dunes behind it. It was hard to see details this late, but he knew from his research that it was two stories, built in the Florida Vernacular style. The buff-colored wooden siding would blend with the dunes in the daylight, and there were covered, whitewashed porches on every level, designed to offer a cool spot to enjoy the ocean view. Right now, though, all he could make out were the wide front steps and a welcoming glow from several of the shutter-framed windows.

Before continuing toward the inn, he took the sandy path that ran parallel to the dunes. Whether the inn was pet-friendly or not, he'd better give Murphy a chance to relieve himself before going in and getting settled. As they walked, Nic was impressed by the sheer size of the grounds, which were crisscrossed by walking paths and planted with a variety of tropical and coastal scrub plants. He stopped to lean against one of the many smooth-trunked palms, breathing in the humid air, richly scented by the jasmine that grew heavy around him. The scent reminded him of the vet tech he'd just met, Jillian. Even over the disinfectant and wet-dog smells, he had picked up on her flowery sweetness, some perfume or shampoo or something.

Straightening, he tugged on the leash and walked back to the hotel entrance. He wasn't here to daydream about pretty brunettes or to soak up the night air. He had a location to scout. Caruso Hotels was very interested in this bit of land, and he was tasked with determining if they should make an offer to the current owners.

There was plenty of room here for a modern beachfront resort once the original inn was torn down. Most of the property was underutilized, a diamond in the rough. A high-rise hotel could change the entire community—bring in tourist dollars, chain retailers and more. A Caruso Hotel would move the town into the modern age, make it a hot spot on the Florida coast.

At the top of the stairs, the large carved door of the Sandpiper Inn opened smoothly, bringing him into the lobby, an eclectically decorated but surprisingly elegant room. Native pine floors gleamed in the light of an old-fashioned chandelier. An antique table to his right served as the check-in desk, and across the room overstuffed furniture offered a cozy place to read or chat. Bay windows with a view of the night sea were directly opposite him; a native coquina fireplace accented the wall to the left.

Bookcases held everything from leather-bound tomes to contemporary bestsellers, with conch shells and chunks of coral for bookends. The antique and modern mix was nothing like the seamless, well-planned lobby of a Caruso Hotel, but welcoming in a way no modern resort could match. For once, he felt like he was stepping into something real, a true home away from home, instead of yet another commercial space.

"Are you checking in?" The question startled him for a moment, returning him to the present business. A young girl—she couldn't be more than eighteen—had come in from a doorway behind the check-in desk.

"Yes, Dominic Caruso. I have a reservation."

She tapped keys on a slim laptop computer, concentrating on the screen in front of her. "I don't see mention of a pet in the reservation notes. Will the dog be staying with you?"

"Yes, but only for one night. Is that a problem? Your website did say you were pet-friendly."

"Oh, no problem. I'll just send up a dog bed and some bowls for him. We have a small selection of pet food, as well, if you'd like." She smiled at Murphy, ignoring Nic in favor of his canine companion, and was rewarded by a mannerly wag of the tail.

"No, thank you, that won't be necessary." Jillian had fed Murphy some kibble before they left the clinic, and had packed him some more for the morning.

"Okay, sign here, then. You're in room 206, just up the stairs and to the left. Breakfast is served on the patio from seven to nine, and coffee and tea are always available in the sitting room. If you need anything, just let me know."

"Thank you very much. I'm sure we'll be fine." He pocketed the key, a real key, not a plastic key card, and headed up the staircase he had passed when he came in. The finely carved banister was smooth beneath his hand, worn to a soft glow by generations of guests and hours of polishing. Upstairs, the hall was quiet and softly lit; most of the other guests were probably sleeping, or perhaps out for a late stroll on the beach.

Grateful for the quiet, he let himself into the compact but tasteful room she had assigned him. Too tired to note much of his surroundings, he stripped off his filthy clothes on the way to the shower, where he stood under the hot, stinging spray to rinse off the mud, sweat and stress of the day. Resting his head on the cool tile, he let the water massage his back and tried to think of nothing, to just be. Instead, his thoughts kept circling back to Jillian, to her pale blue eyes, dark ringlets and those perfect, kissable lips. In a different place, a different time, he would love to explore those lips, and maybe more. But no, he had to work. Hell, he always had to work. At least he was good at his job. Dating, on the other hand, was a series of disasters. It seemed he had a target on his back visible to every gold digger for a hundred miles. His brother adored the attention the family name brought, but as far as Nic was concerned, being single was better than being used.

Annoyed, he turned the faucet to cold, hoping to clear his head. When even that didn't work, he toweled off, then collapsed on the big antique bed. Maybe it was the soft snores of the dog at the foot of the bed. Maybe it was the lull of the waves outside his window. Or maybe he was just that tired. Whatever the reason, for once he didn't have to fight his usual travel-induced insomnia. Tonight, sleep came quickly, the kind of dreamless deep sleep that only came to him when he was home.

Chapter 3

Jillian's morning was a blur of fur and files. There had been countless puppy kisses, but she had also been bitten, scratched and peed on. And that was only the first appointment—new puppy exams for a pair of Labradoodles. Since then, she had struggled to balance her time between assisting in the exam rooms, completing vital laboratory work and counseling owners on proper pet care. Officially, the clinic closed at noon on Saturdays, but it was already almost one, and she still had charts to write up before she left.

Grabbing a diet soda from the break room, she sat at the back desk, away from the barking and hissing, with her stack of charts. But no matter how hard she tried to concentrate, her mind kept returning to Murphy and, if she was honest, to the man who had found him. Lots of men came through the clinic, but not many looked like some kind of Roman god.

And as if being gorgeous wasn't enough, his compassion toward Murphy had bumped him up even higher on the sexy stranger scale of attraction. She had forgotten to ask him what had brought him to town. She knew he wasn't a regular; Paradise was so small, she'd have heard about him if he had been here long. No, more than likely he was one of the few vacationers that occasionally found their way to Paradise.

The island definitely didn't qualify as a tourist mecca; there were no giant, high-end resorts, nightclubs or theme parks to draw people in. But the beaches were pristine, and half the island was a dedicated wildlife refuge, so they did get the occasional nature lover. Somehow, though, Jillian couldn't quite picture the well-dressed man she'd met last night as a bird watcher.

She sighed. Not thinking about him wasn't working; maybe she should be proactive instead. Mrs. Rosenberg should be home by now. If she was fast, she could pick Murphy up at the inn, get him back to his owner and still have time to grab a quick bite before the meeting of the Island Preservation Society this afternoon. Once the Murphy situation was handled, she could move on and stop thinking about the mysterious Nic.

Decided, she grabbed the phone and dialed Mrs. Rosenberg's cell phone number. "Hi, Mrs. Rosenberg. It's Jillian. I'm just finishing up here at work, and wanted to let you know I'll be by with Murphy shortly."

"Oh, dear, I was just about to call you. There's been a slight change in plans. We girls decided to stop over at the outlet malls on the way back, and then, before we knew it, we were at that all-you-can-eat steakhouse. We've given our credit cards a workout, I'm afraid. But as soon as we finish lunch we'll be on our way. I should be in town before three, and you and Murphy and I can have a nice visit then. I'll make us some sangria with a wonderful red I picked up on the winery tour."

"I'm afraid I'll have to take a rain check on that sangria, Mrs. Rosenberg. The Island Preservation Society meeting is this afternoon. I need to head there right after work." Jillian twisted the phone cord, thrown off by the change of plans. "I can bring Murphy by after the meeting, as long as that isn't too late for you. I think we should wrap up by dinnertime."

"That's fine, dear. I can't wait to see my naughty boy. I'm so glad he's okay. I do hate how he keeps getting into scrapes. Won't you reconsider keeping him? I'd feel so much better if he was with someone young and energetic like you."

The elderly woman's request tugged at Jillian's heartstrings. She loved that dog, but there was no way she could keep him. "I'm sorry, Mrs. Rosenberg, you know I'd love to, but my landlord won't allow it. Maybe when my lease is up…" But that was just wishful thinking. Paradise Isle didn't have many apartment buildings, and none allowed dogs Murphy's size. Renting or buying a house was out of the question on her current salary.

Somehow, she, the girl who had grown up wanting nothing more than a houseful of kids and pets, had ended up alone in a small apartment, without so much as a goldfish. That was why she had joined the Island Preservation Society. If she couldn't have the Norman Rockwell life she'd always wanted, she'd have to settle for protecting her picture-perfect community instead. Paradise Isle was her home, and people like Mrs. Rosenberg were her family. "I'll call you when I'm on my way. Have a safe drive back."

"I'll try, but Avril Clookie is driving this time, and you know what a flighty young thing she is."

Mrs. Clookie was at least sixty years old, and about as flighty as a St. Bernard, but Jillian let it go. After saying her goodbyes, she found the consent form Nic had signed last night. His full name was Dominic Caruso, which sounded familiar somehow, and he'd left both his room number at the inn and his cell phone number in the contact section. When he didn't answer at the room number, she dialed the cell.

"Hello?" He sounded out of breath, and she could hear wind blowing in the background.

"Hi, Nic, it's Jillian."

"Ready to pick up your patient?"

"Actually, there's been a change in plans. It seems Mrs. Rosenberg won't be back for a few more hours. I have a meeting after work, so it would probably be best if you brought him to the clinic. I can leave him here while I'm at the meeting, then take him home after that. I'm sorry to change things up on you." She hoped he wasn't too annoyed by the change of plans; his corporate look had screamed "type-A personality" last night.

"No problem. I just finished a run on the beach, figured I'd get some exercise while I was waiting to hear from you. If you want, I can—"

"Wait, you took Murphy running on the beach? His paws haven't healed! He shouldn't—"

"Whoa, slow down! Murphy's upstairs sleeping, more than likely in my bed. I've only taken him out long enough to do his business, and I even rinsed his paws off afterward." Nic's voice was harsh, and Jillian felt herself flush. She shouldn't have assumed. "I'm not an idiot—I do know how to take care of a dog."

"You're right, and I'm sorry. I'm just annoyed that I couldn't take care of Murphy myself. I'm grateful you offered to take him in—really, I am. I'm afraid I let myself get flustered by the whole switch in plans. I hope all this hasn't been too much of an inconvenience."

"It's fine. But listen, I still don't like leaving him in a cage. Why don't you just give me his owner's address, and I'll take him there myself? That way she gets her dog back and you can go to your…what was it?"

"A meeting over at the library. But really, I could figure something out. You've done more than enough already."

"I wouldn't offer if I didn't mean it. I'd like to see him safely home, if that's okay. We've bonded."

"Bonded, huh?" She felt herself smiling; he seemed to have that effect on her.

"Sleeping together does that," Nic deadpanned. "He's a cover hog—don't let him tell you otherwise."

The image of Nic in bed, dog or no dog, was one Jillian did not need in her head. "Fine, I'll give Mrs. Rosenberg your number. If it's okay with her, she'll call you and give you her address, arrange a time." Jillian paused, "I really do appreciate everything you've done for Murphy."

"Well, if that's the case, there is a way you could pay me back."

"How?" Maybe he wasn't so altruistic, after all. If

he was looking for a reward, he was out of luck; neither she nor Mrs. Rosenberg had the extra cash.

"Have dinner with me."

"Dinner?" Her jaw dropped.

"Yeah, you know, the meal after lunch? I'm assuming your meeting will be over by then. I thought you could take me somewhere interesting, somewhere the locals go."

"Well…the locals mainly eat at Pete's. It's not fancy, but they have great burgers, and the seafood is fresh." Jillian tried to picture Nic in his business suit in the more-than-rustic atmosphere of Pete's. "Or we could go to the mainland. There are plenty of restaurants over there, nicer places—"

"Pete's sounds great, exactly what I'm in the mood for. Where can I pick you up?"

"I'll pick you up, at the Sandpiper," she countered. Even small-town girls knew not to get in a stranger's car. "Is six thirty okay? The deck fills up fast on a Saturday night."

"Perfect, it's a date. I'll see you then." A telltale click signaled the end of the call.

She hung up the phone slowly. A date? Since when did she go on dates with random strangers, no matter how sexy they were?

At three o'clock that afternoon, Nic was parked outside a small pink stucco house with a very eager border collie. Murphy strained at the leash on the way up the front walk, apparently as eager to go home as he had been to escape. Nic rang the bell and tried to quiet the dog. Almost immediately, the door was opened by a diminutive woman in a teal tracksuit and rhinestone glasses. Her close-cropped hair was a shade of red that was not, and never had been, anyone's natural color. Nearly blinded by the combination, he was caught off guard when she dove in for a hug, her short stature leaving her head resting just above his navel.

"Thank you! Thank you! Thank you!" Each thank-you was punctuated by a surprisingly strong squeeze. "You saved my precious baby. My sweet boy. Such a sweet, naughty, naughty boy!" With that, she crouched down to hug the canine in question. Murphy, for his part, took the praise as no more than his due.

Finished with her exuberant greeting, she straightened to her full height, which he guessed to be no more than four and a half feet, and tugged on his hand. "Come in, come in. I'm about to open some fabulous wine that I found on my trip. You must have a glass and tell me everything that happened."

Nic followed, intrigued by the tiny dynamo. He knew Florida was known for its active senior lifestyle, but he had a feeling Mrs. Rosenberg surpassed even that stereotype. Besides, he wanted to find out how Murphy was pulling his little escape act.

The house was immaculate, and filled with over-stuffed furniture in shades of mauve and teal. Paintings of tropical flowers were on the walls, and a large brass manatee served as a centerpiece atop the glass coffee table. Through the doorway to the right he could see a small galley kitchen; shopping bags currently covered every inch of counter space.

His hostess dug through the bags, removing multiple bottles of wine before finding what she was looking for. Her wrinkled but capable hands deftly wielded the corkscrew, then poured them each a generous portion. He accepted the proffered glass and took a seat on the overlarge love seat, sinking into the soft surface. His hostess's much smaller body perched on the chair across from him as she raised her glass to toast. "To Murphy!"

"To Murphy." He sipped cautiously. It was surprisingly sweet, but certainly drinkable.

"Good, isn't it? Grown right here in Florida. It's made with native grapes. Lots of antioxidants." She winked, then drank.

He nodded, not sure what to say to the winking, booze-pushing senior in front of him.

"So you found my boy. Jillian says he was all the way across the bridge this time! I am in your debt, son—if you hadn't stopped, there's no telling what could have happened to him. A car could have gotten him, or an alligator! We have those here, you know."

Nic did know, but hadn't thought about it at the time. Which was probably a good thing. Changing the subject, he asked, "Mrs. Rosenberg, do you know how Murphy escaped? Jillian said this wasn't his first attempt. I'd hate to see him get out again."

She shook her head, neon hair flying wildly. "It's a mystery to me. I left him locked in the house, with his food and water. The neighbor was going to let him out for me at bedtime, but she says he was already gone. If he'd been outside, I might think he dug out, since he's done that before, but from inside the house? That doesn't seem likely." She frowned in thought, her be-dazzled spectacles sliding down her nose.

"Do you mind if I look around, see if I can find his escape route?"

"Look wherever you like, son. I'll just sit here and finish my wine." She took another healthy swig. "You let me know if you find anything."

Curiosity getting the better of him, Nic decided to start at the front of the house. Murphy, who'd been lying happily at his feet, jumped up, eager to follow wherever he led. The front door offered no clues, and the windows appeared secure. No loose locks or broken panes. The bedroom windows were the same. Murphy, thinking there was some game afoot, pranced and barked as he searched.

When they got to the kitchen, the dog ran ahead and jumped up onto the kitchen door. Wondering, Nic stopped, and watched. Sure enough, Murphy jumped again, this time his paws hitting the lever door handle. If the dead bolt hadn't been in place, the door would have popped right open. "Mrs. Rosenberg, was the kitchen door dead bolted when you were away?"

"The kitchen door? No, the key for that lock got lost a long time ago. But I did push the button in, on the doorknob. That locks it from the inside, and it opens with the same key as the front door." She paused, eyes wide, "You don't think someone broke in, do you?"

"No, not a break-in," he assured her. "Just a break-out. See these scratches on the door? I think Murphy was jumping at the door to follow you, and his paws landed on the handle. That lock opens automatically from the inside as soon as you turn the handle. He just let himself right out. Then I imagine the storm blew it shut again. If you're going to keep him in, you're going have replace that lever-style handle with a good old-fashioned doorknob."

"Oh, my goodness. What a smart boy! Opening doors!" Mrs. Rosenberg beamed at her black-and-white escape artist. "But I see what you mean. We can't have him gallivanting around town. I'll have to ask around about a handyman—I'm afraid tools and such just aren't my area of expertise."

"I could do it," Nic said before he could stop himself.

"Would you? Oh, that would be such a load off my mind. I worry so about poor Murphy. I know this isn't the best home for him, but I'd be sick if anything happened to him." Before Nic could think of a way to extricate himself, she pressed a wad of cash into his hands. "Palm Hardware is just around the corner. You must have passed it on the way here. Just pick out whatever you think is best."

Thirty minutes later, Nic was tightening the last screw with, of all things, a pink screwdriver. Murphy had been banished to the bedroom after getting in the way a few too many times, and Mrs. Rosenberg was thrilled. Straightening, he couldn't help but grin as he packed up the pastel tool kit. Project Dog-Proof was a success, and despite his initial reluctance to get involved, it felt good to know he'd been able to help. Getting his own hands dirty was a lot more satisfying than just signing a work order.

"I have to say, I'm so glad Jillian had that meeting

today, and you came instead. Not that I don't love Jillian," she clarified hastily. "Murphy adores her and I do, too. But I wouldn't have felt right asking her to change a doorknob. I'm a bit too old-fashioned for that."

He grinned. Of all the ways he might describe Mrs. Rosenberg, "old-fashioned" wasn't one of them. "What sort of meeting she was going to?" He told himself he was only interested as part of his research on the island. He certainly wasn't prying into the pretty vet tech's life. Not very much, anyway.

"The Island Preservation Society. Jillian is one of the founding members," Mrs. Rosenberg said proudly. "I don't attend the meetings—meetings give me heartburn—but I donate when they have their annual rummage sale, and attend the dinner dance they do in the spring."

His shoulders tensed. "What exactly does this society do?"

"They mostly work to preserve the historic buildings, protect the coastal habitat, anything that has to do with maintaining the way of life Paradise is known for." Her eyes shined with pride. "Our little town isn't as fancy or popular as Daytona or Miami or those other beach places, and that's just fine with us. We like things the way they are, if you know what I mean."

Nic was afraid he did know. From what she was saying, he was going to have a fight on his hands, and Jillian was playing for the other side.

Jillian walked quickly across the hot asphalt parking lot, sticky with sweat and humidity. Ahead, the air-conditioned coolness of the Palmetto County Library beckoned like a mirage, a refuge from the last gasp of summer. Stepping inside, she took a deep breath, embracing the smell of old books that permeated the air. Fortified, she climbed the single staircase to the crowded conference room where Cassie and Mollie were waiting for her.

"We saved you a seat." Mollie waved, her pixie-like face lighting up at the sight of her friend. "I was afraid you wouldn't show, and you know I only come to these things because of you." Formal meetings of any sort were definitely not Mollie's thing. Grateful, Jillian hugged the petite woman in appreciation.

"I appreciate you making the sacrifice. These meetings really are important, especially now. Rumor is that the Sandpiper's new owner wants to sell."

"Sell the Sandpiper Inn? That place is an institution! I can remember Dad taking me there as a kid for the annual fish fry and the Christmas tree lighting ceremony. And just a few years ago, he and mom had their twenty-fifth anniversary party there." Cassie's eyebrows furrowed. "It's bad enough that they don't do the community events anymore, but sell it? To who?"

"I don't know." She shrugged. "They haven't even officially put it on the market yet. I think that happens Monday. I only know about it because another one of the Island Preservation Society members, Edward Post, told me about it when I saw him at the grocery store yesterday. He was always close with the Landry family, and had hoped when their daughter inherited the Sandpiper she would bring it back to its glory days. But she's got her own retail shop over in Orlando, and isn't interested in being an innkeeper. He thinks she'll take the first good offer she gets."

Jillian's heart hurt just thinking of the stately inn being taken over by outsiders, or worse, torn down. A beacon on the Paradise Isle shoreline, the Sandpiper had stood for more than a century. Its spacious grounds had always served as an unofficial community center, the gregarious owners often hosting holiday events, weddings, even a prom or two. She'd fallen in love with the grand building the first time she saw it and had always imagined she'd bring her own family to events there, one day. Now it might be destroyed before she ever had that chance. It just didn't seem fair, or right, to let it slip away without a fight.

As the meeting got under way, she found it hard to concentrate on the details of the historic post office renovation, or a proposal for a bike lane on Island Avenue. Normally she was the first volunteer for a Society project, but right now she was too on edge about the fate of the Sandpiper Inn.

And if she was honest with herself, the issue with the Sandpiper wasn't the only thing making her palms sweat. A good number of the butterflies fluttering in her stomach were about her upcoming date. It wasn't as if she'd never been on a date before; at twenty-seven, she'd had her share of relationships. But always with local, familiar, safe men. Nothing serious. After a few dates, they'd ended up just friends, leaving her wondering if she was even capable of more intense feelings.

But Nic, with his towering good looks and confident

manner, was another kind of man altogether. One that had her squirming in her seat, unsure if she was eager for the meeting to be over or afraid of what came after it.

Finally, the last item on the agenda was addressed. Edward Post stood at the front of the room, faced the folding chairs and cleared his throat. "I know that a few of you have heard rumors about the Sandpiper Inn. I'm afraid those rumors have been confirmed. Ms. Roberta Landry, the current owner, has decided to sell the inn and return to her job in Orlando." Shifting his weight nervously, he continued, "The board of the Island Preservation Society has spoken with Ms. Landry, and she has agreed to at least entertain the idea of the city purchasing the inn for community use."

"Can the city afford to buy it?" someone from the crowd asked.

Edward pushed his glasses up his nose, to see who had spoken. "No, not without help. We're preparing an application to the State Register of Historic Places. If we can get the Sandpiper listed, we may be able to get a grant toward its preservation, which would help offset the purchase price. Our chances are good, but the process can take several months. If there is another offer before that happens, Ms. Landry is within her rights to sell without waiting for the outcome of our application."

At that point the meeting broke down, voices rising as friends and families discussed the odds of success. Everyone already knew, without being told, that with land prices finally going up, a new owner was likely to raze the inn and parcel the land up.

Heartsick, Jillian avoided the speculating citizens

and quietly made her goodbyes. Descending the stairs, she vowed to contact Edward and volunteer to write the grant application herself. Tonight she'd start researching the process, figure out their best way forward. She was going to do whatever she could to increase their chances of getting that grant. This was her home, and she wasn't giving up without a fight.

Chapter 4

Nic waited for Jillian on the wide shaded porch of the Sandpiper, where a surprisingly efficient ceiling fan kept the air moving and the mosquitoes at bay. Palms and tropical plants he couldn't identify crowded up against the white railing, as if ready to take over the old inn if given a chance. Farther off, he could hear a woodpecker tapping for his supper, and under all of it was the hypnotic lull of the ocean moving against the shore. He'd traveled the world, stayed at the most luxurious resorts in the most exotic locations, but he couldn't remember ever enjoying an evening more than he was right now.

Something about the seclusion of the location, nestled as it was against the wildlife sanctuary that made up almost half the island, allowed him to let down walls that he'd spent most of his life putting up. The friendliness of the island people was a part of it, as well. He'd wandered up and down Lighthouse Avenue, the main street through town, and every person he'd seen had greeted him openly, willing to talk about the town, their businesses and their families. He'd learned that the mayor had held office for forty years, and was running again in the spring. The streetlights came on at dusk and the shops closed soon after, but the local diner opened early for the fishermen and commuters. He'd also been warned, with a wink and a nod, that alcohol sales were banned on Sundays, so if he wanted to pick up a six-pack to watch the game with, he'd better get it today. The traditional pace of life here was worlds away from the life he'd known, but right now, sitting on a porch swing waiting for a pretty girl, it definitely had its perks.

Tires crunching over gravel signaled a car pulling into the lot hidden by thick green foliage. Leaving the sheltered sanctuary of the patio, he took the steps two at a time, then followed the winding footpath to the large gravel and sand parking lot. A bright blue compact car was in the first spot, its engine still running.

As he started toward it, the door opened, long legs swinging out. Then she stood, facing him, and he was stopped in his tracks, paralyzed. He'd remembered her as pretty, but now, in the light of day, she was stunning. Gone were the shapeless scrubs. Today she wore snug-fitting jeans and a casual but fitted navy tank top that clung to her generous curves. She'd left her hair loose, a mass of ebony curls tumbling down her back. Her striking blue eyes sparkled in the sunlight, framed by dark lashes he knew his sisters would kill for. But it was her smile, innocently seductive, that nearly knocked him over.

"Hi," she said softly, gripping the door handle. "I hope I'm not late."

"No, right on time." He forced himself back into motion, heading for the tiny car. "I heard you pull in, thought I'd save you the walk up."

"Ah, okay. Well." She started to walk toward him, then stopped. "Guess we should be going, then."

"Right, you said it fills up fast, and I'm starving. I think it's all the fresh air." He opened the car door and folded himself carefully into the seat. Although roomier than it had first appeared, it was still a tight fit for his six-foot-two frame. "Is it far?"

"Nothing's far on Paradise Isle."

"Right, I keep forgetting." He grinned. "Here on the beach, it seems the sand goes on forever. It's hard to remember that the actual town is so small."

"Most of the island is taken up by the wildlife sanctuary and public beach access. Only a small portion is actually developed." Her tone indicated that she liked things that way, and he tried not to think about how things would change if Caruso Hotels built a resort here. Instead, he focused on the view as they wound their way down the coast along the beachfront road. Pelicans dove and rose, searching for their evening meal, disappearing and reappearing from behind grass-covered dunes. Some kind of vine also grew on the dunes, with big purple flowers soaking up the evening sun.

"I didn't know flowers could grow in sand," he said, pointing to the tough-looking vines.

She smiled, either at his interest or at the flowers themselves, he wasn't sure. "That's railroad vine. They call it that because it just keeps chugging along the dune, sometimes growing a hundred feet long. The roots help hold the sand in place, protecting the dunes. Best of all, it flowers all year-round. The tall, grasslike plants around it are sea oats—not as pretty, but just as important for the dunes."

Intrigued, he had her point out a few other interesting species as they drove. By the time they reached the restaurant half a dozen names, like coco plum and wax myrtle, were spinning through his head. Impressed, he told her so.

"It's my home. To protect it, I had to learn about it," she said simply.

Another stab of guilt knifed through his stomach. At this rate, he'd be too knotted up to eat a thing. Changing the subject, he focused on the rustic, almost tumbledown appearance of Pete's Crab Shack and Burger Bar—serving the "coldest beer in town," if the worn sign above the door could be believed.

He could see what looked like a small dining area inside, but most of the patrons were sitting on the spacious, covered deck, enjoying the ocean view along with their baskets of food. Jillian led him to one of the few empty tables and passed him a plastic menu. Scanning the offerings, he quickly decided on the grilled snapper BLT, fries and a sweet tea.

"A man that knows what he wants," Jillian commented, raising her head from behind her own menu.

He met her eyes and sparks flew, hotter than the heat lightning flashing in the clouds behind her.

He knew what he wanted.

And it definitely wasn't on the menu.

Jillian felt her cheeks become flushed from the heat in Nic's eyes. Somehow, her innocent comment didn't feel so innocent anymore. Embarrassed, flattered and more than a little confused, she bit her lip and tried to think of something to say. His eyes caught the movement, narrowing on her lips. Oh, boy. Her previous casual dates had not prepared for her this level of... intensity.

Desperate to ease the tension she turned away, hoping to signal the waiter. Instead, she saw Mollie, weighed down by a giant paper sack, cutting across the deck to their table. Knowing there was no way to stop her, Jillian waved her over.

"Hey, Jillian, who's the handsome stranger?" Mollie batted her eyelashes theatrically at Nic.

"Mollie, this is Nic. He's Murphy's most recent savior. Nic, this is Mollie. She's the receptionist at the clinic, and a good friend." She gestured to the overflowing bag. "Stocking up for a hurricane?"

"Picking up dinner for Emma and me. Cassie got an emergency call, and her parents couldn't babysit, some concert or something. I said I'd swing by and pick the munchkin up, take her home and feed her. I wasn't sure what she likes, so I had Pete throw in a bit of everything." She shrugged. "I figure Cassie can eat whatever is left over when she gets home."

"An emergency? That's odd—I didn't get a call from

her." Jillian dug in her purse for her phone. Cassie usually called her for assistance in emergencies.

Mollie grabbed her hand. "Chill out. She didn't call because she said you were, and I quote, 'on a hot date.'" She scanned Nic from head to toe, slowly. "I guess he qualifies." Jillian kicked her under the table. "Seriously, no worries. She said she had it handled, something about a pug having an allergic reaction. She just wants to observe it for a while at this point, make sure the medication is working."

"Oh." Somewhat appeased, she put the phone down. "Well, I'm available if she needs me."

"No, you aren't," Mollie said, winking at Nic. "Hot date, remember?" Avoiding another kick from Jillian, she took her paper bag and strolled out, obviously pleased with herself. Nic, for his part, looked incredibly amused by the entire situation.

"Something funny?"

"Nope, just enjoying myself. And the view," he added, looking pointedly at her.

Those butterflies were rapidly morphing into pterodactyls. Thankfully, Nic's flirting was curtailed by the arrival of the waitress. Jillian ordered the crab cakes, and Nic his sandwich.

The perky waitress, in shorts that covered less than most bikini bottoms, couldn't take her eyes off him, and really, who could blame her? He looked every bit as masculine and commanding in jeans and a casual button-down shirt as he had in his professional clothing the night before. If anything, the more relaxed attire highlighted his chiseled features and hard body.

Annoyed with Ms. Skimpy Pants and irritated with herself for caring, Jillian drummed her fingers on the paper placemat. Nic smiled at her frustration, but to his credit kept his eyes on her, not the scantily clad waitress, who thankfully was called away to another table.

By the time the red plastic baskets of food arrived, Jillian felt a bit more relaxed. Nic, despite his tendency to make her breath catch and pulse race, was a pleasant dining companion. They chitchatted about the weather, which was still warm, even in October, then he relayed the story of his rendezvous with the eccentric Mrs. Rosenberg. His description of her enthusiastic greeting and the way she had bamboozled him into changing her doorknob had her breathless with laughter. "I'm sorry. I should be thanking you instead of laughing at you." She shook her head. "Seriously, thanks for helping her. I'm sure she didn't give you much choice, but thanks, anyway."

"She was definitely persuasive." He sipped his tea, then continued, "But I would have done it, anyway. I'm sure she's very capable for her age, but she's not up to replacing doorknobs. And it needed to be done."

His simple answer spoke volumes about him. Most single guys didn't go around acting as handymen for little old ladies. That Nic didn't realize how uncommon his charitable streak was made it even more appealing. She found herself wanting to know more about this mystery man, and how he'd come to be so chivalrous. "Where did you learn how to change a doorknob, anyway?"

"My dad taught me. That, and a lot of other things.

He didn't believe in paying someone else to do what you could do yourself. So he taught us about household repairs, car maintenance, that kind of thing."

"Us?"

"I have a brother and two sisters. I'm the oldest."

"He taught the girls to do that stuff, too?"

"Definitely. No gender discrimination there. And we all learned to cook, too, no exceptions."

"Your dad cooked?" Jillian was flabbergasted. None of her foster fathers had, of course, but most of their wives hadn't, either. She'd grown up on frozen dinners and boxed mac and cheese.

"Of course he cooked, he's Italian. But my nana is the one that taught us kids. When Mom and Dad were in the kitchen, they were busy, you know, trying to get food on the table in a hurry. Nana had more time and patience, so she taught us all. We would start with tossing salads, easy stuff, and then move up to more complicated things when we were ready. By the time we were in high school, we could all cook reasonably well." He popped a fry in his mouth. "Except for my brother, Damian. He does more than reasonably well. He just finished culinary school, and now he's in Italy getting advanced training. He's a magician with food."

"What about your sisters…what are they like?"

"Smart," he answered without hesitation. "Both are really smart, but complete opposites. Claire is a total bookworm. She's studying for a masters in English at NYU. Isabella is more practical. She has an MBA and works for a big investment firm."

His pride in them was obvious; she could tell just

from his tone how much he cared for his family. A small stirring of envy clawed at her, but she pushed it away. She'd spent much of her childhood wishing for a family like his, with siblings and parents and grandparents. But she was an adult now; she'd had plenty of time to learn that wishes didn't always come true.

Nic enjoyed talking about his family, but the questions about their careers made him nervous. He knew it was dishonest, but he didn't want her to ask what his father did or what *he* did. He'd had too many women want him just because of his family, or rather the family fortune. Of course, in this case, his family being the driving force behind Caruso Hotels didn't seem like news she'd be happy to hear, with the Sandpiper being up for sale. If she knew he was here to look into buying it, well, that would definitely wipe the smile off her face.

And it was a knockout of a smile. Her whole face glowed, and her nose scrunched up, just a little, in the most adorable way. In the end, business would have to stay business. His father and the whole company were counting on him to make this deal. If he was going to take over from his dad one day, he needed to prove he could handle the job. But in the meantime, he couldn't help but want to spend some time with a woman who seemed to like him, not his money or his glamorous lifestyle.

Hoping to change the subject, he asked casually, "So what about your family? Do they live around here?" Her face blanched, just briefly, and he saw a flash of pain in her eyes that had him reaching for her hand as she caught her breath. Caught off guard by her reaction, he kept silent as he waited.

She looked down at their joined hands, then into his eyes.

"I don't have any family."

When he didn't react, other than to squeeze her hand reassuringly, she continued. "My parents died in a car accident when I was two years old. They were caught in a bad storm and lost control of the car. I'm told they died on impact, but paramedics found me buckled in my car seat, not a scratch on me."

He didn't know what to say, had nothing to offer, other than "I'm sorry."

Smiling at that, she said, "Yeah, so am I. They—I—didn't have any family, at least that anyone knew of. I ended up in foster care, moving every year or so. Eventually I ended up here, on Paradise Isle. When I was in high school, I got an after-school job at the clinic, back when Cassie's dad was still running things. Later, when my foster parents moved to Jacksonville, I convinced the social worker to let me stay here. I had some money saved up, and I got some financial assistance from the state. I finished out my senior year living in a motel room. After I graduated and could work full-time, I found an apartment and started classes at the community college. A few years ago, I passed my State Board exams, and got certified as a veterinary technician."

"You've been on your own since high school? With no help?"

"I had my friends, and Doc Marshall, Cassie's father, helped by convincing the case worker not to put me back in foster care. I was almost eighteen and with foster homes so scarce, it wasn't a hard sell. But without him backing me, and giving me a job, it never would have worked."

Nic couldn't even imagine that kind of self-reliance. His family had always been involved in his life—sometimes too involved. But as much as their expectations and demands could feel like an albatross around his neck, they had always been there for him when he needed them. They were the only people he could truly count on.

No wonder Jillian was so attached to the community—it was all she had. The guilt he had pushed aside began chewing a fresh hole in his gut. If he greenlighted the Caruso Hotel project, it would completely change the island, and although he'd assumed that change would be for the better, he had a feeling she wouldn't agree.

Carefully, he tried to feel her out on the subject. "So why Paradise? Of everywhere you lived, what made you stay here?"

Jillian smiled. "Because it felt like home. Nowhere else ever did. Here, the people I met really seemed to care, to want to know me. No one brushed me off as just a foster kid, or acted like I was a lost cause. The town is small enough that people really get to know each other—there are no strangers. And everyone looks out for each other. It's the closest I've ever come to having family." Her voice quavered at her last few words, leaving no doubt as to the extent of her loyalty.

Nic wanted to argue, to offer some counterpoint, but he couldn't. Even in his short time on the island, he'd seen the camaraderie she was describing. Her friend Mollie's willingness to give up her Saturday night to help a friend was just one more example. He wished he could say there were plenty of places like Paradise, but if there were, he'd never seen them.

Of course, small towns, isolated from the fast pace of modern life, weren't his usual haunts. Caruso Hotels were found in the busier tourist destinations; some of their larger resorts became cities unto themselves. On paper, Paradise Isle had seemed like a blank canvas, waiting for development. Choosing an unknown place wasn't their usual mode of operation, but he'd thought it a brilliant and cost-saving strategy, one that would pay handsomely when they transformed Paradise Isle into a tourist hot spot.

Now, seeing the town for himself, he realized how arrogant he'd been. Paradise might be small, but that didn't mean it was insignificant. A revelation that was a bit too late in coming. How could he tell his father, the CEO of a world-renowned business, not to purchase a prime piece of property because "the people are really nice"? It was absurd. He'd just have to figure something out.

And find a way to live with himself afterward.

Jillian hadn't meant to go on and on about her childhood; she hated it when people felt sorry for her. But

Nic didn't look as if he pitied her. If anything, he looked thoughtful as she talked about Paradise, her adopted hometown. She found herself wondering what his hometown was like, but before she could ask he was signaling the waitress for the check. "No, I'm buying," she protested. "We agreed. I'm treating you, to thank you for being Murphy's knight in shining armor. And for helping Mrs. Rosenberg. "

"I changed my mind." He handed his credit card to the waitress without even looking at the check. "What kind of knight lets the princess foot the bill? Besides, I'm the one who should be grateful. You stayed late to help a stranger—"

"Murphy isn't a stranger—" she objected.

"No, but I was. And you didn't know it was Murphy when you let me in. And you've kept me from eating alone or worse, falling prey to our waitress over there." The woman in question was still making eyes at him, none too subtly.

"A fate worse than death," she teased. "Better watch out, she's headed our way."

He just grinned, and signed the offered receipt without taking his eyes off Jillian. The waitress, realizing she was being ignored, practically stomped off. *Not so perky anymore*, Jillian thought, more pleased than she had a right to be.

She knew she had no claim on this gorgeous man, but she was enjoying his company, and the way he made her feel. He listened to her, really listened, and when he spoke, he was funny and engaging. And of course, he wasn't exactly hard on the eyes. Several times she had embarrassed herself by staring at him; thankfully he didn't seem to have noticed. She'd never been so quick to be attracted to a man before, but Nic had intrigued her from the first minute she'd seen him.

When he took her elbow to guide her down the steep stairs she didn't object, nor did she protest when he opened her car door for her after she unlocked it with the remote. His actions were quaintly old-fashioned, and that appealed to her more than she would have expected.

She turned on the air conditioner as soon as she got in, hoping to relieve the oven-like temperature, zooming the windows down to let some of the hot air escape. Once on the road, she put them back up, cocooning them in a car that suddenly seemed quite claustrophobic. His scent permeated the air, some kind of aftershave or cologne that smelled clean yet spicy.

As she merged onto the main road, he reached over and rested a broad hand on hers where it gripped the gearshift. An innocent touch, but it had her pulse racing. All at once the drive to the Sandpiper felt too long and yet not long enough. She was still debating how to handle things when she pulled into the Sandpiper's secluded parking lot.

Should she take her hand back? Kiss him? Let him kiss her? Or maybe she was misreading the whole thing, and the attraction was completely one-sided.

Confused, she turned to find him watching her, searing her skin with his gaze. Energy was radiating off him in waves. Frozen, she could only blink as he reached to brush a lock of hair from her face, twirling it around one finger. They both seemed to hold their breath as he gently tugged, then untwined it curl by curl.

She moistened her lips, and he shifted his attention to her mouth. Sensuously, he traced a finger over the swollen nerve endings, the sensation causing her eyes to flutter closed. There was a whisper of air as he leaned toward her, and then his mouth was on hers.

His kiss was gentle at first, a request, not a demand. But when her lips parted on a sigh he accepted the invitation, deepening the kiss. As his tongue teased, she reached for him blindly, finding his broad shoulders, clutching him to her, not wanting him to stop, not able to stop. Never had she experienced a connection like this. This was so far beyond a kiss; it was some kind of magic, and she never wanted it to end. Straining toward him, but trapped by the seat belt, she whimpered in frustration.

Immediately he let her go, backing away to his side of the car. "Did I hurt you?" His worried eyes darted over her, obviously mistaking her whimper for a sign of pain.

"No," she managed, her voice shaky. "No, that definitely didn't hurt." Finding her composure, and realizing he really was concerned, she explained, "The seat belt was in my way."

"Oh."

She could see now that he was breathing as hard as she was. So she had affected him, too. A bit of feminine pride crept over her.

"Tomorrow. What are your plans tomorrow?" His tone was insistent, compelling her to respond.

"Um… I usually go to church in the morning, the early service, but otherwise, I'm not sure. I don't really have any." Until now, painting her nails and catching up on reality TV were generally the highlights of her weekend.

"Spend the day with me." When she hesitated, he pushed. "Show me your island, give me the grand tour."

She considered. She certainly wanted to spend more time with him, and it was an innocent enough request. But this man was trouble wrapped up in sin. If he could get her this worked up over dinner and a short car ride, who knows what would happen with a full day together? He knocked down walls she didn't even know she had, and she wasn't sure she was ready for that.

As if sensing her hesitation, he withdrew as far as he could in the small confines of the car and said, "I'll be a perfect gentleman, I swear."

He really was cute. Giving in, she nodded. "All right, what time do you want me to pick you up?"

"How about ten thirty? And no offense, but I'd rather we take my rental. More legroom."

He had a point; he barely fit in her little compact. But she knew enough about basic safety to avoid giving out her address to a man she barely knew. "Let's meet at The Grind, a coffee shop on Lighthouse Avenue, a few blocks from the clinic. They've got great coffee, and they carry pastries from the local bakery if you want something sweet."

"I think I just had something sweet."

She felt her cheeks heating again at his casual innuendo. Flashing her a very male, very satisfied smile, he let himself out of the car. She watched him walk confidently toward the inn, as if he hadn't completely rocked her world.

Dear heavens, what on earth did she just get herself into?

Chapter 5

The cool dimness of the All Saints sanctuary never failed to soothe Jillian. The scent of incense clinging to the walls and the flicker of dripping candles made her feel as if she'd stepped out of the ordinary world, and into someplace timeless.

Most of the old wooden pews were empty this early in the morning—the eleven-o'clock service was much more popular. Which was the main reason she avoided it. Seeing all those happy families squeezed into the pews, children whispering, parents trying to keep them quiet, made her ache for what she had missed out on. So she came early, and then had the rest of the day for errands and chores.

Today, the stillness of the old building was particularly welcome. She'd had a restless, sleepless night, tossing and turning while reliving Nic's kiss. Of course, now, in the light of day, she felt silly getting so worked up over a single kiss.

As she prayed, waiting for the service to start, she

felt the bench shift, signaling that someone had joined her in the pew. Her peripheral vision caught the familiar motions of the sign of the cross. Finished with her own prayers, she eased back into her seat and turned to greet her pew mate. *Nic?* "What are you doing here?" she whispered.

"Praying?" he whispered back, all innocence.

"No, seriously, what you are doing here? Are you some kind of stalker or something?"

"What, I can't just be here for my own redemption? Remember, big Italian family, church attendance comes with the territory." At her narrowed brows, he admitted, "Okay, so I'm not going to win any attendance awards. But I did grow up in the church, was an altar boy and everything."

She tried, but could not picture this wickedly sexy man as an altar boy. He might have been an innocent child once, but you'd never know it now. When she continued to glare at him, he confessed, "I talked to my mom on the phone last night, and it came up that I was meeting you after church. I thought I would score big points by saying I met a nice girl." He rubbed his neck ruefully. "But she just wanted to know why I wasn't going to church, too. By the time I got off the phone I had promised I'd go, and that I'd say a prayer for Aunt Irene's cataract surgery."

Jillian stifled a chuckle, aware that their conversation was starting to draw attention. Nic might be a grown man, but he obviously still respected his mother. Definite bonus points. "So, did you pray for Aunt Irene yet?"

His answer was cut off by the processional hymn.

Standing, she stood shoulder to shoulder with him, his masculine presence impossible to ignore. He held out his hymnal for her to share, and although she appreciated the gesture she was flustered enough to stumble over the words more than once. He had no such issue, his rich baritone voice carrying the notes clearly. She was still feeling unsettled when they sat to listen to the readings, but eventually was carried away by the familiar readings, songs and worship. By the end of the service she found she was actually enjoying his company, and told him so as they filed out into the sunlight.

"Sorry I acted so startled in there. I'm not used to having company in church, but it was nice."

"How long have you been going here? It seemed everyone in there knew you by name."

"Most of them do. When I turned eighteen, my case worker gave me a packet with all my information in it, including my baptism certificate. I was so young when my parents died, I don't have any real memories of them, but I do know that my mom attended church, and that religion was important enough to her to have me baptized. Saying the prayers she said, singing the hymns she sang, it makes me feel closer to her somehow." She stopped, wary of oversharing. "That probably sounds silly."

"Not silly. It makes perfect sense. I'm sure she'd be very proud of you." He stopped, looked at his watch. "So we have most of the day left to play. Do you still want to hit the coffee shop? Or something else?"

She squinted at him; the bright sun overhead had already heated things up considerably. She sized him up and made a decision. "You go get the coffee, and I'll meet you there—I just need to run home first. Cream and sugar, please. Oh, and pick out some muffins or scones or something." She paused. "And get a couple of bottles of water. You're going to need them." Then she walked off before he could ask any more questions. This time, she was in charge, and she liked it that way.

Nic had no idea what Jillian was planning, but he might as well go with the flow. Tomorrow he had to meet with a city council member to discuss infrastructure plans, look into possible traffic and utilities issues, and then write up his findings before getting on a cross-country flight to Las Vegas. So today, he was going to enjoy himself as much as possible. He'd promised himself that much. Everyone and everything else could wait.

He stretched out his legs beneath the small sidewalk table outside the coffee shop. The sun was hot enough that he had chosen khaki shorts and a golf shirt instead of slacks this morning, deciding that was dressy enough for church, given the steamy weather. As he sipped from the eco-friendly paper cup he watched the Sunday morning street life ebb and flow around him. Children with dripping ice cream cones and sticky smiles, parents with shopping bags or grocery lists, all smiled or nodded a greeting to him as they passed. From his shaded vantage point under The Grind's awning he could see quite a bit of Lighthouse Avenue.

Across from him was the Sugar Cone, an old-fashioned ice cream parlor. Treasures of the Sea, a gift shop of some kind, abutted it on one side, and a used bookstore called Beach Reads was on the other. On his side of the street, there was a pharmacy to his left, and beyond that Framed, which looked to be some kind of art gallery and photo studio. To his right was a bicycle shop, and farther down were restaurants, a grocer and a clothing boutique.

On his drive over he had also passed a post office, medical clinic and the hardware store. There were no big box stores on the island, no shopping malls or dance clubs. There was one bar, more tavern than nightclub, over on the beach side, near Pete's, but there was not much in the way of nightlife. That would mean that a Caruso Hotel built here would need an on-site nightclub to satisfy its usual customer base. Recognizing he was still in work mode, he gave himself a mental shake. Surely he could spend one day focused on pleasure, not business.

Recommitted to that goal, he munched on one of the donuts he'd picked out and went back to soaking up the beach town ambiance.

Spotting a woman approaching, he blinked in surprise. Was that Jillian? She'd changed into tight athletic shorts, a spaghetti-strap tank top the color of daisies, and had her hair pulled through the hole in a white ball cap. Struggling a bit, she was pushing a metallic-green bike with oversize tires.

"What is that?" he asked, pointing to the odd-looking bike.

"It's a fat bike, for riding on sand. And it's yours, for the day, anyway. Here—" she shoved the bike at him "—hold this, I'll be right back with mine."

Bemused, he propped the bike against a pillar and waited while she went back into the bike shop. She soon came out with a similar, if slightly smaller, blue version of the first bike. Leaning it with his, she plopped down in the seat across from him and snatched one of the donuts. "Those are easier to ride than push," she commented, before taking a large bite of the sticky confection.

"I certainly hope so. It's been a while since I've ridden a bike, other than the stationary one at the gym."

"Well, you know what they say—you never forget how." She tasted the coffee next, and he got to see her eyes close in a look of pure bliss. "Best coffee on the island."

"So what's the plan?" He eyed the bike uncertainly. He hoped she was right about not forgetting how to ride. The last real bike he'd ridden had been a ten-speed in junior high. And that had been on pavement, not sand.

"First, I'm going to eat another donut and finish this coffee. Then sunscreen—don't make that face, because the sun's brutal here and even tough guys wear sunscreen—then we bike down the avenue, and take Palmetto. That's the way you would have come in on, over to the coast road. We'll take the ramp down to the beach and ride all the way to the Sandpiper." She grinned. "If you're a good boy, we'll stop for lunch along the way."

"Oh, I'm very, very good," he responded, rising to the bait. While she finished the last donut he disposed of the trash and secured a water bottle to each bike. He noticed she had an insulated bag attached to the rear rack of her bike, and wondered what other surprises she had in store.

He'd wanted something different, something outside of his normal routine, and he was getting exactly that. He even let her mount and ride ahead of him—although it chafed his ego a bit—since she was the one giving the tour.

"Follow me, watch for pedestrians and holler if you need to stop," she called over her shoulder, merging into the meager Sunday traffic.

He immediately realized there was a definite upside to taking up the rear position. Namely, the good view he had of her rear end. Shapely and athletic, it was more than enough to take his mind off his rusty biking abilities. Watching her ride, her black curls blowing in the wind, firm legs pumping up and down, he was so distracted that they had ridden several blocks before he remembered he was supposed to be taking in the scenery. Forcing himself to look away, he made himself notice the tidy storefronts as they continued down Lighthouse Avenue. He'd seen only one franchise business, and that was a gas station. All the other stores were obviously run and owned by locals, and seemed to be thriving despite any problems in the larger economy.

Paradise Isle might be a small town, but it certainly was flourishing. Not having a direct connection to I-95 had kept it isolated, but the town didn't seem to be hurting from the lack of exposure. As they turned into a more residential area, passing picturesque Spanish-style stucco homes alongside the small wooden "shotgun"-style cottages, he couldn't help feel that the people he saw mowing lawns and walking dogs were not going to be eager to have the floodgates of Florida tourism thrown open. Normally that wasn't something that he would even think about. But now, every time Jillian turned back to smile at him, he felt his sense of duty pulling him down like a weight, one he didn't know how to escape.

By the time they reached the beach, Jillian was sweating, but exuberant. The sight of the ocean, as common as it was to an islander, never failed to thrill her. Nic had been a great biking companion, staying far enough behind for safety, but close enough to hear if she needed to give directions. Not that she had doubted his athleticism, not with that body.

Stopping to rest under the shade of the sea grapes that grew around the access ramps, she freed her water bottle from its rack and drank her fill. Nic did the same, his head tilted back, tanned skin gleaming with sweat as he gulped the cool water. Watching, Jillian's mouth went dry. She raised her own bottle again to cover her slack-jawed staring.

He finished drinking and looked around. "This was a great idea—definitely more fun than the bike at the gym."

"Not much of a compliment, but I'm glad you're enjoying it. But before you get too enthusiastic, remember, we still have the beach ride."

"I'm game if you are." Daring her, he pushed off and started down the beach, leaving Jillian to catch up. She laughed out loud, and stood on the pedals to get more speed. When they hit the hard-packed sand near the water, he paralleled the coast and slowed for her to catch him. Nodding, acknowledging his win, she pulled abreast and set a more leisurely, and safer, pace down the fairly crowded beach.

Just like every other weekend there were bronzed teenagers, slick with suntan lotion showing off for their friends, eager children digging in the sand while their parents watched, and surfers on colorful boards fighting for the perfect wave. But even as everything looked the same, it felt different. She felt different. She felt…happy.

Being with Nic made her happy in a way that nothing else ever had. There was a warmth deep inside that was filling her up, as if the sun's rays were somehow penetrating all the way to her heart. In such a short time this one person had filled a hole in her life, in her heart, that she had spent years trying to ignore.

But as wonderful as he made her feel, she was scared to death of what that feeling meant, and what would happen when he left town. She'd lost her heart too many times in her life to be willing to risk that kind of pain again. Her parents, foster parents, foster siblings…they had all left, and she had the emotional scars to prove it. Sure, someday she wanted a family of her own, but getting attached to a tourist was a bad bet. Of course, that didn't mean they couldn't have a good time today, enjoy some food and activity, and then part as fond acquaintances, if not friends.

Resolved, she turned and smiled, shoving down the tingling that shot through her when he grinned back, boyish enthusiasm lighting up his face. Unlike a lot of the guys she had dated, he had nothing to prove, and was secure enough to be silly and have fun without worrying he'd look less manly. A refreshing change, one that made it hard to keep her guard up.

They cruised along, eventually leaving the populated part of the beach for the deserted stretch between the public access area and the Sandpiper. Awed, as always, by the pristine beauty, she slowed her pace to take it all in. White sand stretched for miles in either direction, marred only by the tracks of the industrious little sandpipers the nearby inn was named for. Even the ocean was at peace here, swelling slowly and stretching to the shore in a smooth arc, rather than crashing and foaming against the beach.

Signaling to Nic, she slowed, and then stopped. "I'm ready for a break, if that's okay with you."

He wiped the sweat from his forehead and ran a hand through his damp hair, his fingers mussing the dark waves. "Sure, you're the boss." He drank from his water bottle and looked around at her chosen resting point. "This is amazing. I've been on beaches all over the world, but this is something else. I feel like we're on a deserted island. I can't believe how close this is to the main part of town. It feels so far away."

"I know. It's amazing to have something this pristine only a bike ride from home. And the Sandpiper is only a little ways around that bend. They don't get busy enough to disturb this part of the beach." Sitting down on the sand, she removed her tennis shoes, stuffing her socks into them. "Come on. Let's get our feet wet, cool off a bit."

After a moment's hesitation, Nic followed suit, toe-ing off his boat shoes and following her to the ocean's edge. The water was perfect, just cool enough to be re-freshing but not cold. "Wow, that feels amazing."

She walked a little ways down the shore, splashing like a kid. There was nothing better than sun, sand and surf to clear the mind. Nic strolled with her, gradually easing closer. Trapped, she couldn't move away from him without getting into deeper water.

When he took her hand, she knew she should say something, remind him that they were just friends. But her voice caught in her throat, and she reveled in the touch of his warm, calloused palm, swinging their arms as they walked.

She was so focused on that point of contact that it took her several moments to realize how far they had strayed from the bikes. Stopping, her hand tugged on his, turning him to her. She wanted to tell him that they should go back, but his eyes locked on hers, and the words wouldn't form. He used their linked hands to pull her toward him, close against his chest. His left hand was still tangled in hers; he buried his other in her hair, anchoring her as she stood in the swirling water. She felt her heart tumble as if buffeted by the waves around him, all of her arguments washed out to sea. Logically, this was a bad idea, but she had left her good sense on the beach with the bikes and their shoes. Instead of pull-ing away, she arched up to him, ready to meet his kiss.

Splash!

Sprayed with water from head to toe, Jillian jolted, stepping back as far as his grip on her hair would let her.

"What the heck?" Nic let her go and wiped the salty water from his eyes. "What on earth just happened? Is this some kind of practical joke?"

"A pelican." Jillian, now free, retreated another step. She shook her head at the dumb luck of it. "He was diving for a fish. Usually they don't come so close to people, but a few get enough handouts from fishermen to make them pretty bold. I've never been quite that close, though." Heart pounding from the near miss with the bird, and the even nearer miss with Nic, she headed for the bikes, her steps quick and precise. She was going to have to be much more careful from now on, if she wanted to keep her pride, and her heart, intact.

After the pelican's untimely interruption, Nic found straddling a bike to be a tricky business. Luckily, his baggy shorts camouflaged the extent of his response. But discomfort aside, it was best they move on, putting the near kiss behind them. He was leaving tomorrow, and when he came back, if he came back, it would be to buy the inn she was so desperate to save. Under those circumstances, kissing her, sleeping with her, would be unethical. He had been raised better than that.

He'd never lied to a woman to get her into bed; hell, he'd never needed to. Not once they found out he was an heir to the Caruso fortune. And although he hadn't exactly lied to Jillian, he wasn't being honest, either.

There was no way around it—she and that hot body of hers were off-limits. Not that she was chasing him down; she'd all but run once he'd let her go. Something he should be grateful for.

"The Sandpiper's just ahead. We'll have lunch there on the back deck, if that's okay." Jillian pedaled easily alongside him, as if nothing had happened. Fine, if she wasn't going to bring up their near kiss, he certainly wasn't going to.

"Sounds good to me." He figured they'd order in or get something from the small kitchen at the inn, but when they parked their bikes, she unstrapped the insulated bag from hers, tossing it to him.

"Lunch is served."

Intrigued, he carried the bag up the stairs to the wide, covered deck of the Sandpiper. Shaded by an upper-level balcony and boasting several paddle fans, it was at least ten degrees cooler than the beach below. Cushioned lounge chairs at one end and an outdoor dining area at the other looked out over the water below.

He set the bag on the table and started fishing out the contents. Instead of the typical sandwich and chips, he found several plastic containers filled with obviously homemade food, as well as a small loaf of crusty bread and a thermos of lemonade. "This looks a lot better than the soggy peanut butter and jelly sandwiches I remember from picnics as a kid." He held up one of the containers. "What is all this stuff?"

"The smaller container is a smoked fish spread, made with locally caught amberjack. There are crackers to go with it. Then those two have salads in them, greens with cold chicken and a citrus dressing. And that last one has a couple of slices of key lime pie in it." She opened the smoked fish and spread some on a cracker for him. "Try it, it's good stuff."

Starving, Nic shoved the cracker in his mouth. Smoky and sweet, the flavors exploded across his taste buds. "Wow…that's seriously good," he managed to get out around the mouthful of food. "I wonder if I can buy this stuff at home." Not that he was ever home long enough to bother grocery shopping. Ignoring that depressing thought, he reached for the dish and began loading up another cracker.

Jillian sorted out the rest of the food, and he eagerly accepted his share of salad, a hunk of the crusty bread and a paper cup of lemonade. Chewing, he ate in silence, determined to keep his eyes on the view of the ocean and not on the way her shirt, damp now from the pelican encounter, clung enticingly to curves he wasn't supposed to notice. A losing battle if there ever was one.

"Penny for your thoughts."

Had she seen him staring? She was chasing a piece of lettuce with her fork, and didn't seem upset, so maybe not. "Just thinking how impressive the view is." And not just of the beach.

"It is. It's been a while since I've sat back here." Her eyes went soft, as if she was seeing something he couldn't. "Lots of memories here."

"You've stayed at the Sandpiper?"

"As a guest? No. But before the last owners died, they would host all sorts of community events. Fish fries to raise money for the fire department, Fourth of July fireworks displays, a big Christmas tree lighting party, that kind of thing. The place was pretty much the heart of the island for decades. Toward the end they were too frail to run things the way they wanted to, and when their daughter inherited, she was too busy for that sort of thing." Her mouth curved into a small smile. "Some of us are hoping to get it listed on the register of historical places. That would mean grant money, which would allow the city to buy it when it goes up for sale. I'd love to see it back in the center of things."

She paused, as if weighing if she should continue. "The thing is, when I was a kid and came here alone, everyone else was with their families. I'd always hoped to bring my own family here one day. So I offered to write the grant proposal myself. Saving the Sandpiper would be a way to hold on to that childhood dream."

The creamy pie turned bitter in his mouth. The hope in her eyes tore at him. The better part of him wanted to respond to that innocent dream, to help her achieve what she so obviously wanted. But it was impossible. His duty was to his family, to his company, not to this siren of an orphan, no matter what spell she had cast on him.

So he would do his damn job, do what he had to do. But that didn't mean he had to keep lying to her about it. He'd just have to find a way to explain things. Even if it made her hate him.

Chapter 6

Nic had been quiet ever since their picnic at the Sand-piper. He'd definitely seemed distracted on the bike ride back into town; she hoped he wasn't still upset about the kiss. Correction, the nonkiss. She'd been about to jump into his arms, and then had practically run away. Talk about mixed signals. Not something he usually dealt with, she was sure. He probably had his pick of women back home, wherever that was. She needed to get him talking about where he was from, to remind her brain that he was just a temporary distraction. Maybe then the weird tingling sensation running through her body would go away.

"So, where are you from, anyway? You never really said." Watching him out of the corner of her eye, she baited her hook with a piece of squid and executed a near perfect cast over the pier's guardrail. Fishing at the Paradise Isle Pier was a favorite way to relax, and something she'd wanted to share with him, ridiculous as that was. She really knew so little about him, other than that he wore expensive suits, cared for stray dogs and old ladies, and was way better looking than any man had a right to be.

"I'm from New Jersey, at least originally. I've got a place in Manhattan now, but I still don't think of it as home."

"You don't like New York?"

"I like it fine. You know, it's true what they say—it is the city that never sleeps. There is always something to do—anytime, day or night. I just never seem to find the time to actually do any of those things." He rubbed the stubble on his face, as if just noticing it. "I work a lot. Pretty much all the time. Spending a day like this, just enjoying myself, going with the flow... I can't remember the last time I did that." He cast his line out almost as well as she had her own. "It's a curse for a lot of us in the city. We move there for the culture, the plays, the museums, the nightclubs, and then work so damned hard we never actually see any of it."

"That sounds awful." She worked hard to support herself, but even back when she was taking classes at night and working days at the clinic, she'd always had time for walks on the beach, or a few hours fishing on the weekend.

"I shouldn't complain. I do well for myself, and a lot of people would kill for my job. And it's not like I'm working every day. But I'm out of town more than I'm home, and the rare times I am there and have a day off, I feel like I need to spend it with my family." He turned to her, earnestness shining in his eyes. "I realize I probably sound like a jerk, complaining about family, when

I should just realize how lucky I am to have them. But I don't mean it like that. I love my family, and I love spending time with them. It's just…"

"Overwhelming?"

He flinched at her word choice. "That's pretty terrible, isn't it?"

Was that shame she saw in his eyes? She put a hand on his arm. "No, I think I understand. You want to be there for them, but you want a life that's your own, too." She'd always romanticized the idea of big families, but maybe it wasn't always picture-perfect.

"Right. I just feel like I have so much responsibility at work, so many people counting on me, and then there's my family, counting on me, as well. Keeping everyone happy is a nearly impossible job." He turned back to the water, watching his line with more intensity than it probably warranted.

Sensing he was uncomfortable revealing so much, she kept her tone casual, her eyes on the water. "Wanting your own life, your own destiny, that isn't terrible. You just need to find a way to do it."

"It's not that simple." He tugged hard at his line, reeling it in and then whipping it back out.

"Why not?" She stopped pretending to watch the water, and faced him head-on. "Why can't you work less, or just tell your boss you need more time off?"

"Because I work for my family. It's a family business. If I don't get the job done, I'm not just slacking on the job, I'm betraying my family." The muscles around his eyes were tense, his jaw hard. "My parents raised me to believe that family comes first. Loyalty matters.

My dad always wanted me to take over one day, or at least play a significant role in the company. He started it from scratch and built something he could be proud of. I need to live up to that. I won't let him down. I owe him."

"Wow. Okay, that does complicate things." She was in over her head here; she had no experience balancing family and work, let alone managing them both together. But it was easy to see that he was both intensely loyal and proud. With no advice to give, she was better off just listening. "So what kind of business is it, anyway?"

Nic set his pole into one of the holders screwed into the railing, and faced her, shoulders squared as if preparing for a blow. "Hotels. My family owns Caruso Hotels."

"But…" She tried to think, get her bearings. Caruso Hotels? They were one of the biggest hotel chains in the country, catering to high-end tourists. There was even one opening in Orlando soon. She'd read something about it in the paper, and from the sketches it had included, it was going to be a world-class resort. "The Caruso Hotels? The ones with the fancy resorts all over the East Coast?"

"We're expanding out West, too. I'm flying to Vegas tomorrow to handle some issues with a land deal out there." His voice betrayed not a single shred of emotion.

"Wait—land deal?" Her heart sunk. Bits and pieces of their conversations coalesced, forming a picture she didn't want to see. She had to physically force the question past the lump in her throat. "What exactly is it you do for Caruso Hotels?"

"I'm Vice President in Charge of Acquisitions." He hesitated.

"Go ahead, tell me." She wasn't letting him get away with anything less than the whole truth, late though it was.

"I scout out new locations for our hotels, negotiate sales and make sure the building process goes smoothly."

"So you aren't just here on vacation, are you?" she accused, the words like acid in her mouth.

"To be fair, I never said I was." His denial was too little, too late. As if he realized it, he continued. "I came here to check out a potential new location, a property that recently came up for sale."

Her stomach clenched; she knew what he was going to say, but she had to hear him say it. Fisting her hands, she asked, "What location? What property are you looking to buy?"

"The Sandpiper." She rocked back as if he'd hit her. He was here to buy the Sandpiper? The city didn't stand a chance against a corporate giant like Caruso Hotels. At least now she knew why he'd been wearing a designer suit when they had first met; he'd probably been wheeling and dealing all day. And now he was here to do the same.

She'd trusted him. Told him about her childhood, her dreams for the future. And all the while he'd been planning to crush those dreams like so much sand beneath his feet. How stupid was she, to imagine he felt something for her? Here she was, thinking how he was the first man to make her heart beat faster, and he'd just been looking to get the inside scoop on the island.

Tears stung her eyes, but she refused to let them fall. "So today was just another day on the job for you, huh? Market research or whatever?" She swiped at her face. "So glad I could be of service."

Hurt flashed in his eyes before he composed his features. As if he had the right to be hurt. She was the victim, not him. "What, can't stand the truth?"

"Today wasn't about business. Hell, it's probably the first day I've had in almost a year that I didn't work." He shook his head, pacing the pier. "I have meetings scheduled for tomorrow, but this weekend was supposed to be an attempt at some downtime. Maybe try on the idea of a personal life for once. You were a part of that. This place was part of that."

"Right. Well, excuse me for thinking that a tour of the island's best tourist spots might be of professional interest to someone intent on exploiting the town for his financial gain. I might not have been part of the original plan, but hey, sometimes you just get lucky."

"Seriously? I don't want to exploit anyone. I'm just trying to do my damn job. People are counting on me. My family is counting on me."

"Right, it's all about family. How could a poor little orphan understand something like that? Obviously, I have no idea what it's like to care about people." The anger and the pain tangled within her. How could she have been so naive? How could he have been so deceitful?

"That isn't what I meant. None of this is what I

meant, what I wanted to happen." He reached out toward her, grasping her arm. "You have to believe me."

Locking down her heart, she shook him off. "Tell it to the fish. Maybe they'll believe it."

Nic watched her storm off, mired in guilt. He'd totally screwed up. Yes, his hands were tied, but that didn't justify the way he'd hurt her. And he had hurt her; he could see the pain shimmering just beneath her anger. He didn't blame her; he'd behaved badly. But it *was* business.

He should let her go before he made things worse. Just move on, get back to work and do what needed to be done, like always. Somehow, though, that didn't feel right. He had gotten this far in life by going with his gut, and right now his gut said he needed to make this right. Not because he thought he had a chance with her—he knew that was out of the question—but because, business or not, she'd gotten to him. The whole damned place had gotten to him.

Mind made up, he started after her. His own stride was twice the length of hers, and he was able to catch up before she was even halfway down the long wood-and-stone pier. "Hey, wait."

"No." She quickened her pace.

"Let me make it up to you."

"What? Now you want to bribe me? Maybe that works in New York City, but here we put people before profit. I don't want your money." Her shoulders shook. "I don't want anything from you."

"What if I help you with the grant?"

"What?" She stopped, faced him, eyes wide, brows raised.

Uh-oh, where had that idea come from?

Not one to go back on his word, he scrambled for mental traction. "Well, I could help you write the grant. If you get it, I'll back off, let the city buy the property."

"Why would you do that?" Her steady stare bored into him, daring him to lie.

"Because if the Sandpiper is listed as a historical site, it could mean a legal battle when we tear it down." Which was true.

They had the legal means to fight any challenges, but the press would be ugly, making it a huge hassle none of the executives would want to deal with. Of course, they also wouldn't want him to help write the grant proposal, but that didn't matter right now. "Listen, I've got some connections, and a lot of background dealing with properties of various importance. I'll help you however I can, and if the grant goes through I'll find somewhere else to build."

"And if it doesn't?"

"Then Caruso Hotels will make an offer." He wasn't going to lie. He was already kicking himself for his earlier misrepresentation. He'd always been a man of his word, and any hint of dishonor disgusted him. For his own sake, as well as hers, he wanted to make it up to her, and to do that they had to trust each other.

Appearing to consider his offer, she bit her plump bottom lip, forcing him to look away before he forgot this was about business, not pleasure. Thankfully, even if she took him up on his offer, they'd be collaborating long-distance; he obviously had control issues when it came to her.

"How would you even do this? You're leaving for where? Reno? The application process isn't something that can be done in one night."

"Vegas, and no, I'm not planning to do this tonight." In fact, he planned to stay far, far away from her tonight. "I work on the road all the time. Between video conferencing and email, we should be able to get it done without any real face-to-face contact." He should be relieved that there would be so much distance between them, but instead an odd heaviness settled in his bones. He drew a deep breath, suddenly exhausted. "I'll leave my contact info with the Sandpiper before I go. Just email me the forms and I'll take a look at what we're dealing with."

Shading her eyes against the setting sun, head cocked, she asked, "Who *are* you?"

"I thought we just covered that. Nic—technically, Dominic—Caruso. Do you want to see my identification or something?"

"No, I mean, I don't know. I just don't get it. One minute you're saving puppies, then helping old ladies, and now you are going to help me try to save the property you came here to buy. I don't understand. Why are you doing all this?"

"Honestly? I have no idea."

Chapter 7

Nic was still trying to understand his own motives when he got back to his room that evening. Yes, he'd felt guilty about withholding his true intentions from Jillian, but that wasn't enough to explain his impulsive, and honestly reckless, offer to help her. The last thing he needed was another person looking at him to fix everything; he got enough of that from his job. And yet here he was, taking on exactly that. Maybe he was just a masochist. What other explanation was there? Sure, he was attracted to her, but attractive women weren't exactly in short supply. So why was he willing to risk a business deal for one? Maybe it was because, unlike his family or the women he tended to date, she didn't have any preconceived expectations of him? She'd certainly been shocked when he offered to help.

Pushing away his muddled thoughts, he entered the room and absently noted that it had been tidied and the bedcovers turned down. After tossing down his wallet and keys on the nightstand, he headed straight for the shower, where a stack of clean white towels awaited him. He certainly couldn't fault the service at the Sandpiper, or much else about it, for that matter.

He turned the shower knob to hot and stripped down. When the temperature was sufficiently close to scalding, he stepped in, letting the water pound his knotted muscles. High-stakes deals, red-tape snarls and near constant travel made tension his normal condition, and he'd long ago found that a hot shower did more to relieve the stress than a bottle of whiskey. Of course, the whiskey was more fun, but with meetings back-to-back tomorrow, he couldn't afford the hangover.

He braced his hands on the cool tile and lowered his head, letting his mind wander as the jets of water worked their magic on his neck and back. Behind his closed eyelids he saw Jillian again, how she'd looked at the pier with the setting sun burnishing her skin. How she'd leaned in for the kiss that hadn't quite happened, how her tank top had clung to curves that shamed every bikini-filled billboard from here to Miami. Frustrated in more ways than one, he gave up on relaxing and shut off the tap.

As he toweled off, he caught the familiar ring of his cell phone. Crap, he'd forgotten. He always called his parents on Sunday evenings, just to touch base. It kept his mom happy and out of his hair, and let him and his dad do a bit of strategizing before the workweek started. Normally, he called around seven, and it was after nine.

Grabbing the phone, he perched on the edge of the bed, still dripping despite the towel around his waist. "Hi, Mom…sorry I didn't call, I just got back to my room a little bit ago." He shifted farther onto the bed as they talked about his sisters, his grandmother and whether he had in fact gone to church. Suitably pacified, his mother turned him over to his father, who, like always, was ready to talk business. Nic half listened as his father reiterated the issues with the Vegas deal, issues they'd already discussed several times this week. But Lorenzo Caruso took the Boy Scout motto of "be prepared" seriously, and wanted to make sure they'd covered every contingency. Normally Nic was just as obsessive as his father, but tonight he just didn't have it in him.

"So what do you think of the Sandpiper property?" his father asked, grabbing his wandering attention.

Not the conversation Nic wanted to have right now. "It's got a good view, and most of the property is undeveloped. I'll know more after I meet with the people at City Hall tomorrow."

"We already knew all that, son. What I wanted to know were your impressions of the place. Is it good enough to be a Caruso property?"

"It's got potential," he hedged.

"Something wrong? Any problems down there I should know about?"

"Just some rumblings in town. It seems the Sandpiper is something of a local landmark. People aren't very happy about the idea of it being sold." One person in particular.

"They're just nervous about change. When they see the sketches for the resort, they'll love it. People always do. And the tourist money it brings in will shut down any complaints."

"Maybe."

"You okay, son?"

"Yeah, I'm fine. Just tired. It's been a long weekend." He explained about finding Murphy, helping Mrs. Rosenberg and touring the island. He left out any mention of his attraction to Jillian, or her feelings about the sale of the Sandpiper.

"So the dog's okay now, right?"

His father was a shark in the boardroom, but a big softie when it came to animals of any kind. "Yeah, he's healing up fine, according to Jillian."

"And this Jillian, she's a pretty girl?"

"What? Where did that come from?"

"You don't expect me to believe it was your mother's persuasive powers alone that got your butt in a church pew this morning, do you?" His father's chuckle carried over the line easily, despite the miles.

"Listen, it's not like that. Besides, have you ever tried telling Mom no?"

"Absolutely not, I'm no fool. But don't change the subject. This is the first time I've heard you talk about someone or something not related to work in longer than I can remember. I can only assume there's something special about her."

A mental picture of Jillian came unbidden. He rubbed a hand across his eyes and tried to sound disinterested. "She's pretty enough, and we had a good time. Nothing wrong with that."

"Agreed, nothing wrong with that at all. In fact, I'm

happy to hear you had some downtime. Your mother and I worry about you. You work too hard."

"I do what needs to be done," he answered, hating how defensive he sounded.

"You do, and I'm grateful, and proud of your work ethic. But there's more to life than work."

"I do date, Dad. I'm not a monk." Although, come to think of it, he couldn't remember the last time he'd been out on a date. He'd given up on the idea of a real relationship years ago after the last in a string of girl-friends let it slip that she was more into his money than him. He wasn't willing to be anyone's sugar daddy.

For a while after that, he'd contented himself with casual flings. There had been a time when he'd been more than happy to pick up a girl in a hotel bar, but somehow he'd outgrown that lifestyle without really noticing. No wonder he was reacting to Jillian like she was a pool of water after a summer drought.

His dad laughed, triggering a wave of latent home-sickness. Since when did he get homesick? "No one could accuse you of celibacy. But I didn't mean…dates. I'm talking about family, love, kids. The things that are really important in life, just as important as the job. I couldn't have gotten as far as I have without your mother by my side, you know that."

"Geez, Dad. I take it Mom's pining for grandkids again?"

"It's not just her, you know. I'd like to have a chance to get to see another generation of Carusos before I'm in the grave."

"You're not exactly elderly yet. But I'll make a note that providing the next generation of Carusos is another of my obligations to the family." He couldn't help the bitterness that crept into his voice. It was just never enough.

"Obligation? Hell, what's gotten into you? You think your mother's an obligation to me? Or you kids? Something I put on the schedule like a meeting with my broker?"

Now he'd stepped in it. He knew that his father adored his mother—he'd never seen a couple more in love. And they had raised their kids in that same love. Which was why he refused to settle for anything less now. "No, sir. I know that's not how it is."

"Damn straight. Love, family, those aren't obligations, they're blessings. The best part of life. I thought we'd raised you to know that. Your mother and I don't want you to miss out on that. We want the best for you, for all you kids."

Nic cleared his throat. "I'll keep that in mind." Good Lord, this was all too much right now.

"See that you do."

After exchanging goodbyes, Nic hung up the phone without getting out of the bed. Stretching out, still in nothing but his towel, he let his eyes drift closed. He'd get up and work on some reports in a few minutes.

But the exhaustion of the day had caught up with him, and he soon fell into a restless sleep, his dreams cluttered with barking dogs, bicycles and a blue-eyed siren he was forbidden to touch.

"Hey, Jillian, you there?"

Her head snapped up; she'd been daydreaming again. "Yes, sorry. Cassie, did you need me?"

"Just wanted to know if you were going to eat out back with Mollie and me. It's too nice to stay inside today." Cassie tossed her lab coat on her desk, and left by the rear clinic door, not waiting for an answer.

A break in the heat was rare this early in the year, and always welcome. Shaking off her lethargy, she closed up the chart she'd been working on and headed for the little seating area Cassie's father had built when he owned the clinic.

Stepping outside, she took a deep breath, relishing the lack of humidity for a change. By tomorrow the weather would probably be back to the normal sauna-like conditions, but today was pleasant and mild, with a taste of fall on the breeze. Cassie and Mollie were already sitting at the old-fashioned picnic table, a pitcher of iced tea between them as they ate their lunches.

Jillian set her own lunch on the table with the others, leftovers from the picnic she'd made for Nic yesterday. Remembering their uneasy arrangement had her stomach tumbling like a Tilt-A-Whirl. Unable to eat, she sipped some of the sweet tea instead, readying herself for the interrogation to come.

"So, spill it. How'd the date with Mr. Tall, Dark and Handsome go?" Mollie never was one to mince words. She called it like she saw it, usually an endearing trait. Not so much right now.

"Yeah, give us all the details so I can live vicariously through you," Cassie demanded, waggling a carrot stick at her.

"It wasn't a date. Just a…thank-you dinner."

"No hanky-panky?" Mollie asked.

"No!"

"Not even a good-night kiss?" Cassie prodded.

Jillian felt the heat rise in her cheeks.

"You're blushing!" Cassie clapped her hands in excitement. "You *did* kiss him! Was it amazing? God, I miss kissing."

"I am not blushing. I just got a lot of sun yesterday." As if they were going to buy that excuse. Her face was always a dead giveaway. "And yes, if you must know, we kissed. But it was just once…well, almost twice, but really just once."

That piqued both women's interest, the questions coming fast and furious.

"Whoa, slow down. There's nothing really to tell. We had lunch, he kissed me goodbye and then the next day, we did some biking and fishing."

"Two dates in two days, but there's nothing to tell? What happened?" Mollie's eyes crinkled in confusion. "I would have sworn I saw sparks flying when I ran into you at Pete's. Did he end up being a dud?"

Remembering the way she'd felt pressed against him, the way he'd made forgotten parts of her anatomy tingle, had her shaking her head. "No, not a dud. But things got…complicated."

"It's been a while since I've been with a man, but I don't remember it being that complicated. Slot A, Tab B, that kind of thing," Cassie countered.

"Cassie! Seriously? Get your mind out of the gutter. What I meant is, he isn't who I thought he was. He's not here on vacation, for one thing." At their blank looks, she added, "You know Caruso Hotels, right?"

"Of course," Cassie answered. "They've got that giant resort and casino down south, and I heard they're building one in Orlando, too. It's supposed to have its own water park and two nightclubs." She stopped, mouth dropping open. "Wait, Nic Caruso…he's one of *those* Carusos? What's he doing here?"

"He's here to see about buying the Sandpiper, that's what. They want to tear it down and use the land for one of their mega-resorts." The thought still stung. Sure, for him it was a job, not a personal attack, but the idea of her home being turned into some kind of twenty-four-hour tourist trap sure felt personal. At least being angry about it felt more useful than the tears did.

"What a lousy piece of—"

"Hold on, Mollie, it isn't settled yet. He says Caruso Hotels won't buy it if the grant goes through—they don't want the bad press of tearing down an historical site. And…he's going to help me with the grant application."

That bombshell had even Mollie speechless for once. Cassie regained her composure more quickly. "Wait, why would he help you if it would mess up his own plans?"

"Honestly, I'm not sure." She had lost hours of sleep trying to figure that one out. "He said he felt bad about not telling me who he was, but… I just don't know."

"I wouldn't trust him," was Mollie's response.

"Don't worry, I won't." Trust was earned as far as she was concerned; she'd learned that the hard way, growing up in foster care. Too many times she'd counted on someone, trusted them, only to have them leave without a backward glance. Better to rely only on yourself than to have your heart broken. She would never let someone shatter her that way again. No matter how tempting he was, she planned on keeping Mr. Nic Caruso a safe distance from her heart.

Chapter 8

Jillian had overslept again today, after another night of tossing and turning. In fact, she hadn't slept well in weeks, not since she'd started working on the grant to save the Sandpiper. So much was riding on that application; she felt she had to get everything just right. If it wasn't for Nic's help, she would have gone crazy by now. She'd tracked down important events in the building's history using the library, but most of the technical work had been on his shoulders.

He had brought in an architect he knew to help them make sure they were describing all the building's attributes correctly, and then arranged for the land survey required. She just hoped it was enough. There was only so much grant money to go around, and as beautiful as the Sandpiper was, looks alone wouldn't cut it. Without any ties to important historical figures, the odds were long at best.

She'd mailed off the paperwork this morning, so now it was a waiting game.

That Nic was coming into town tonight hadn't helped her nerves, either. Having him call or chat on Skype every single night had been bad enough. The application didn't really require daily communication, but not a night had gone by that he hadn't spent time talking with her, asking her about her day, getting under her skin in a way that she hadn't expected.

Then he had offered to take her to dinner to celebrate the completion of the grant paperwork. She'd told herself it wasn't a date, not really. Just two friends marking the end of a business relationship. If she'd spent extra time choosing a dress to wear tonight, well, that was just because she didn't often get a chance to go somewhere as nice as Bayfront, where he'd made reservations. The sheer black dress had been a fun splurge, one both Cassie and Mollie had approved of when they had seen her hang it in the break room this morning. And the queasy feeling in her stomach was because she'd been too busy to eat lunch, nothing more.

At least after this it would be over. She'd gotten a bit too comfortable with their routine, snuggled into the couch, talking to him for hours every evening. That kind of closeness wasn't a good idea with someone like him, someone from a world so different from hers. She'd miss their chats, she could admit that, but that was all the more reason they needed to end. She'd have dinner with him tonight, but that would be their last contact until there was news of the grant, one way or the other.

Hoping to take her mind off the Sandpiper—and Nic—she grabbed the chart for the final patient of the day. She'd worked through lunch, and hoped this would be a quick case. She was eager for dinner, and still needed to change before Nic arrived. Before she entered the exam room to get the patient's vitals, she skimmed the notes Mollie had made.

Oh, God—no—this couldn't be right. The patient, Bailey, was a favorite at the clinic, a young beagle who'd never met a stranger. His owners, newlyweds in their late twenties, were just as friendly. Jillian always looked forward to their visits, which until now had consisted of routine checkups and the occasional ear infection. But, according to the notes in the chart, this was something altogether different.

It seemed that Bailey had been injured when jumping off the bed a few days ago, and at first he had been only mildly stiff. But instead of getting better, he'd gotten worse, and now was dragging both hind legs. Apprehensive, Jillian entered the room, hoping the young owner had exaggerated the symptoms. Maybe Bailey was just limping a bit, a little sore. One look, however, confirmed the worst. The normally exuberant pup was crouched in the corner, shaking instead of prancing for a treat, as was his normal habit. Elle Hancock, the beagle's mistress, was red-eyed from crying, and obviously struggling to hold it together.

Jillian felt like crying herself, but fought down her own emotions. She needed to project confidence for Bailey's sake, and Elle's. Gently lifting Bailey onto the table, she checked his temperature, pulse and respiration rate while Elle watched with concern.

"That's a good boy. You sure got yourself in trouble, didn't you, buddy? Don't you know better than to scare your mama like this? That's it, easy now." She finished her tasks and, reassuring Elle as much as she could, went to fetch Cassie. She found her in the lab, looking over an earlier patient's blood work results.

"Cassie?"

"One minute." She finished reading the report, then set it on the counter. "Who's next?"

"It's Bailey, and it's bad." She forced herself to be clinical. "I'm worried it's his back. You're going to need to take a look, but if we want to catch Dr. Rainer before he leaves for the day, I should have Mollie call as soon as possible." Dr. Rainer, the best veterinary neurologist in the state, was at least an hour's drive away. If they were going to transfer the paralyzed patient they'd need to start the process soon, or he wouldn't make it there before closing time.

"Oh, no, Bailey? Is he ambulatory?"

"Nope, totally down in the rear, not able to stand or walk at all."

"In that case, yeah, go ask Mollie to give Dr. Rainer a heads-up, then come join me in the exam room."

Cassie's very thorough exam was not encouraging. She tried to offer some hope, but cautioned that, with cases like this, there was a possibility the paralysis would be permanent—or worse—progress further. The prognosis wasn't good, and everyone in the room knew it.

With an increasing sense of dread, Jillian carried the patient beagle to the car. Elle followed with a copy of Bailey's medical records and driving directions to the specialist. As if sensing her unhappiness, Bailey squirmed, angling himself to lick her face in reassurance. The sweet creature was trying to comfort her, when he was the one so gravely injured. Touched, her tears spilled silently down her cheeks, soaking into the soft brown fur. Settling him on the seat of the car, she turned and hugged Elle, who had tear streaks of her own on her face. "Good luck. He's a strong, healthy dog, and Dr. Rainer's the best. You'll like her, I promise."

Elle simply nodded and got into the car. Jillian watched her drive away, then walked back inside, her legs almost too weak to carry her. Dazed and overwhelmed, she stood in the empty waiting room, unsure of what to do next. Intellectually, she knew that weeks of sleep deprivation and a skipped lunch were as much to blame for her reaction as concern for her patient, but the fear and grief were like a living thing, crushing her from the inside. On autopilot, tears still falling, she headed for the treatment room. There were patients that needed medications and lab equipment that needed to be taken care of before she could leave. She just had to get through the next half hour or so, then she would curl up somewhere and let the numbness swallow her.

For once traffic was cooperating, and Nic was fairly confident he could catch Jillian at the clinic before closing time. Maybe a smarter man would have stayed in Orlando after finishing his meetings, instead of heading for Paradise again. But being so close to Jillian without seeing her would take a stronger man than he had ever been or could ever hope to be. It was like he was addicted, and she was the drug. She'd slipped into his system somehow, and now he couldn't get her out. More surprisingly, he didn't want to get her out. Or let her go.

Of course, there was a chance that after seeing her in person, he'd find that she was just a woman like all the others, looking out for herself. Not the near-angel he'd come to think of her as during their nightly conversations. It had been her looks that caught his attention, but what had him reaching for the phone every night went deeper than that.

As they had worked on the complicated government forms, he'd found she had a sharp intellect tempered by an easy wit. Even more impressive was her determination. She had grit, and there was nothing he admired more. She certainly had to be tough to have made it through foster care, then living on her own and putting herself through school. He couldn't think of a more independent woman, and he'd certainly known his share, growing up with his mom and two sisters.

It was her independence, as much as anything, that made him feel comfortable getting as close as they had. He'd avoided entanglements for years, unable to handle being responsible for even one more person, as weighed down as he felt by work and family already. He hated that he sometimes resented the long hours and constant travel that he felt obligated to do. Even worse, he was starting to think of his family only in terms of the job, lumping them in with the rest of his to-do list.

Having one more person pushing him to be more, do more, might send him over the edge. And that's what women he dated always wanted: for him to work harder, make more money, gain more power for them to bask in. He didn't think Jillian was like that, but only time would tell. The more jaded part of him said that finding out wasn't worth the risk of being used again.

So why was he, even now, crossing over the Intracoastal, on his way to see a woman he had no business seeing? Because he couldn't do anything else, that's why. Being this out of control was a new feeling, one that didn't sit well. At least driving to Paradise Isle was taking action, and action was always better than inaction. He'd see her, take her to dinner to celebrate the grant process being over, and maybe even get her out of his system for good.

Keeping that in mind, he pulled into the clinic parking lot just before six. He noted her tiny compact in the lot. Good, he hadn't missed her. Pleased that things were going according to plan, he locked his rental, the same style of SUV he'd rented before, and examined the building in front of him; he'd been in too big a hurry last time to notice many details. The low-slung building was in the same Spanish-style stucco as many of the other buildings on the street, with large glass windows lining the front, tinted against the brutal Florida sun. A nicely landscaped path took him to the front door, where he chuckled at a discreetly placed container of doggy pick-up bags. Swinging open the heavy door, he strode to the front desk, where Mollie and the doctor— Cassie something—had their heads together, whispering worriedly. He didn't see anyone else in the waiting area; from the state of the parking lot, he assumed the last clients must have already left.

"Hello, Mollie, Doctor. Is Jillian still here?" He'd seen her car, but it seemed presumptuous not to ask.

The two women looked at each other, as if conferring silently. The hair prickled on the back of his neck. Something wasn't right here. Something to do with Jillian. "What? What's going on? Where's Jillian?" Fear made his voice harsh, but damn it, how did they expect him to react?

The veterinarian spoke first, silencing Mollie with a gesture. "Jillian is in the back, finishing up with some overnight patients." She paused, as if she wasn't sure how to phrase what came next. "She…had a hard day. She might not be up to dinner tonight. Maybe you could postpone?"

"Not possible. I'm only in town one night. I flew in this morning to finish up some details on our Orlando project, and I fly back out in the morning." What was going on here? "We've got reservations in an hour." He'd secured the seats at the elegant restaurant on a whim, one he was seriously rethinking. "Listen, if she doesn't want to go, or has other plans, just say so."

Mollie stood up, ignoring the other woman, and quickly made for the doorway to the next room. "I'll tell her you're here."

Nic turned back to the doctor. "You still haven't answered my questions, Doctor. So either you tell me what's going on, now, or I can force my way back there and see for myself. Either way, I'm not leaving until I know Jillian's okay. You choose." Someone was going to give him some answers, fast.

"Please, call me Cassie." The petite woman smiled,

not in the least intimidated by his assertive demands. Oddly, that made him like her more, but he wasn't going to back down on his threat. "Jillian's a bit upset, that's all. One of her favorite patients just came in, critically injured. We've transferred him to a specialist, but his chances aren't good. It hit all of us hard, but Jillian particularly so. She's…not herself right now. I'm a bit worried about her being alone, so all in all, it's probably a good thing that you're here."

"Murphy?" He swallowed hard.

"Oh, no, not Murphy. Another patient, a sweet dog with really nice owners."

Hearing that the rascally border collie was safe had him relaxing the fists he hadn't known he'd been clenching. "But don't patients get hurt all the time? I mean, I get it, it's sad, but isn't that kind of business as usual?"

"Sure, and usually everyone handles it very professionally. You learn to keep your emotions in check, to be kind, but not get drawn into it. You have to. But sometimes…sometimes something happens and it's like all the pain is there at once, all that emotion you've managed to ignore over a hundred different patients swallows you up for a time. It happens to all of us, when we're tired, or stressed out, or just not up to par. A pint of rocky road and a good cry are the usual treatment, and then, when you finish crying, you're ready to do it all over again, see that next patient, face whatever the next challenge is." Her smile was weak, and couldn't hide the strain on her face.

He'd never really thought about how hard a job like this could be. It made his issues with zoning boards and contractors seem petty. That these women dealt with this kind of emotional trauma on a regular basis had him in awe. He'd be a basket case trying to deal with all that. So tonight he'd make sure to keep things light, cheer Jillian up, show her a good time. No problem.

Nic heard the treatment room door open behind him, and turned, a smile in place. Then he saw her, and his heart stuttered in his chest. Her face was tearstained, her normally pale skin blanched an unnatural white. He had to grip the counter in front of him to keep from picking her up and carrying her out of there.

Instead, he let her come to him. Gently, he placed a palm on her cheek, needing to touch her, but afraid she might shatter like a crystal if handled clumsily. She didn't so much as blink, just pressed her own palm against his hand, holding him to her. Her eyes, red from crying, pleaded with him, but for what? What could he do?

"She's been like this how long?" He kept his attention on Jillian, but his words, bitten past the lump in his throat, were for Cassie.

"About twenty, thirty minutes. She'll be okay. She just needs a little TLC."

"I just want to go home." Her words were clear, if quiet.

"I'm going to get you out of here, okay, honey?" He moved his hand down to her waist, steering her toward the front door. "Are you hungry?"

"She skipped lunch. We got swamped today, so I know

she hasn't had anything since breakfast, if then," Cassie interjected, concern showing in the lines on her face.

"I… I didn't have breakfast, I overslept. But I'm not hungry right now. I'm fine, really."

Her voice sounded stronger, but he could see what the effort was costing her. She was ready to collapse, no two ways about it. No way was he letting her go home by herself. Cassie was right; she was in no condition to be alone right now.

Or to go to a fancy restaurant.

Fine. Problems cropped up in his work all the time; this was no different. He'd just come up with a new plan. Gears turning, he accepted the small purse and slinky black dress that Mollie retrieved for Jillian, then waved a brief goodbye as he escorted her out of the building.

When she stumbled, he held her tighter, half carrying her slender form by the time they reached his car. Using the button on the key fob to unlock it, he used his free hand to open the door, then simply lifted her up and into the seat. She was like deadweight in his arms, and her lack of protest scared him. She just sat there, eyes closed, so he reached over and buckled her in himself. Careful not to catch her hair in the door, he closed her in and ran around to the driver's side, starting the car with no real idea of where to go or what to do.

He headed for the Sandpiper. He'd reserved a room earlier, and they'd be able to get food there. Besides, it was as close to a home turf as he had right now.

Driving carefully, ridiculously afraid to jar her, he kept one eye on the road and one on her pale face. She appeared to be almost asleep, probably the best thing right now. His panic abating, he wanted to shake her for letting herself get so run-down. He'd known her to be resilient, practically invulnerable; seeing her this fragile made his heart ache in a way he didn't want to acknowledge. Instead, he focused on the task at hand, getting her to the inn, getting some food in her and then giving her hell for scaring him like this.

Plan in place, he pulled into the closest spot he could find in the Sandpiper parking lot. Rounding to her door, he touched her arm, again struck by how cold she felt. Her eyes opened at his touch. "Hey, honey, we're here. Can you get out?"

She nodded, taking in their surroundings without a word. If she was surprised he'd brought her to the inn instead of her apartment, she didn't show it. She could question his motives later. Right now, he just wanted to get her to his room safely. After that? He didn't have a clue.

Chapter 9

Jillian wandered the lobby of the inn while Nic checked in with the front desk. It had been a while since she'd seen the inside, but not much had changed. The natural orchids in the coquina fireplace caught her eye; it must be too early in the year for a fire. Too bad, she would appreciate the warmth right now. She was cold down to her bones. Served her right for skimping on meals and sleep. Nic must think she was an idiot, acting like some kind of trauma victim over an injured dog. She would have tried to explain in the car, but she was just too tired. Just thinking about putting that many words together was exhausting. She desperately wanted to flop down in one of the lobby chairs, but if she sat down, she might not get back up again.

Finished at the desk, Nic motioned for her to follow. Maybe he wanted to drop his stuff off before taking her back to her place? Why else would he have brought her here? Or did he bring her here so she could change into her dress? Did he still want to go out to dinner? Nothing made sense to her frazzled brain, and trying to figure it out made her head hurt. Better to go along with whatever he was planning, and figure it all out later.

He led her up a flight of stairs, catching her elbow when she almost missed a step. At the landing he went right and opened the last door off the hallway. Watching her, he paused, then gestured for her to go in.

Of course, ladies first. Always the gentleman. An absurd giggle threatened to bubble up, another sure sign she was way over her emotional limit for the day.

Inside, he locked the door, set her purse on the nightstand and strode directly to the bathroom. Left to wait again, she checked out the room. She'd never been in one of the Sandpiper's guest rooms, and this one was certainly worth seeing. A king-size sleigh bed dominated the room, its carved cherry headboard an art piece in itself. A small sitting area with two wingback chairs sat in front of the balcony doors, and a low dresser with a flat-screen television on top completed the furniture. Turning to take it all in, she found Nic standing at the bathroom door, watching her.

"I ran you a bath, put whatever bubble stuff they had in it. It should warm you up. I'll order the food while you're taking your bath." His words were clear, but she couldn't wrap her head around his meaning.

"You want me to take a bath?"

"You're cold, and you're upset. My sisters swear by long baths when they're upset. My mom, too. I thought it might help."

"I don't know…"

"Just take the bath. Then we can talk, or not talk,

whatever." He scrubbed a hand over his face. "Listen, I'm not trying to seduce you or anything, okay? Just take the bath, please?"

It was the "please" that got to her. She knew adding it on had cost him. And really, a bath did sound wonderful. Her apartment only had a glassed-in shower stall, no tub. Stretching out in the big claw-foot one behind him would be heavenly. And warm, so very warm. Giving in, she nodded. "Okay."

He stepped aside so she could pass, saying nothing, but looking relieved when she went into the bathroom and shut the door. Stripping quickly, ignoring her appearance in the mirror, she sank into the fragrant bubbles. The scent of lavender and honeysuckle rose up on the steam, making her feel like she was floating on flower petals instead of water. Heat seeped into her, releasing the muscles she had been clenching in a desperate attempt to keep from falling apart. Letting herself slide down the tub, she submerged to her ears, and tuned the world out for a few blessed minutes.

Cocooned in the fragrant water, her thoughts turned to the man that had brought her here. Who would have thought a straitlaced corporate executive would have such a sensitive side? She would have bet money he was going to bail when he saw her falling apart like that—she'd seen the fear and confusion in his eyes— but instead he'd rushed to her side, supported her, been there for her.

Nothing in her background had prepared her for that kind of reaction. No one had ever really been there for her, taken care of her. The Marshalls, Cassie's family, had tried, but she'd been too distrustful to let them get close. So they'd mostly let her take care of herself, which was exactly what she'd wanted and needed. Foster care and living on her own so young had taught her to be independent, no matter what.

As much as she said she wanted a husband and a family someday, the idea of actually letting down her guard, being that close, that dependent on anyone, had always terrified her. But with Nic it felt natural. Easy. Safe. Who knew that giving up a bit of control could feel so right?

Creak...

She sat bolt upright at the sudden sound, only to immediately slosh back under the bubbles when she saw Nic at the door. "What are you doing in here? Get out!"

"I knocked, but you didn't answer. I was afraid you'd fallen asleep in there." He had one hand over his eyes; the other was clutching a stack of clothing. "I brought you some sweatpants and a T-shirt. I thought you might want to change when you were done, and that dress didn't look very comfortable."

She wouldn't have heard his knock with her ears submerged. But still! "Just leave them there and get *out*." Mortified, she slid farther under the water, hoping everything was covered. She didn't trust him not to peek between his fingers. Just the thought of him seeing her nude warmed her blood, despite the rapidly cooling water. Nic Caruso definitely heated things up, that's for sure.

When she was sure he was gone, she jumped out of the tub, then darted to the door to lock herself in.

Heart pounding, she grabbed a towel and dried herself hurriedly, feeling exposed despite the locked door between them. She threw on the too-big clothes, the soft shirt falling nearly to her knees. The pants she cinched with the drawstring, and then rolled up the legs so she wouldn't trip.

Fully covered, she stopped to catch her breath and mop up the water she'd sloshed onto the floor in her mad dash to lock the door. She ignored the fogged-up mirror; a quick finger comb of her curls was the best she could do appearance-wise, anyway. Her makeup was in her purse in the other room. Not that she was trying to impress him. They both knew that anything between them was completely impossible. No point in getting worked up over what was, in the end, just a business relationship.

After closing the door, Nic sank down onto the edge of the bed. He really had been concerned she might have fallen asleep in there. But his brotherly compassion had flown the coop when she'd jolted into a sitting position, suds streaking down her slick skin. He'd covered his eyes as quickly as he could, but not before he'd seen more than he should, more than was good for him. The image of all that creamy skin, slick and rosy from the bathwater, was going to be branded in his brain forever.

Adjusting his suddenly too-tight pants, he debated calling down to room service again to ask for some whiskey, something to take the edge off. On the other hand, if he was going to have any hope of taking care of her needs, rather than focusing on his own less honorable ones, he needed to stay sober. Otherwise, he was liable to forget what a bad idea being together was, and in her weakened condition that would be unforgivable. He might be a hot-blooded guy, but he knew not to take advantage of a woman; his father had drilled that lesson into him by the time he hit puberty. Which meant he needed to keep his libido locked down, even if it killed him.

The click of the bathroom door signaled her return. She edged out around the door, and he knew he was doomed. Seeing her in his shirt, his clothes, was like a sucker punch to the gut. The soft material clung to her curves, her hair was damp and curling around her face, and her big eyes were even darker against her still-too-pale skin. She was softness, and vulnerability, and everything he thought he didn't want, didn't need, all bundled up in a package hot enough to melt steel. Absently, he pressed a hand against the aching in his chest. Dear God, what was he going to do with her?

Worse, what was she doing to him?

"I'm sorry."

Her voice jump-started his stalled mental capacities. "What?" Yeah, that sounded brilliant.

"I said I'm sorry. I don't know what got into me. I'm never like that." She fiddled with the drawstring to his too-big sweatpants. The innocent movement had his hormones swirling again. The lady was killing him slowly and she had no idea she was doing it.

"Like what?"

"Weak." Her eyes dropped at the word.

Crossing to her, he lifted her chin, his fingers burning where they met her skin. "Not weak. Human. We all have a breaking point, honey. Today, you hit yours."

She offered a shy smile, then broke contact by stepping past him, toward the sitting area. "I shouldn't have skipped lunch, it was stupid. We were just so busy and—"

"And you were taking care of everyone else but yourself. Am I right?" He cocked an eyebrow, daring her to contradict him.

She raised her chin, defensiveness radiating off her. "That's my job. It's not like I was doing my nails or something. I was busy."

Good, she was getting her spunk back. "I get that. I get busy, too. But you've got people and their pets depending on you, so try for some balance, okay? Stock some snacks in the break room for when you're busy, or protein shakes, whatever. Being busy doesn't have to mean letting your blood sugar crash. You're smarter than that." He really did hope she would listen; she'd scared the crap out of him. If pushing her buttons would get her to take better care of herself, he was more than willing to do it.

Looking chastened, she shrugged. "You're right. It was dumb."

"Like I said, we all have bad days."

"I bet you've never cried on the job."

The image of him crying in the middle of some business deal had the corners of his mouth twitching. "No, I guess not. But I do yell, and I bet you don't do that."

"No, I guess I don't," she conceded. Her stomach

rumbled audibly. "I'm too hungry to keep arguing. I think I could eat a horse."

"Well, horse wasn't on the menu, but hopefully burgers and fries will work. I'd planned to take you out for steak and champagne, but comfort food and a movie on pay-per-view seemed like a better idea, given the circumstances."

"A burger sounds heavenly right now. Then we'll see about a movie."

A knock at the door signaled the arrival of room service. Nic opened the door for a teenager pushing a wheeled cart with an assortment of covered dishes. The food was transferred to the sitting table, along with two sodas, napkins and tableware. Nic signed the receipt, gave a generous tip and closed the door. Turning back to the table, he let Jillian choose her chair, then settled in the one opposite. "I hope soda is okay. I thought it might help get your blood sugar up quickly, in case you weren't ready for a meal yet."

"It's fine, and I'm more than ready to eat, trust me."

Trust. She threw the word out casually, but they both knew it wasn't as easy as all that. Trust had to be earned, and even then you could still get burned. He trusted his family, sure, but he'd seen too many handshake deals gone wrong, seen too many wealthy men used by women as nothing more than a meal ticket, to be willing to accept anything or anyone at face value. That Jillian, sitting there, barefaced, in his old clothes, could make him want to let down his hard-won barriers was absolutely terrifying. He'd been worried about not hurting her, but now he realized she held the power to hurt him, as well. And that was something he could not allow.

Jillian attacked her burger with a vengeance. She felt like her stomach was turning itself inside out, she was so hungry. Her embarrassing outburst had sapped her remaining reserves, leaving her hollowed out in more ways than one. The juicy burger would fill some of that emptiness, but not all of it. Work, her friendship with Cassie and Mollie, her church, the animals, they helped, but at the end of the day there was still a dark hole deep down inside. One she hadn't been aware of until she met Nic.

Rolling her eyes at her own melodrama, she concentrated on the good food in front of her instead of the man across the table. He must think she was some kind of basket case. No need to make it worse by mooning over him. Only when the last fry was gone, and as much of the burger as she could stuff in, did she risk conversation.

"So I never did ask why you had to come back to Orlando. I thought you were working over in, where was it—South Carolina—this week?"

"I was able to wrap up that deal yesterday, but there were some environmental issues to address at the Orlando site, so I flew in this morning. I met with the landscape architect and the environmental group, got them to come up with a compromise that provided the drainage we need while protecting the native species in the area. And of course, I wanted the chance to celebrate with you."

"I'm sorry we missed our reservations." Her burger suddenly felt heavy in her stomach. He'd had such a long day, then driven all the way out here to treat her to dinner, and instead of a celebration he'd ended up playing nursemaid.

"Hey, I told you, you have nothing to be sorry for." His deep voice brooked no argument. "Besides, I'd rather eat burgers in a T-shirt than lobster in a suit any day."

He did look content, and all male, leaning back in that big chair, long legs sprawled out in front of him. His T-shirt—he must have changed while she was in the tub—stretched across his broad shoulders and well-defined chest, making him look more like a male model than a businessman. But the casual clothes did nothing to detract from the energy that radiated off him. Men like him didn't need power suits to be intimidating; they were just born that way.

Watching him, mesmerized by all that maleness, she didn't even notice the buzzing coming from her purse.

"Is that your phone?"

"My phone? Oh, crud, yes, my phone! I forgot to turn it off vibrate when I left work." She dove onto the bed to grab her purse, retrieving her phone before the voice mail could kick in. Spotting Cassie's number on the caller ID had her burger threatening to come back up. *Please, please, don't be bad news.*

"Hey Cassie, do you have news on Bailey?" She listened to Cassie's report, tears stinging her eyes, heart in her throat. "Are they sure? Oh, thank God! Does Elle know? Wonderful! Okay, let me know if there's anything I can do." She gave Nic a quick thumbs-up when he sank down on the bed beside her. "All right, see you Monday. And thanks again for calling."

She hung up and turned, the tiredness gone, her smile stretching so wide she thought her face might break in half.

"Good news, I take it?"

"The best. His test results looked better than expected, and he's already responding to the intravenous medication they're giving him. It will take a while, but they think he'll make a full recovery. He's going to be okay!"

Overwhelmed, she threw her arms around him, hugging him in celebration. Her face pressed to his shoulder, she inhaled his clean, spicy scent as he returned the embrace. He felt strong and safe, his muscles hard beneath her hands. Then his arms tightened around her, and that quickly the moment shifted. Her breathing quickened as one of his hands began to rub sensuous circles up and down her back. Melting, she yielded to the pressure, arching into him, her head bowed back to the kiss she craved as much as her next breath.

He met her halfway. His mouth came down over hers, tasting and then plundering as he lifted her into his lap.

Her hands roamed his body, testing the muscles beneath. His fingers wrapped in her hair, pinning her in place as their tongues danced to a silent rhythm.

Head spinning, she clung to him, fists bunching in his shirt as heat pulsed beneath her skin. Every cell in her body was screaming that this was right, he was right. Deep inside, something clicked, as if the tumblers of a lock were falling in place.

Greedy, hungry for more, she pressed even closer, swept up in the magic he wove with his hands and lips, knowing now that she needed him, more than she'd ever needed anyone.

Holding Jillian was like holding a live wire, her soft curves lighting up his body wherever she pressed against him. Her hands electrified nerve endings everywhere she touched, daring his body to respond. Nuzzling his way from her lips to her slender neck, he tumbled them both to the bed, angling her so her compact body landed on top of his own hardness.

"Ouch!"

A sharp pain shot through his back, just below his rib cage. "What the..." Moving Jillian to the side, he rolled and reached for the unseen weapon. "A fork?"

"What? Oh, no, I must have dropped it when I was grabbing for the phone. I was so worried it would be bad news, I forgot it was in my hand." Giggling, she bit her bottom lip. "Are you okay?"

She was laughing? The most intense kiss in his life ends with him being stabbed in the back, and she was laughing at him? Lobbing a pillow at her head, he grunted out, "It's not funny. I could have been seriously injured."

"Uh-huh."

"This is serious." He tried to sound stern, but knew he'd failed. The truth was, it was serious, way too serious, given that he was leaving first thing in the morning. They'd come very close to crossing a line, one he had promised himself he wouldn't cross, not while she was weak and vulnerable.

As if trying to diffuse the situation, Jillian scooted up to the top of the bed, carefully keeping to her side, and grabbed the remote. Eyes averted, she focused on the flat-screen television across from the bed. "You promised me a movie, didn't you?"

Willing to play along, knowing this wasn't the time to push things, he stretched himself out next to her, plumping a pillow under his head. "Yes, ma'am. Lady's choice."

Less than an hour into the movie, Jillian's slow, even breathing told him she had fallen asleep. Should he wake her up, take her home? She didn't have to work tomorrow; he knew it was her one weekend off this month. It seemed a shame to disturb her when she was so tired. If she stayed, it would be torture to lie beside her all night, without touching, but the idea of waking up beside her was oddly tempting.

Ignoring the warning bells in his head, he kissed her forehead and pulled the covers over her, settling himself in for a long night. Despite the lingering sexual tension, listening to her breathing proved more relaxing than he would have predicted. He was on the verge of drifting off himself when he heard her cell phone ringing.

Please, not more bad news, not now. Teeth clenched, he grabbed the phone from the table and answered it himself, as she slowly stirred beside him.

"Hello?"

"Who's this? Where's Jillian?" The voice sounded oddly familiar.

"This is Nic. Jillian's right here. Can I tell her who's calling?" Jillian was sitting up now, reaching for the phone, rubbing her eyes.

"It's Vivian Rosenberg, that's who! Now let me talk to Jillian!" Handing the phone to Jillian he made the connection. Rosenberg? As in Murphy's owner? Had something happened to the dog? Listening to Jillian's reassurances that she'd be right there, wherever *there* was, he quickly found and put on socks and shoes, handing Jillian hers, as well. Keys in hand, he was ready to go when she hung up.

"Murphy got away again. Mrs. Rosenberg had the senior group over tonight for cards, and in the confusion of everyone leaving, he slipped out." She slipped on her shoes, then grabbed the plastic bag he'd given her to put her clothes in after her bath.

"We'll find him," he assured her, already unlocking the door.

"We? Oh, Nic, you don't have to come. You can just drop me off at the clinic. I've got my car there."

"No way. I'm going with you. It's late, and however safe Paradise is, you shouldn't be running around in the dark by yourself."

She rolled her eyes, but didn't protest. "Fine, let's just hurry."

They made for the car and were on the road within minutes, both of them scouring the streets for signs of Murphy on the way to Mrs. Rosenberg's. As they entered her neighborhood, he remembered something he'd been wondering about. "Why did she call you, not the clinic, or animal services or something?"

"Well, I've been going over there every day to take Murphy for a run, do some training with him. She knows I love him just as much as she does, that I'd want to be the one to look for him. Plus, he knows me, so he's more likely to come if he hears me calling."

"You go over there every day?"

"Well, not tonight, obviously. But yeah, either before or after work, ever since his last escape attempt. She still wants me to keep him, but since I can't, this is the best I can do, and the exercise keeps him out of trouble. Usually." She smiled, but it didn't reach her eyes. "It's almost like having my own dog."

They rode in silence the rest of the way, him wondering at the bond she'd forged with Murphy, and the dedication it took to go take care of yet another animal after a full day of doing just that at the clinic. Every time he thought he knew her, she impressed him again. That someone so dedicated to pets couldn't have one of her own struck him as incredibly sad, but she had made the best of it, like she did with everything. Hopefully, she'd be able to do the same if Caruso Hotels bought the Sandpiper.

Sobered by the thought, he let Jillian take the lead when they reached Mrs. Rosenberg's. The elderly woman handed out flashlights, clutching a fuchsia robe around her, seemingly unconcerned that Nic was with Jillian at this late hour. He'd wondered if she'd say something, and was glad when she didn't. He didn't want Jillian having to deal with small-town gossip about their relationship. Especially since he hadn't figured out how they could ever have a relationship. He had a job to do, and he couldn't ignore it for the sake of one woman, no matter how bewitching she was. Which meant he'd keep the Caruso legacy moving forward, and hope it didn't push her out of his life entirely.

Chapter 10

Flashlight in hand, Jillian tried to figure out where to start looking. Her head was such a tangle right now, she wasn't sure she could find her way out of a paper bag, much less locate a stubborn pup with a nose for trouble. "I always use the same route when I take him on his run, and dogs can be creatures of habit. Maybe he was frustrated because I didn't come today, and followed it on his own."

"Makes as much sense as anything. Lead the way." Nic held a flashlight, a bottle of water and Murphy's leash. Jillian had dog treats and the other flashlight. Together they started down the quiet suburban street, taking turns calling for the dog. At each clump of trees, she'd stop and check the shadows before moving on to the next bush, the next yard, the next block.

The moon was bright above the horizon, creating a silver-tinged landscape that would have been romantic under any other circumstances. Jasmine blew on the breeze, sweetening the evening, despite the fear that gripped her. Poor Murphy. His training was progressing, but with the limited time she had to spend with him, he still wasn't trustworthy around doors. And Mrs. Rosenberg, bless her heart, wasn't up to the challenge he presented. If he was hers full-time, she could have had him well under control by now, but her landlord wasn't budging. Just one more dream that wasn't going to come true.

Watching Nic as he checked yet another hedge, she sighed. He was another dream that wasn't going to be realized. The past few weeks, she'd gotten to see the man behind the business suit, and she liked what she saw. His workaholic nature was driven not by blind ambition, but by a desire to do right by his family. She knew he looked up to his father, that he was determined to live up to the trust placed in him. That kind of family loyalty was rare, and she couldn't help but respect him for it. Even though that same family loyalty could mean the destruction of her little island sanctuary.

"Do you think he would have gone this far?" Nic asked as they crossed yet another deserted street.

"I honestly don't know. He's fast, so he could have covered a lot of ground pretty quickly if he wanted to. On the other hand, if he was sniffing every fence post and fire hydrant, it could take him all week just to circle the block." She huffed to blow her hair out of her face. She hadn't thought to grab a hair tie when they ran out of the hotel. "If it was daytime, we could ask if anyone had seen him, but as it is…" Her voice trailed off.

"Yeah, this place really does roll up the streets after dark, doesn't it?"

They hadn't seen anyone since they'd started their walk. Most of the houses were quiet, the warm glow of porch lights acting as sentries against the night. "I guess Paradise is pretty boring after Vegas and New York City, huh?" She kicked at some mulch that had spilled over onto the sidewalk from its assigned flower bed. This might be her idea of perfection, but to him it was just some Podunk town. No wonder he was so eager to bring in tourists and nightclubs, to make it another Daytona or South Beach.

"Boring? No, that's not how I would describe it. Peaceful was more what I was thinking. It's actually kind of nice to be somewhere where everyone goes home at night, has dinner with the family and turns out the lights. I'd forgotten people still lived like this."

His wistful tone took her by surprise. Had she been wrong to assume he couldn't see what she saw? "Before I moved here, I didn't know people could live this way. I love seeing kids playing in the yards every evening, old men hanging out at the hardware store in the morning. Life on the mainland is always changing, but here on the island, they've managed to hold on to what's important. That predictability makes me feel...safe, I guess."

The rhythms of Paradise Isle were like a security blanket she tucked around herself to help her sleep at night. After so many moves, changes and families, she had finally found a place where she felt secure. That he could tear that all apart was the elephant in the room, a fact both of them were unwilling to confront.

"The town I grew up in was like this, but I guess I thought that because I had changed, everyone else, everywhere else, had changed, too." He looked directly at her, as if holding her with his gaze. "I'm glad I was wrong."

Before she could decide exactly what he meant by that, a faint sound had her attention shifting. "Did you hear that?"

"What?"

She heard it again…a high-pitched whine, almost a whimper. "That!"

"Maybe…yeah, I hear it. Think that's Murphy?"

"I don't know, but it doesn't sound good." Pacing, she tried to locate where the sound was coming from. Maybe it was a bit louder, a bit stronger in that direction. Maybe.

Frustrated, she walked more quickly. "Murphy! Is that you, boy?" An answering bark and more whining had her running, Nic's footsteps heavy behind her. The distressed sounds grew louder, coming from behind the last house on the block.

Ignoring Nic's protest, she darted right into the yard and around the side of the house. At this point, she could hear two animals; the whining one was, hopefully, Murphy. But what was that hissing, growling noise? A possum? They could really do some damage; a raccoon would be even worse. Heart in her throat, she scanned the small backyard, hoping the poor dog wouldn't be too injured.

There, in the corner, she could make out Murphy's white patches in the moonlight. Approaching cautiously,

Nic at her side, she brandished the flashlight like a weapon, hoping desperately she wouldn't have to use it.

Nic grabbed Jillian's arm, slowing her before she could barrel headfirst into whatever had Murphy cowering in the shadows by the fence. Didn't she understand how dangerous this was? They were in a stranger's yard late at night, chasing what might be some kind of rabid beast. And she was ready to jump in without thought to her own safety, an idea as foolhardy as it was admirable. "Let me go first, see what we're dealing with."

"No way. I'm the one with the animal background, and I'm more familiar with the wildlife around here," she snapped, trying to pull away from him.

His instinct was to argue, but before he could come up with something that sounded like more than macho rhetoric, the clouds parted, letting moonlight flood the yard. There, only a few feet away, standing guard on top of a large trash can, was Murphy's would-be attacker.

"Oh, Murphy..." Jillian's reproach dissolved into a full-fledged laugh.

A cat. The creature they'd heard hissing and screeching was nothing more than a big old tomcat, defending his territory from the hapless canine.

Shaking his head, Nic ignored the angry sentry and went to the trembling dog. "Big tough dog like you, afraid of a little pussycat? You should be ashamed of yourself." He gave the dog a good-natured pat and reached for the bag of treats Jillian had brought. "Here you go, liver treats. Maybe they'll give you some courage." The cat, assured of its victory, stretched and then proceeded to carefully groom itself. Still, Nic gave it a wide birth, if only to spare Murphy any further trauma.

"We'd better get out of here before whoever lives here comes out to investigate," Jillian warned, her eyes darting to a light that now glowed in an upstairs window.

"Good idea." Explaining this ridiculous rescue mission to a half-asleep homeowner didn't sound like fun. And they really needed to get Murphy back to Mrs. Rosenberg before the poor lady made herself sick with worry. "Let's move."

They'd made it a full block before his pulse settled down, and he was able to appreciate the humor in the situation. Murphy was back to his normal carefree self by then, as well, and he danced at the end of the leash, eager to be home.

As he walked with the happy dog down the quiet street, Jillian by his side, he was struck by the normalcy of it all. The longing behind that thought surprised him. Sure, he'd become disillusioned with the constant travel of his current lifestyle, but did that mean he wanted something so completely different? Lately, he had toyed with the idea of shifting some travel responsibilities to other people in his department, spending more time at his office in the city. But would that be enough? He had thought it would be. But then why did he feel more at home, more at peace, here on this tiny island, than he ever had in New York City?

Shoving away the questions that circled him like hungry sharks, he chose to focus on the here and now. Right now he was strolling under a starry sky with a beautiful, intelligent, courageous woman. Reaching out, he caught her hand in his, letting them swing together as they walked. She accepted the gesture without hesitation, perhaps trapped by the same magic that had him wishing for things that weren't his to wish for. If there was a way to freeze this moment, keep it and take it out whenever he wanted, he would.

They reached the street that Mrs. Rosenberg lived on far too soon, his steps slowing as they approached the house. When they reached the walkway, Jillian slipped her hand away, a shy smile on her face. The spell that had entangled them was unraveling, taking a part of him with it.

"Is that you, Jillian? Did you find him? Is he okay?" Mrs. Rosenberg called from her front porch, peering out into the night.

"Yes, Mrs. Rosenberg, we have him. He's fine, other than some bruising to his ego. He got cornered by a cat over on Hibiscus Street."

The elderly woman waved them over, eager to be reunited with the dog that gave her so much trouble. "You poor thing, was that cat mean to you? Mama will make it up to you, don't you worry." Murphy accepted her praise and subsequent petting with a big doggy grin, tongue hanging out one side of his mouth. "You two, do you want to come in and have a drink or a snack? I've got plenty of cookies left from our little card party."

Jillian responded first. "No, but thank you. It's been a long day, and I really need to go home and get some sleep."

The older woman scrutinized the younger and then

nodded, apparently accepting her excuse as valid. "You do that then, and sleep in tomorrow, too, if you can. Murphy can wait for his run until later. I'll keep him locked down until then."

"Sounds good," Jillian replied.

"And you, young man. Don't think I'm not wondering why you were with my Jillian at this hour. I'm just too well-mannered to say anything about it. But I'm watching you, and you'd better have the right kind of intentions, if you know what I mean."

The right kind of intentions? Who said things like that? He might have laughed if she didn't look so very serious. Not wanting to hurt her feelings or dig himself any deeper, he decided to play it safe. "Yes, ma'am. I understand." Which was a bold-faced lie. Right now, he didn't understand anything, least of all his intentions toward Jillian.

Jillian settled into the comfortable bucket seat as Nic drove her home. She was exhausted, too many near catastrophes in too short a time, but the energy crackling between them kept her alert. The passionate embrace at the inn had ignited more sparks between them, and the walk with Murphy had layered a new element of sweetness onto the sultry feelings he inspired.

Chemistry was crazy that way. She'd been on numerous dates with totally suitable men, men from her own neighborhood with similar lifestyles and goals, and felt nothing more than curiosity. But Nic, who was all wrong for her, and completely unattainable, made her pulse throb and her knees weak every time he came near. Totally unfair, and at the moment, incredibly disturbing.

Would he expect a kiss when he dropped her off? Or more—would he want to pick up where they'd left off before an errant piece of silverware had so pointedly interrupted them?

Of course, the most likely scenario was that he was berating himself for that lack of judgment and trying to figure out how to let her down easy. After all, this was just one stop in his busy schedule. For all she knew, he had dinner, and maybe more, with women at every job site. Not to mention that currently she and the Island Preservation Society were a huge thorn in his side with regards to his business dealings. And with Nic, nothing was ever just business; it was always personal, always about how best to impress his family. Which meant if the grant fell through, his connection to her wouldn't be enough to stop him from buying, and destroying, the Sandpiper. For him, it was a matter of family loyalty, something she would never begrudge him, no matter how it affected her personally.

Hoping to avoid an awkward scene, or the lack of one for that matter, she had a hand on the door handle, ready to jump out the minute he pulled up to the clinic. "Thanks for the ride, and dinner, and helping with Murphy and, well, everything," she fumbled, nerves getting the best of her. "I'll, um, talk to you later."

Nic, with his quick reflexes, bounded out of the car and was at her side before she finished extricating herself from the SUV. He reached into the backseat, retrieving her purse and dress, both of which she'd nearly forgotten in her cowardly bid at a quick getaway. He ignored her attempt to take them from him, instead carrying them to her car, where he took the time to put them on the passenger's seat before opening the driver's door for her. His automatic chivalry gave her weary heart yet another jolt. His touch, a soft brush of his knuckles against her cheek, nearly broke her.

Their eyes locked, heat and longing and something more spilling into the stillness between them. She watched, helpless to stop him, not wanting to stop him, as Nic leaned into her, then closed her eyes against the sudden, sharp sting of tears when he only placed a gentle, chaste kiss on her forehead.

"We need to talk about us, Jillian. Not tonight, but soon. I'm not done here." His voice was husky; hers had abandoned her entirely. A simple nod was the best she could manage before retreating into the relative safety of her car. She somehow shut and locked the door in a single motion. Locking him out, or herself in?

Chapter 11

It had been a full week since Murphy's last escape and everything that had happened that night. She'd spent much of that time dodging Nic's phone calls. Now that the work on the grant proposal was over, there was no reason for him to contact her, but he still called every night, like clockwork. What had he meant when he said he wasn't done? What more was there?

It was not like they'd been dating, or even friends really. They'd had a moment of passion, some tender moments. They both knew that wasn't enough to build a relationship on. So any lingering emotion was misplaced and should be ruthlessly ignored. To that end, she'd agreed to meet Mollie for an afternoon at the beach; a few hours of sun and sand could fix pretty much anything. And just in case, she'd picked up Murphy on her way over. Now that his paws were healed, he was in need of some playtime, and his high spirits were guaranteed to chase any blues away.

She held the leash tight and let Murphy sniff each

weather-beaten stair step on the way down to the sand. His nose quivered with delight at all the new smells, and his black-and-white plume of a tail wagged high over his back. His enthusiasm was impossible to resist. Happier already, she kicked her flip-flops off and left them at the base of the stairs before breaking into a jog over the hot sand, heading for the cooler, hard-packed sand closer to the water. Murphy barked with delight, happy to chase the pipers and gulls that skittered along the shoreline.

At Murphy's bark, Mollie, comfortably situated in a low-slung beach chair right at the water's edge, looked up from her book and smiled. "I didn't know you were bringing this handsome guy. Has he been behaving himself lately?"

"More or less, depending on the day. But no more escape attempts. I figure a few hours at the beach should wear him out enough to keep him home for a while." She passed the leash to Mollie so she could put down the chair she'd been carrying, unfolding it and situating it next to Mollie's. From her bag she withdrew a rubber ball. Murphy spotted it and immediately crouched down in the famous border collie stance, ready to leap the minute it was tossed. Unsnapping the leash, she threw the toy into the waves before settling into her chair.

"So has he called yet?" Mollie asked.

"Who?" Jillian feigned ignorance.

Mollie wasn't fooled. "You know who. Mr. Caruso Hotels himself. Have you heard from him?"

"Yes. I mean, no." At Mollie's raised eyebrow, she continued, "He's called. A lot. I just don't answer. He'd promised to help with the grant, and he did, but that's over now. There's no reason for us to talk now."

"No reason at all, except the guy is crazy about you."

She dropped the dripping ball she'd been about to throw, her fingers unresponsive. "What? You're crazy. It was just business."

Mollie lifted her sunglasses to scrutinize her friend. "Are you telling me nothing happened between you?"

Jillian looked down to watch the water creeping closer to her chair. "There's some...chemistry. I won't deny that. But he's probably got women throwing themselves at him all the time. A girl in every port, you know." Just saying the words hurt, but she might as well face the truth.

"I don't buy it. If just any girl would do, he wouldn't have driven all the way from Orlando to take you to dinner." The petite brunette shook her head, her short hair swinging. "No, that wasn't some booty call. The man cares about you. Otherwise, he would have ditched you the other night when he saw what a basket case you were."

"I was not a basket case."

"Sweetie, you were in rough shape. Most men would have run fast and far from that kind of drama. Instead, he went all protective alpha male—I swear I thought he was going to pick you up and carry you off. I may have even swooned a little."

The image of tomboy Mollie swooning made Jillian smile. "He *was* awfully sweet," she conceded. "But the fact is, there's nothing going on between us, and no reason to keep in contact. At least not until we find out about the grant."

Mollie frowned. "What do you think the chances are of saving the Sandpiper?"

"Not great." She sighed, absently rubbing Murphy's ears. "We applied late in the year, so there won't be much money left, even if they like the proposal. And although the Sandpiper is certainly old enough and still reflects the original architecture, most of the buildings that are selected have some kind of tie-in to Florida history or to a famous person. The Sandpiper is meaningful to us, but that isn't enough to impress the committee."

"If it doesn't go through, will Nic really buy it and tear it down? Even though he knows how much it will upset you?

"It's not really his call. Caruso Hotels is a giant corporation. He's just doing his job." Why was she defending him?

"But he has to have a say in it. He's a vice president, isn't he? Can't you get him to back off?"

"What, ask him to set aside a multimillion-dollar project because it would hurt my feelings?" Jillian scoffed.

"Yes! I'm telling you, he cares about you."

"Even if he does—and I don't think that's the case, at least not the way you mean—but even if he does, he cares about his family more. When push comes to shove, he's going to do right by them, and if I get hurt in the process, well, that's simple collateral damage."

After all, family always came first, and she wasn't anyone's family.

* * *

Cold pizza and a lone beer of unknown age. The state of his refrigerator was pathetic. He could order some Chinese takeout, but he didn't want to wait for it. Resigned, he grabbed a slice and the longneck bottle. Twisting off the top, he leaned a hip against the counter, content to eat standing up after ten hours hunched over a desk. This was not turning out to be a stellar Saturday.

He'd gotten into town yesterday morning and had spent the whole day in various meetings at Caruso headquarters. Today he'd been stuck at his desk, dealing with the inevitable paperwork that those meetings generated. Somehow, he'd managed to put off any questions about the Sandpiper, but he knew it was only a matter of time before his father would expect a status update. Burying himself in reports and sales figures was nothing more than the urban version of hiding his head in the sand. If he kept busy enough, he wouldn't have to think about how to handle the Sandpiper or, worse, how to handle Jillian.

He had tried calling her at least a dozen times in the past week, but had gotten her voice mail every time. She'd obviously started screening his calls, and it hurt more than he wanted to admit.

Hearing her voice, discussing his day with her, had become second nature. Somehow she'd become the person he bounced ideas around with, the person he went to for advice, or just a listening ear. Obviously she didn't feel the same way. He should have expected this. Once the grant proposal was denied, and despite their best efforts, he knew it probably would be, Caruso Hotels would buy the Sandpiper and Jillian Everett would kick him out of her life for good. Maybe she was just trying to do him a favor by ending their friendship, or whatever it was, now, before things got really ugly.

He understood her reasons for fighting against Caruso Hotels—hell, he was actually starting to agree with her. Which just made everything more complicated. His instinct was to fly down there, make her see him, but that was the last thing she seemed to want. Which left him standing here, alone, trying to figure out a way to go on with his life. Or, more accurately, get a life.

A check of his watch showed it wasn't even eight yet; he could still go out. He was young, single and had money to burn. A night out was just what he needed after yet another long week.

Before he could change his mind, he pulled his cell phone from his back pocket and dialed his brother. Damian was supposed to have gotten back from Florence sometime last week, but he'd been too busy to call and ask him about his trip. A lame excuse. Tonight he'd make it up to him. Buy him a drink and listen to all the ways European cooking was superior to anything in America.

Three rings in, Damian picked up. "Hey, wow, was wondering if you'd call. Are you in town?"

"Yeah, sorry... I've been busy. Got in yesterday and just came up for air."

"Dude, you work too much. Seriously, you've got to live a little."

"Agreed. Starting now. Want to meet me for some drinks at Dry?"

Damian was silent for several seconds. "You want to go have drinks? At a club? Who are you, and what have you done with my brother?"

"Ha, ha, very funny. What's wrong with wanting to go out on a Saturday night?"

"Nothing, bro. It's just not like you. But, yeah, I'm up for it. Meet you there in an hour?"

That should be plenty of time to shower, change and get a cab over to the trendy bar, named for its famously dry martinis. "Yeah, that works. See you soon."

He called down to the doorman to request a cab, then took a quick shower. The scruffy look was still fashionable, right? No need to shave. Searching his seldom-used closet, he found designer jeans and a button-down dress shirt. The owner of Dry, Andrew Bennet, was a family friend, so getting in wasn't an issue, but he didn't want to look out of place, either. Keys in hand, he headed out the door, ready for whatever the night might bring.

Nic made it to Dry before Damian, so he elbowed his way to the main bar and sent his brother a text to meet him there. Music pulsed from hidden speakers, enticing the more adventurous onto a dance floor commanding most of the exposed second level. Spotting the bartender, he ordered a scotch on the rocks and then surveyed the action. Lots of what were probably young professionals, looking to unwind after working way too many hours. And of course, lots of people looking to hook up, men as well as women. Skintight and low-cut seemed to be the trend of the day, the couture clothes designed to showcase bodies perfected by spin classes and personal trainers. He had never realized how frenetic it all was, with everyone rushing to cram as much fun as possible into the meager downtime their lean-in lifestyle permitted.

By the time Damian appeared at his elbow, he had an empty glass and a full-on headache. Damian placed his own drink order and motioned to Nic, asking if he was ready for another. "Sure." Maybe the booze would drown out the pounding in his skull. Had this place always been so loud?

"So why are we here?" Damian asked, skipping over the usual pleasantries.

"To drink." He tipped up his glass, taking a large swallow of the fiery liquid. "Why else?"

Damian's eyes roamed the room, then came to rest on a particularly well-endowed blonde enthusiastically sucking on a lime. "There are other reasons. Thought maybe you were ready to come off whatever self-imposed dry spell you've been on. This place is practically dripping with possibilities."

His brother had a point. There was no shortage of attractive women, including the bombshell doing the tequila shooters. He certainly could appreciate the display, but nothing about her or the other women that had attempted to make eye contact drew his interest. They were trying too hard, making him feel like a conquest, a prize to be won. Not that he could explain that to his brother, so he just shrugged. "Maybe."

Damian quirked up an eyebrow at that, but didn't comment, content to drink and listen to the music.

One hour and three drinks later, Nic's head was a bit fuzzy, so he was slow to react when a leggy redhead with surgically perfect features moved in a little too close. He had nothing against a bit of harmless flirting, but she seemed to have more ambitious goals in mind. When her roaming hands started heading south, he realized he'd had enough.

Turning to Damian, he shouted over the music, "I'm leaving." Damian looked questioningly at the handsy redhead, but shrugged and followed him out.

"What happened? She seemed into you."

"What she was into was my pants pocket, with her hand. She was trying to get a grip on the goods, if you get my drift."

"And?"

"And I like to know a girl's name before she starts massaging the family jewels. I'm old-fashioned that way."

"Damn, Mom was right. I hate it when she's right."

"What the heck are you talking about?"

"Mom. She said you'd fallen for someone, some girl down in Florida. That she had you going to church and everything."

Great. "I haven't fallen for anyone, not like that." He scowled, hoping to intimidate his younger brother into dropping this line of questioning.

Damian was undeterred. "She says that you talk to her all the time—that you even hung up on her so you could talk to this chick."

"It's business, that's all. I'm helping her with some real estate stuff." That the help he was giving was in direct opposition to the goals of Caruso Hotels didn't need to be mentioned. "And I didn't hang up on Mom, for crying out loud. I'd already talked to her for half an hour, so when Jillian called on Skype I told Mom I had to go."

"Skype? What is she, some kind of cybersex babe?"

Damian barely had the words out of his mouth before Nic had him shoved against the brick wall of the club, one arm across his throat. "Don't talk like that about her, understand?"

Damian, eyes wide, nodded, unwilling or unable to speak while his trachea was being crushed.

Nic stepped back, breathing hard. Crap, what was he doing? He scrubbed a hand over his jaw, feeling the bristles, taking the time to calm down and think clearly, or as clearly as the alcohol would let him. "Damian, I'm sorry, I had too much to drink, I shouldn't have—"

Damian's hoot of laughter cut him off. "Oh, boy, you are totally messed up over this girl." His idiot brother was grinning from ear to ear. "No worries. I'll even be your best man, just let me know when the wedding is."

"Very funny." Great, if this got back to his parents, he'd be signed up for a tux fitting before he knew what hit him. "Like I said, she's just..." Hell, he didn't know. A friend? A colleague? The woman that kept him up at night, aching? "She's just someone I met. Besides, that's all over with. I haven't even talked to her since I was down there last week." Mainly because she wouldn't answer his phone calls.

"Wait, you saw her last week? I thought you were in Orlando last week?"

He was never drinking again. Ever. "Yeah, well, I drove over to Paradise Isle while I was there."

"Orlando to Paradise Isle? That's quite the booty call." Damian ducked this time; he was smaller and more sober, and easily eluded Nic's drunken punch. "Sorry, dude, that was just too easy."

"You're a jerk, you know that?"

"Yeah, I know. But I'll buy you a late dinner to soak up that booze, to make it up to you. Let's get out of here."

"Fine."

"Oh, and Nic?"

"Yeah?"

"Mom was definitely right." Nic glared, but didn't have a response, at least not one that Damian was going to buy. Not after seeing how riled up he got over a few remarks about Jillian. He was still hot about it, could still feel the temper simmering within him.

Which told him, more than Damian's taunts had, that his mom was right. He was really falling for Jillian. Maybe it was time he let her know it.

Chapter 12

A long afternoon at the beach with Murphy had scorched her skin but cleared her head. She'd even let Mollie talk her into dinner, and then drinks, at Pete's. Her canine buddy had been worn-out when she'd dropped him off, and now, climbing the stairs to her apartment, she felt about the same way. It was a good kind of tired, though, and she was glad she'd taken the time to catch up with Mollie. Sure, they saw each other at work every day, but it wasn't the same. Chatting with her friend had reminded her she had people in her life that cared, that she wasn't dependent on Nic Caruso or any man to keep her entertained.

After unlocking the door, she crossed the small living room and headed straight for the bathroom. She stripped off her tank top, shorts and bathing suit, leaving them in a pile on the floor, and turned the water on full force. Nothing felt better than a hot, soapy shower after a day at the beach.

She took her time, using her favorite deep conditioner to rehydrate her curls after the salt water. A tingly, ginger-infused body wash got rid of the sticky sunscreen residue and left her feeling refreshed. She chose one of her biggest, softest bath towels for her body, and another for her hair. An orange-and-ginger-scented body lotion slathered on from head to toe finished her mini home spa treatment. She really should do this more often; she didn't need to wait for a big date to pamper herself a little. Feeling soft and pretty was its own reward.

A glance at her cat clock with the waggling tail told her it was already late, but after the beer she drank she should hydrate before going to bed. So she slipped into her favorite old nightshirt and went to the kitchen to pour a giant glass of water. Minutes later, she was perched on her hand-me-down couch, scanning the channels and sipping her drink. An old sitcom marathon was the best she could find, unless she wanted to watch endless infomercials for products she'd never heard of.

By the third episode her eyelids were sagging more than the punch lines. She really should go to bed, but getting off the couch sounded like a lot of work. Easier to just curl up right where she was. She snuggled farther into the cushions and snapped off the flickering television. Drifting off, she was in that lovely not-quite-asleep haze when the phone buzzed.

"Hello?" she managed to mumble, answering it without thinking to check the caller ID.

"Hi, Jillian. It's Nic. Did I wake you up? I didn't realize it was so late." His deep voice rumbled through the phone, a wakeup call to every sleeping nerve in her body.

"Um, no. I mean, well, not quite. I'm camped out on the couch and was just kind of dozing. Too lazy to get up and go to bed. I don't even know what time it is."

"Oh. It's almost midnight, I think. I shouldn't have called so late. I'll let you get back to sleep."

"No!" She scrambled to a sitting position. Now that she could hear his voice, she wanted him to keep talking, to ignore all the reasons she'd been avoiding his calls. "No, I'm awake. Really, it's fine. What's up? Did you hear something about the grant?"

"The grant? No, not yet. I'm sure you'll hear something soon."

"Hopefully." Why did he call if it wasn't about the grant? Did he just want to torture her, string her along a little longer?

"Yeah. Hopefully."

The silence echoed, stretching her nerves until she couldn't take it any longer. Maybe she would regret asking, but she had to know. "Nic?"

"Yeah?" His soft, husky voice sounded only inches from her ear, tempting her heart into wishing for things that weren't there.

"Why did you call?" Breath held, she waited.

"Because—well, I just wanted to talk to you, but you've been kind of hard to get ahold of lately. I care about you, you know."

Guilt formed a knot in her throat. Swallowing past it, she forced some cheer into her voice. "Oh, I'm fine. Went to the beach today with Mollie. I took Murphy.

You should see him chase the ball in the waves. He's a real fiend about it."

"Yeah, I bet that's something." He cleared his throat. "In fact, when I come down there, maybe—"

"Maybe what, Nic?" Her embarrassment and guilt fused into anger in the space of a heartbeat. "Maybe when you're down here directing the demolition of the Sandpiper, you'll find some time to hang out on the beach? Show me where you're going to put in the first high-rise, and the water park, and who knows what else? Maybe you can take me on a tour this time, show me the new and improved vision for Paradise Isle, with all the tacky T-shirt shops and after-hours nightclubs? Is that what you think, Nic?"

His words were low and controlled when he spoke. "I wasn't thinking anything of the kind, Jillian."

"Good! Because I don't think anything of you or your plans to ruin the only home I've ever known." She was sobbing now, her voice cracking. "So stop pretending we're friends, or that you're going to come down here and we'll have some kind of romantic reunion, you, me and Murphy. Stop acting like you care, and stop calling me." She pressed the end-call button and threw down the phone, mortified.

Where did that come from? Hadn't she told Mollie just this afternoon that she agreed with Nic's motives, if not his plans? And yet here she was, throwing it all in his face, acting like a crazy woman. Because he was going to destroy the Sandpiper?

Or because he was going to destroy her heart?

Was she angry with him or with herself for letting her guard down, letting someone in?

Not that it mattered. That display of theatrics was guaranteed to keep him out of her life. Too bad it was a bit too late. No matter what she told her friends, this pain in her heart could only mean one thing. Somehow, she'd managed to fall in love with Nic Caruso, a man destined to destroy her world, and her life.

Sunday was usually Nic's chance to sleep in, at least on the days he didn't have an early flight. And since he'd lain awake for hours last night, trying to puzzle out his disastrous phone call to Jillian, he really needed the extra rest. A detail that his sister Isabella didn't care about in the least. When he'd ignored her phone call, she had just sweet-talked the doorman into letting her in. At least that's what she said. Eyeing his take-no-prisoners sister, he figured she'd most likely bulldozed whatever unlucky man had gotten in her way.

Right now she was standing in his dining room, towering over him while he slowly drank a cup of much-needed coffee. She was wearing jeans and a tailored blouse instead of her usual designer suit, but she still oozed the kind of confident power that had made her successful in the male-dominated world of investment banking. But if she thought that kind of power play was going to work on him, she was sorely mistaken.

"I'm assuming there is a reason you barged in so early?"

"It's only early to people that were up late getting drunk."

Great. Damian didn't waste any time tattling. "It wasn't that late, and I wasn't drunk." At least the first part was true; he had been home at a decent hour.

"You were drunk enough to shove Damian around."

"Since when do I need to be drunk to want to mess around with Damian?" He certainly felt like beating on his brother right now. How much had he told her?

"Okay, you have a point." Dropping the tough interrogation act, she sat down next to him, her golden eyes filled with concern. "But seriously, what's going on with you?"

Oh, boy. He could stand up to her tough-girl talk all day long, but he couldn't resist his sisters when they turned mushy. "Listen, it's not a big deal, okay? Some girl hit on me at the club, and I turned her down."

"Why?"

What, did all his siblings think he was some kind of playboy? Was turning down a girl that earthshaking? "No real reason, she just didn't do it for me."

"Maybe." She watched him closely; she had always been too perceptive for her own good. "Or maybe she was the wrong girl. Maybe there's someone else you're interested in."

"Yeah, well, sometimes the right girl is still all wrong," he muttered, shoveling in another bit of cereal.

"Aha! So there is a girl. Okay, well, by 'wrong,' do you just mean it might take some actual effort on your part? 'Cause, big brother, I have to tell you, you have gotten lazy."

He nearly choked on his cornflakes. Lazy? She had to be kidding.

"Don't you look at me that way, Dominic Caruso. I know you work hard, but when it comes to women, you've never had to lift a finger. They just throw themselves at you, and the most you have had to do is decide which one you want. I'm betting that for once, you've found one that won't come running when you snap your fingers. Am I right?"

He didn't want her to be right. He definitely didn't like the picture she was painting of him, but there was some truth to her words. "Let's just say that when I tried to talk to her last night, she hung up on me, crying."

Isabella's smug smile seemed completely out of place. "Oh, that's nothing. Just give her some flowers and grovel. Totally fixable."

"I don't think it's that easy."

"That's because you've never really groveled. Trust me, it works." The glint in her eyes told him she'd seen her share of such men.

"There's more to it than that. There are other...complications."

"So tell me about them. You know you're dying to tell someone. And unlike Damian, I won't go running my mouth to the rest of the family."

That much was true. Isabella's brain was like a vault. Nothing spilled out without her express permission. And maybe talking it out would help him to make sense of things. Drinking hadn't. So he explained, as best he could, the situation, telling her about the town, Jillian, the Sandpiper and Caruso's plans to transform the island. By the end of his story, his sister had tears in her eyes and a sappy smile on her face. "What? Why are you looking at me like that?"

"Because it's so romantic," she gushed, fanning her face to stop the tears from ruining her makeup.

"It's not romantic, it's a mess." Standing, he carried his dishes to the kitchen, loading them into the dishwasher with more force than necessary.

"Well, yeah, it's a mess. But it's romantic, too. The two of you are star-crossed lovers, like Romeo and Juliet."

"And look how they ended up."

"Okay, bad example. But seriously, it has to be fate that the two of you met. If you really have feelings for her, if you love her, you have to find a way. You can't let anything stop you."

"Whoa…who said anything about love?" He staggered back, knocked off-kilter by the idea. "We've only known each other a few weeks, nowhere near long enough to be throwing the *L* word around."

"Oh, yeah?" Isabella advanced on him, coming in for the kill. "And exactly how long did Mom and Dad know each other before they got married?"

"Three weeks." *Oh, man.* "But that was…different."

"Not so different. And you know they're just as much in love now as they were then."

Nodding, he rubbed his chest, struggling to even out his breathing. His parents *were* very happy, but he'd always thought their whirlwind romance was the exception to the rule. Certainly nothing that could happen to him. His father was undeniably a risk taker in every facet of his life. A whirlwind romance, a risky business idea: that was Lorenzo Caruso's modus operandi. Nic, on the other hand, was methodical to the bone.

Someday he'd planned on falling in love, preferably with someone he was already friendly with, and only after a long courtship. They'd date casually at first, then more seriously, then after a year or so announce an engagement at just the right time. That was the right way to go about things.

Isabella interrupted his tumbling thoughts with a dilemma of her own. "I actually didn't come by here just to give you a hard time. I wanted to ask you to put out some feelers for me."

"You're looking for a new job?" He knew she'd been under a lot of stress, working longer hours than even he did, but he hadn't thought she was that unhappy.

"Yeah, it's time. I took this position as a stepping stone, a chance to get experience in a big company. But I'm tired of doing grunt work. The pay is great, but I want a chance to make real decisions. Instead, I'm spending all my hours crunching numbers, just for some executive to ignore them and do whatever he wants, anyway. I need a new challenge, a different way to use my skills. Maybe something with some travel. I've always envied you, getting to stay in all sorts of interesting places, meeting new people. Me? My biggest adventure is getting a new flavor of nondairy creamer for my coffee."

"It's not all glamorous, trust me."

"Nothing is, but I didn't come here to complain, just to ask you to keep an ear out. Let me know if you hear of anything that sounds interesting."

"Sure, I can do that. I don't have a lot of contacts in finance, but if you're looking for a change, there are lots of businesses that would jump at a chance to have someone with your experience. It's just a matter of who has openings."

"Thanks, I know it will take some time. Just fix your woman problems, and by then I'll probably have my dream job all lined up." As confident of her success as ever, she let herself out, leaving him alone with his thoughts. And if any of what she'd accused him of was true, he had plenty of thinking to do.

Chapter 13

Jillian regretted her angry outburst at Nic, but what had her nerves twanging like a tautly strung banjo wasn't the fight, it was discovering how deep her feelings for him ran. He might think he was interested right now, but she was realistic enough to know that any feelings he had couldn't last, not long-term. Anyone could see they were all wrong for each other. Even without the controversy over the Sandpiper, there were so many reasons they could never work as a couple. He was a rolling stone, constantly traveling. She was a homebody, with a need to plant deep roots. He was wealthy, with powerful family connections. She was happy to finally be able to afford rent and her own car. And of course, his life centered on his family, and she was an orphan who didn't know the first thing about those kinds of blood bonds.

Added all up, it equaled disaster. And yet, somehow she'd managed to fall for him, anyway. Hook, line and sinker. The only bright point was that he didn't know how she felt. In fact, after that last phone call, he probably assumed she hated him. Better that than to face humiliation on top of rejection. This way she could nurse her wounded heart in peace, with no one the wiser. Surely, after a while, it would heal. She'd lived through worse. She'd live through this, too.

Her coping strategy of the moment was to spend time with Murphy, her wannabe dog. She'd increased her training sessions with him, and he was really turning into an obedient little guy. He loved the extra attention, and she found comfort in his furry friendship. Mrs. Rosenberg had asked a few times about Nic, but when Jillian refused to talk about him, she had backed off. Even Cassie and Mollie had stopped asking about him, instead focusing on the future of the Sandpiper and Paradise Isle. The first thing anyone asked when they saw her was if she'd heard about the grant decision yet. The stress of waiting for news was almost worse than the heartbreak over Nic. Almost.

Arriving home after another long day at work and then an hour working with Murphy, she was ready to call it a night. Out of habit she stopped at the row of metal mailboxes, using her tiny key to access a stack of what looked like bills and junk mail. Shoving them in her purse, she climbed the stairs to her second-floor apartment, trying to decide on dinner. Sandwich? Soup? What the heck? Might as well have both.

Once inside, she tossed her purse and mail on the kitchen counter, the envelopes fanning out across the tan Formica. She found a can of alphabet soup and heated it up on the stove, letting it simmer while she made a quick ham sandwich. Cooking didn't seem worth it when there was no one to cook for, so this would have to do.

She ladled the soup into a bowl and started nibbling the sandwich, sitting at the breakfast bar that extended from the counter. Too tired to read, she let her mind wander. She ought to wash her car this weekend. Organize the pantry. Oh, and clean out the mail basket; there were ads and coupons and bills all mixed together in a jumble. She had a tendency to just pile it up, and then she didn't have the coupons when she wanted them, and it was a pain to find the bills and pay them. Really, she should start that now. Go through the stuff she'd just dropped on the table, sort it out. It would at least be a start.

She put her dishes in the sink and scooped up the scattered mail, taking it to her desk in the entryway. Pulling out the wastebasket she kept under the desk, she began sorting. Advertisement, bill, craft store coupon, bill, political brochure and a plain brown envelope with the State of Florida seal on it. Her hands trembled. Maybe she shouldn't open it. Maybe she should give it to the Island Preservation Society, let them open it.

"Don't be such a baby," she scolded herself, ripping open the envelope before she could chicken out again. She unfolded the single page, holding her breath as she quickly scanned the typewritten lines. *We regret to inform you...*

None of the other words made sense after that, or even mattered. There would be no grant money. The city wouldn't be able to purchase the inn; it wouldn't be listed as an historic place. It would be torn down, and in its place would be some mega-resort with everything the busy traveler could want—for a price. They'd overrun the beaches, crowd the streets and take over the restaurants. The Paradise Isle she'd come to love would no longer be the quiet sanctuary of her dreams. And there was absolutely nothing she, or anyone else, could do about it.

Sinking to the floor, she tucked her head against her knees and let the tears come. She cried for the sheer ugliness of what was going to happen, for the upheaval sure to come, but mostly for the loss of yet one more place, one more dream. Would she ever find a safe haven of her own?

A good cry helped to wash the pain out of head and heart, leaving an empty numbness in its place. Soon, she'd have to figure out the details and set up a meeting of the Island Preservation Society to break the bad news. For now, though, there was an even bigger hurdle to clear. She needed to let Nic know. And then face the consequences, whatever they were. She was sure he'd be nice about it, of course. He didn't want to hurt her, of that she was sure. But hurt her he would, and she couldn't even work up any righteous anger about it.

As much as she hated what he was going to do, deep down she admired his devotion to his family, his loyalty. She couldn't ask him to betray the trust his family had placed in him when they brought him into the company. Which meant that there was nothing left to do but move on and make the best of it.

Unfolding herself from her cramped position on the floor, she stood tall, bracing herself for the coming conversation. She needed to be strong—she wouldn't, couldn't, let him hear her pain. No, she'd be professional, impart the information he needed, and that would be the end of her dealings with Nic Caruso.

She dialed with steady hands, calming herself through sheer force of will. She could do this. The phone rang. Her stomach flopped. She hadn't talked to him since their big fight. What if he didn't want to talk to her, wouldn't answer? Another ring. Just as she lost her nerve and started to hang up, he answered.

"Jillian?" He sounded cautious, but not angry. That was a good sign. At least he wasn't going to hang up on her.

"Hi, Nic. I'm sure you're wondering why I'm calling. And I won't keep you. I just wanted to inform you that I received a letter from the State Registry of Historical Places, and they were not able to grant us any funds."

"Oh."

She tried to finish quickly, get it over with. "So, just thought you should know, so you can make arrangements, do whatever it is you do. So anyway—"

"Hey, listen, for what it's worth, I'm sorry."

She didn't want to hear that. She wasn't going to be able to hold it together if he started pitying her. "Well, be that as it may, the fact of the matter is, you win. You get what you want."

"Jillian, I need to talk to you—"

She hung up. She'd told him what she had to tell him; she wasn't going to torture herself by staying on the line, making small talk, pretending things were just fine between them. How could she? He had stolen from her the one thing she'd come to count on: her home. She had wanted to raise a family here, on the quiet and safe streets she'd grown to love. But now those streets would be overrun with tourists, the small shops replaced with chain stores and after-hours nightclubs. She'd lived in other places where tourism had taken over, and had no desire to repeat the experience. She knew some people thrived on the hustle and bustle, but she craved peace and a sense of community that those busy cities couldn't provide.

And, beneath that hurt, there was a deeper, sharper pain, one that tore at her battered heart.

How could it hurt this much to lose a man she should never have fallen for in the first place?

Chapter 14

As much as Nic had come to dislike the constant traveling his job required, he had never actually dreaded a trip before. Of course, it had never been so personal before. Boarding the plane to Florida, all he'd been able to think about was Jillian and how badly he'd messed things up. Not that he could think of a different way to have handled things, other than never meeting her at all. He couldn't have prevented the bond that had formed between them any more than he could prevent his next breath. Heaven knew he'd tried. But she'd gotten stuck inside him somehow, and now he was trapped, forced to either hurt the woman he wanted to protect or betray the man that had given him everything. He couldn't do that to his father.

So his only option was to try to minimize the impact of the hotel on the island and hope that would be enough to show Jillian how he felt. It wouldn't be easy, and most of the changes couldn't be prevented. But he had to try. He only hoped that would be enough for Jillian to forgive him. Maybe then he'd have a chance with her. It wasn't a great plan, but what else could he do?

The flight, for once, felt too short. In what seemed like no time he was loading his luggage into yet another rental car. The motions were familiar, but the anxiety chewing through his gut was not. He'd always been a confident person, and years in the field had assured him he had the skills needed to complete the task at hand. So it wasn't fear of failure that nagged him now. It was the cold, hard fact that this time, he didn't want to succeed.

Shrugging off his melancholy mood, he concentrated on navigating the horrendous traffic that Orlando was famous for. Caruso Hotels would definitely have to arrange for some kind of shuttle from the airport, so vacationers didn't show up to the resort already in a bad mood. Maybe even a helicopter service for the VIP guests; they'd love that. The noise would be an issue, but in the scheme of things, the prestige would be worth it. He'd send a memo to the development team so they could work a landing pad into their plans. Focusing on the details let him avoid thinking about the ramifications of what he was about to do.

That strategy worked well until he approached the spot where he'd rescued Murphy, and all the memories of that first weekend came flooding back in Technicolor clarity. Her gentle touch with the injured dog, her eyes so big and blue, her lips and how right they'd felt on his own. Just thinking about it had his body responding, his blood pressure rising.

Damn, if he was this wound up just thinking about her, how much harder was it going to be to see her? And he was going to see her. Even if he couldn't convince her of his feelings, he didn't want to end things like they had, with her angry and hanging up on him. He wanted a chance to explain, to apologize, to tell her his plans to make the transition as easy as possible. And, if he was honest with himself, he just couldn't stay away.

Which was why he found himself climbing her stair-case as dusk was falling, knowing she would, most likely, slam the door in his face. When his knock was met with silence his first assumption was that she was, in fact, avoiding him. It was only when he scanned the parking lot and didn't find her car that he realized his mistake. She was probably taking her nightly run with Murphy; he'd somehow forgotten her commitment to the pet she couldn't have. He could sit and wait for her, but his growling stomach gave him a better idea.

There was a diner around the corner; he could pick up food for the both of them, a peace offering of sorts. Deciding to walk rather than drive, he once again noted the Norman Rockwell quality of the town. Everywhere he looked, he saw kids playing in the twilight, fami-lies gathering in neat little houses, older folks rocking on front porches, as they probably had every evening for decades, watching the comings and goings of their neighborhood.

Even Mary's Diner was picturesque in its own way, a throwback to the 1950s, with red booths and chrome accents everywhere. A few single men sat at the bar; the tables were filled mostly with young families grab-bing a bite out after a busy day. The service was quick and friendly. A matronly woman wearing a frilly apron took his order, and within minutes he had two meat loaf dinners and a lemon pound cake packed up and ready to go. The aromas tantalized him as he made his way back; hopefully she'd be hungry enough to let him in, at least long enough to eat.

She arrived a few minutes after he did, pulling into the parking lot directly across from where he sat at her front door. He knew the minute she saw him; her eyes narrowed, as if just the sight of him caused her pain.

What had he been thinking, coming here?

It was too late now. He only hoped he could reassure her somehow, make things even a little bit right for her. Because as much as he knew he should just walk away, he couldn't do it. Not yet.

The last thing Jillian had expected when she finally got home that night was Nic Caruso at her door. They had no business left to discuss, and she thought she'd hinted pretty clearly that she wanted no personal contact with him, either. Obviously subtlety was lost on him. She'd just have to tell him, politely but firmly, to go. Whatever he thought he wanted, he wasn't going to get it from her. She wasn't equipped to deal with the emotional maelstrom he triggered—she was too raw. The sooner she got him out of her life, she sooner she could pick up the pieces of her broken heart.

When she had stomped up the last step, she saw the bags of food. Damn him. She was starving; no way was she going to turn down food from Mary's. Fine, they'd eat—quickly—and then he could leave. Whatever he had to say, he'd have to say fast, before she finished devouring whatever was behind that wonderful aroma.

She refused to ask him why he was there as she pushed past him to open the door. It didn't matter, anyway. "Put the food on the counter. I'll get plates and drinks."

He did as she instructed, opening up Styrofoam containers to reveal savory meat loaf, mashed potatoes and carrots. Her stomach rumbled, betraying her interest in his culinary olive branch. She assumed that's what it was, and it annoyed her that it had worked. Just having him in her apartment was a major mistake, one she wouldn't have made if she had been thinking with her head instead of her stomach. The irony was that now that she'd seen him, the only thing she had an appetite for was him.

Get a grip. She couldn't let him see how much she wanted him. She couldn't lose her pride on top of her heart.

She forced herself to set the plates down on the breakfast bar rather than slam them, not wanting to show more emotion than necessary. Crossing to the refrigerator, she considered the options, then closed it again and grabbed a bottle of red wine off the counter. A little liquid courage to get her through this. She silently handed him the bottle and corkscrew, then fetched the wineglasses. He poured generously, then clinked his glass against hers. "Salute."

She looked up, unfamiliar with the toast, and her eyes met his over the raised glasses. She read regret there, and concern, emotions a little too close to pity, and she wouldn't be pitied. Not again. She'd gotten over being the poor little orphan girl long ago, and didn't need him feeling sorry for her. He might as well pour salt on her wounds.

"So, I assume you're here to buy the Sandpiper, tie up all the loose ends or whatever. Then you'll be off to your next conquest." *Soon*, she added silently. The sooner he was gone, the sooner she could try to forget the way he made her feel. Even now, knowing what he was here to do, she found herself wanting to let down her guard, recapture the closeness that had sprung up so quickly between them.

"Not just yet. I need to schedule more land surveys, have various inspections done, that kind of thing. And I'm going to order an environmental survey, as well. It isn't strictly required, since the zoning won't change, but I'm going to do my best to limit the impact to the beaches and wildlife. I want to make this work, and I want to do right by Paradise Isle. I want to do right by you."

"So that's why you're here?" She gestured to the apartment around her. "You came to my home, knowing how I feel about all this, to tell me it won't be so bad, after all?" She didn't know if she should laugh or cry at his brazenness.

"Well, yeah. And to bring you dinner." He smiled cockily, melting her defenses in the space of a heartbeat.

"That was a dirty trick." But she took a bite of the meat loaf, anyway. She *was* hungry, and heaven help her, she couldn't keep up the bitch act around him. She liked him too much. Liked him? Who was she kidding?

She was head over heels for him. Just watching him sit in her kitchen, in faded jeans and an old band T-shirt that stretched enticingly when he moved, had her hormones working on overdrive.

But it was more than his looks; it was who he was as a person that had gotten her to let down her guard. Even when they should have been enemies, they still slipped into the easy banter that had become so natural between them. She loved hearing about the exotic places he had traveled, and he always seemed genuinely interested in the stories she told him about the animals at work. They'd found they also shared similar views on politics, religion and literature, but were, of course, rivals in football and baseball. His family was another frequent topic of conversation, one that often had her crying tears of laughter as he told stories of his childhood.

"Is Damian back yet from Florence?" she asked, reaching for more wine.

He filled her glass, and topped off his own. "Yeah, he got back a few weeks ago, even more arrogant than he was before."

She grinned. A certain level of self-confidence was a trait the brothers shared, whether Nic acknowledged it or not. "So I take it you got a chance to see him the last time you were home?" With his crazy schedule, he didn't always get time for family visits on his brief trips to New York.

"Um, yeah…sure, I saw him," Nic mumbled, suddenly very interested in the last few carrots on his plate.

"What? What happened?" She smelled a story here. When he didn't answer, she grabbed his arm, spinning his bar stool toward her. Facing him, she demanded, "Spill it!"

"Nothing happened, really. I had a few drinks and, well, things got a little tense. But it's fine now, no big deal."

Jillian had heard enough about the family to know that a scuffle between the brothers was nothing new. But something about his reaction had her curiosity piqued. "What was the fight about?"

Again, he didn't answer. Now she had to know. She slid off her stool into the space between them. Taking his face in her hands, she pulled him down so she could look into his eyes. "Hey, seriously, what started it this time?"

Sighing, he knocked back the rest of his wine. "It was just a misunderstanding. He was trying to get a rise out of me, and it worked. I mentioned that you and I had been talking on Skype a lot, and he insinuated I was using you for cybersex."

Speechless, she felt the blood rise in her cheeks. She wasn't a prude, but wow, she hadn't expected that. Unbidden, seductive images streaked across her mind's eye.

"Don't worry. I made it clear to him that's not the situation. At all."

"That's…good." Suddenly she realized how close she was standing to him; only inches separated them. There wasn't enough oxygen, not enough space. She needed more distance, physically and emotionally. She tried to clear her suddenly dry throat. "Obviously that's not the kind of thing that would happen with us."

"Oh, I don't know," he answered, reaching out to brush a stray curl from her face. "I can't say the idea *never* occurred to me."

Her mouth parted in shock and Nic took full advantage of the offering, lowering his lips to hers, tasting, testing, gently seducing. His tenderness was her undoing. Time stopped, the world spun away. Distantly, she knew this shouldn't happen, but there was no way she could stop it. Nothing else mattered, just him. Just this moment and this man.

He'd never paid much attention to descriptions of heaven, but it couldn't be better than this. She was warm and soft in his arms; her lips were a silken seduction tempting him to explore and linger. Holding himself back, ignoring the fire in his body that demanded to be fed, was like holding back a raging river. It took all his willpower but he kept his touch light, sampling rather than devouring the mouth she so innocently offered up for him.

When his resolve was strained nearly to the breaking point, he forced himself to pull away. Panting, he leaned his forehead against hers. "I didn't expect that."

Her eyes were glazed, but she shuttered them quickly, turning away at his words. "I'm sorry." Her voice trembled, plucking at his guilt.

When she tried to walk away, he grabbed her arm, stopping her. "Don't be sorry—I'm not."

Shaking him off, she pulled out of his grip, backing into the living room, putting as much space between them as was possible in the small apartment. "This can't keep happening." Her eyes pleaded with him, pain reflecting in the smoky depths.

"It can, if you'll just let it." He shoved his hands through his hair. "Damn it, I can't force you to admit what you feel, but I'm done hiding how I feel. And I'm sure as hell not to pretend I'm sorry, that I regret kissing you. And I don't think you regret it, either."

"I think you should go now." Her arms were wrapped around her body, her gaze refusing to meet his.

"Don't do this. I know you want—"

"What I want is for you to go." Her voice cracked with emotion. "Please...just go."

Damn it. Look at what he was doing to her. He'd been a fool to think he could see her and keep his hands off her. All he'd wanted was to make things a bit better, a bit easier for her. Instead, he'd made of mess of everything, leaving her worse off than before. But he'd told her the truth; he didn't regret that kiss, or any of the others for that matter. He only regretted hurting her. His instinct had been to protect her, but for now the best way to do that was to leave.

"I'll go." He'd brought nothing with him other than the food; there was nothing to collect, no way to stall on his way to the door she held open for him. He wanted to stay and fight, to make her let him stay, but the tears spilling onto her cheeks stopped him when no argument or harsh word would have.

"Goodbye. And Nic? Please don't come back."

Her final words haunted him as he drove through the night. He had reserved a room at the Sandpiper, but he took the highway back to Orlando instead. He didn't trust himself to stay away with so little distance between them. Even now, knowing how badly he'd hurt her, he had to fight to keep from turning around and forcing her to let him back in.

Maybe he'd been wrong about them, about making it work. She obviously wasn't going to forgive him. And he didn't blame her; he'd attacked the one thing she held dear—her community.

Being without her might kill him, but if seeing him was going to hurt her, then the only solution was to leave the island, leave the project. He'd have to find someone else to take over; there was no way he could be there, day after day, and not see her, even if only accidentally. He'd never walked away from an assignment before, but right now his reputation was the least of his worries. He'd turn over his notes to one of the up-and-coming executives, give them a chance to prove themselves. He could spin it that way, make it sound like he was mentoring someone, helping them move up in the ranks.

His father would be a hard sell, but certainly by now he'd earned some discretion. The project would go forward, and Jillian would get the space she'd asked for. He should have done this weeks ago, as soon as he started getting involved with her. But he'd always managed to keep his business and personal lives separate before; he hadn't expected it to be a problem.

But there was no way to compartmentalize his feelings for Jillian. She permeated every facet of his life; he'd even started dreaming about her. Right now he should be thinking about work, about finding the right person to take over the project, and figuring out how to streamline any collaboration. Instead, he kept seeing the tears on her face, each one another slice at his soul.

He'd dated dozens of beautiful women, so why did this one bring him to his knees?

The answer was obvious. He was in love with her. Only he'd figured it out way too late.

Furious with himself, with fate, his job, he pounded his fist on the steering wheel, relishing the sting. Physical pain faded quickly. Much worse was this throbbing ache in his chest, threatening to consume him. Maybe with some distance he'd be thinking more clearly and would find a way out of this mess. Because the alternative was unthinkable.

Chapter 15

Jillian knocked quietly on Cassie's door, not wanting to wake Emma if she was already asleep. What time did four-year-olds go to bed, anyway? Not that she knew what time it was. She'd spent longer than she should have indulging in tears after Nic left, then had gone on a cleaning spree, taking her angst out on her kitchen. She now had gleaming tile and the beginnings of a plan. Talking to Cassie was the first step to putting it in motion.

Her friend opened the door, ushering her into the small but cheery 1950s cottage she'd purchased when Emma was born. Soft throw rugs were scattered on the terrazzo floor, creating a welcoming and child-friendly space. Family photos and pictures of various pets intermingled with books on the large, built-in bookcases, the only real decoration other than a few jewel-toned throw cushions. Jillian kicked off her shoes at the door and sat cross-legged on the taupe microfiber couch. Cassie joined her, settling slightly sideways so she could face her friend.

"Thanks for letting me in, I know it's probably late. I hope I didn't wake Emma."

"You know you can come by anytime. And Emma sleeps like a rock—a five-piece band wouldn't wake her up. But it is late, at least for you, so I assume it's important."

Jillian took a deep breath, steadying her nerves. She'd practiced a speech on the way over here, but now it seemed so scripted. Maybe she should just lay it all out there, and then deal with the aftermath. "I'd like to tender my notice of resignation."

"Excuse me? What did you just say? I must have misheard. I would have sworn you just said you were quitting."

"That's exactly what I'm saying. I've stayed in Paradise a long time, longer than anywhere else I've lived. I stayed because of the kind of place it is, but that's all changing, so there's no reason I shouldn't move on, try something new."

Cassie narrowed her brow. "Funny, I would have thought your best friends being here might be a reason to stick around."

Crap. She didn't want to offend Cassie, but she had to move. She couldn't stay in Paradise with Nic parading in and out of town constantly. And once the resort was built it would be a constant reminder. She would never be able to put him behind her if she stayed here.

Maybe she just wasn't meant to have a real home. Some people never settled down; they moved whenever the urge hit them. Just because she'd always dreamed of putting down roots didn't mean it was the right thing or that this was the right place. She knew better than most that dreams didn't always come true. "I love you guys, you know that. But just because I won't live here doesn't mean we can't still be friends. I'll call, we can talk on Skype, email, text. And when I'm settled you can come visit me."

"Settled where?" Cassie threw her hands up in the air. "Do you even know where you want to go?"

She'd anticipated that question. Unfortunately, she hadn't come up with an answer yet. "Not yet. But I will. I'm going to start checking ads, see who's hiring. Maybe try somewhere up north for a change."

"So let me get this straight." Cassie had shifted to what Jillian thought of as her doctor voice. "You have no idea where you want to go, nothing planned out, and yet you are quitting your job—a job I was reasonably sure you liked—leaving your best friends, and deserting the town you love. And you are doing this why?"

"When Caruso Hotels buys the Sandpiper—"

"Ah, Caruso, that's what this is about. Nic Caruso, to be specific. Damn him. What happened? If he hurt you, I know how to castrate—"

"That won't be necessary." She managed a smile at the image, pleased by the show of solidarity if not the dramatic suggestion. "He didn't do anything, really. Other than be the wrong man at the wrong time." She needed Cassie to understand. "He came by tonight. He's in town to start negotiations to buy the Sandpiper. He wanted to tell me he was sorry things turned out this way, that he would try to make the transition as pain-less as possible, even though we both know there isn't much he can do to minimize the impact of thousands of new tourists." She focused on her hands, resting them carefully in her lap. "He brought me dinner."

"What a bastard," Cassie said drolly.

Jillian continued without pause. "We talked, and for a while it was like before. Then it got...tense, sort of. And then he kissed me."

"And?"

"And it was wonderful, okay? The best kiss I've ever had. But then I stopped it. I can't go there when I know it can't work, not long-term." She swiped angrily at her eyes, refusing to cry over him anymore. "I get that he has to do his job, has to build the hotel. I fell in love with him, anyway. I'll find a way to get over him, but I can't keep seeing him. It hurts too much." Her voice cracked, but she didn't break down this time. No more. She'd learned to be strong a long time ago, and no man was going to break her. Not even Nic Caruso.

"Oh, Jillian... I'm so sorry."

"Don't feel sorry for me, okay? Just help me move on. Accept my resignation."

Cassie started to say something, then stopped. Get-ting up, she moved to the desk in the corner where she kept her computer. "Well, come on. Let's start searching those job databases. We need to find you somewhere fantastic, somewhere fun for me to visit."

Nic sat in one of the leather chairs facing the oak desk where his father conducted all his business. He'd waited until the end of the day to approach him, not wanting to chance their conversation being interrupted. Even still, he'd found Lorenzo Caruso tied up in a conference call with the marketing department.

Tapping his fingers on the leather, he took another swallow of the whiskey he'd helped himself to, trying to contain his nerves. He was generally given free rein with business decisions; as a vice president, he technically didn't need approval to hand off the Paradise Isle project. But his father would be curious, and it was better to head off any questions, rather than be put on the defensive later. At least, that was the plan.

His father waved a finger at him, signaling he would only be another minute. Good: the sooner this was over, the sooner he could get to work on something else, anything else. A new place, a new challenge—that was what he needed. Hopefully Dad would have something ready for him, something meaty that would take all his concentration. Something to get his mind off his impossible situation with Jillian.

Finally, his father hung up the phone, circling the desk to envelop Nic in a crushing hug. "What are you doing here? I didn't think I'd see you until next week!"

He returned the embrace, happier to see his father than he would have expected. The older man returned to his desk, settling on the edge of it rather than sitting behind it.

"Were there any problems?"

"No problems, Dad. As expected, the grant I told you about didn't go through, so there's no issue there. In fact, it should be a straightforward enough project that I'm going to have Mike Patrullo head this one up. He's been doing good work, and I think it would be a positive experience for him."

His father pursed his lips, swirling his own, mostly empty glass of whiskey, the golden liquid dancing in the light. "You've never turned an assignment of this magnitude over to someone else before."

"No, but this seemed like a good time to try it, let someone else take their shot."

"And this decision wouldn't have anything to do with a young lady your mother was telling me about, would it?"

Great. Was his whole family obsessed with his love life?

"And don't go blaming your mother. You know she just wants you to be happy," his father added before Nic could voice a complaint.

Cornered and not willing to lie to his father, he conceded the point. "Yeah, I guess it does have to do with her. I messed things up, badly."

"So you're running away? I thought I raised you better than that."

"I'm not running. She asked me to leave. Staying there would just make things harder for her, and—"

"And you're willing to make a sacrifice if it means you can help her out, is that right?"

"Yes." He relaxed a bit more into the buttery leather; he should have known his father would understand. He might be a savvy businessman, but he had raised his boys to be gentlemen, as well.

"Do you love her?"

The blunt question ripped through his careful posturing, resurrecting the headache he'd almost managed to forget about. Knowing his father wouldn't leave it alone, he gave the only answer he could. "Yes." Dropping his head back, he closed his eyes against the overhead lighting. "But that doesn't seem to matter."

"Dominic, love is the only thing that does matter."

Those were not the words he'd expected to hear from his ambitious father.

"You don't understand. She deserves things I can't give her. She needs someone that wants the same things as her, someone that can be there day in and day out, home for dinner, with kids and a dog in the backyard."

"Ah, I see." His father rested his hands together, steepling his fingers. "And that's not the kind of life you want."

"No. I mean, I don't know. But either way, it's not the life I have. Heck, I'm barely home long enough to read my mail, let alone have a relationship."

"True. And after investing so much time and effort into your work, you wouldn't want to change things now."

"It's not about what I want. It's about what needs to be done. I've got responsibilities. You know that— you're the one that taught me about responsibility."

"Yes, I did. And I've always been proud of your work ethic. But maybe I didn't do a very good job of teaching you about priorities."

"What's that supposed to mean? I should just drop everything, run off to Florida because I met a pretty girl?"

"No, not if that's all she is. But this isn't about playing beach blanket bingo with some random girl, is it?"

Nic shook his head, then got up and walked to one of the large windows overlooking the street far below. From this distance, the frantic pushing and shoving of evening commuters looked almost choreographed. Were any of them as twisted up inside as he was?

His father stepped up behind him. "You won't find the answers out there, son, and I don't have them, either. You're going to have to do some hard thinking. But I trust you to find your way in this, just as you have in everything else."

Nic stayed at the window long after his father left, hoping for some inspiration in the place where so many pivotal decisions had been made.

A knock at the door found Jillian elbow deep in a box of books, trying to figure out the best way to arrange them for maximum space. Happy for a reprieve, she stretched out her aching muscles. Packing was harder work than she remembered, although really, this was the first time she'd ever had much worth packing. Increased pounding hurried her to the door. "I'm coming. Keep your pants on."

Impatient as always, Mollie had already let herself in by the time Jillian got there. Taking in the boxes, packing paper and all-around mess, she let out a long whistle. "You didn't waste any time getting started, did you?"

Jillian huffed at a curl that had escaped the bandanna she'd used to cover her hair. "No, I want to be ready to go as soon as I hear back on a job. And if you're here to talk me out of it, you can just leave now." Hands on her hips, she silently dared her friend to challenge her.

"No, I said I'd help, and I will. That doesn't mean I have to like it, or that I agree with what you're doing, but it's your life."

"Exactly."

Kneeling next to the box again, she gave up on efficiency and just piled the books in however they fit. It wasn't like boxes were hard to come by—the clinic got enough shipments of dog food and medications to keep her well supplied. "I'm doing the bookshelves first, then the pictures, then we can start on the hall closet."

True to her word, Mollie pitched right in, grabbing another box and a stack of books. "So, any leads yet?"

"A few nibbles. I have a phone interview with a place in New Mexico on Tuesday."

"New Mexico, huh? What about New York? Did you find any openings up there?"

"I didn't really look," Jillian lied. She'd spent quite a bit of time and ink printing job ads for New York City, only to toss them in the trash.

"Well, you should. If you're going to be selfish enough to move away from us, you should do it for a good reason. Moving to be with the man of your dreams qualifies. Running away, on the other hand, does not."

"I'm not running away, I'm getting a fresh start."

"You say to-*may*-to, I say to-*mah*-to."

"Juvenile."

Mollie stuck her tongue out, undeterred.

"And I'm not moving to New York City. First of all, Nic has given me zero indication that he has any interest in making things work between us."

"Maybe that's because he thought you would never agree to relocate. You made such a big stink about how Paradise Isle is the only place you've ever felt at home, he probably never even considered asking you to be near him. And yet here you are, moving away, leaving everything."

Mollie had a point. She had made it sound as though she would never leave, for anything. Until just a few days ago, she hadn't thought she ever would. But that didn't mean anything, did it? "It would be pointless, anyway. Even if I did move up there, which I won't, he's almost never home."

"Maybe he's never had anything worth going home for?"

"Right...gorgeous guy, lots of money, apartment in the city. He's been starved for female companionship, I'm sure." Her eyes rolled so hard she almost sprained something.

"Maybe not. But love is different, it changes things. If love is powerful enough to make you pick up and run from the one place you've always said you'd never leave, don't you think it would be enough to get him to spend more nights at home?"

All Mollie's talk of love was making her head spin. "He's not in love with me. Anyway, I'd probably hate a city that big. I've always said I want to start a family somewhere small, with a hometown feel to it. You know that."

"Sure, and that's a great dream. But it seems to me, you're looking at this from the wrong angle. What's important about a home is the people in it, not what zip code it's in." Shrugging her shoulders, Mollie went back to packing the box in front of her.

Jillian looked into her own box, then at the things still waiting to be packed. She'd spent so much time and energy searching out things that would make this apartment feel special, feel homey. But no matter how she decorated, it never had the kind of inviting vibe she was going for. Sure, she'd been burned by people in the past, but had that somehow taught her to invest her emotional energy into a place, instead of people? Was she so afraid of being hurt again that she'd ignored the importance of love in her search for the perfect home? So many times she'd prayed and hoped for a real family, but when had she stopped believing that wish would come true? Had she traded her dreams of love for security?

If that was her coping strategy, it wasn't working very well. Wasn't that why she tended to stay at work late, or go by Mrs. Rosenberg's in the evening? She thought about the houses she'd envied growing up— all were filled with people that cared about each other. Even the clinic, with all its sterility, felt welcoming because Cassie and Mollie were there. Despite herself, she had wonderful people in her life. Was she really going to let her old insecurities drive her into leaving them, running away from everyone that mattered, in a misguided attempt to protect herself?

Was that hidden fear the reason her romantic relationships had never gone anywhere? Because she was afraid of being abandoned again? Had she pushed Nic away, too, because of her distrust? Maybe she had been too quick to assume things between them could never work out, too quick to shut the door on what could have been. She had missed her chance to fix things with him, but that didn't mean she had to keep repeating the same pattern.

Energy rising, she stood, dumping the half-filled box, the books thudding to the floor. "You're right."

Mollie nodded, her short hair bouncing. "Always. But in what way, specifically?"

"About me, about people being more important than places. I've always said that I'd stay in Paradise forever, right? So leaving just because things are changing is crazy."

A smile filled her friend's face. "Totally insane. And stupid."

"Don't go overboard." She smiled. "But moving isn't what I really want. Paradise might be different, but my friends are the same, and I'm not going to give them up." She felt her own grin growing. "I'm staying. Which means—"

"That we need to unpack all these boxes." Mollie sighed. "Do you have any wine? This is going to take a while."

Nic wasn't sure how long he had been in his father's office, alternating between pacing the floor and staring blankly out the window. Long enough that the offices had grown quiet other the bustle of the janitorial staff somewhere down the hall. He really should leave, but instead he sank into his father's worn desk chair. In front of him a small city of photographs populated the desk, as if guarding the stacks of paperwork enshrined there.

One, older than the rest, caught his eye. The frame was a plain, wooden square, aged but sturdy. The picture inside was faded, the sepia tones revealing two men, one middle-aged and bearded, the other young and clean-shaven with an adventurous gleam in his eye. Father and son shared similar dark features, features that Nic had inherited, as well.

He hadn't thought about his grandfather, his *nonno*, in quite some time. His health had kept him from visiting the past few years, but before that he had made a point of staying in touch with his descendants in America, despite the distance. Picking up the picture to look more closely, Nic could make out the bow of a boat in the background, one they had probably built together. Nonno had been a shipbuilder, as had his father before him. Lorenzo, Nic's father, had been taught the craft at a young age, with the expectation that he would continue the family tradition.

But the youngest Caruso had had other dreams. He'd worked for passage to America, sure his destiny was there. And it had been. He'd used his business expertise and natural charm to find jobs, saving until he could buy the rental home he'd been living in. He might have never owned more than a property or two, but wise investment and a healthy dose of luck had allowed him to channel his legendary determination into what was now one of the premier resort chains in the country.

And no one was more proud than Lorenzo's own father, who had made it his personal mission to stay in every single Caruso Resort. If he'd ever been upset about his son's choice to immigrate, Nic hadn't heard about it.

The family ties that spanned the two continents hadn't broken or strained over time, only strengthened. That was an accepted fact of Nic's family history, but one that he was now seeing through new eyes. There had been no disloyalty in his father's decision to leave the family shipbuilding tradition or the country of his birth. Maybe it had caused some tension; surely there had been concerns, but never hard feelings. So why did he feel so trapped by his own relationship with his father? Had he confused his connection to his father's business with his connection to the man himself?

Yes, his father had wanted a son to take over the business—he'd made no secret of that—but he'd also never indicated his love for his children hinged on it. No, the blame was his own. Success in business had become a way to prove his loyalty to his father, a way to earn his respect. And that was still important; it always would be. But following blindly in another man's footsteps, even a man as wise as his father, wasn't a life. It was time to make his own decisions. He needed to respect himself enough, trust himself enough, to follow his own heart.

His father had left part of his family on another shore, but in doing so he'd expanded the family in other ways. Vision finally clear, Nic grabbed the desk phone. Dialing from memory, he waited for her to pick up, fingers absently tracing the faded photograph.

"Hey, Isabella? We need to talk."

Chapter 16

"Up you go." Jillian lifted the elderly schnauzer into a cage lined with clean, soft towels. Mr. Snappers was recovering from his dental extraction, and was still a bit loopy from the medication. She checked his IV again and adjusted the fluid rate, then placed a hot water bottle wrapped in a soft cloth next to him. The warmth would help him recover more quickly and would feel good to his old bones.

Finished with her midday patient checks, she washed her hands, then walked to the front desk to see if the first afternoon patient had arrived. Dan Jameson was there, talking to Mollie, his dalmatian focused on the cat cowering in a carrier a few feet away. "Hey, Dan, how's Flash doing?" The lanky, white-whiskered man was a security guard at the county courthouse, but volunteered with the small island's fire department and considered it his civic duty to keep the fire station mascot in good health.

"Right as rain, Miss Jillian, right as rain. I just

stopped by to pick up his special food." Flash had a genetic condition that caused bladder stones; a prescription diet helped keep them at bay.

"Wonderful! And you're only giving him the special prescription treats now, right?"

"I keep a jar of them at the station house and some in my pocket for when we're out and about. The kids like to make him do tricks, and he likes to show off, don't you, boy?" He patted the handsome animal, pride showing in his face. They were a great pair, and an example of everything she loved about Paradise. How could she have even considered moving?

Mollie handed Dan his receipt and then turned to Jillian. "Dan was just filling me in on some news. It seems the sale of the Sandpiper is moving forward."

Her stomach tumbled as if tossed by a rogue wave. Counting to ten silently, she steeled her spine. If she was going to stay in Paradise—and she was—she would have to come to terms with the sale and the changes it unleashed. "Well, that was to be expected."

Dan shook his head. "Maybe so, but it sure seems to be happening fast. A lady over in the clerk's office told me that the survey was already ordered, and the seller is hoping to be done with it and back in Orlando within the month."

"I didn't think it could happen that quickly." She swallowed and reminded herself that the sooner it was done, the sooner Nic would be onto the next project and out of her life.

"Me, either, but I guess when you've got money, the wheels turn a bit more quickly than they do otherwise."

"I guess so." Rubbing Flash's silky ears, she sighed. Gesturing to the bag of food on the counter, she asked, "Can I take this out for you?"

Eyes wide, he shook his head. "No, ma'am, I can't have a lady carrying my things for me. The boys at the station would never let me live it down."

She laughed, recognizing the truth in his words. "I'll get the door for you, then, if it won't hurt your reputation too much."

"Just don't tell anyone." He winked, then hefted the bag without letting go of the waiting dog's leash. She beat him to the door, swinging it open for him, then took a minute to appreciate the breezy fall afternoon. A light wind stirred the palms that dotted the street and carried the smells of the Sandcastle Cakes with it. "Hey, Mollie, when's the next appointment due? Do I have time to run and grab a coffee?"

"You've got five minutes, but I just made a full pot, so why do you need to run out?"

She grinned ruefully. "Because I like my coffee with a side of pumpkin spice scone. I can smell them from here."

"Ooh, yum. Get me one, too. But hurry."

"I'm already gone. Tell Cassie I'll grab her one, too."

"Grab me one what?" Cassie asked, walking in past Jillian, returning from her lunch break.

"A scone and a coffee. The smell of pumpkin spice is too much to resist."

"Ooh, perfect. I knew I had a light lunch for a reason. Whose turn is it to buy?"

"Mine," Jillian answered. "I'll be right back."

Heading for the sweet shop across the street, she felt her shoulders slide down, her tension over the discussion of the Sandpiper soothed by the normalcy of the errand. The new influx of tourists might make her daily coffee run take a little longer, but surely places like the Sandcastle would stick around, at least until one of the national donut chains chased the crowds and opened up shop. Grimacing, she entered the quaint storefront, where the warm aroma of sugar and spice reminded her of her mission.

"Something wrong?" Grace Keville asked, pausing from wiping down a gleaming display case chock full of decadent desserts.

"Nothing one of your delicious scones won't fix. Three pumpkin ones, please, and some cappuccinos to go with them." Sandcastle Cakes didn't offer the variety of coffee creations that The Grind did, but the freshness and sheer number of drool-worthy treats made it her favorite place for an afternoon pick-me-up. Her mouth watering, she scanned the glass cases. Scrumptious muffins, cookies the size of her hand, layer cakes dripping with buttercream. How did Grace stay so skinny? Just the scent of all that yumminess was probably adding an inch to each of her own thighs.

Seeing her order was ready, she tore herself away from the wonderland of confections. "Thanks, Grace, this is just what I needed."

"If only all my customers were so easily pleased." She wiped a smudge of flour from her face with the edge of her apron. "I've had to do three mock-up cakes for one of my wedding clients. If it's this hard to decide on a cake, I don't see how she ever managed to pick a groom."

Laughing, Jillian pocketed her change and took the cardboard drink carrier and white bakery bag. "Good luck with Ms. Indecision. I'd better go before Cassie sends out a search party for me."

Walking as quickly as she could without spilling coffee, she pondered how to protect small business owners like Grace from the influx of commercialism that was on the horizon. She'd bring that up at the next Preservation Society meeting; there might be zoning issues or other changes they could make if they hurried.

Unfortunately, it was too late to protect her heart; that was a restoration project with no end in sight.

Nic adjusted his tie for the umpteenth time, hoping his impatience wasn't overly obvious to the man on the other side of the desk. He'd dealt with dozens of mortgage officers at banks across the country, and they all seemed to move in the same lethargic time warp as this guy. The minute hand on the large wall clock ticked by with maddening precision, a metronome for the musical shuffling of papers and clacking of keyboards. No other deal had been this nerve-racking, but he'd also never had a deal with so much riding on it.

He needed this to go through smoothly, without any last-minute changes or red-tape snags. He'd spent hours going over the business plan, the revenue projections, the zoning regulations. Everything was there; he just needed this one poorly paid employee to stop overestimating his own importance and sign off on it. He'd seen the glint in the man's eye—he was enjoying making someone with the Caruso name wait on tenterhooks. It might be the only time he got to be in a position of power with someone like Nic, and he wasn't letting it go sooner than he had to. Recognizing the situation for what it was, Nic had forced himself to smile, to make small talk. And now, he forced himself to wait.

"Well…it seems everything is in order." The mousy man with thinning hair and an ill-fitting suit looked up. "I know you've called in some favors to fast-track this. I find that highly irregular, and not the proper way of things. But Mr. Ackerman, the bank president, has instructed me to proceed. Everything will be ready for you at the closing, as you arranged."

Thank heaven for small favors and the connections his father had made over the years. He needed this deal to close as soon as possible. He shook the man's limp hand and was out the door, on to his next appointment. He had a meeting with an architect in twenty minutes, and then a landscape specialist after that. If all went well, he'd have the big items on his list checked off by late afternoon and be back in New York by nightfall. He had some shopping to do, and the limited options on Paradise Isle just weren't going to cut it for this particular task.

He was almost to the architect's when he saw her. She had darted across the street, almost directly in front of where he was stopped for a red light. She hadn't recognized him in a different rental car, but he'd know her anywhere. Her dark curls bounced as she walked, and her cheeks were reddened by the wind. His body hardened as he watched her. Would it always be like this? Would he always want her, need her so badly, that just the sight of her nearly drove him mad?

A car honked behind him. The light had turned green without him noticing. He drove through the intersection, fighting the urge to turn around, to go to her. But that wasn't part of the plan. He had things he needed to do, and he couldn't let his hormones, or his heart, distract him.

He pulled into the small parking lot in front of Island Architecture with five minutes to spare. Time enough to make a quick phone call.

"Hey, Dad, just finished up at the bank. Your phone call did the trick."

His father's voice rumbled back. "Are you sure you want to go through with this?" Concern echoed over the airwaves.

"I'm sure. The numbers make sense."

"It's not the numbers I'm worried about. You're more important to me than any of that."

"I know, Dad." And he did know. They'd had a long talk, late into the night, after he'd met with Isabella. They were on the same page now, and that felt good. Really good.

"I'll call you after the closing, let you know when everything's settled. And Dad?"

"Yes?"

"Thanks again for understanding."

"You got it. Now, get back to work. You've got a big project on your hands."

"You're right, I do. Bye." He hung up and did what his father had advised, what he did best. He got to work.

"I wish I had better news for you, but if there's a way around this, I can't find it."

Jillian absorbed the Preservation Society president's words, knowing they were no more than the truth. She and Edward had been poring over zoning regulations, municipal codes and city ordinances for hours, hoping to find something they could use to stop the spread of the large chain stores they both were felt was inevitable. It wasn't that she was averse to commercialism—she liked to shop as much as the next girl—she just wanted to protect the small businesses that gave Paradise so much character. She'd hoped there would be something already on the books, but it looked as though they'd have to start from scratch. A process that would take more time than they had.

She shouldn't have gotten her hopes up. She had been so sure they would find a way to protect the charm of Paradise amid the changes the new resort would bring. But the town's elected officials had never anticipated this kind of rapid progress; no one could have predicted this.

Heart heavy, her neck stiff from hunching over the conference table so long, she stood and stretched. "You're right, Ed. There's nothing more we can do about it tonight, anyway. I knew the Caruso lawyers would have triple-checked everything as far as the hotel itself, but I had wanted there to be something we could do about all the other changes coming." She started stacking up the books and reams of paper they'd torn through. "Looks like we don't have a leg to stand on."

"Don't give up just yet. I'll ask around, see if there's anything else we can do."

"Thanks, Ed. I'll try to stay positive.

"That's the way. Remember, the people here won't change, not just because there are a bunch of new stores and tourists crowding up the place."

"Good point, and exactly what I needed to hear." On impulse, she hugged him, making him blush like a schoolgirl instead of the middle-aged man he was. This learning-to-trust business was hard, but he was right. She needed to remember that the people wouldn't change just because everything else did. Maybe someday expecting the best from people would be second nature, but for now she appreciated the reminders. She'd probably need a lot of them as construction got under way. Leaving Ed flustered, but smiling, she said her goodbyes and left the small library room that served as the society's headquarters.

At least she hadn't run into Nic yet. She was on pins and needles every time she left the house, certain she would bump into him on the street or in a café. The constant anxiety was draining her; she needed to relax. Maybe she'd check out a book before she went home, something lighthearted. Romance was out, but maybe one of those funny vampire books, where everyone wore designer clothes twenty-four hours a day. Something to take her out of her head for a bit.

Browsing the stacks, she found a few that looked interesting, and started for the checkout area. Reading the back cover of one of her picks, she walked right into one of the other patrons in line. "Excuse me, I wasn't looking where I was—"

"Jillian."

"Nic. Wow. I didn't expect to see you here. I mean, here, the library, not here, Paradise." Off-kilter, she tried to look anywhere but at his face. The book in his hand caught her attention. "*Native Florida Plants for the Landscape Beginner*, interesting choice. I hadn't pegged you as the gardening type."

"Just some research. How about you?" He gestured to the paperbacks she was clutching.

"Some pleasure reading." She tried to hide the covers from him. Why did all the novels have to feature such erotic images on the front? He was going to think she was sex-crazed if he saw them. Which admittedly was pretty accurate where he was concerned. They were in a library, of all places, and he still had her blood thrumming through her veins, her body warming in all the right places. At least the sudden jolt of lust offered a bit of a distraction from the ever-present ache in her heart. Hormones beat heartache any day.

"Good, you deserve a bit of relaxation."

"Seemed like a good idea. Things have been a bit stressful."

He winced at her not-too-subtle indictment. "I suppose I deserved that."

"Yes, you did." If only she could really hate him, that might make things easier. But she couldn't.

Moving forward in line, he handed his book to the librarian at the desk, presenting a Paradise Municipal

Library card. When had he gotten that? The library did issue short-term cards to nonresidents for a fee, but not many people took advantage of the service. It seemed like a lot of trouble for a short-term business trip.

He wasn't planning on extending his stay, was he? He had to go. Soon. Being this close to him, and not having him, was agony. Even breathing hurt. He had to go so she could try to forget him and move on with her life. Every run-in would be like ripping off a newly formed scab. She needed space and time for the wounds to close, for her heart to mend.

He'd finished with his transaction, and was watching her, his eyes soft. "I had planned to call you tonight."

Keeping her face averted, sure he'd see the turmoil in her eyes, she handed her books to the impatiently waiting librarian. "I don't think that would be a good idea."

"No, I can see that." He hesitated. "Have a good night, Jillian."

Not able to trust her voice, she only nodded. Accepting her silence, he turned and walked out of her life once more.

Chapter 17

Nic paced the whitewashed boards of the Sandpiper's wraparound porch. After that last run-in with Jillian, it was obvious that a straightforward approach wouldn't work. Hell, the way she'd treated him had him rethinking his plan altogether. Maybe he'd done enough damage and should cut his losses and run.

Except he wasn't built that way. For better or worse, he didn't quit, and he didn't walk away, not when it mattered. He might be making some changes in his life, but he was, at heart, still the same guy. Which meant he needed to find a way to get Jillian to listen to him, no matter how angry or hurt she was. She might push him away forever after that, but at least he would know he tried.

Frustration spurred him down the stairs and onto the soft sand of the beach below. Maybe a walk would clear his head. Leaving his shoes by the steps, he started for the shore. Then he went back and moved his shoes farther out of sight, under a step. He knew it was ridiculous—crime was almost nonexistent in Paradise—

but New York habits died hard. It was going to take a while to adjust.

Satisfied he wouldn't be the victim of a random shoe-napping, he started off at a brisk pace. Most of the young families had already packed up for the day, and in their place were older couples walking hand in hand, enjoying a simple Friday night. He knew from the local paper that the beach was also a favorite of the high school crowd, come the weekend. He had read that one student had broken his arm on this beach, trying to play tackle football by moonlight. If that was the worst trouble the young people got into around here, he figured they were doing pretty well. This place really did seem like a tropical version of a 1950s sitcom.

His feet kept time with the waves, carrying him farther down the coast. Ahead, he spotted a dog chasing seagulls, barking in delight as they kept just out of reach. Smiling, he wondered what Murphy thought of the birds. He knew Jillian took him for regular runs on the beach; maybe they were old hat by now. He still couldn't get over how dedicated she was to that dog, caring for him better than many people did their own pets.

He stopped. Murphy—that was his answer. Jillian might not be willing to meet with him, but she'd do anything for Murphy. It was a dirty trick, but he just needed it to work once. Hopefully she'd agree the ends justified the means. And if not, well, he wouldn't be any worse off than he was now.

It turned out Mrs. Rosenberg loved his scheme and was happy to lend Murphy to the cause. When he'd spoken to her last night, she'd agreed to have the dog ready at five thirty today. She had already called Jillian to tell her not to stop by to exercise Murphy, saying she had family coming by that wanted to see him. All the other details were taken care of, and, checking his watch, he decided it was time to head over to collect the dog.

He had directions with him, but felt pretty confident he could find her house without them. He'd become much more familiar with the island over the past several days. Driving along the coast, he marveled yet again at the constantly changing view. Today he saw nothing but blue sky and a single osprey silhouetted darkly against it. The big bird was perched on a light post, where he, or she—he had no idea how to tell the sexes apart—had built an enormous nest. He'd seen quite a few of the precariously balanced constructions, and every time wondered how they kept the things from tumbling to the water below. Maybe he should pick up a book about the local birds the next time he hit the library. He'd never been much of a reader, but he'd been doing a lot of new things lately. Given the scope of his plans, it made sense to continue to research the area.

Turning onto one of the main thoroughfares, he kept an eye out for any businesses that might be interested in putting together vacation packages, things that could be bundled with a hotel stay. The dive shop seemed like a good bet, and maybe the kayak outfitter, as well. He was also hoping to work out some arrangements with local restaurants for picnic baskets to be delivered directly to the beach for lunching families. Driving by the photography studio's window display had the gears turning in his head, and he made a mental note to drop by with a business card and proposal next week.

Soon he was past the last of the commercial buildings and navigating the residential neighborhood where Mrs. Rosenberg's house was. The houses here were older than on the other side of the island. Most were small, single-story bungalow types with stucco or siding to protect them from the harsh Florida sun. Mrs. Rosenberg's was easy to spot, the pink paint standing out among the more neutral colors of her neighbors' homes. A few plastic flamingos were the only thing keeping her house from being a Florida cliché.

Shutting the car door, he started up the walk. At his knock, Murphy's enthusiastic barking greeted him, followed by Mrs. Rosenberg's muffled voice as she shushed the eager border collie. Once she opened the door for him, he held up a treat he'd stashed in a pocket. Murphy, knowing the routine, plopped his furry rear end on the floor, then accepted the treat with dignity. Nic ruffled the dog's fur and took the leash that Mrs. Rosenberg had already secured.

"Thanks again. I really appreciate you letting me borrow him."

Her brightly painted lips turned up as she regarded man and dog. "I'm happy to do it. I don't usually condone sneaky behavior, but it's for her own good. She has some issues with change, I know she does, but sometimes you have to embrace change if you want to move forward. Besides, if you don't take him, he's liable to drive me crazy, with her not coming to play with him tonight."

"Well, I'll take good care of him. Any particular time you want him back?"

"No rush. I went ahead and told the girls in my senior group to come over—didn't want to be lying to Jillian. We'll wait up together to hear how things go."

He had no doubt they'd be gossiping about it all night. Heck, there might even be bets placed. But at the end of the night, he would be the one taking the risks, and the stakes were high.

Jillian put the final coat of polish on her freshly manicured nails. The pretty golden color was unlikely to last, given how hard she was on her hands during the workweek, but it was a Saturday, and she figured she deserved a bit of pampering, even if she had to do it herself. The meticulous process also gave her something to focus on other than Nic Caruso, Caruso Hotels and the entire mess that had become her personal life.

Since she'd run into him, she had cleaned her apartment, decluttered her closet, baked and frozen more muffins than any one person could ever hope to consume, and gotten an early start on her Christmas list, thanks to the wonders of online shopping.

But no matter what activity she threw herself into, the pain was still there, gnawing away at her. There was an empty spot inside of her, a deep hole that no amount of manic cleaning or self-improvement could touch. Even when she closed her eyes, exhausted and desperate for sleep, she saw him. His dark eyes, chiseled jaw and teasing smile followed her into her dreams, dreams that left her needy and restless.

It seemed there was no cure for heartbreak, other than, hopefully, the tincture of time. She'd gotten through other disappointments, but this time was different. She had finally learned to open her heart, only to have it squashed like one of the many lovebugs stuck to her windshield.

Still, the hurting couldn't last forever. She'd just have to keep her chin up until then. She could do that. Focus on work, and her friends, and maybe take up a hobby or twelve. Reading hadn't worked; every hero in every story had reminded her of Nic. Maybe knitting or golf. Golf was popular.

She was searching golf lessons on the internet, and becoming increasingly intimidated by the prices, when the phone rang.

Desperate for a new distraction, she grabbed the phone without checking the caller ID. "Hello?"

"Hey, Jillian, it's Nic. Please don't hang up."

"Why not?" This was crazy—how many times did she have to tell him to leave her alone? Her stupid heart was beating a happy tune just hearing his voice, but her head knew there was only pain down that path.

"Because I need help, or rather Murphy does. He's here, running on the beach. I don't know if I can catch him on my own."

Well, crap. This was really starting to get old. She'd have to talk to Mrs. Rosenberg again about being more careful. "Fine. I'm on my way. Keep an eye on him until I arrive, and keep your phone on. I'll call when I'm there."

Fuming, she got her keys and stomped down the

stairs. She was supposed to be pampering herself. Now, she'd be torturing herself instead, teasing her heart yet again with the one man she wanted but couldn't have. Maybe she needed to get away. Not move, she'd ruled that out as cowardice. But there was no reason she couldn't take a long-overdue vacation, maybe go camping in the state forest or drive up to St. Augustine for a few days. Anywhere would be better than here, if being here meant constantly running into Nic.

By the time she got to the Sandpiper, she had a vacation itinerary mapped out. She parked and noted that other than a few cars in the employee section, and a single rental car that must be Nic's, the place was empty. Odd, but then again, with the sale so soon, maybe they'd stopped taking reservations. Crunching over the gravel, she punched Nic's number into her phone. It rang three times before she got a breathless answer.

"Hey, are you here?"

"Yeah, walking up now. Are you still on the beach?"

"No. Yes. Just…come around to the back." And the phone clicked off.

He'd sounded a bit off; maybe Murphy was giving him trouble? Or maybe he wasn't thrilled to have to see her, given how she'd treated him the past few times. She'd blown hot and cold so often she felt like a hair dryer on the fritz. He had every right to be a bit wary of her mood. Or just frustrated to once again be saddled with a delinquent dog. Either way, she'd get Murphy, and herself, out of his hair as quickly as she could. Her pockets were stuffed with liver treats, more than enough to guarantee the canine's cooperation.

If only the human male could be wrangled so easily.

She took the steps two at a time, ready to get this over with so she could continue with the business of getting on with her life. The front door was right there, but it was just as easy to go around via the wraparound porch. Between cleaning, baking and pampering, she'd been cooped up inside for too long, and the longer route gave her a few more minutes to brace herself before she saw him.

Skirting potted orchids and patio furniture, she made the trek around the stately building. Not a single guest to be seen—in fact, if it wasn't for the murmur of voices drifting up from the beach, she would have sworn she was alone on the island.

Reaching the final turn, she saw Nic in one of the wicker lounge chairs, Murphy sitting expectantly at his feet. Surprised, she watched as Nic tossed the dog a treat, then ruffled his fur. Man and dog looked completely at ease, as if they were just enjoying the afternoon air. If there had been any kind of crisis here, it was long over. So why had he called?

Chapter 18

Nic felt like a suspect waiting for a jury verdict. He'd prepared his case, would make his arguments, but in the end the decision was out of his hands. At least he had Murphy as a character witness.

Wait, was he really so far-gone that a dog was his best chance of success?

Sadly, yes, yes, he was. If an actual dog would keep him out of the proverbial doghouse, he wasn't going to fight it. He stroked Murphy's coat, more to calm his own nerves than settle the animal. In fact, Murphy seemed perfectly content. He figured the continuous consumption of liver treats probably had a lot to do with that, so he tossed the happy dog another one.

"You're going to make him sick if you give him too many of those."

Busted. "They're really small."

"And very rich. We'll take him home in your car. If he yaks, you can deal with it."

Nic looked down at the mostly empty bag of treats

in his lap. Maybe he had been a bit overgenerous. Murphy nosed his leg, maybe to show support, more likely to search for more treats. "You heard her, no more."

"So, I thought you needed help. Seems like you're doing just fine on your own."

"I don't suppose you'd believe that I just now got him under control?"

"You're not sweating, he's not panting and it doesn't look like either of you have any sand on you at all."

Sand. He hadn't thought about that. Oh, well, the ruse had gotten her here, so it had served its purpose.

"Are you going to tell me why you dragged me over here?"

Her blue eyes were like icicles, her lips pursed in righteous indignation. She was angry as hell, and still knock-you-on-your-butt gorgeous. Her mood didn't matter when it came to his feelings, or his libido. He wanted her, in his arms, in his life, in his bed. But wanting didn't mean having. If he didn't play his cards right, she was going to walk out of his life, leaving him right back where he started. And he wouldn't, couldn't, let that happen.

"I had to show you—and tell you—some things. If you give me this, I promise I won't bother you again. I'll leave town tomorrow if that's what you want."

She narrowed her eyes. "If I listen to you now, you'll leave town? No more running into each other, no more emergency phone calls, no more anything?"

"You have my word. You tell me to leave, and I'll go." Sweat trickled down his back. Everything was on the line—there would be no second chances.

"Fine. Let's get this over with."

Not exactly a vote of confidence, but he'd take it. "Come with me, we'll walk Murphy while we talk."

"While *you* talk. I don't have anything left to say."

"Either way." He started to reach for her hand, but figured that would be pushing it. Instead, he grabbed Murphy's leash and headed around the side of the building, hoping she would follow. She did, and his lungs loosened a bit. Drawing a deep breath, he spoke. "As you can see, the structure of the building is sound, but a lot of the siding needs to be replaced, and in several places the porch railing shows signs of dry rot." He gestured to an area where the weathered boards, bleached by the sun, were peeling away. "The good news is I've found a contractor who has experience working on buildings from this time period. He should be able to match everything, make it look just like the original."

Jillian stopped dead. "Replace? What's the point of replacing stuff when you're just going to tear it—"

"No questions yet. I'm not done, and you promised to listen."

Jillian's mouth opened, then closed. He definitely had her interest now.

"There are obviously some improvements that can be made inside as well—a new computer system, some upgrades in the kitchen, that kind of thing. More updating than remodeling. But really, what I wanted to talk to you about are the grounds." He chanced touching her, taking her elbow to steer her down the stairs to the walking path below.

"The majority of the land is undeveloped. Other than

a few fruit trees, and of course the benches and paths, nothing had been touched out here."

"Right. Your point?" She was still prickly, but he could tell she wanted to hear more.

"Well, I'm thinking we can add some interest to the landscape and still keep the natural feel of the place. For instance, a butterfly garden with a gazebo at the center. There's a nursery on the mainland that can set one up using native plants. It will add some color, but blend in with the natural surroundings."

"A gazebo?"

"Yes, I think it's exactly what we need, if we want to hold weddings here again. Didn't you say this used to be a popular place for them?"

"Yes, but wait—what about the giant resort?" He could almost see the wheels turning in her head. Grinning, he ignored her question and continued walking, taking her past the parking lot to the south side of the inn.

"Take a look at this spot." He pointed to a shady clearing amongst the scrub pines. "What do you think of a playground here, the kind made mostly of wood, so it doesn't stand out too much? Maybe some picnic tables or benches for the parents."

"Playgrounds. Gazebos. Weddings. New siding. Am I crazy or are you? Because I don't see how any of this makes sense when you're just going to bulldoze the place."

"Maybe I'm crazy, maybe I'm not. But I one thing I can say for sure, no one is bulldozing this place."

"Excuse me?" Jillian felt as though she were on some kind of carnival ride, her head was spinning so fast.

Nothing made sense. She had to have heard him wrong or misunderstood. "I could have sworn you just said you aren't going to tear down the Sandpiper."

He gave her a smug little grin and tucked his thumbs in his pockets, as if there was nothing strange about her question or the whole situation. "That's right. I'm not tearing it down. It's got good bones and a history. I don't want to lose that."

"But, then, what are you going to do?" She suddenly understood how Alice felt when she fell into Wonderland. Up was down, down was up and the man in front of her was mad as a hatter.

"That's what I've been trying to talk to you about. For starters, we'll remodel the inn itself, repair what we can and replace what we can't. That's the easy part."

"None of this sounds easy."

"Easy in that we already have a blueprint and the contractor just has to replicate what's already here. No big changes. It's the rest of it that I wanted your input on."

"My input?"

"That's right. I want to bring the Sandpiper back to its glory days, and to do that I need to know more about it. I need to know what the community is missing, what it needs and wants. You know Paradise better than anyone, so I thought you would have some insight into what needs to be done."

She had some thoughts all right, but getting them sorted out would take a while. "Let me get this straight. You are not going to tear down the Sandpiper or build some giant luxury hotel?"

"Right."

She plowed on, trying to grasp what was happening. "And you called me—tricked me, in fact—to come out here, so that I could tell you where and how to build a playground?"

"Among other things, yes."

He really was insane. It was the only explanation.

And now he was walking away, veering off the path and cutting through the clearing he'd designated for the playground. She scrambled after him, catching up to him in a grassy area that backed up to the bluffs, with a view of the beach below. Grabbing his arm, she spun him toward her. "You said other things. What other things?" How much more bizarre could this get?

"You said there used to be community events here. What kinds?"

"Well, charity stuff, mostly. They used to sponsor a yearly fish fry benefit for the library and a chili cook-off for the fire department." She tried to think of what other events she had attended over the years, as well as the ones she'd heard about from Cassie from before she'd moved here. "There used to be a big Christmas tree lighting every year, with caroling and hot chocolate. And I think there was a fall festival, too, but that was before my time." She looked out over the ocean, spotting a cruise ship against the horizon. "They would do the fireworks here, too, on the Fourth of July. Sometimes there was a pig roast or a clambake first."

She turned back to him, and realized he was actually taking notes on a small notepad. "Did you get all that? Or should I repeat it for you?" She tried to infuse as much sarcasm as possible into her voice, but he either didn't pick up on it or tuned it out.

"I got the basics. But thanks." He tucked the pad into the back pocket of his slacks. "Next question. What do you think about this spot for a house?"

"Whose house?"

"The innkeeper's house, of course. There's a suite in the Sandpiper, but I'm thinking that a house makes more sense. It opens more room up for guests in the main inn and offers some privacy for starting a family."

"I can't imagine Caruso Hotels makes a habit of building custom homes for the management staff."

"No, but Caruso Hotels doesn't own the Sandpiper. I do. And I want a house."

Her knees buckled, and she leaned against a well-positioned pine. The rough bark scraped through her thin T-shirt, grounding her. He bought the Sandpiper? Not Caruso Hotels? He was staying? Permanently? There would be no way to avoid him, not if he was running the inn. And what was that he said about starting a family? Was she going to have to watch him date, get married, have children? She'd said she would stay in town, but how could she do that when Paradise was turning into her own personal version of hell?

Jillian looked as though she'd been sucker-punched. The color that had heated her cheeks while they argued had vanished, leaving her as pale as the white clouds floating overhead. Eyes wide, she stared at him. Maybe he shouldn't have blindsided her, but she hadn't left him much choice. She never would have come if she'd known that he, not his father's company, was the new owner of the Sandpiper. Still, her silence had his gut churning. "Are you okay?"

She nodded, straightening almost imperceptibly against the tree she was braced against. "You don't mean you bought it for yourself, right? You must mean you bought it on behalf of Caruso Hotels."

"No. I couldn't do that if I wanted to, since I'm no longer an employee of Caruso Hotels. I turned in my resignation the last time I was in New York."

"But…you can't just quit. You're a vice president, for crying out loud. "

"Not anymore. My sister Isabella now has that title, and good luck to her."

"Your sister? I thought she worked at some fancy Wall Street investment firm."

"She did, but she hated it. She was tired of doing work in the background, never getting to make a decision. She wanted something different, and with her business background and her degree, she'll do a great job."

Jillian threw her hands up, more flustered than he'd ever seen her. "But, it's not just about the job—it's about who you are."

"Who I was. I don't want to be that person anymore." He shoved a hand through his hair. How could he explain this to her, when he was just starting to figure it out himself? "I wasn't living my own life. I was just doing what I thought everyone wanted me to do, what I thought I had to do. But that's not a real life, and it's not what I want. I need to do something for myself, find my own path."

"And that means being an innkeeper?"

"It's as good a job as any. I can use what I know about the industry, but be truly involved. I won't just be setting things in motion. I'll get to follow through. I can create my own vision, instead of following someone else's. And I'll get to put down real roots. I'm tired of living out of a suitcase."

The shock and horror on her face were easy to read, but hard to accept. He had planned on her being surprised, but the anguish on her face, that was something else entirely. Had he misunderstood everything? Imagined her feelings in order to justify his own? He'd convinced himself that she was fighting the same losing battle he was, but maybe she was already over him or had never really wanted him in the first place.

No. He couldn't think like that. Couldn't go there. He'd second-guessed everyone he loved too many times, trying to live up to expectations they'd never really had. If he'd learned anything in the past few days, it was that the only real freedom came from honesty. He had to act on what was in his own heart and then let the chips fall where they may. At least he would have no regrets.

"What about your family?"

"My family wants me to be happy. I don't know how I convinced myself that the only way to make them proud was to be a part of the family business, but I know now that isn't true. I did some hard thinking about our family and what has kept us all together. It isn't the business or a set of expectations. It's love."

He took a deep breath to steady his nerves. His eyes

searched hers; he needed her to see the truth in his words.

"I stayed in the job because of love. And I left it for love, because love is the most important thing in the world. I bought the Sandpiper for love, for you. Because I love you."

He saw the tears coming, and before he could stop and think, he took her in his arms. She clung to him, her shoulders shuddering as she sobbed. At a loss, he stroked her hair and let her cry herself out, wanting nothing more than to keep her protected in his arms forever.

Jillian couldn't believe she was blubbering all over Nic, but she was powerless to stop. All the worry and pain and sadness had built up, and now, hearing his words, she couldn't hold it back anymore. It flowed out of her on a river of tears, clearing the path for the warmth that was taking over, everywhere her body touched his. Was it possible? Pushing away, she wiped her blurry eyes. She had to hear it again, had to know he'd really said it, that it wasn't her emotions playing tricks on her. "You did all this because of me? Because you love me?"

"I did it for us. I bought it for us. I wanted to show you how I feel, and the Sandpiper seemed like the perfect way to do that. You love it, and I love you. Pretty simple."

"But...you really love me?"

He laughed. "Were you not paying attention?"

"I just need to hear it again." Her voice was shaking,

one more thing out of her control. "I've never heard it before."

He smiled. "That's because I've never said it to you before. But I'll say it again. I love you."

Something fluttered inside, breaking free. She felt the tears starting again, but this time she laughed through them. "No, I meant I've never heard that before, from anyone." She smiled. Were her feet even touching the ground? "I'm glad you were the first."

Taking her trembling hands, he pulled her against him. "I'm so sorry, I didn't think... With foster care, your parents. I just didn't think. I should have said it before now, but I promise I'm going to make it up to you. I'm going to say it so often you'll get sick of hearing it." Stopping, he tilted his head to the side. "Wait, does this mean you love me, too?"

She stretched onto her toes, angling for a quick kiss. Lips nearly touching, she whispered against his lips, "I love you—"

He took her mouth, silencing her. She responded eagerly, no longer afraid of the feelings he triggered. When his tongue teased, she parted for him, letting him explore her mouth, answering him with her own bold invasion, needing to taste and feel and love the way she had wanted to since she first saw him standing at the door of the clinic. She held nothing back; she gave him everything. Heart and soul went into that kiss, and he met her passion moment by moment, until her head was spinning and the only thing keeping her upright were his arms firmly wrapped around her body.

Slowly, gradually, he gentled the kiss, nibbling at her

bottom lip before putting a few inches of distance between them. "I have more I want to show you, tell you."

"More?" She felt half-drunk; how much more could there be? She had everything she wanted right here, in him.

"Plenty more, of everything," he answered, his husky voice sending shivers through her body. Practically giddy, she let her imagination paint pictures of what could be.

"But for now, let's start with where we should put the gazebo. I want you to pick the spot."

"Me?"

"Didn't I say I bought this because of you? You're the one that knows it, that loves it. You should be the one that helps it come alive again. Besides, a gazebo is all about romance, and as the female of the species I'm willing to bet you have more expertise in that particular area."

"Hmm, I suppose that's true." She grabbed his hand, dragging him with her as she looked for the perfect spot. "You said it would be used for weddings, right?"

"Right."

"Okay, so you want a good view and enough room around it for guests to gather." She nearly floated across the grass, heading for what she knew would be the ideal location. Tucked away, just off the walking path, was an open area framed by towering palms and a clear view of the ocean. "Here," she declared confidently.

"You're sure?" He squeezed her hand.

"Positive. It's the perfect setting. The sea as a backdrop, plenty of room for folding chairs, easy access from the parking lot—this is the spot."

"Well, if you're sure." He walked to the center of the spot she had chosen, Murphy following at his side. Pulling a small box out of his pocket, he knelt down on one knee and looked up at her.

"Wait...what are you doing?" He couldn't be... could he? Even Murphy looked confused, his gaze going from her to Nic and back again before finally laying his head on Nic's bent knee, as if waiting to find out what was happening.

"I told you, I want to start holding weddings here again. And I want the first wedding to be ours, if you'll have me." He held out a ring, the large diamond scattering rainbows as it caught the setting sun. "Jillian Everett, will you marry me?"

Her throat closed over another round of tears, stealing her voice. Pulling air into her lungs, she swallowed and tried again. "Yes." And then, offering a shaking hand, "When?"

He laughed, the hearty laugh she'd learned to love, and slid the ring over her trembling finger. "As soon as we can get the gazebo built, if that's what you want."

Tugging on their joined hands, she pulled him back up, leaning into his body. "Nic?" She slowly kissed her way along his jaw, letting her hands roam his back, his chest, his arms.

He groaned; whether in frustration or pleasure, she wasn't sure. "What?"

"Build fast."

Chapter 19

Nic figured he'd probably broken a world record in gazebo construction, if there was such a thing. He had ended up having to order most of the supplies—there wasn't much of a lumber selection in Paradise—but once everything had arrived he had attacked the project like a man possessed.

He had spent years supervising construction, massive projects with hundreds of crew members. But this was the first time he had actually built something from the ground up on his own. When the last board was in place and the last coat of paint applied, he was as proud of it as he ever had been of a high-rise hotel.

Of course, it turned out that planning a wedding involved more than just building the gazebo. Thankfully, Jillian was handling most of the other preparations. He was much more at home wielding a hammer, however inexpertly, than he was in a florist's shop. He'd be forever grateful that his main contribution was preparing the physical surroundings.

With the gazebo finished, he had turned his energies to the Sandpiper itself. The previous owners had canceled all the reservations, and the hotel was isolated enough that there was no one to disturb as he hammered and sanded and painted until the wee hours. They were going to hold off on the grand reopening until after the wedding, but he wanted the old building to be at its best when his family came for the ceremony. His parents, siblings, aunts, uncles and maternal grandparents would be on hand, filling the Sandpiper to capacity. His father's parents weren't able to make the transatlantic trip on such short notice, but they had insisted the happy couple visit while on their honeymoon tour of Italy. He had been so afraid of losing his family, but the upcoming wedding had only brought the generations closer together.

Checking his watch, he decided he had enough time to shower before the last of them arrived. He'd just finished moving his things into the suite he and Jillian would be living in while their new house was built. Construction was slated to start next week, but for now this little grouping of rooms would be home. Their home. The irony of living in an inn after protesting his suitcase lifestyle for so long wasn't lost on him. But now, instead of moving on, he'd be putting down roots, becoming part of the community.

More important, he'd have Jillian at his side—and in his bed. She'd suggested, since they had already waited so long and the wedding was so soon, that they should wait to make love until after they had said their vows. Something about heightening the anticipation. He, as a gentleman, had agreed, but after three weeks of sleepless nights and countless cold showers he was regretting that particular act of chivalry. As far as he was concerned, anticipation was highly overrated.

At least they wouldn't have far to go. They had decided to spend their wedding night here at the Sandpiper before catching a plane for Rome tomorrow afternoon. The less time between the saying of the vows and the consummation of the marriage, the better. If he had his way, they'd skip the reception entirely and go straight to that part, but that wasn't going to fly with Jillian or their guests.

Forcing himself to think of something other than getting his soon-to-be wife in bed, he stripped down in the large bathroom they would soon be sharing. Waiting for the water to heat up, he eyed the shower stall. They could probably both fit in there, with some creative positioning. Steam rose as he contemplated the possibilities.

But this was no time for fantasizing; he had a wedding to get to. Resigned, he braced himself, and turned the faucet to cold one last time.

"All set?" Cassie asked, straightening Jillian's veil.

Jillian nodded. She'd been ready since the moment Nic had asked the question. But as excited as she was to marry him, she hadn't wanted to give up her girlhood idea of a dream wedding, either. So, with Cassie and Mollie's help, she had crammed months of wedding preparations into a few short weeks. Now, after what felt like a mad dash to nuptial bliss, she was more than ready to get to the "I do" and become the newest member of the Caruso family.

She had worried that Nic's parents would resent her, blame her for him leaving the company. Instead, she had been inundated with offers to help with the wedding. Both of his sisters and his mother, Marie, had flown down as soon as they heard of the engagement to take her dress shopping. Then, while everyone else was oohing and aahing over her final choice, Marie had quietly made arrangements with the shop owner to pay for it herself. She'd insisted that it was her honor, making Jillian cry for what was probably the hundredth time since Nic had proposed.

Now they were all waiting for her, seated around the beautiful gazebo Nic had crafted. She just had to walk down the path and her new life would start.

Taking a deep breath, she watched Cassie and then Mollie, dressed in simple pastel gowns, walk down the aisle to the strains of a single violin. Then Emma, in the pink flower girl dress she'd picked out herself, started down. She held a posy of flowers in one chubby hand and Murphy's leash in the other. The canine ring bearer trotted beside the pretty girl, trained to home in on Nic, his new master. Mrs. Rosenberg had given them the dog as their first wedding present. There was a mountain of gift-wrapped boxes waiting for them inside, but nothing else could compete with him.

When the music shifted to the traditional wedding march, Doc Marshall, Cassie's father, gave Jillian's hand a squeeze. "We're on, sweetie. Your fella's waiting."

Taking his arm, she let him guide her out of the

trees and into the clearing. Nic, in an elegant linen suit, waited for her in the gazebo he'd worked so hard to build. As she started down the aisle he smiled, the love in his eyes unmistakable.

The officiant said the standard words, and she was sure there were readings and hymns and all the usual things. But all she heard were the vows they said to each other, and the declaration that they were man and wife. And then even that proclamation was wiped from her mind when Nic's mouth met hers in their first kiss as husband and wife.

The rest of the evening was a blur of tears and laughter, new family and old friends. Finally, as the stars came out, the guests began to make their farewells.

"Miss Jillian, you forgot!"

Jillian looked down from her plate of cake at a very sleepy Emma. "What is it, honey? What did I forget?"

"The flowers. You forgot the flowers."

Jillian looked around at the garlands artfully decorating the wraparound porch. "There are plenty of flowers, Emma, enough for you to take some home even, if you want."

The little girl furrowed her eyebrows. "No, not these flowers. The ones you throw. So someone else can get married."

"Oh, the bouquet. You're exactly right, princess. I did forget the bouquet. Were you hoping to catch it?

Wide-eyed, she shook her head, curls swinging. "No, I don't wanna get married. I wanna help you throw it."

Laughing, she tucked the child's hand in hers. "Okay, let's do it."

She found Cassie quickly and told her the plan. Then, upstairs, she led Emma out onto the main balcony, handing her the bouquet of tropical blossoms. "Here you go, Emma. I'll pick you up, and on the count of three, you throw it as hard as you can, okay?

The little girl's eyes beamed. "Okay."

Shouldering the girl, she saw Cassie and Emma, Nic's sisters, and even Mrs. Rosenberg gathered on the lawn with the other single ladies. As soon as the crowd spotted the duo on the balcony they started the countdown. "One—two—three!"

The cheer that went up almost drowned out Emma's shout of "Mama, catch!" But everyone saw her smile when the bundle of flowers landed directly in Cassie's hands.

"Now it's all over, right, Jillian?" the tired girl asked, stifling a yawn.

All but the best part, Jillian thought, suddenly as eager as Emma to move the guests along.

It took another hour, but finally they were standing on the front steps, waving goodbye to the last of their guests. Even the cleaning crew had finished, leaving only Nic's family, most of whom had already retired to their rooms.

"Good night, Jillian, and welcome to the family." Lorenzo Caruso, the last to go up, gave her a crushing hug, squeezing a laugh from her.

"Thank you so much. And do let us know if you need anything during the night."

"Are you kidding? It's your wedding night. My wife and son would kill me if I even thought about disturbing you."

"You've got that straight," Nic agreed, wrapping his arms around her. "Now go, before Mom comes looking for you."

"Nic!"

"No, he's right. He's waited long enough to have his bride to himself. We'll see you in the morning." He patted her arm, then retreated into the inn.

The minute the door was shut, Nic swung her around, pressing her against the railing, his mouth coming down hard on hers. A throbbing hunger rose up at his touch, and tasting him only made it stronger. His hands crushed her dress as he molded her to him. Maybe she should care that he was ruining the lace, but she was too desperate for his touch to stop him.

Her own hands sought skin, pulling and pushing at the layers of formalwear. "Nic, I need—" she panted in his ear.

"I know, baby." His husky voice vibrated along her neck, sending chills zinging along her skin. In an instant, she was in his arms, being carried across the threshold and up the stairs, into the master suite.

They somehow managed to undress as they tumbled onto the bed, buttons flying, mouths nipping, hands seeking. He expertly teased her to a fast peak, leaving her gasping and aching for him. "Now, Nic, please, now."

And then they were one, and it was everything she had ever wanted or needed. He whispered words of love as she met his pace, then urged him on. Perfectly matched, they raced for completion together, each swallowing the other's cries as they climaxed.

Afterward, he rolled her on top of him, so her head

rested on his chest. Hearing his heart galloping, she smiled and snuggled closer.

"Don't get too comfortable, Mrs. Caruso. That was just the opening act," he rumbled, stroking lazy patterns up and down her bare skin.

"So was the wait worth it?" she teased.

"Let just say we have a lot of work to do, to make up for lost time." As if to punctuate his words, she felt him growing ready again.

"Speaking of time, I know it probably makes more sense to wait to start a family until the house is built—"

Cutting her off with a kiss, he flipped her beneath him. "I can build fast, remember? Nine months should be plenty of time."

* * * * *

A VALENTINE
FOR THE VETERINARIAN

Ean, for picking up the slack
and never complaining about it.

My mom and my son, Michael,
for babysitting the littles when I had a deadline
and needed some quiet.

My agent, Jill, for guiding me through the process.

And my editorial team, especially Carly and
Jennifer, for finding my (numerous) mistakes
and making me look good.

Chapter 1

"Grace, you just saved my life. How can I ever repay you?"

The woman behind the counter rolled her eyes. "It's just coffee, Dr. Marshall, not the fountain of youth. If you leave a few coins in the tip jar, we'll call it even."

Cassie clutched the cardboard cup like a lifeline, inhaling the rich aroma. "I had an emergency call last night, ended up performing a C-section on a schnauzer at three a.m., and then was double-booked all day. So right now your caffeinated nectar is my only hope of making it through the meeting I'm going to." She paid for her coffee and took a cautious sip of the scalding brew. "You're my hero."

"That kind of flattery will get you the last cinnamon scone, if you want it."

"Have I ever turned down a free baked good?" Cassie accepted the small white bag with the proffered pastry. "Thanks. This ought to keep me out of trouble until I can get some dinner."

"Speaking of trouble, here comes that new sheriff's deputy. I'd be willing to break a few rules if it would get him to notice me." Grace craned her neck to see more clearly out the curtained front window. "Don't you think he looks like a man who could handle my rebellious side?"

Cassie nearly spit out her coffee. If Grace Keville, sole proprietor of Sandcastle Bakery, had a rebellious side, she'd kept it well hidden. Even after a full day of baking and serving customers, she looked prim and proper in a crisp pastel blouse and tailored pants. From her lacy apron to her dainty bun, she was the epitome of order and discipline. Not to mention she was happily married and the mother of three. "You've never rebelled a day in your life."

Grace sniffed. "Maybe not, but that man makes me consider it. Hard."

Rebellion wasn't all it was cracked up to be. She'd been there, done that, and had considerably more than a T-shirt to show for it. She started to say as much, but stopped at the jingle of the door chimes behind her. Turning at the sound, she caught her breath at the sight of the intense man heading toward her with long, ground-eating strides.

No wonder Grace was infatuated. The man looked like he'd just stepped out of a Hollywood action movie rather than the quiet streets of Paradise, Florida. Thick, dark hair framed a chiseled face with just a hint of five-o'clock shadow. His eyes were the exact color of the espresso that scented the air, and reflected a focus that only men in law enforcement seemed to have. Even without the uniform she'd have known him for a cop. Sexy? Sure. But still a cop. And she'd had her fill of those.

"I'm here to pick up an order. Should be under Santiago."

Grace grabbed a large box from the top of a display case. "I've got it right here—an assortment of cookies, right?"

"That's right."

"What, no doughnuts?" Uh-oh, did she say that out loud?

He gave Cassie a long look before quirking up one side of his mouth. "Sorry to ruin the stereotype."

Grace glared at Cassie before attempting to smooth things over. "Deputy Santiago, I'm Grace. I'm the one you spoke to earlier on the phone. And this is Dr. Cassie Marshall, our resident veterinarian."

"Nice to meet you Grace, Dr. Marshall." He nodded at each in turn. "And off duty it's Alex, please." He smiled then, a real smile, and suddenly the room was too warm, too charged, for comfort. The man's smile was as lethal as the gun strapped to his hip—more potent than any Taser. Unsettled by her instant response, Cassie headed for the door. It wasn't like her to speak without thinking; she needed to get out of there before she embarrassed herself more than she already had.

"Let me get that." He reached the door before her, balancing the large cookie box in one hand and pulling open the door with the other. After her own snide comment, his politeness poked at her conscience.

"Sorry about the doughnut remark." There, her conscience was clear.

"I've heard worse." His expression hardened for a minute. "Don't worry about it."

She wouldn't; she had way too many other concerns to keep her occupied. Including the meeting she was going to be late to, if she didn't hurry. She nodded politely, then made a beeline for her hatchback. Setting the coffee in a cup holder, she cranked the engine and popped in a CD of popular love songs. She had less than ten minutes to put aside all the worries tumbling through her mind and get herself in a Valentine's Day kind of mood.

Alex watched the silver hatchback drive away, noting she kept the small vehicle well under the speed limit. Few people were gutsy enough to speed in front of a sheriff's deputy—but then again, the average person didn't spout off jokes about cops to his face, either. There had been resentment in those blue eyes. She'd disliked him—or at the least the uniform—on sight. He was used to gang members and drug dealers treating him that way, but a cute veterinarian? His gut said there was a story there, but he didn't need to make enemies in his new hometown. He had plenty of those back in Miami.

A loud bark snapped him out of his thoughts.

"I'm coming, boy."

At this point, he and his canine partner, Rex, were in the honeymoon period of their relationship, and the dog still got excited whenever he saw Alex return. Unlocking the car, he couldn't help but smile at the goofy expression on the German Shepherd's face. As a trained K-9, Rex was a criminal's worst nightmare, but to Alex he was the best part of his new job.

He'd never expected to live in a small-time town like Paradise, had never wanted to leave Miami. But when he testified against his partner, the department had turned against him. It didn't matter that Rick was guilty. Alex was the one they turned on.

He'd known that refusing to lie during his deposition meant saying goodbye to any chance of promotion. He could live with that. But when his name and address were leaked to a local gang he'd investigated, things changed.

Putting his own life at risk, that was just part of the job. Messing with his family, that was a different story. When his mom had come home one day to find threats spray-painted on her walls and her house trashed, he'd known they couldn't stay.

He could still see her standing in her ruined kitchen, white with fear. She'd aged ten years that humid night.

Guilt clawed at him. What kind of son was he to lead danger straight to her doorstep? He'd resigned the next day and spent his two-week notice hunting down the scum responsible.

Then he'd packed up and looked for a job, any job, where he could start fresh without a target on his back. When a position in the Palmetto County Sheriff's office became open, he'd jumped on it. Working with a K-9 unit was a dream come true; he'd often volunteered time with the unit back home. That experience, plus a stellar record, had landed him the position.

Having the dog around eased the loneliness of being in a new city and made the long night shifts required of newbies seem a little shorter.

Thankfully, his mom had been willing to move, too. She'd lived in Miami ever since she and his father emigrated from Puerto Rico. He'd worried she would fight against leaving, but she'd agreed almost immediately. Her lack of argument told him she was more rattled than she'd admitted.

And of course there was Jessica, his younger sister, to think about, too. She was away at college, but still lived at home on school holidays. His mom wouldn't want her in the line of fire, even if she wasn't afraid for herself.

Now Paradise was their home and all that was behind them.

As he drove down what passed for Main Street, he scanned the tidy storefronts, more out of habit than caution. The tiny island community couldn't be more different from fast-paced south Florida. Instead of high rises and strip malls, there were bungalows and family-owned shops. Miami had a vibrant, intoxicating culture, but working in law enforcement, he'd spent his hours in the less picturesque parts of town. Here, even the poorest neighborhoods were tidy and well kept.

Of course, nowhere was perfect, not even Paradise. Which was why he was missing valuable sleep in order to attend the Share the Love volunteer meeting. The sheriff's department was pairing with the county's department of children's services in a fundraiser, a Valentine's Day dance. The money raised would be used to start up a mentor program for at-risk kids. Some were in foster care and many had parents serving time or were in trouble themselves. When the department had posted a flier about the program, he'd been the first to volunteer. He'd been on the other side of that story; it was time to give back.

It took only a few minutes to cross the island and reach the Sandpiper Inn, the venue for tonight's organizational meeting. The largest building on the island, it often was the site of community events.

Pulling into the gravel lot, he was surprised to see most of the parking spaces were full. Either the Sandpiper had a lot of midweek guests or the meeting was going to be larger than he'd expected.

He grabbed the box on the passenger seat and left the engine running, thankful for the special environmental controls that kept things safe for his furry partner. Late January in Florida tended to be mild, but could sometimes still hit dangerous temperatures. "Sorry, buddy, but I think this is a human-only kind of thing."

Rex grumbled but settled down, his big head resting on his paws when Alex locked the car.

"Are you following me?" The voice came from behind him and sounded hauntingly familiar.

The prickly veterinarian from the bakery.

She was standing where the parking area opened onto the shaded path to the inn's entrance. Her strawberry-blond hair caught the rays of the setting sun, strands blowing in her face with the breeze. Eyes snapping, she waited for him to respond.

"I'm not stalking you, if that's what you mean." His jaw clenched at the insinuation. "I'm a law enforcement officer, not a criminal."

Her face softened slightly, and he caught a glimpse of sadness in her eyes. "Sorry, it's just that in this town, there isn't always a difference."

Chapter 2

Well, that was embarrassing. Cassie truly did try to think before speaking, but some days she was more successful than others. What had she been thinking, accusing him of following her? It had been months since the accident; she needed to stop jumping at shadows.

"Mommy, look what Miss Jillian helped me make!" Cassie's daughter, Emma, came bounding down the stairs of the picturesque inn with the energy and volume befitting a marching band, not a four-year-old. "I made Valentine's cards!"

Behind, at a more sedate pace, came Cassie's best friend and employee, Jillian Caruso. With her mass of black curls and pale skin, she looked like a princess out of a fairy tale, despite her casual jeans and sweater. Right now she also looked a tad guilty. "Before you say anything, this wasn't my fault. I told her I would help her make some, but all the ideas were hers."

Cassie arched an eyebrow, but let it go. She was just grateful Jillian had been willing to entertain Emma.

Normally her mom watched Emma after her preschool let out, but today there had been a schedule conflict. Emma was much happier playing at the inn than being stuck with Cassie at the clinic yet again. "Hi, sunshine. I missed you." She swept her up in a hug, letting go of the tension that had dogged her all day. This was why she worked so hard. This little girl was the most important thing in her world and worth all the long hours and missed sleep of the past few months. "Are you having fun?"

"She should be," Jillian broke in. "She's been here less than an hour and we've already played on the playground, looked for seashells on the beach and made brownies."

"Are you a policeman? Did my mommy do something bad?"

Cassie had almost forgotten the deputy behind her. Blushing, she set Emma back down and turned to find him a few feet away, smiling as if she hadn't just bitten his head off.

"Hello, sweetie. I'm Alex. What's your name?"

"I'm Emma. Are you going to take someone to jail?"

"Not today. Unless there are any bad guys here?" His dimples showed when he smiled. Cops should not have dimples.

"Nope, just me and Miss Jillian and Mr. Nic. And Murphy. He's their dog. And a bunch of people for the meeting. But they're going to help kids, so they can't be bad, right?" Her little brows furrowed as she thought.

"Probably not. Helping kids is a good thing. Are you going to help?"

Emma's curls bounced as she nodded. "Yup, I get to help with the decorations. Mommy said so. And I get to come to the big Valentine's Day dance. I'm going to wear a red dress."

"A red dress? Sounds like a great party." He raised his gaze to the third member of the group.

"Hi, I'm Jillian. Welcome to the Sandpiper Inn." She offered her hand to the handsome deputy.

"Nice to meet you. Alex Santiago. Thanks for offering to host the meeting here."

Jillian smiled, her face lighting up. "We're happy to do it. I grew up in foster care myself—I know how hard it can be. Even the best foster families often can't always give the kids as much attention as they need. It will be great if we can get a real mentor program started."

If Alex was surprised by Jillian's casual mention of her childhood, he didn't show it. He just nodded and held out the box he'd picked up at the bakery. "I brought cookies, if you have somewhere I can put them. I figured at least a few people might not have had a chance to grab dinner yet."

Oh, boy. Shame heated Cassie's cheeks. She'd been stereotyping him with the old cops-and-doughnuts line when he'd actually been buying refreshments to share with others—at a charity event, no less.

The sight of the uniform might set her teeth on edge, but that was no reason to be openly rude to him. The car accident that had injured her father so badly had been caused by a single out-of-control deputy, but she couldn't blame the man in front of her just because they both wore the same badge.

"Ooh, can I have a cookie?" Emma looked up at Alex, practically batting her eyelashes. "I've been very good."

He laughed, and the lines around his eyes softened. "That's up to your mom, princess."

Emma turned pleading eyes to Cassie, whose heart melted. "Since you've been good, yes, one. But just one. Jillian said you've already had a brownie, and I don't want you bouncing off the walls on a sugar high." She nodded a thank you to Alex for letting her make the decision. "Now, let's see those valentines you were telling me about." She brushed off the niggling bit of envy that she hadn't been the one making valentines with her daughter. Maybe that was why Jillian looked concerned about them?

"Cassie, maybe you should wait and read those later?" Jillian cautioned, nodding toward Alex.

Cassie darted a glance at the cop still standing on the stairs with them. He shrugged, then moved past them. "I'll just go find a place to set these down. See you inside."

Why was Jillian acting so tense over this? They were just paper hearts and glitter, not a manifesto. Taking them from Emma's slightly grubby fist, she continued up to the massive front door of the Sandpiper.

The first card boasted a crudely drawn bouquet of flowers, and the words MOM and LOVE circled by pink and purple hearts. "Thank you, sweetie, I love it." She shuffled that one to the back and opened the next one. This time there were happy faces covering the pink paper, and Jillian's name, misspelled, at the center. "Beautiful!" Smiling, she opened the last heart-shaped card and then froze, almost stumbling as her daughter pushed past her into the warmth of the lobby. The words on the page had instantly imprinted on her brain, but she read them again anyway.

To Daddy. Painstakingly spelled out in red and gold sequins.

She felt a hand on her shoulder. Jillian's eyes were wide with sympathy. "I'm sorry. I didn't know what to do. I told her I'd help her make valentines, but I had no idea..."

Cassie straightened her spine. She'd talk to Emma about it. Make her understand, somehow, that this particular valentine was going to remain unsent. Her head began to throb.

"Don't worry. It's not your fault," Cassie told Jillian. *It's mine.*

Alex kept an eye on the door as he mingled and shook hands in the spacious lobby. Observation was second nature at this point, and he wanted to see how that little scene out front played out. What was the big deal about a couple of valentines? Maybe it was nothing, but an overactive sense of curiosity came with the job.

He was munching on a tiny crustless sandwich when Cassie entered the room. Her daughter and friend followed, but she was the one that drew him, made him want to know more. There was something about the fiery redhead that made her impossible to ignore. Yes, she was pretty in a girl-next-door way, with a petite build and freckled complexion. But it was more than that. Her quick temper should have been off-putting. Instead, her transparency put him at ease. Every emotion showed on her face—there was no hidden agenda. In his line of work, he spent most of his time trying to figure out what someone wasn't saying, but this woman was an open book.

And right now, she looked like she needed a friend. Her pale skin was flushed, and she had a tight look around her eyes, as if she was fighting off a headache. Moving toward her, drawn by instinct more than conscious thought, he offered her a drink. "Water?"

"Hmm?" She looked down at the unopened bottle he held in his hand. "Yes, thank you." Taking a tentative sip, she screwed the cap back on. "Listen, about the coffee shop. I'm sorry I was rude. It was a dumb joke. I just…well, it wasn't about you, specifically."

"Not a fan of cops, are you?"

She winced. "That obvious?"

"Let's see. You made a cop joke in front of a cop. Then you equated law enforcement with criminal behavior. It wasn't a hard case to crack."

Her eyes widened, and then she smiled. A heart-stopping smile that reached her eyes and made him wish he could do more for her than hand her a bottle of water. This must have been how Helen caused all that trouble in Troy. His heart thudded in his chest, warning him to look away.

His eyes landed on her daughter, who had snuck to the far side of the table to liberate another cookie. "She's beautiful."

The smile got even brighter. "Thanks."

"Just like her mother."

Instantly her smile vanished, and her gaze grew guarded. "I should go find a seat, before they're all taken."

He hadn't meant the compliment as a pick-up line, but she obviously thought he was hitting on her and was putting as much space between them as possible. She wasn't wearing a ring, but he'd heard medical people didn't always wear them because of the constant hand-washing. Great. She was probably married. Now she had a reason to dislike him personally, rather than just cops in general.

Unable to come up with a reason to follow her, he hung back to watch the proceedings from the rear of the room, a small crowd filling the seats in front of him. These were his neighbors now, his community. Getting to know them had to be top priority if he wanted to be effective at his job. Hopefully volunteering like this would be a step in that direction. He had other, more personal reasons for wanting to volunteer, but no one needed to know that. He didn't need his past coloring his chances at a future here.

At the front of the room, the woman he'd spoken to earlier, Jillian, stood and called for everyone's attention. "Welcome to the Sandpiper, and thank you for taking the time to help with such a worthwhile project. As most of you know, I was a foster child myself, so I know firsthand how hard that life can be. And what a difference a caring person can make. I'm really thankful we have so many people interested in volunteering, and that, in addition to working with children's services, we will also be partnering with the Palmetto County Sheriff's Department. They will be sponsoring a group of kids for the program as well, kids who are in a difficult spot and might need some extra help. Deputy Santiago is here representing the department tonight and will be volunteering his own time to this important project." She smiled at him, and he raised a hand in acknowledgment. Several of the townspeople turned and sized him up. Many offered warm smiles; a few nodded in acceptance.

Jillian finished, then introduced the chairwoman of the event, Mrs. Rosenberg, a diminutive senior citizen decked out in a leopard-print track suit. As she listed off the various jobs, he made a mental note to sign up for the setup crew. A strong back would be welcome when it came time to move tables and hang decorations, and it sounded a heck of a lot better than messing with tissue paper and glitter for the decorating committee.

Finally, the talking was over. Everyone milled around, catching up on gossip as they waited to sign up on the clipboards on the front table. He started that way, easing through the crowd as best as he could, given that everyone there seemed to want to greet him personally. He'd exchanged small talk with half a dozen people and was less than halfway across the room when he felt a tug on his sleeve.

"Deputy?"

It was the chairwoman, now sporting rhinestone spectacles and wielding a clipboard.

"Yes, ma'am?"

"You're new in town, aren't you?" The question was

just shy of an accusation, and the shrewd eyes behind the glasses were every bit as sharp as a seasoned detective's.

"I am." He extended a hand. "Alex Santiago. Nice to meet you."

She gripped him with a wiry strength, then spoke over his shoulder. "Hold on, Tom, I'll be right there." Turning her attention back to him, she smiled. "I have to go handle that. But don't worry. I'll get you signed up myself."

Grateful that he wouldn't have to fight the crowd, he backtracked to the front door. He was almost there when it hit him. "Mrs. Rosenberg?"

From across the room she turned. "Yes?"

"Which committee are you signing me up for?"

"Oh, all of them, of course."

Of course.

Cassie spent most of the drive home trying to figure out what to say to Emma about her valentines. She still wasn't sure how to explain things in a way a four-year-old could understand, but she'd come up with something. She always did.

She set her purse down on the counter and put the old-fashioned kettle on the stove. "Emma, go put your backpack in your room, and get ready for your bath, please. I'll be right there." It was so late she was tempted to skip the bath part of bedtime, but changing the schedule would undoubtedly backfire and keep the tyke up later in the long run. Besides, after an afternoon romping on the beach and exploring the Sandpiper's sprawling grounds, her daughter was in dire need of a scrub-down.

Enjoying the brief quiet, she kicked off her sensible shoes and opened the sliding door to the patio. The screened room was her favorite part of the house, especially at this time of year. The air was chilly by Florida standards, but still comfortable. Right now she would have loved to curl up on the old chaise with her tea and a cozy mystery, but tonight, like most nights, there just wasn't time.

"Mommy, I'm ready for my bath."

"Okay, I'm coming." Duty called. Taking a last breath of the crisp night air, she caught the scent of the Lady of the Night orchid she'd been babying. It would bloom for only a few nights; hopefully she'd get a chance to enjoy it. But for now, she closed the door and went to find her daughter, stopping to fill her mug with boiling water and an herbal tea bag.

Emma was waiting in the bathroom, stripped down to her birthday suit and clutching her favorite rubber ducky. "Bubbles?" she asked hopefully.

"Bubbles. But only a quick bath tonight. It's late."

The little girl nodded solemnly. "Okay, Mommy."

Cassie's heart squeezed. No matter how stressed or tired she was, she never got tired of hearing the word *Mommy* from her baby's lips. She couldn't say she'd done everything right, but this little girl—she had to be a reward for something. She was too good to be anything but that. There was nothing Cassie wouldn't do for her. Which was why it broke her heart to know she couldn't give Emma her biggest wish.

"So did you have fun today at the Sandpiper?" She watched the water level rise around her daughter, the bubbles forming softly scented mountains.

"Yup. I played with Murphy and ate brownies, and we saw a butterfly, and Mr. Nic pushed me super high on the swings."

Nic was Jillian's husband. He had bought the Sandpiper for Jillian just a few months ago, and the playground was one of the first things he'd added to the grounds. He and Jillian were hoping for a child of their own soon, but in the meantime the paying guests—and Emma—made good use of it. "That sounds like a real adventure."

"Uh-huh. And then Miss Jillian helped me make my valentines. I made one for her, and you, and for a daddy. We just need to get one so I can give it to him."

Darn. The child hadn't forgotten, not that Cassie was surprised. Emma had perfect recall when it came to what she wanted. Now to figure out a way to let her down without breaking her heart. "Honey, I can't just go get you a daddy."

Emma frowned up at her.

Okay, that didn't work. "You are going to have a wonderful Valentine's Day. You're going to have a party at school with cupcakes and candy and everything. And then we'll go to the big dance. It's going to be great, you'll see."

"It would be better if I had a daddy. Then he could be our valentine. Like Mr. Nic is Jillian's valentine. I heard him say so."

Cassie blinked back the sudden sting of tears. She'd

tried to be everything for Emma, to provide enough love for two parents, but the older Emma got, the more she realized something was different. Something, someone, was missing.

"A daddy would be nice," she conceded. "But you have me. And we're a great team, you and I. So if you don't have a daddy right now, that's okay, because we have each other, right?"

Emma looked thoughtful, her nose crinkling as she considered. "But why don't I get to have a daddy? Lots of kids at school have one."

The pounding behind Cassie's eyes returned with a vengeance. Rubbing her temples, she tried to explain to her daughter what she still didn't understand herself. "That's just how it is sometimes. Some kids have mommies, and some kids have daddies, and some kids have both."

"Oh, and some kids don't have a mommy or a daddy, right? That's why we get to have the Share the Love party, to help them, right, Mom?"

Cassie sighed in relief. "Right, honey. Those kids are in foster care with people that take care of them until they get a new mommy and daddy. Every family is different, and we just have to be happy about the one we have."

Her face falling, Emma nodded slowly. "Okay."

Watching her daughter's solemn expression, Cassie felt like she'd kicked a puppy. The guilt sat heavy in the pit of her stomach, reminding her of how her choices had led to this. Her impulsiveness, her recklessness, had created this situation. For the millionth time, she fought the instinct to regret ever meeting her lying ex. But of course, without him, there would be no Emma. And that was simply unthinkable. Being a single parent was hard, but it was worth it.

That didn't mean that she didn't sometimes wish she had a partner in all of this. As she toweled Emma off and got her ready for bed, she wondered what it would have been like to have a man to talk to once her daughter was asleep. Instead of eating ice cream out of the carton, she'd have someone she could talk things out with, someone to share her fears and frustrations with.

But letting someone into her life, relying on him like that, was too big a risk. She'd let her emotions carry her away once, and look how well that turned out. No, she needed to keep doing what she was doing and leave the idea of romance alone. She wasn't any good at it, and she couldn't afford to make that kind of mistake again.

Chapter 3

Alex was still shaking his head over Mrs. Rosenberg's sign-up shenanigans ten hours later. And puzzling over the intriguing veterinarian, despite the way she'd blown him off. She was fire and ice, and definitely not interested, but he couldn't quite get her out of his head. Between her and Mrs. Rosenberg, the island definitely had its share of headstrong women.

He'd spent the long night patrolling the quiet streets of Paradise and the connecting highway across the bridge, alone except for Rex and his own thoughts. He was grateful for the lack of crime, but the slow shift gave him too much time to think, too much time to remember the chain of events that had brought him here. Not that this was a bad place to be.

When he'd accepted the position with the Palmetto County Sheriff's Department, he'd expected to be working at the county headquarters in Coconut Bay. Instead he'd been assigned to the small substation serving Paradise. The island was too small to support a city police force, so it, like some of the rural ranching areas across the bridge on the mainland, was under county law enforcement.

As dawn approached, he made a last loop along the beach road to catch the sunrise over the ocean. Stopping in one of the many parking spaces that bordered the dunes, he got out and stretched, his neck popping loudly. At Rex's insistence, he opened the back door as well, snapping the dog's leash on and walking him to a grassy area to relieve himself. When the dog had emptied his bladder, they strolled together to one of the staircases that led down to the sand.

Here he had an unobstructed view of the water and the already pink sky that seemed to melt along the horizon, the water turning a molten orange as the fiery sun crept up to start the day. Sipping from the lukewarm coffee he'd picked up a few hours ago at a gas station on the mainland, he let himself enjoy the quiet. No jarring static from the two-way radio, no traffic, just the soft sound of the waves rolling on the sand and Rex's soft snuffling as he investigated the brush along the stairway.

Alex had made a habit of doing this since he moved here. In the clear morning light, he could feel good about himself, his job, the direction his life was taking. The fresh start to the day was a reminder of his own fresh start, one that he hadn't asked for, but probably needed.

He was over thirty now, as his mother never failed to remind him. Maybe here he'd find a life beyond his work. He wasn't a family man; nothing in his background had prepared him for that kind of life, but a place like Paradise made him want to settle down a bit, make some friends, maybe join a softball team or something.

Chuckling at the image, he turned to go. Rex, trained to stay with him, uncharacteristically resisted the tug on the leash. Maybe he was tired, too.

"Here, boy! Come on, it's quitting time. Let's go."

The dog stood his ground, whiskers trembling as he stared into the dark space under the steps.

"What it is it, boy?" Alex found himself lowering his voice, catching the dog's mood. He was no dog whisperer, but obviously there was something under the stairs. Something more than the broken bottles and fast-food wrappers that sometimes got lodged there.

"Is somebody there?"

There was a scrambling sound, but no answer.

Rex whined, the hairs on his back standing up in a ridge. Feeling a bit silly, but not willing to take a chance, Alex removed his Glock from its holster, finding confidence in its weight even as he sent a silent prayer he wouldn't have to use it. Crouching down, he aimed his flashlight under the wooden structure, his gun behind it. He couldn't see anyone, but there was an alcove under a support beam that was hidden from his light. He'd have to go around.

He circled around to the other side, leaving Rex pacing back and forth at the foot of the stairs. Repeating his crouch and waddle move from before, Alex inched up under the overhang, scanning the area with his light. Nothing.

Woof!

Alex jumped, rapping his head on the rough boards of the stairway. A lightning bolt of pain shot through his skull as he quickly crab-crawled back out of the cramped space beneath the stairs. He heard Rex bark again and rolled the rest of the way out, careful to keep the gun steady.

"What is it, boy?"

A quick series of staccato barks answered him from the landing above.

"Stop! Sheriff's Deputy." The logical part of his mind knew that it was probably just a kid sneaking a smoke or a surfer who had passed out after too many drinks, but he'd had more than one close call in his career and wasn't going to chance it. Standing up, cursing the sand spurs now embedded in his skin, he followed the dog's line of sight.

There, clearly visible in the breaking dawn, was the menace that had his dog, and him, so worked up. A tiny kitten, barely more than a ball of fluff, was huddled against the top step.

"Rex, hush!" he commanded, not wanting the big dog to scare it back under the stairs. He was not going into those sand spurs again if he could help it.

The kitten was gray, its fur nearly the same shade as the weathered boards he was clinging to. If Rex hadn't made such a fuss, the kitten could have been directly underfoot and Alex would have missed it. Putting the dog into a down-stay, he dropped the leash and tucked away the gun and flashlight. Then he eased up the stairs as quietly as his heavy boots would allow.

The kitten watched him, eyes wide, but didn't run. A small mew was its only reaction, and even that seemed half-hearted. The pathetic creature looked awfully weak. The temperature was only in the mid-forties right now and had been significantly colder overnight. Plenty of strays did just fine, but this one seemed way too small to be out in the cold on its own.

Scooping the kitten up, he cradled it against his chest with one hand, then leaned down and retrieved Rex's leash with the other. The kitten was trembling, obviously cold if nothing else. Loading Rex into the car, he mentally said goodbye to the sleep he'd intended to catch up on. It looked like he was going to be seeing that pretty veterinarian again after all.

Cassie stared at the teakettle with bleary eyes, as if she could make the water boil faster through sheer force of will. She'd tossed and turned again last night. Maybe at some point she'd get used to the nightmares.

She often dreamed about the accident that had left her father in the hospital and herself with a mild concussion and a mountain of worry. At first, they'd feared her father's injuries were permanent, but he was home now and steadily getting better. She'd hoped that would be enough to stop the dreams from haunting her. But so far, no such luck.

But last night the dream had changed. The broken glass and screeching tires were the same as always, brought back in minute detail to terrorize her, but this time the sirens had triggered something new. Instead of the middle-aged deputy who was normally part of the nightmare, there was someone else. Alex Santiago, the new deputy she'd embarrassed herself in front of.

Suddenly, instead of ambulances and flashing lights, there had been stars and the crash of the ocean. They were alone on the beach, kissing as if there was nothing more important than the feel of skin against skin, tongue against tongue. She'd been unbuttoning his uniform when the blaring of her alarm had woken her up.

She had lain there, hot and trembling, for several minutes before forcing herself to shut the dream out of her head. There was probably some deep, psychiatric reason her subconscious was twisting her nightmare into something totally different, but there'd been no point in lying there, trying to figure it out.

So she'd forced herself out of bed and into a quick shower before throwing on her usual uniform of casual khaki pants and a simple cotton blouse. Now she was desperate for some tea and maybe a bite of breakfast. She had another thirty minutes before Emma would be waking up, and she intended to enjoy the quiet while she could.

The tea was still steeping in her mug when she heard a knock at the door. Dunking the bag one last time, she tossed it in the trash as she made her way to the front of the house. Peering through the wavy glass of the peephole, she could just make out the blue uniform of the Palmetto County Sheriff's Department. Her mouth turned dry, another flashback threatening her still drowsy mind.

Her heart thudded hollowly as she turned the lock. Why would there be a cop on her doorstep? Had something happened to her parents? The clinic? A neighbor? Her mind darted through possible scenarios as she opened the door. Surely this wasn't because of the accident? In the beginning, there had been what seemed like countless interviews and questions, but that had all ended months ago.

Taking a deep, cleansing breath, she swung open the door. There on the stoop was Alex, looking just as he had in her dream. The fear retreated, chased off by other, equally potent stirrings. Her cheeks heated in embarrassment, not that he could possibly know that she'd dreamed about him. Keeping her voice cool, she asked, "Is there a problem, Deputy?"

He smiled at her, all male energy and smooth charm. "I suppose it's too early for this to be a social call?"

"I'd say so." She noticed the shadows under his eyes and realized he'd probably just come off the night shift. "I'm assuming you have a professional reason for banging on my door at dawn. If you could share it so I can get back to my breakfast, that would be helpful."

Before he could answer her, she caught the weirdest impression of movement under his department-issued windbreaker. "What on earth?"

At that moment, a tiny, gray head squirmed out of the neck of the jacket and nuzzled his chin. Darn. Now she had to let him in.

"I know it looks strange, but the little guy was shivering. I thought I could keep him warm in my jacket, but he doesn't want to stay put." He grabbed hold of the kitten as it wriggled its way farther out of the coat.

"Well, come on in. Let's take a look at him." She

motioned for him to continue back to the kitchen, then shut the door behind him. "Where did he come from and how long ago did you find him?" She kept her tone and actions professional, using her clinical manner to maintain some emotional distance. He might look like a Latin movie star, but the Palmetto County Sheriff's Department logo on his shirt was a glaring reminder of the chaos she was currently embroiled in. She'd help the kitten, then send him on his way, before he or the animal got too close.

Alex followed her, his large stature making her cozy cottage feel small. "Rex found him under one of the beach access staircases. We'd stopped for a few minutes and he refused to leave. Somehow he knew the little guy needed help."

"Is Rex your partner?" The name didn't ring a bell.

"Yeah," Alex answered distractedly as he attempted to remove the kitten's claws from his uniform shirt. "He's waiting out in the car."

"He didn't want to come in?" Had the animosity toward her gotten that bad?

"Oh, he wanted to, but I figured it was better not to totally overwhelm you at this hour of the morning."

Right. More likely his partner just wanted to avoid her. Well, too bad. She was tired of feeling like a pariah in her own town. "It's going to take me a little while to check the kitten out, so you might as well tell Rex to come in. No reason to sit out in the cold."

"You're sure?"

"Of course."

While he fetched his partner, she went to the hall

closet to retrieve her medical bag. It was on the top shelf, wedged next to a box of random sports equipment. And a bit too heavy to snag one-handed. She was on her toes, the kitten snuggled firmly in one arm, when she heard the front door open behind her.

Giving up, she turned around to ask for help. "Hey, could one of you hold the kitten while I—"

Her voice died in her throat. Standing directly in her path was the largest German Shepherd she had ever seen, taking up most of the limited real estate in her tiny foyer. Suppressing a completely unprofessional squeal at the sudden intrusion, she cautiously observed the behemoth before deciding the doe-eyed canine meant no harm. Probably. Intuition and years of experience gave her the courage to edge around him, keeping the kitten out of his reach, just in case.

She was relieved to find Alex in the foyer, apparently not eaten by the mammoth canine. "You aren't going to tell me Rex found that guy under a staircase, too, are you?" No way was this regal giant a foundling.

"What?" Alex's eyes narrowed in confusion. "Found who?"

She waved her arm toward the dog. "Him. Where did he come from? Obviously your partner didn't find him when he found the kitten."

Alex's full-throated laugh filled the air, erasing the tired lines that had creased his face a moment before. Unable to resist smiling along with him, she rubbed the kitten's head with her free hand and waited to be let in on the joke.

"Rex is my partner." When she only raised her eyebrows, he continued, "I mean, the dog is Rex. My partner."

Understanding belatedly wound its way through her sleepy brain. "You're a K-9 officer?"

"Yeah. I just assumed a local veterinarian would have known that."

She thought back. She *had* heard rumblings of a new K-9 unit, but she would have sworn the idea had been tabled when it was determined there wasn't enough money in the budget. "I thought the department couldn't afford a K-9 unit? Trained dogs have to cost a fortune."

Alex ruffled the big dog's fur, a wry smile on his face. "He's worth every penny, but you're right. He's way outside Palmetto County's price range. The department was able to get federal and state grants to cover the purchase cost, and Miami-Dade County let me train with its K-9 unit on my off time before I came. The department still has to foot the ongoing costs for veterinary care and our continued training, but that's less expensive than paying the salary for another officer. In the long run, having a K-9 on staff should save the department manpower and money."

Watching Alex's eyes shine with pride in his job and his dog had her swallowing hard. She'd been too quick to think she was being avoided, to assume she was being treated badly. Had she gotten so cynical that she assumed the worst of everyone?

If so, she needed to stop. That wasn't who she wanted to be or what she wanted to teach her daughter. Which meant she needed to bite the bullet and at least try to be open-minded, try to be friendly. Even with the sexy cop standing in her living room.

If Alex had been a little less tired, maybe he would have picked up on Cassie's confusion earlier. As it was, the look on her face when she'd found the hundred-plus-pound dog in her house had been priceless. He gave her credit, though; she'd stood her ground without flinching. She'd correctly read Rex's body language and known he wasn't a threat, despite his size. Heck, even some of his fellow officers were skittish around Rex.

Tough and beautiful. A dangerous combination. He'd once described his ex, a fellow cop, the same way. Then she'd dropped him for an assistant DA and he'd shifted his assessment from tough to cold-hearted. But Cassie, although she'd been less than friendly when he'd first met her, didn't seem to have the calculating nature that had doomed his relationship with his ex. Cassie tried to hide them, but her emotions were right there on the surface, reflected on her face like the rays of the sun off the ocean.

She had her eyes closed as she felt her way over the kitten's body from head to tail. Watching her slender but capable fingers skim the soft fur had him wondering what her touch would feel like. Her husband, if she did turn out to be married, was one lucky bastard.

Who probably wouldn't be happy to find a stranger staring at his wife this way.

Not that she'd even noticed. She'd all but forgotten Alex. Her brows knit in concentration. All her focus was on her small, purring patient.

Better take it down a notch. Focus on the issue at hand. "Is he going to be okay?"

Cassie made a noncommittal noise, then slid the earpieces of a stethoscope into place. A few tense minutes later, her face relaxed into an easy smile. "Lungs sound good, no evidence of any kind of infection, and his heart sounds great. At least, what I can hear over the purring." She nuzzled her face against the now ecstatic creature. "He seems none the worse for wear, just hungry and cold. It's lucky you found him when you did—the forecast is calling for another cold front to roll in by the end of the day."

He suppressed a shudder, despite the warmth of Cassie's cozy kitchen. An image of the kitten, all alone in the cold, flashed through his head, and he made a mental note to pick up one of Rex's favorite chew bones at the store later. The big dog deserved a reward, for sure.

As if reading his mind, Cassie opened a whitewashed cupboard and pulled out a box of dog biscuits.

"Can the hero here have a treat?"

"Of course. He's off duty, and he's definitely earned it."

"What about you?" She tipped her chin toward the kettle on the stove. "I've got hot water for tea, or I can make a pot of coffee. If you have time, I mean."

"Tea would be fine, thank you." He normally stuck to coffee, but there was no point in her making a whole pot just for him. Maybe the coffeepot was strictly for her husband, although it didn't look as if it had been used yet this morning. Her mug, purple with pink paw prints on it, sat alone on the empty counter, smelling of peppermint and flowers.

Come to think of it, there'd only been one car in the driveway. Her husband could have left for work already, but there was nothing in the kitchen to indicate a male presence. Surreptitiously, he scanned the room. No dirty breakfast dishes, no mugs other than hers. Even more telling, the decor ran to pastels and flowers. The evidence was circumstantial, but certainly enough to introduce reasonable doubt as to the existence of a Mr. Marshall.

Accepting the tea, he told himself it didn't matter one way or the other. She'd made her opinion of him, and his profession, perfectly clear when they first met. But as he sat across from her in the cozy kitchen, his dog at their feet and a kitten in her lap, a new, friendlier relationship seemed possible. Which didn't explain why he cared if she shared her home, or her bed, with another man.

He'd obviously been up too long. That was all. Sleep deprivation could mess with your mind. Everyone knew that. After a few hours' sleep, he'd remember all the reasons he wasn't looking for a relationship, especially with the firecracker of a redhead sitting across from him. For now, he'd drink his tea and enjoy a few minutes of company before going home to his empty apartment.

When he'd first taken the job in Paradise, he'd suggested he and his mother share a place, but she'd just chuckled and said he would need his own space for "entertaining." Right. He'd had only one other person in his apartment since he moved to Paradise, and that was the cable guy. Between the new job and the extra training sessions he'd signed up for with Rex, he hadn't had the time or energy for dating. Which was fine by him.

Although right now, enjoying the morning light with a beautiful woman, he wondered if he wasn't missing out after all.

Unwilling to explore that thought, he finished his tea and stood, the chair scraping against the terrazzo floor.

Startled by the noise, the kitten leaped onto the table, nearly overturning the china cups.

"Sorry about that. I'll get this guy out of your hair and be on my way." He scooped up the kitten with one hand. "Thanks for checking him out—I didn't know where else to take him."

Cassie stood to escort him out. "What will you do with him now?"

Good question. One he hadn't thought through yet. He'd been worried about the little guy making it. "I'll have to keep him for a few days, I guess, while I ask around, try to find him a home." Frustrated, he rubbed his eyes with his free hand. "Guess I'd better stop and pick up some food for him first." He nearly groaned with frustration. His tired body was crying out for a bed, but he couldn't let the little guy starve.

"The stores won't even be open for another hour." Cassie's eyes went from man to kitten. "I can take him to the office with me, get him fed, wormed and cleaned up, and then you can pick him up before you start your shift tonight. How does that sound?"

"Like you're my guardian angel. Thank you."

She blushed, the pink accentuating her soft coloring.

"I'm not doing it for you. I'm doing it for him." Her firm tone was a contrast to the camaraderie they'd shared in the kitchen. The friendly interlude was over, it seemed.

"Either way, I appreciate it just the same. What time do you need me to come get him?"

"The clinic closes at six, so any time before then is fine."

He could get a solid stretch of sleep and still have time to get food and the cat before his shift started. Thank heaven for small favors. And the angels who delivered them.

Cassie had spent way too much time thinking about Alex today. Really, any time thinking about Paradise Isle's newest lawman was too much. But between Emma's incessant questions over breakfast and the knowing looks and suggestive remarks from her staff, she'd found her attention forced to him more times than she could count. Not that it took much forcing. The sight of the rough-around-the-edges deputy cuddling an orphaned kitten had triggered something inside her, reminding her she was still a woman, not just a mother and veterinarian.

She eyed the gray bundle of fur that had triggered today's chain of events. "You're a troublemaker, you know that?"

The kitten in question was currently exploring her office after being evicted from the patient care area by Jillian. "He hates the cage and his crying is getting the other patients upset," she had said when she'd deposited him on her desk an hour ago.

Absently, Cassie balled up a piece of paper and tossed it in front of the cat. Thrilled, the tiny predator pounced on it, rolling head over heels in his enthusiasm.

Once upon a time, she'd been that carefree, that eager to chase adventure. But she'd been knocked down too hard to be willing to risk tumbling end over end again. She almost envied the kitten its bravery. He'd nearly frozen to death last night and yet he still seemed fearless. Meanwhile, she was afraid of her own shadow most days.

Having her ex leave her had made it hard to trust people, but the aftermath of the car accident she and her father had been in certainly hadn't helped. Naively, she'd assumed that the drunken deputy who hit her would face jail time, that he would pay for his actions. Instead, he'd gotten what seemed like a slap on the wrist. She'd tried to push for more, pointing out Jack's obvious alcoholism, but the department had closed ranks around him. According to them, he'd made a simple mistake and she was just stirring up trouble. A few people had even suggested the accident might have been her fault, despite all evidence to the contrary. Logically, she knew they were wrong, but that didn't make the nightmares or the guilt any better.

"Hey, Cassie?" Mollie, her friend and the clinic receptionist, spoke over the intercom. "Emma's here."

Cassie glanced at her watch. How was it already five o' clock? "Send her back and let her know her little friend is still here." Her daughter had fallen in love with the kitten when she saw it this morning. She'd be thrilled it hadn't been picked up yet.

"Mommy!" Her daughter flew into the tiny office, tossing her backpack down to give Cassie a big hug. "Mollie said he's still here! Where is he?"

Cassie laughed and pointed to the wastebasket in the corner of the room. "Look behind the trash can. I think he'd hiding back there."

Emma, always excited by a new visitor to the clinic, scrambled out of Cassie's lap to check it out. "Found him!" she whooped, clutching the kitty to her chest.

"Careful. Don't squeeze him too hard."

"I know that, Mom. I'm not a baby." The indignation on her little face was better suited to a teenager than a preschooler, but she did have a point. Emma had grown up with foster animals and convalescing pets around the house and knew how to handle them.

"Well, this one is a bit of a troublemaker, so just be careful." Even as she gave the warning, the little guy was trying to climb out of Emma's arms and to scale the mini-blinds over the window. Delighted at his antics, Emma gently untangled him.

"You sure do get into trouble," she scolded the kitten. "That should be your name—Trouble."

Cassie laughed. "I think you're right. That's the perfect name. I'll have Mollie put that on his chart."

"Will the policeman mind that we named the kitten without him?"

"I'm sure he won't mind." Time for a change in subject. "So did you have a good day at school?" Emma had started half days at the preschool affiliated with their church only a few months ago.

"Oh, yeah! John Baker brought a snake into school today for show-and-tell."

"A real snake?" She shivered. There was a reason she hadn't specialized in exotic medicine, and that reason was snakes. Professionally she knew they were legitimate pets, but personally she found them cringe-worthy.

Her daughter nodded with glee. "Uh-huh, a baby one. He had stripes and was really pretty. Can we have a snake, too? I'd take really good care of it."

"Absolutely not. No snakes."

"But you said we could get a pet ages ago and we still don't have one." She stuck her lip out in a perfect pout.

"We will when the time is right."

"When will that be?"

When? When her father was able to work again? When the nightmares went away?

"Soon."

Emma shot her a disbelieving look and went back to snuggling the kitten.

Great, just one more way she'd let her daughter down.

Alex had overslept, then cut himself in his hurry to shave and shower. Now he was standing in the pet food section of Paradise's only grocery store, still bleeding, and confused as heck. Was growth food the same as kitten food? Or should he get the special indoor formula? Or sensitive? What did that even mean, sensitive? And then there were all the hairball options. By the looks of it, half of America's cats were fighting some kind of hair trauma he had no desire to understand.

Dabbing again at the cut on his jaw, he decided on the bag marked Growth, mainly because it had a picture of a kitten on the front. That had to be a good sign.

Taking the smallest bag, he added it to his basket, which already contained a box of protein bars, new razor blades and the chew bone he'd promised Rex this morning. Thankfully, the checkout line was short, and he was in the car and tearing into one of the protein bars in a matter of minutes. He washed down the makeshift meal with some bottled water and nosed the vehicle south on Lighthouse Avenue. A few quick blocks later and he was pulling into the small parking lot.

Rex woofed hopefully.

"All right, you can come in." He got out and then let Rex out, snapping on his leash. The dog trotted at his side, nose working the breeze. The K-9 was probably picking up a full buffet of smells from all of the pets that had been through there recently.

Once inside, Rex honed in on the treat container in the reception area, sitting prettily directly in front of it.

"Hi, handsome!" The pretty brunette behind the counter, Mollie, according to her name tag, smiled at the panting dog, then turned to Alex. "You must be the man that rescued the kitten this morning, right?"

"Guilty as charged. Although really Rex was the one who found him. He deserves all the credit."

"I'm not sure *credit* is the word." She made a wry face. "Maybe *blame* would be more accurate. That little guy has been driving everyone nuts all day. They had to move him into Cassie's office because he was getting the other patients all worked up with his yowling."

Alex winced. "Sorry. I probably should have taken him with me, but I wasn't exactly prepared for a surprise kitten at six this morning."

"Don't be silly. It's not your fault he's so rambunctious. And Dr. Marshall's daughter is in love with him. She's back there playing with him now."

"Emma's here? Surely her mother doesn't bring her to work every day?"

The receptionist tipped her head, studying him. "I didn't realize you'd met Emma already. Her grandparents dropped her off a little bit ago. They watch her in the afternoons."

He nodded. "Emma and I met at the Share the Love meeting the other day—she asked if I was going to take anyone to jail. She's quite the character."

Mollie laughed. "That she is. Not a shy bone in her body, that's for sure. Have a seat. I'll let them know you're here."

Alex chose the seat farthest from the door, across from an older man snuggling a Persian cat. Rex ignored the cat, preferring to keep an eye on the treat jar.

Only a few minutes later, he was called into an examination room. He was surprised to recognize one of the owners of the Sandpiper, Jillian, waiting for him, dressed in scrubs.

"Deputy Santiago, good to see you again." She offered a wide smile, then crouched down to pet Rex. "And nice to meet you, Rex. I hear you're quite the hero."

"He's going to get a swollen head from all the compliments the women in this place give him. And call me Alex."

"Okay, Alex. Well, Dr. Marshall should be with you in just a minute. She was checking on the kitten's lab results, but he seems plenty healthy."

"Yeah, I heard he's been a handful. Sorry about that."

"Please. If we can't handle a two-pound kitten for a few hours, we're in trouble."

"Well, thank you anyway. I have to admit, I'm surprised to see you here. I thought you ran the Sandpiper?"

"Oh, no, I'm one of the owners, but my husband's the one who really runs it. Nic grew up in the hotel business, so he handles all the day-to-day stuff. I've been working here in the clinic since I was in high school. I can't imagine doing anything else."

He nodded in understanding. He could respect that; it was how he felt about being a cop.

The door opposite the one they came in from opened and Cassie entered, her daughter behind her. In Emma's arms was the kitten.

"He looks better," Alex commented. "Jillian said he's doing okay now."

"He's doing more than okay," Cassie told him. "He's got a belly full of food and has been given more attention today than he's probably ever had in his life."

As if to prove her statement, the kitten began purring, his throaty rumbling surprisingly loud given his small size.

"That's good, because he's going to be on his own

tonight. I did stop and get him some food. And I can make him a bed up, with towels or something."

"Good. What kind of litter did you get?"

Uh-oh. "Um, well…"

Cassie watched his face, then burst into laughter. Her shoulders shook as she spoke. "You've never had a cat before, have you, Deputy?"

Her laughter was almost worth the embarrassment. Almost. He had a college degree and had solved numerous criminal cases, yet he couldn't figure out how to take care of a simple cat? She must think he was an idiot.

Still chuckling, she put a hand on his arm. "I'm sorry I laughed. I should have given you a list this morning or at least told you what to get."

Her hand on his arm was warm, the casual touch sending a jolt of heat through his body. Pulling away, he cleared his suddenly dry throat. "You did more than enough. This was my fault." He rubbed a hand over his jaw. "I don't suppose you sell that stuff here? I've got to be on patrol in a bit, and, well—"

"Why don't we take Trouble home with us, Mommy?"

Alex looked from the bright-eyed girl to her mother. "I don't think—"

"Please, Mommy? You said we would get a pet. And this one needs a home. And he loves me so much, I know he'd miss me. And," she said, pointing at Alex triumphantly, "he doesn't know how to take care of a cat. He doesn't even have a litter box."

Put in his place by a child. So much for making a good impression. He'd be offended, except she was right. He had no idea what to do with a cat. He'd grown up with dogs, but cats were a new experience. Still, he didn't want to put Cassie out more than he already had.

"I'm sure I can figure something out for tonight, and I'll pick up a book at the library tomorrow. It can't be that hard, right?"

Cassie nodded slowly, but her eyes were on her daughter. Remembering her earlier conversation with Emma, she gave Alex a half-hearted smile. "I'm sure you could figure it out, but Emma's right. I did promise her a pet." And since she couldn't give her a dad, she might as well give her a cat. Because that made sense. Not.

"Really, Mommy? Really-really?"

"Really-really. But you'll have to take care of him yourself. He'll need to be fed and his litter box scooped. It won't just be about playtime and snuggles." Her lecture was lost on the girl, who was already whispering into the kitten's ear. No doubt they were planning all sorts of adventures.

"You didn't have to do this. I would have managed."

Alex looked uncomfortable with the change in plans. The poor guy probably wasn't used to being overruled by a four-year-old.

"I'm sure you could have handled it, but Emma's right. I did promise her a pet. I've been saying it for a while now, and since we aren't fostering any pets right now, it's a good time to do it. And a kitten's better than a snake."

"A snake?" He arched an eyebrow.

"It's a long story." A thought struck her. "You didn't want to keep him yourself, did you? I really should have asked before basically catnapping him from you."

He grinned at her pun, one side of his mouth tipping up higher than the other. The crooked smile made him look boyish and devious all at once. A potent combination that had her pulse tripping faster. "No, I wasn't planning to keep him. Between the new job and Rex, I'm not looking to take on any more responsibilities."

Her libido cooled as quickly as if he'd dumped a bucket of ice water on her. Avoiding responsibility was a definite turnoff. "Right, well, it's good you know your limitations. Too many people don't take that into account until after the damage is done."

"I just want to do right by the little guy. If you and Emma are willing to give him a good home, well, I can't imagine a better place for him." He paused. "Do you need to run this by your husband before bringing a new pet home? I don't want to cause any problems."

She fumbled with the stethoscope around her neck. "No, that won't be necessary."

"It's just Mommy and me at home," Emma piped up. "We're a team."

Cassie was used to looks of pity when people found out she was a single mom, but Alex's eyes showed only admiration.

Turning back to Emma, he crouched down so he could look her in the eye. "Well, then. Do I have your word that you're going to take good care of him? Feed him and clean up after him and whatever else your mama says?"

Her eyes wide, she nodded solemnly. Then, without warning, she ambushed him with a hug, nearly knocking him, the kitten and herself to the floor. "Thank you for finding Trouble, and for giving him to me! He's the best present ever!"

No one could resist Emma when she turned on the cute, not even a hardened lawman like Alex. He hugged the girl right back. Then, once she released him, he stood and called Rex to his side. "Rex here is the one who found your kitty."

Awed by the massive dog, she asked quietly, "Does he like little girls?"

"Of course he does. Little girls are his favorite kind of people."

That was all the encouragement Emma needed. She wrapped her arms around the giant dog's neck, burying her face in the thick fur. Cassie started forward, visions of police dogs and bite suits flashing through her mind.

Alex stopped her with a touch. "They're fine."

He was right. Rex had his tongue lolling out of his mouth, panting in the way of happy dogs everywhere.

"I'm sorry. I normally wouldn't worry, but I haven't had much experience with police dogs. I wouldn't want—"

"No need to explain, I get it. Honestly, I wouldn't suggest she try that with most K-9s, but Rex really likes kids. I've even done some demonstrations at the school. He was chosen for our department partly because he's so social. He's the first dog here, and if he gets a bad reputation, that would be the end of the Palmetto County K-9 unit."

As she watched the dog, her instincts agreed with Alex's words. Rex did seem as comfortable with Emma as any family pet.

"You take Rex to schools?" Emma had lifted her head to speak, but kept her arms around the dog.

"Sometimes." He winked, then stage-whispered, "I think he likes to show off."

Oh, my. The combination of the wink and the dimples, not to mention the low gravel of his voice, had Cassie clutching the edge of the exam table. This man was so potent he needed a warning label.

"Could you bring him to my school for show-and-tell? That would be even cooler than John Baker's silly snake."

"Well—"

"Emma, Deputy Santiago is a busy man. He and Rex have a very important job to do."

"That's right, we do."

Emma's face fell.

"But show-and-tell sounds pretty important, too. And Rex sure would love to see you again."

Sexy, confident, good with dogs and kids. If she hadn't had a hang-up about the Palmetto Sheriff's department, she would have said he was perfect.

Why couldn't he have been a doctor or a lawyer, or even a mechanic? No, he had to be part of the good old boy network that passed for law enforcement in this area. Yeah, she was cynical. But for good reason, darn it.

Pasting a smile on her face, she remembered this wasn't about her. It was about her daughter. "Thank you, Deputy Santiago. I know the kids will love having you come. I'll have her teacher contact you about the details, if that's okay."

"Sure, no problem at all." Patting Emma's strawberry-blond curls, he extended a hand to Cassie. "Thank you again for taking the kitten. Let me know if it doesn't work out, and I'll figure something else out."

His hand was warm on hers, firm but gentle. Letting go abruptly, she stuck her tingling hand in her pocket. "We'll be just fine, Deputy. Thank you."

As Alex passed by the receptionist's desk, Cassie caught Mollie checking out his rear end, and who could blame her? The deputy said he didn't want to cause trouble, but from where she stood, he was exactly that.

Chapter 4

Alex stood in front of the double doors of All Saints School, feeling as if he was eight years old again. He'd gone to an elementary school very similar to this one and had spent more than his fair share of time in the principal's office. But that was a long time ago, and he was no longer a messed-up little kid in trouble for fighting. He was a grown man; there was no reason to be intimidated.

Rex whined, looking between him and the door. Sometimes having a dog so in tune with his emotions wasn't a good thing.

"It's okay, boy. They invited us. You'll show them your tricks, and then we can go home." He'd scheduled this visit for his day off and was looking forward to a nap and then maybe stopping by his mom's place for dinner. Just the thought of her empanadas had his stomach grumbling.

"All right, let's go." He squared his shoulders and opened the door, stepping into the relative warmth of the building. It even smelled like a school, of crayons, newly sharpened pencils and that odd industrial soap all schools seemed to use.

Rex's nails clicked on the industrial linoleum floor as he walked to the door labeled Administration. An older woman with a neat bob of silver hair sat behind a massive oak desk. Spotting him, she stood as he came in. "Deputy Santiago, I'm Eleanor Trask, the assistant principal. I want to thank you for coming. Our pre-schoolers are really looking forward to this."

"I'm happy to do it."

She stepped past him through the door, motioning him to follow. He walked beside her down the wide hall, then down a side passage with doors every few feet. Paper-plate snowmen with children's names on them lined the walls. He smiled, knowing that most of the artists had never seen a single flake of snow.

"You like children, Deputy?"

"Yes, ma'am, I do. Children are honest, and I don't see much of that in my line of work."

She paused and then nodded. "I've never thought of it quite that way, but you're right. They are honest in a way refreshing to most adults. I find that people who don't like children usually have something to hide."

He thought of his own childhood and agreed. "I suppose that's true."

They stopped in front of a door toward the end of the corridor. "This is it. We decided to bring in the other two preschool classes as well, given the exciting nature of this particular show-and-tell. You should have quite the audience."

Swallowing, he let her open the door and introduce him. From the doorway, he could see about thirty small children seated in rows on the brightly-colored carpet. After Ms. Trask reminded the students to be on their best behavior, she left, leaving him wondering what he'd been thinking. He'd faced hardened criminals less intimidating.

"Hi, Rex!" The familiar voice carried over the whispers of her classmates. Rex woofed in return, setting all the kids into fits of giggles. Emma was front and center, her red-blond curls in pigtails and her face alight with joy. Smiling back, he felt a heavy tug on his heartstrings. It seemed both the Marshall women knew how to get to him.

Alex spent the next half-hour telling the students a bit about police dogs before moving on to some demonstrations. Rex did his various obedience moves, then used his nose to find a hidden object in the room. He determined which of two pencils had been held by Alex. Delighted by the dog's tricks, the children all begged to pet Rex. He let them, one by one, monitoring closely. Rex might like kids, but that many children could overwhelm any dog.

Emma's excitement was contagious. By the end of his talk, all the kids were in love with Rex, and half wanted to be K-9 handlers when they grew up. Definitely a success. Before leaving, he handed out shiny sheriff's deputy stickers, hoping they would keep the kids distracted enough for him to make his getaway. He was just slipping out when Emma stopped him.

"Deputy Alex?"

"Yes?"

"Do you have anyone to be your valentine yet?"

Where on earth did that come from? "Um, no, I guess not. Other than Rex here."

She rolled her eyes at him. "A dog can't be your valentine. It has to be a people."

"Oops, sorry. I guess I don't, then."

"Would you like one?"

Was he being propositioned by a four-year-old? "Um, sure, I guess. I hadn't thought about it much yet."

"Perfect. I'll tell her you said yes." Flush with success, she waved goodbye and ran back to her friends.

Had he just agreed to something? And if so, what?

Cassie managed to snag one of the few open parking spots; maybe that meant her luck was changing. The school secretary had called an hour ago to tell her that Emma had forgotten her lunch again. Stuck in surgery, she hadn't been able to leave until twenty minutes ago, only to find the abandoned Hello Kitty lunchbox on the backseat of her car, tucked under a sweater. And after baking in the hot car all morning, the contents were less than edible. It might be January, but in typical Florida fashion the temperature had climbed twenty degrees in the past few days. Then, what should have been a quick trip to the corner store for more food had stalled out when the person ahead of her paid with loose change—counting and recounting three times.

But she was here now, and lunch period didn't start for another ten minutes. Slamming the car door closed, she made for the main entrance, only to have the door open as she reached for it. Off balance, she did a stutter step to keep from falling.

"Whoa, sorry. Are you okay?"

Alex Santiago and his dog were staring at her, concern showing in both their gazes. How could she have forgotten today was the show-and-tell thing? "I'm fine, really. I just have a habit of tripping over my own feet, that's all."

"Are you sure?"

His deep voice set off tingles in all the right places. Stomping down on her libido before she said something stupid, she held the lunch box out in front of her like a shield. "I'm good. Just going to drop off Emma's lunch. She forgot it this morning. How about you—how was show-and-tell?"

He winced. "Loud. Very loud. I'm not quite sure how such small people make so much noise. But other than that, I think it went well. And Rex put on a good show."

"I'm sure he did." Awkwardly, she ducked past him into the building. "I'll see you around, I guess."

"Oh, you will. Mrs. Rosenberg was helpful enough to sign me up for every committee there is for the Share the Love dance. We're bound to run into each other."

"Mrs. Rosenberg is a force to be reckoned with." Shaking her head at the image of the elderly lady pulling a fast one on the tough cop, she suddenly realized something. "Does that mean you'll be at the decorating committee meeting tomorrow night?"

"So it seems. And you?"

"Yes, that's the only committee I signed up for."

"You've got plenty on your plate already with Emma and the clinic, I'm sure."

"You're right, I do." And yet she'd been standing there making small talk when it was almost time for Emma's lunch. "Speaking of which, I'd better get this to Emma."

"Of course. See you tomorrow." He exited via the door she'd just come through, Rex trotting at his side.

Shaking her head to clear her thoughts, she went to the front office to sign in and get a visitor's pass, then headed for her daughter's classroom. She should have just enough time to say hello before getting back for afternoon appointments. Her own lunch would have to be a protein shake between patients, but that wasn't anything new.

Emma was lining up at the front of the room with her friends, but ran for a hug when she saw Cassie walk in. "Thanks, Mom. Sorry I forgot it."

Cassie guided her back into line and walked with her toward the cafeteria. "You know, one of these days I'm going to just let you starve." Rolling her eyes, Emma reached for her hand as they walked.

They both knew that wasn't going to happen, mainly because Cassie was just as forgetful, if not worse. If she didn't have Mollie to keep her on track at work, she'd be in deep trouble. Sticky notes and alarms on her smartphone were a big help, but it would be a few years before Emma could make use of those. "Just try to be more careful. Okay?"

"I will. I was just so excited about seeing Rex and Deputy Alex that I couldn't think about anything else."

Another shared trait—a fondness for handsome men and good-looking dogs.

"Oh, and Mommy, guess what?"

"What?"

"Deputy Alex is going to be your valentine!"

"What?" Several heads had turned at Emma's enthusiastic statement. No doubt there would be talk in the teacher's lounge later.

"I asked, and he said he doesn't have a valentine. And you don't have one, either. So you can be each other's. It's perfect."

Emma's innocence made Cassie's heart squeeze. "Oh, honey, it's not quite that simple. Just because we're both single doesn't mean we're going to be valentines with each other."

Emma frowned. "Why not? Don't you like Deputy Alex?"

"Of course I do." More than she should. "But someday, when you're a grown-up, you'll understand that things like valentines are more complicated than just liking someone."

"I don't ever want to be a grown-up. It makes everything complicated."

No kidding, kid. No kidding.

Cassie gave Emma a quick hug at the cafeteria door, then headed back out to her car and her very grown-up, way-too-complicated life.

Back at the clinic, Cassie had little time to dwell on her lack of a valentine or her daughter's ridiculous matchmaking. A terrier with kennel cough had one exam room shut down until it could be fully disinfected, causing the rest of the appointments to be delayed. She'd soothed the last cranky client of the day only a few minutes ago and was going over the day's receipts when Jillian knocked on the open door.

"Got a minute?"

Cassie stretched her arms over her head, her vertebrae popping at the movement. "Sure, what's up?"

Her friend pushed her dark curls off her face, fidgeting, her eyes looking everywhere but at Cassie.

Gut clenching, Cassie put down the stack of papers she'd been reading. "What is it? What's wrong?" Jillian was her best friend, the closest she'd ever gotten to having a sister.

Jillian's big brown eyes filled with tears, which she quickly wiped away. "Nothing. I mean, nothing's wrong. It's just…well…" She placed a hand on her flat belly and met Cassie's gaze. "I'm pregnant."

"Oh, my goodness, really?" Jumping up, Cassie stared at Jillian's hand, as if she could see through it to the baby growing underneath. "That's amazing! But why are you crying? I thought you and Nic wanted to have kids right away?" A horrible thought hit her. "The baby's okay, right? And you're okay?"

"We're both fine. I saw the doctor on my lunch hour and she says everything is perfect."

"Oh, thank goodness." She sat back down. "And Nic's happy about the baby?"

"He's over the moon. He was drawing out plans for the nursery when I left."

That sounded like Nic. The former hotel magnate

had recently discovered a latent talent for carpentry. "So then why are you crying?"

Laughing through her tears, Jillian shook her head. "I don't know! It just keeps happening."

Relief sang through Cassie. Embracing her friend, she found her own eyes filling. "Hormones will make you crazy, but who cares? You're going to be a mommy! You have to let me throw your baby shower, promise?"

"Of course you can. So you aren't upset?"

Cassie pulled away. "Upset? Why on earth would I be upset?"

"Because of all the inconvenience. I'm not going to be able to take X-rays, and I think I'll have some limits on lifting, and it's just going to make more work for everyone," she finished with a sob.

"Oh, sweetie, don't worry about all that. Mollie can cross-train some and help out in the back, and you can help her up front. We're all in this together, right?"

A fresh round of tears soaked Jillian's smiling face. "Right. Thanks. And I am happy. I just didn't think it would happen so soon, you know?"

"I've seen the sparks between you and Nic. Honestly, I'm surprised it took this long."

Jillian grinned through her tears. "Speaking of which, I've seen the way that new deputy looks at you, the one with the Shepherd. Anything going on there?"

"Hardly." She turned her gaze back to the paper printouts on her desk.

"Well, why on earth not? He's hot, single and likes dogs." She ticked off the traits on her fingers.

"And works for the sheriff's department. No thank you."

"Cassie, the entire sheriff's department is not against you. Besides, Alex wasn't even working there when all that happened."

"It doesn't matter." She forced a smile. "I've got my hands full anyway, with work and Emma and the charity dance. And on top of all that, I've got a baby shower to plan. Who's got time to think about men with all that going on?"

"Right." Jillian didn't look convinced, but good friend that she was, she dropped the subject. "If you don't have anything more for me, I'm going to go. Nic wants us to call and tell his family about the baby tonight."

"Go, then. I'm almost done here anyway. And congratulations again. You're going to make a wonderful mother."

And she would. Despite Jillian's lonely childhood, bouncing from one foster home to another, or maybe because of it, she would be an excellent mother. And her baby would be lucky enough to grow up with a father, as well. He or she would have two stable, loving parents, the kind of family Emma was so hungry for and Cassie would never be able to offer.

Chapter 5

Alex parked his department SUV in the gravel lot of the Sandpiper and tried to psych himself up for the scrutiny and pointed questions he knew were coming. It wasn't that he disliked socializing, but being the new guy in a small town meant everyone thought they had a right to his life story. Thankfully, so far the gossips had been too well-mannered to press him, but his luck couldn't hold forever.

"Come on, boy. Jillian said you can come in as long as you're nice to her dog."

Rex woofed, nearly toppling Alex in his eagerness to get out and explore. The inn billed itself as pet friendly, and no doubt there were a myriad of smells for the big dog to enjoy. Not to mention, letting him amble a bit on the way in meant a few more minutes before he was put under the microscope by the committee ladies.

Rex was intently sniffing a coco-plum hedge when his ears suddenly pricked up. A moment later, the sound of footsteps on gravel signaled someone coming up the path behind them. The dog's frantic tail wagging indicated a friend, so it was no surprise when Cassie came around the bend. "He remembers you."

"He remembers the treats I gave him, don't you boy?"

Woof.

"Sorry, I don't have any on me right now. But don't worry, I bet Emma will sneak you some out of Murphy's stash."

"Is Emma with you?"

"My mom dropped her off here after dinner, so I wouldn't have to make an extra trip to pick her up."

He angled his steps beside hers as they headed for the main building. "It must be a big help, having your family around."

"I couldn't have done it without them. My dad is a vet, too. He owns the clinic, in fact. But he hasn't been able to work since the accident, leaving me with longer hours. It's a bit better now that Emma's in preschool, but that's only part-time. Knowing she's with family or with a friend like Jillian after school keeps me from going totally insane."

Accident? He was about to ask her about it when the front door swung open. A tall, dark-haired man stepped out and embraced Cassie, nearly sweeping her off her feet.

"Can you believe it? Jillian said she told you today."

Cassie laughed and gave him a peck on the cheek. "Yes, she told me, and of course I can believe it. You two are meant to be parents." She turned back. "Nic, this is Alex Santiago. Alex, meet Nic Caruso, proprietor and father-to-be."

Alex's offered hand was enveloped in a very enthusiastic handshake. "Thanks for letting us use your place for the meeting. It's very generous of you."

"That's all Jillian. She's the one in charge."

Cassie grinned. "And don't you forget it."

"I won't. She won't let me. In fact, I'd better go see if she needs anything else before the meeting starts."

Alex watched him duck through a swinging door into a private hallway. "He seems like a nice guy."

"He is. They're really lucky to have each other."

At her wistful smile, an ache started deep in his chest. Her vulnerability triggered all his protective instincts. Someone had done wrong by this woman, and he wouldn't mind a few rounds alone with whoever it had been.

Breaking the silence, Cassie indicated the French doors that were the rear entrance. "We'd better get started before they get it all done without us."

He followed her gaze across the casual yet elegant room. Overstuffed furniture was arranged around a native coquina-stone fireplace. Beyond that, large windows were open to the crisp night air. Over the sound of the sea came the rise and fall of voices; it seemed everyone else was out back.

As soon as they stepped outside, they were greeted by a chorus of welcomes. Mrs. Rosenberg was there, of course, and she nodded approvingly when she saw them. Jillian was seated next to her at a large picnic-style table, and a number of other women filled the deck chairs scattered along the wide whitewashed porch that wrapped around the building. As expected, he was the only male member of the decorating committee. Well, except for Rex and Murphy, Jillian and Nic's dog. The border collie had been sleeping under the table, but at the sight of Rex had bulleted through his mistress's legs to greet his new playmate.

"Murphy, don't make a pest of yourself. Rex is a serious working dog, not your new partner-in-crime," Jillian admonished. She smiled up at Alex. "Sorry, he means well, but he's still stuck in the puppy phase. Possibly permanently."

"No problem. Rex likes other dogs and could do with a buddy." Rex held still as the younger dog sniffed him all over, then returned the favor. Canine introductions over, they both looked up at Alex, as if waiting for permission to play. "Is it okay if I let him off his leash? I don't want him to get tangled with Murphy."

"Of course. Maybe Rex's good manners will rub off on him. Either way, I've got the gate to the yard closed off, so they can't go far."

At the click of the lead unsnapping, both dogs bounded off for the far end of the porch, away from the crowd. Keeping one eye on the dogs, Alex settled onto a white bench next to Cassie and across from Jillian. "I hear congratulations are in order."

The mother-to-be blushed. "Yes, we just found out. We're both a bit overwhelmed."

"Understandably. I'd be quaking in my boots, but fatherhood never has been on my radar. Nic seems to be taking it in stride, though."

"You didn't see his face when I told him. I thought he was going to pass out right in front of me."

Mrs. Rosenberg patted her hand. "They all get a bit jumpy when they find out. I know my Marvin did. But before you know it they're passing out cigars and acting like they're the first person to ever make a baby."

Next to him, Cassie fiddled with the edge of her sweater. Most of the women he knew loved baby talk, especially the experienced mothers. Cassie, however, looked as if she'd sooner face a firing squad than swap maternity tales. Jillian must have seen it, too, because she took one look at her friend's face and changed the subject.

"Cassie, can you and Alex work on the banners? Mrs. Rosenberg and I are going to go inside and put together the centerpieces."

"Sure." Cassie looked to Alex. "Does that sound okay to you?"

Alex nodded. "Sure, as long as there are some instructions somewhere. I'm kind of clueless with arts and crafts."

Mrs. Rosenberg pointed to the stacks of paper and craft supplies on the table as she stood up. "Cassie knows what to do. Just stick with her and you'll be fine."

He looked expectantly at Cassie. "I hope you're a patient teacher. I'm afraid I failed cut and paste in school."

That got a grin from her. "Well, big guy, you're going to get a crash course in it tonight. Not to brag, but as a surgeon, I'm an expert at precision cutting. All you have to do is watch me."

No worries there. Seeing her there, bathed in moonlight, he couldn't have taken his eyes off her if he tried.

Cassie never would have imagined she'd enjoy spending an evening cutting out hundreds of construction-paper hearts. But talking with Alex had made the time fly by. He'd entertained her with stories of growing up Puerto Rican in Miami, teasing her when she couldn't pronounce the name of his favorite food. She'd shared some of the funnier animal encounters she'd had over the years, and then they'd both cracked up when Murphy ran in with an entire string of pink twinkle lights wrapped around his body.

After they untangled the dog, he had been banished to Jillian and Nic's private quarters, where he'd kept Emma company watching cartoons. Rex, worn out by the younger, more rambunctious dog, had curled up under the table with his head on Cassie's feet.

In fact, the only awkward part of the evening had been when Jillian and Mrs. Rosenberg were comparing stories about their husbands. They hadn't meant any harm, but remembering her own early pregnancy was hardly a pleasant experience. Nic might have been over the moon about the new baby, but Cassie knew too well that not all men got past the initial shock and fear. Certainly her ex never had. He'd called her a liar, then suggested the baby wasn't his after all. Learning that he'd walked out on her had been almost a relief after the awful things he'd said.

His reaction might have been extreme, but it wasn't

all that uncommon, in her view. Even Alex had commented on how frightening the idea of fatherhood was.

Thankfully, once the subject was changed, the rest of the evening had been more pleasant than she'd expected. Now it was probably time to get going. She finished stringing one more heart on the banner in front of her and reluctantly stood up. "It's late. I need to get Emma home and into bed."

He looked down at his watch. "Wow, it is late. She must be exhausted."

"Actually, she's probably passed out on Jillian's bed. She can fall asleep anywhere."

"Seriously?" His eyebrow cocked in disbelief. "We haven't exactly been quiet out here."

"I'm telling you, she could fall asleep in Times Square. The clock strikes eight and she's out for the count. She's been like that since she was a baby. Come, I'll show you."

She grabbed his hand, pulling him up to follow her. Awareness snaked up her arm like heat lightning on a summer's night. Dropping his hand, she stumbled back as if she'd literally been shocked.

Alex stared, the heat in his eyes a match for the surge she'd felt in his touch. All she had to do was lean forward and he'd kiss her, and it had been so long since she'd been kissed.

But a kiss wouldn't be enough, not by half. Accepting that and knowing it couldn't be more, she drew a deep breath and turned away. She wasn't running away. She was being sensible. So why did the sound of his footsteps behind her have her increasing her pace?

She stopped just inside Jillian and Nic's private suite, taking a moment to calm herself before waking Emma up.

"Wow, you were right." Alex's husky whisper sent a shiver down her spine.

Emma was passed out in a heap on the floor, her head resting on Murphy's snoring form. "She's always fallen asleep easily, but she's a bear when you wake her up."

"Then let's not wake her." Alex stepped past her and gently scooped Emma into his arms. Cassie meant to stop him, to insist that she could handle things, but the way his jeans molded to his body when he bent over left her temporarily speechless. Oblivious to her ogling, he effortlessly carried the girl past her and toward the front of the inn. Scrambling after him, she rushed to open the door while waving a hasty goodbye to her friends. Jillian's lips quirked up at the sight, but she thankfully didn't comment.

Outside, the cooler air calmed her senses and her libido. There was no need to get all worked up. Alex was just being chivalrous. But all her rationalizations didn't stop her heart from aching at the sight of her daughter cradled in his strong arms. This was the kind of thing Emma had missed out on by not having a father around.

In the parking lot, Alex silently slid Emma into her car seat, then managed the buckles like a pro.

"Thanks."

"Anytime."

Right. One time was more than was smart, if her jumping pulse was any indication. If she wanted to protect her heart, she was going to have to stay far away from Alex Santiago.

Chapter 6

"So, I hear you met the new K-9 officer?"

Leave it to her dad to touch on the one subject she was hoping to avoid. He'd had a knack for that all her life.

"I've run into him a few times. And he found an abandoned kitten that Emma talked me into keeping." Across the kitchen table in her parents' home, her father watched her carefully.

"Emma told me about that. She's taken quite a shine to him."

"Well, kittens are pretty hard to resist."

"I was talking about the man, not the cat."

Well, he was hard to resist, too. But that was more than her father needed to know. Turning her eyes back to the laptop in front of her, she chose her words carefully. "He seems very nice."

Her father looked over his glasses at her. "Very nice?"

"Yes, he seems nice." No way was Dad going to get her to admit to more than that. She'd come over so they could go over the clinic books together, not so he could play matchmaker.

He leaned over her shoulder and tapped at the keyboard, printing out the most recent month's statistics. "Well, that should make things easier."

"Make what easier?"

"I'm getting to that. You see, before the accident, I'd agreed to help the sheriff's office with the new K-9 unit. Nothing major, just routine checkups and some help with the training runs."

She closed the laptop. Obviously that wasn't why her dad had called her over anyway. No, he had something else up his sleeve.

"So anyway, with me still not up to par, that leaves you."

She stared at him. "Leaves what to me, exactly?"

"Like I said, routine medical care. And some training."

"Medical care, sure. But training? You want me to put on a bite suit or something?" What on earth had her father gotten her into?

"No, nothing like that. But they want the dogs to do search work and need some volunteers. I'd planned on doing it, but as it is..." He pointed to his injured leg.

"Fine. I'll do it." Darn him, he was actually smirking. "You know, you don't have to look so pleased about the whole idea."

"Who, me?" He winked at her. "I really do feel bad about backing out, so I'm glad you're going to take my place. But yes, I am also happy about you spending some time with a young man. A very nice young man, I believe you said."

"Who just so happens to work for the sheriff's department. You know, I wouldn't think you'd be so eager to help them after everything that happened."

"Cassie, honey, we've been over this. You can't hold the whole department responsible for what happened. And this Alex fellow wasn't even here back then."

Logically, she knew her father was right. But that didn't keep her from breaking out into a cold sweat at the sight of the blue sheriff's uniform or jumping every time she heard a siren. She'd made some progress, thanks to a therapist recommended by the ER doctor who had treated her. And it was true that Alex didn't trigger the usual panic. But he caused a whole different kind of emotional overload, one she wasn't up for dealing with.

"I said I'll help. Don't push for more, okay?" She was agreeing at all only because she still felt guilty about the accident. No, she hadn't caused it, but she'd been the one driving, and she couldn't help but second-guess herself. Especially when she saw the pain her father was still in.

"How's the physical therapy going?" She gestured to his knee, now supported by a brace.

"Good." He beamed. "I should be back at work in another week or so."

"Is that what Jen said?" Jen Miller was her father's physical therapist and an old schoolmate.

Her father rubbed the knee absently. "It's what I'm saying. You're doing a tremendous job, but you can't run that clinic on your own forever. That's why I asked you to come over. I can at least start doing the paperwork." He ran a hair through his still-thick gray hair. "If I don't do something, I'm going to go crazy."

"He's right, much as I hate to admit it." Her mom

walked in, a load of laundry in a basket on her hip. "I know he enjoys spending time with me and helping with sweet Emma, but if he doesn't get back to the clinic soon, he's going to drive both of us crazy."

Her father snaked out a hand and pulled his still-trim wife into his lap. "Lady, I'm already crazy, over you." He planted a loud kiss on her lips, then let her up.

Cassie turned back to her computer, never sure what to make of her parents' affectionate displays. She was glad they were so happy together; plenty of her friends growing up had come from divorced or unhappy homes. But she couldn't help wonder what was wrong with her, that she had never found that kind of happiness herself.

Clearing her throat, she tried to bring the conversation back on track. "I get that you're frustrated, and yes, I'm happy to have you take over the bookkeeping. But please, follow Jen's advice." Veterinary work was often physically difficult, and as much as she felt crushed under the workload, she didn't want her father having a relapse, either. She'd have to talk to Jen and get the real prognosis, and if Dad was rushing things, she'd have a heart-to-heart talk with her mom. Her father might be bull-headed, but he would listen to his wife. Love had that effect on a man, or so she'd been told.

Cassie waited in the cool, casually decorated lobby of the Paradise Physical Therapy clinic, watching the minute hand tick its way around her watch. Stopping by without an appointment had been a mistake; it seemed the practice was much busier than she'd expected. It wasn't that she didn't have the time—Emma wasn't due to be picked up for another two hours and Mollie had cleared the rest of her appointments for the day—just that she hated waiting.

Flipping through an out-of-date magazine filled with celebrities she had never heard of, she wondered when she'd lost track of pop culture. Probably about the time she became a single mother. Between work and child-care, there hadn't been much time for movies or concerts, and her television habits had been reduced to educational cartoons. Although if half of what the magazines said was true, she hadn't missed much.

"Cassie?"

Her childhood friend looked the same as she had in high school, trim and athletic with curly brown hair pulled back in a neat ponytail. "Hi, Jen. Thanks for seeing me on such short notice."

"No problem. Thanks for waiting. Come on back. I'm going to grab some coffee in the break room before my next appointment."

Jen led her down the hall to a small but tidy room, then offered her a drink.

"Water would be great, thanks."

Jen handed her a bottle from the refrigerator, then poured a cup of coffee. "So what brings you by here? Is there a problem with your father?"

"No. Well, sort of. I'm just worried that he's pushing too fast. He says he's going to be back in the office in a week or two, and although I'd love the help, I'm afraid he's going to end up hurting himself worse."

Jen sipped her coffee. "I can't discuss his medical records with you. You know that. But I can say that, professionally, I don't see a problem with that plan. He'll be sore, but it shouldn't set his recovery back, if that's what you're worried about."

What felt like a hundred pounds of dead weight lifted from her shoulders. "Really? You think he's doing that well?" He'd been in such bad shape after the accident, it was hard to imagine him finally back at work. But she trusted Jen's opinion, so if she said he was up for it, then he was.

"Like I said, I can't release details, but since you are business partners, I can tell you the same thing I would put in a note for an employer. He's still got some hurdles to overcome, but yes, he should be clear for light duty in a few weeks if he feels up to returning."

"That's wonderful. Thank you, Jen. I know you're the reason he's done so well."

Jen dumped the last bit of her coffee in the sink and rinsed the cup. "I've done the best I could for him, but the truth is, your father is a strong man with an incredible work ethic. He gets full credit for his success."

Cassie laughed. "I think what you are trying to say is that he's tough and a bit bull-headed."

"You said it, not me," Jen replied, a grin on her face. "But really, it was good to see you. We should get together soon."

"I'd like that. Maybe once Dad is back up to speed, I can meet you for lunch or something."

"Sounds good. Just give me a call." Jen looked down

at her watch. "Sorry to rush off so fast, but I've got another patient."

"No problem. I can see myself out." She gave Jen a quick hug goodbye, then navigated the twisting hallway back to the front lobby. Outside, the bright sunshine echoed her mood. Her father's recovery had been so long in coming, it was amazing to see the finish line after so many months of therapy.

"How come you never smile like that for me?"

Cassie startled, then saw it was just Alex, carrying a white prescription bag from the pharmacy next door. "Sorry, I didn't see you there."

"No apology needed. You just looked so happy I had to ask why."

"Well, I just talked with my father's physical therapist, and he's doing really well. In fact, he's going to be able to come back to work in a few weeks, if everything goes well."

"That's great news—in fact, how about I buy you a hot chocolate to celebrate?"

She did have a bit longer before she had to get Emma, and the only thing waiting for her back at the office was a stack of paperwork. She'd told herself Alex was off-limits, that getting involved was a bad idea. But it was just hot chocolate, not really a date. And when the choice was a sexy man with dimples to die for or writing up charts, there wasn't much of a decision to make.

"Hot chocolate sounds great."

Walking down Paradise's Main Street, she could feel everyone's eyes on her. They probably were wondering what she was doing with the new hot deputy when she hadn't been on a date in known memory. Small towns were great most of the time, but they didn't allow for much privacy. Luckily, the Sandcastle Bakery was only a few blocks away and served all sorts of hot beverages.

Inside the bakery, she stepped up to the glass display counter where Grace was sliding a tray of cinnamon scones onto a shelf. Normally, the pastries were a favorite of Cassie's, but right now she was too focused on the man beside her to care about food.

"Well, Cassie and Alex, what a surprise to see you two here…together." She winked at Cassie, no doubt remembering their earlier conversation about the good-looking deputy. "What can I get for you?"

"Two hot chocolates, please." Alex pulled out his wallet and paid for both, a move that had Grace raising an eyebrow in surprise.

"We're just celebrating Dad's recovery. Alex bumped into me as I was leaving the physical therapy clinic, and when I told him the good news, he suggested we come here."

"Well, that's very sweet of you, Alex." She handed him his change and then passed over the two cups, each with a hefty dollop of whipped cream on top. "You two have fun, now."

Alex held the door for her, and they walked back onto the sidewalk, Grace no doubt peeking out after them. This was why she didn't date. Well, one of the reasons why. The minute you said hello to a man, the entire town was all up in your business, watching your every move. She loved Paradise, but sometimes it felt like living in a reality show. Although having Alex as a costar in their own little romance was pretty tempting.

He was in khakis and a polo shirt today, looking strong and sharp and altogether too good for her. Not that he seemed to realize it. He hadn't taken his eyes off her since they ran into each other, his heated gaze warming her core faster than the hot drink in her hand. Desperate to change the subject, she tried to come up with a topic of conversation.

"So, my dad told me you need some help with Rex's training."

"We do. The department's been trying to find some volunteers. I guess the original plan was to have your father help, but even with all the progress your dad is making, I can't imagine he's going to be up to traipsing through the woods for quite a while."

"No, he's not." Again the guilty voice in her head reminded her that even though she'd been driving, her dad was the one in the brace. "But since he can't do it, I told him I would. Just tell me when and where you need me."

Alex stopped walking, his hot chocolate nearly sloshing over the side of the cup. "Really? You'd do that for me?"

"I'll do it for my father," she clarified. "I'm just filling in for him. That's all."

He grinned, his dimple winking at her. "Of course, and I appreciate it. Can you meet me at the wildlife refuge Saturday afternoon, around four o'clock?"

"I'll be there. Do I need to bring anything?"

"No, I'll have a pack for you and supplies. All you

have to do is show up and enjoy yourself. It's really pretty straightforward."

Right. A day in the woods, purposely getting lost, while trying to avoid her growing feelings for a man she had no business falling for. What could possibly go wrong?

Chapter 7

Alex ducked his head farther into his hooded sweat-shirt. The relative warmth of the last week had broken this morning when a cold front blew in. Yesterday afternoon had been a balmy seventy-five degrees; today the mercury had stopped in the low forties and was expected to drop further at dusk. All over the island, people were putting sheets over prized rosebushes and bringing their potted plants indoors in advance of the expected freeze tonight. He'd thought about resched-uling the training session, but being able to work in all weather was part of the job description. Training only in perfect conditions wouldn't create a reliable dog, and with lives possibly in the balance, that was unacceptable.

"So tell me again. What do I have to do?" Mollie squinted up at him, shading her eyes from the bright but cool sunshine. She'd shown up with Cassie, a last-minute surprise volunteer. She seemed eager to work and hadn't complained once about the weather, which earned her points in his book. Right now, she was bouncing on the balls of her feet, waiting for instruction.

"You're going to wander away and find a place to hide. Spend about fifteen minutes or so walking before you stop. If you have any problems, you can use the radio, but otherwise try to keep quiet if you can. I want Rex to use his nose, not his ears."

"And he'll really be able to find me just by my scent?"

"That's the idea. He's going to be smelling the rafts of cells that fall off your body. Sometimes those fall right where your footsteps are, but sometimes they're blown around, pooling in invisible eddies of air. My job is to help interpret the wind patterns, as well as any terrain or temperature issues that might affect where the scent pools."

"I'm not sure if I'm fascinated or intimidated." Mollie's pixie-like features grinned up at him. "But I'm curious to see how well it works."

"Well, go hide, then, and we'll see how he does." Mollie gave a mock salute and started out across the scrubland that made up much of the Paradise Isle Wildlife Refuge. A few minutes later, she disappeared into a more densely wooded area shadowed by thick oaks.

With nothing to do but wait, he turned to Cassie, who'd been mostly silent since they arrived. "Sorry it's so cold out. I thought about canceling, but I'm not sure when my next day off is going to be, and Rex needs the practice."

"No, it's fine. I mean, you can't exactly choose the weather during a real search."

"Exactly. And I really want to get him up to speed. Police dogs don't usually do search and rescue, but with the nearest search group a few hours away, it makes sense to try to cross-train him."

"Really?" She cocked her head. "I thought all police dogs did that kind of thing—you know, tracking down bad guys and such?"

"Not all K-9s. And even then, not all scent work is the same. There's tracking, where they stay right along the footprints of the person they are following, and then there's air scenting, which is more what we are doing today. Rex will search in a zig-zag pattern to find the scent, then triangulate in. It's similar to how a police dog might clear a building. And then of course some dogs are also trained to detect drugs, or explosives, or even cadavers."

She shivered, and he had a feeling it wasn't from the cold this time. "That's kind of creepy."

"Well, sure. But at the same time, being able to provide closure for grieving families is pretty amazing."

"You're right. I'm sorry."

"No need. I'm just glad you came. Like I said, Rex needs the practice. He's doing well so far but hasn't made the jump yet to longer, aged tracks."

Cassie leaned down and ruffled Rex's fur. "I've got faith in you, buddy. You'll find her."

Energized by the attention, the dog bounced into a deep play bow, wiggling his butt in the air. "This cool weather has him acting like a puppy. We'd better let him burn off some energy while we're waiting or we won't be able to keep up with him on the trail." He pulled a tennis ball out of the backpack at his feet and tossed it to Cassie. "See if you can wear him out a bit while I double-check the map."

Cassie's face lit up at the challenge. She whipped the ball across the field and Rex tore after it as if it was the last ball on earth. Then, rather than waiting for him to bring it back, she chased after him, initiating a canine version of tag.

Crouched over his maps and log book, Alex couldn't help but notice how much more relaxed she seemed while playing with the dog.

"You should do that more often," he called out after watching them play for a while.

"Do what?" She walked back, the dog panting at her side.

"Smile."

Her back straightened stiffly. "Sorry, didn't realize I was such a downer usually."

Crap. "No, I just meant—well, you looked so happy just now. Not that you seem depressed otherwise, but you do seem a bit more weighed down most of the time." He shrugged a shoulder. "It was nice to see you just having fun. That's all."

"Oh." She bit her lip, an innocent act that had his mouth watering. "Well, I don't get a lot of time to just run and play. So thank you for inviting me out here."

"Hey, you're the one doing me a favor. But I'm glad you're not hating it."

She ducked her head. "Actually, I thought I would. In fact, I only agreed to help because my dad guilted me into it."

"Is it me? Have I done something to offend you? Or is it just the cop thing?"

"It's not you." She gave a wry grin. "I don't have a good relationship with the sheriff's department, that's all."

Well, at least it wasn't him; that was progress. "Anything I should know about? I'm too new to have heard much gossip, so I'd consider it a public service if you'd fill me in."

She smirked. "Public service? That's an interesting way to spin it."

Chuckling, he shouldered his pack. "We should get started now. And seriously, if it involves the department, I'd like to know, but if you're not comfortable sharing, that's fine, too. I didn't mean to put you on the spot."

She fell into step beside him. "It's not exactly a secret. I'm surprised you haven't heard all the details by now. I'll fill you in while Rex finds Mollie."

"If he finds Mollie. Remember, he's pretty new to this." He opened a small Ziploc bag that held a T-shirt of Mollie's and held it down for the dog to sniff. "Search, Rex. Search."

The dog snuffled the bag, then started sniffing around. Working back and forth in front of them, he covered an amazing amount of ground. Soon, his tail flagged up and he started moving in the direction Mollie had taken.

"Now what do we do?"

"Watch him and try to keep up."

Cassie watched the dog work, fascinated at the way he seemed to follow invisible signposts only he could see. Or, more accurately, smell. Alex was tracking each turn in his logbook, and he occasionally called out encouragingly to Rex. His love and pride in the dog and his dedication to his job were obvious. She respected that. And yet she'd treated him badly when they first met without provocation. He deserved to know why.

"Several months ago, my father and I attended a professional lecture over in Orlando. He drove on the way over, so I volunteered to drive home. It was late by the time we hit the Paradise Isle bridge, not much traffic at all. We were so close to home, and then, going through the intersection there at the base of the bridge, we were sideswiped. He didn't even slow down. I don't think he saw us at all, or the red light." She paused and turned to Alex. "The who that ran that light and hit us was an off-duty sheriff's deputy. He was drunk. He kept saying he was sorry over and over, and I could smell the booze on his breath. My dad had to be cut out of the car and still isn't back to work or able to walk without a brace. Jack, however, is just fine." Bile rose in her throat. "So yeah, I'm not a fan of cops right now."

Alex looked concerned, but to his credit he didn't exude sympathy like some people had. She hated pity.

"Jack? Jack Campbell? Older guy, real skinny?"

"Yeah, that's him. Paradise Isle's resident alcoholic. He was suspended, but because it was his first offense, he won't serve any jail time. His lawyer said he was a dedicated public servant going through a hard time, that it was a one-time mistake." Sarcasm coated her words. "No one is willing to acknowledge that he has a real problem. Least of all the Palmetto County Sheriff's Department."

"Wait, so you're saying the guys at the department are covering for him?" The disgust on his face made her like him even more.

"Maybe not covering for him exactly, but definitely in some serious denial. Several of his friends accused me of exaggerating Jack's drinking, saying I was just trying to make trouble. Maybe they're right about it being the first time he's been caught, but given how frequently Jack closes down the only bar in town, I can't believe it was the first time he has driven under the influence. He needs more than just a slap on the wrist, but no one is willing to do anything about it. They act like I ruined his life, like he's the victim in all of this."

"Well, if it matters, I didn't know about any of it. I've been mainly working night shifts since I got here, so I'm a bit out of the loop."

It did matter. Reaching out, she squeezed his hand. "Thanks for listening, and thanks for believing me. I think that's been the worst part of this whole thing, having people not believe me."

He kept hold of her hand, tracing over her skin with this thumb. She shivered, and not from the cold.

"I do believe you. I'm not sure what I can do to help, but you can bet I'll keep my eyes open. Loyalty to fellow law enforcement is one thing, but I've been doing this long enough to know that not everyone lives up to the responsibility of the uniform. And when they screw up, they drag us all down with them."

His eyes had gone cold, as if locking down whatever

pain that lesson had cost him. She could try to find out what had happened, but that seemed too personal just yet. Being here, walking hand in hand through the crisp air—that was enough for now.

Ahead of them the dog was getting more animated, making shorter zigs and zags as he narrowed in on the scent. The oaks were thicker here, the branches forming a living canopy of green above their heads. With the trees blocking some of the wind, it was quieter, the only sound the rustle of old leaves at their feet. It was hard to believe that this quiet oasis of green was only a few hundred yards from the beach and a short drive from the shops of downtown Paradise.

The quiet was broken by Rex's excited bark. "Sounds like he found her." He checked his watch and made a notation in his log. "Now he's supposed to make his way back to us so he can lead us to her."

At his hip, the radio crackled. "Hey, Rex was here, but then he ran off again."

Alex grinned, and spoke into the radio. "Yeah, he's supposed to do that. It's okay. He's coming to get us. We'll be there in a minute."

As he finished, Rex came bounding up, barking at Alex.

"I hear you. Bring me to her. Let's go." Alex broke into a jog behind the dog, and Cassie followed. The excitement of the moment was contagious; it was like being a kid on a scavenger hunt, racing to the next find. They crashed through some low-hanging branches and came into a clearing. Rex was waiting on the far side, getting petted by Mollie.

"Good boy, Rex. Good boy." Alex took a tug toy out of his bag and tossed to it Rex, who caught it in mid-air, then pranced around the clearing with it, shaking it gleefully.

"He's awfully proud of himself," Cassie commented, watching his antics.

Mollie stood and brushed the dirt from her jeans. "He should be. He did a great job. I didn't think it would be that quick."

"He was pretty incredible." Cassie had known in an academic sense how amazing a dog's sense of scent was, but seeing it in action was another thing entirely. "Do you think he's up for another round?"

"I think so. He needs the practice, and he certainly doesn't seem tired." He handed her one of the printed maps. "Take this, just in case."

Cassie shoved the map into her pack, then patted the radio on her belt. "I'll take it, but if he doesn't find me, I'm calling for help. I can't navigate my way out of a paper bag without a GPS."

"Hey, I know. How about I go with you? I'm good with a map, and it will be more fun to hide together," Mollie suggested.

Alex quirked an eyebrow, but after a moment agreed. "I guess that would work. Lost hikers are often in pairs, so it would be worth trying. Just stay close to each other to keep from spreading the scent too far. Oh, and ladies?"

"Yes?" Mollie asked.

He winked. "No talking about me."

"What the heck was that about?" Cassie demanded as soon as they were out of earshot. "And don't give me that line about being good at reading a map. I've been on road trips with you, remember?" Mollie's sense of direction was even worse than her own.

"How else was I supposed to get a few minutes alone with you? So spill it. What's going on with you and Deputy Sexy-Pants?"

Cassie tried, and failed, to hold her laughter in. "You are awful. And nothing. Nothing is going on."

Mollie rolled her eyes. "Please. He can't keep his eyes off you. And you keep checking him out when he isn't looking. Admit it. You think he's hot."

"What are you, twelve?"

Mollie grinned and stuck her tongue out at her. The girl had no shame.

"Fine, yes, I think he's attractive."

"Hot," Mollie corrected her.

"Okay, he's hot." There was no point in denying it; just the thought of his hard body and those bedroom eyes had her temperature rising. She grinned. "Total eye candy."

Mollie smiled in triumph. "And he likes dogs, rescues orphan kittens and is sweet to your kid." She ticked off each trait on her fingers. "In other words, perfect for you. You need to go for this."

Cassie shrugged. "I don't think there is anything to go for. I can't imagine he's looking to hook up with a ready-made family a few weeks after moving here."

Mollie rolled her eyes. "I'm not saying you have to marry the man. But you could go on a date or make out or something. Anything. Do you even remember how to kiss?"

"Mollie!" She smacked her friend on the arm. "And just when am I supposed to do this? While I'm covering my work and my father's at the clinic, or during the preparation for the charity dance, or maybe while I'm attempting to be both mother and father to a four-year-old girl?" It wasn't as if she hadn't thought about dating. But moving from the thinking stage to the action stage took time and energy. And it seemed as if there was never enough of either.

"You have friends and family to help with Emma. And you weren't dating even before the accident, so it's not about that. Your real issue is that you're afraid."

She wanted to argue, but the truth was, she *was* afraid. Afraid of messing up again. Of falling for the wrong guy. Or worse, falling for the right guy and him not feeling the same way. As upset as she'd been when Tony left her, her heart hadn't been broken. He'd been an adventure, not the love of her life, and even then, it had still hurt. How much worse would it have been if she'd really had her heart on the line?

Annoyed, she tromped off through the leaves, angling east toward the ocean. Mollie stayed a few steps away. As they left the shade of the oaks, the landscape changed back to the saw palmettos and sand pines that were typical of the coastal scrub habitat. Picking her way through, Cassie made sure to avoid the sharp teeth of the saw palmettos, keeping an eye out for any other hazards. This area was home to a large number of native gopher tortoises, and stepping in a burrow would be a quick way to get a twisted ankle. They had walked almost to the edge of the boundary marked on Alex's map when she found a burnt-out log, the remnant of some long-ago brush fire. "This looks like as good a place as any to stop."

Resting against the damaged tree, she watched two bright blue scrub jays search for their evening meal as tension seeped from her shoulders. Her dad and Mollie were right; she had needed to get away from her responsibilities, at least for a few hours. And they were right about Alex, too, at least partly. He did seem like a good guy, and it wasn't right to lump him in with the likes of Jack Campbell. That didn't mean she was going to date him or anything like that. But maybe they could be friends, have some fun. What would be the harm in that?

Chapter 8

Alex kept his focus, checking wind currents, watching Rex for signs of a find. But a part of his brain was stuck on how Cassie's hand had felt in his. He wanted to touch her again. Hell, he wanted to do a lot more than touch her. But she wasn't the type for a quick romp in the sack. And he didn't date women with children. Emma was ridiculously cute, but he knew he wasn't cut out for fatherhood. His own dad had failed spectacularly in that department and he had no desire to repeat those mistakes.

Growing up with a father more interested in his next score than his family had left its mark. He'd been ten before he gave up expecting his dad to show up at his Little League games or school parent nights.

He'd been twelve when his father went to jail for the first time.

His dad tried to say it was a bum rap, but the truth was, he'd been busted for possession. He'd sworn he'd get straight, and for about six months after his release, he did. Or at least, he'd seemed to. But then he started missing work and disappearing for days at a time. When the cops finally locked him up for good, Alex had been glad to see him go. Better no father than one who broke his promises as fast as he made them. Drugs or no drugs, he'd never been happy as a family man. He wanted more adventure than a wife and kids and mortgage could offer.

Alex had vowed never to be like him. He'd chosen law enforcement instead of a life of crime, but weren't those just two sides of the same coin? Working the streets of Miami was an adrenaline rush as addictive as any drug. Maybe he'd found a better way to channel his need for adventure, but that didn't mean he was any more suited to family life than his father had been. And unlike his dad, he wasn't willing to start one if he couldn't stick around for the long haul.

Which meant there was no way he could get involved with Cassie. "Look but don't touch" would be his motto.

He could do that. He would do that. He'd wanted to get more involved with the community, to let his guard down a little and make some real friends. Spending time with Cassie could be the first step in that direction.

Rapid barking broke him from his thoughts. Rex was just beyond the tree line, impatiently looking back at Alex as if annoyed with him for taking so long.

"I'm coming. Some of us only have two legs, you know." To pacify the dog, he eased into a run. Breaking through some low-hanging moss, he spotted the women up ahead. Mollie was taking photos of something with a camera she must have stashed in her pack, and Cassie was just standing there, waiting for him. Locking eyes with her, he felt energy crackling between them. Not daring to move closer, he stopped a few feet away.

"You found us," Cassie finally said, moving toward him.

"The dog did all the work." She was almost close enough to touch, but before he could make a move, Rex pushed into the space between them, nosing Alex for the tug toy he knew he'd earned. Nothing like a slobbery dog snout to cool off sexual tension. Tossing the toy to the dog, he marked down the details of the find, then took a swig of water.

"I think that's enough for today. If we stay out much longer, we'll be searching in the dark."

Cassie looked up from playing with Rex. "Can't he search in the dark?"

"Theoretically, yes. But we haven't practiced that yet, and I'd rather end on a high note and a successful find, just in case. When we move to night searches, I'll make it really easy for him at first, then gradually build to longer searches."

"That makes sense." Mollie chewed a granola bar, then stuck the wrapper in her pocket. "Besides, I'm hungry."

"You're always hungry," Cassie said. "It kills me that you can eat all day long and you never gain an ounce. I'm probably gaining weight just watching you eat."

"What can I say? Good genes, I guess."

Alex ignored the friendly banter. He'd learned long ago that there was nothing to be gained by entering into this kind of argument. Not that Cassie had any reason to be concerned. Her athletic curves were in perfect proportion. She must look amazing in a bikini.

Picturing her in one wasn't part of his "just friends" plan, and his body's quick reaction to the mental image was anything but platonic. Hoping to keep anyone from noticing his predicament, he turned to head back. He'd only made it a few steps when the chorus of "Cat Scratch Fever" blasted his ears. Turning, he saw Cassie grab her phone out of her pocket while shooting Mollie a dirty look.

"I change her ringtones every now and then," Mollie explained. "The last one was 'Who Let the Dogs Out.' Cassie isn't always as appreciative as she should be."

"What? When?" Cassie's face went white as she fired off questions. "Did you check under the beds? In the garage? The yard? Wait, what? Oh, my God." She sank to her knees, a look of pure pain on her face.

Crossing the ground between them in two strides, he took the phone from her limp hand. "Hello? This is Alex Santiago. What's the situation?"

He listened carefully. "We'll be right there, and I'll call for backup. Stay by the phone in case they need to reach you."

He turned to Mollie, who had an arm wrapped around her panicked friend. "It's Emma. She's missing."

Chapter 9

Alex risked a glance at Cassie as he navigated the rapidly darkening streets of Paradise. She was staying strong, but he'd seen the tears that she'd silently wiped away. He couldn't imagine how frightened she must be. From what Cassie's father had told him, Emma had accidentally left the back door open and her kitten had escaped outside. They'd looked for it, but after an hour with no luck, the Marshalls had made Emma come in for dinner. Distraught over her pet, the little girl must have snuck back outside when she was supposed to be washing her hands.

Dr. Marshall wasn't mobile enough yet to do much searching, but Mrs. Marshall had searched the yard and house with no luck before calling Cassie. Their house backed up to the wildlife refuge with its acres of undeveloped land. The only good news was that the area he'd chosen for Rex's training session today was less than five miles from the Marshalls' neighborhood.

"I shouldn't have let her take the kitten with her," Cassie said.

"You had no way of knowing this would happen." They'd replayed this conversation several times already, but none of his assurances made a difference. Nothing would, other than finding her daughter, safe and sound.

A crackle of the radio pulled his attention back to the logistics of the situation. Backup was coming, but it would be a while. The deputy assigned to Paradise today was dealing with a serious traffic accident on the other side of the bridge and would be tied up for who knew how long. The main sheriff's office was almost an hour away, and the nearest trained search team was double that. Had the girl wandered off in the daytime he might not be so concerned, but given the remote location and the weather, he was calling in every person he could. In the meantime, he'd scour every inch of those woods himself if need be.

He pulled into the driveway only a few seconds ahead of Mollie, who was driving Cassie's car. Together they approached the house, where a large man with a cane was waiting on the porch. *He must be Cassie's father.*

Taking charge, he held out a hand. "Dr. Marshall, it's good to meet you finally. I'm sorry it's under such circumstances. Can we go inside?"

"Yes, sorry, come in." He led them through the door and back to the rear of the house into a large, comfortable kitchen. "I made some coffee. I didn't know what else to do. My wife's out looking for her, but I'm stuck in here with this damned leg like some kind of invalid." He slammed his cane on the ground, punctuating his words.

"I understand your frustration, sir, but trust me, you're going to be needed right here. First, I need you to get me something with Emma's scent on it. An article of clothing, a favorite stuffed animal—anything like that would work. While you're doing that, I'm going to take a look at my maps and maybe have some of that coffee you made."

The distraught man limped off toward another part of the house, the sound of his cane marking his progress. Alex wished he could offer more comfort, but the best thing he could do right now was work on finding Emma. Pulling out the maps he'd used during the training session, he located the Marshalls' neighborhood on the edge of the refuge. Marking it, he tried to figure out where Emma could have gone. The only road was the one they'd driven in on, and they had seen no sign of her. Which meant she most likely was somewhere in the refuge.

Cassie paced behind him, watching him work. She didn't ask any questions, probably because she was afraid of the answers.

Mollie shoved a cup of coffee in her hand, then placed one on the table next to the maps. A few minutes later, a sandwich joined it.

"Thanks." He took a bite and washed it down with the strong brew. When Cassie didn't join him, he looked up at her. "Eat. I can't afford you getting weak out there because you've got low blood sugar."

She looked as if she might argue, but Mollie steered her to the table and pushed her into a chair. Cassie picked at her food, but did seem to get some down.

Good. There was no telling how long this was going to take; they all needed to be as strong and prepared as possible.

Dr. Marshall came back into the kitchen with a small stuffed bunny just as the back door opened. A tall woman with a noticeable resemblance to Cassie walked in, holding the missing kitten in her arms. "I found the cat, curled up in the shed, but Emma isn't anywhere." Her voice cracked. "I'm so sorry. I'm never going to forgive myself." Sobs shook her shoulders.

Cassie embraced her mother. "You didn't know. And we're going to find her. We have to find her."

Watching the two women cry was more than Alex could take. Shoving away the rest of his food, he stood and shouldered his pack. "Dr. Marshall, can I borrow that stuffed animal? And maybe a plastic bag to put it in?"

"Of course." He pulled out a bag from a cupboard, and placed the small, worn toy into it. "Here you go. It's her favorite. She's had it since she was a baby."

Alex could tell the man was trying to be strong for his family, but the strain was etched into the lines on his face. "Thank you, sir. I'm sure she'll be happy to have it when we find her."

Cassie let go of her mother. "You're going to have Rex search for her?"

He nodded grimly. "It's the best chance we have right now if we want to find her quickly. Once backup arrives, we can start a grid, cover more ground. But until then, with our limited manpower, I think it's our best option."

Mollie broke in, "But you said he wasn't ready for night searches. And Emma's been gone nearly an hour. That's a lot longer than the tracks you had us making for him."

She was right, but there wasn't a better option. "I've been following the rule book with him, but he doesn't care about the rules. He does care about Emma. He'll do what he has to to find her."

Dear Lord, let that be the truth.

Cassie gripped a flashlight and waited on the back deck for the rest of the group. She'd stepped outside while Alex talked with the deputy team headed in their direction. It seemed the county search team was already deployed farther north and wouldn't be available until morning.

Acid swirled in her stomach at the thought of her little girl alone all night. She'd been wearing only a long-sleeve T-shirt and jeans, no jacket, when she snuck out. The weather was expected to drop below freezing in a matter of hours. Emma couldn't wait until morning. They had to find her now.

As if responding to her thoughts, Alex came through the French doors onto the patio, Rex at his side. Ignoring the hot tears burning her eyes, she knelt down and hugged the dog. "You have to find her, Rex. Please."

"Cassie, he'll find her. But we need to get started. The sooner we go, the easier it will be for him."

What he wasn't saying was that the odds were already stacked against them. Rex would be working a trail aged longer than any of the ones he'd practiced on and under new, nighttime conditions. Alex had assured her on the way over that search dogs worked just fine at night, but they both knew his lack of experience was working against them. He wasn't even a certified search-and-rescue dog, but he was all they had.

Alex opened the bag with Emma's toy in it and offered it to Rex to smell. The dog sniffed the toy, then started moving back and forth across the deck, his nose quivering. Instead of going down the steps to the yard, he circled back to the railing at the north side, where it met the house.

"That's where Emma likes to climb down from. She can reach the ground from that spot if she ducks under the rail." She started to scramble over the rail when Alex grabbed her arm.

"We'll take the stairs. He knows not to get too far ahead of us. He'll wait. And you won't be any good to your daughter if you end up with a sprained ankle."

Her face heated. He was right, of course. She took the stairs two at a time, needing to see what direction Rex was headed in. Alex's flashlight beam found the dog first, his reflective collar a beacon of hope. He was waiting at the edge of the yard, scenting the wind.

"The wind should make searching easier," Alex assured her.

And increase the risk of hypothermia. Damn it, what had Emma been thinking? The wildlife refuge took up almost half the island; there were a thousand places to get hurt or lost. "Emma!" Her voice lodged in her throat, her call coming out a raspy croak. Alex glanced at her, but kept his focus on the dog. Rex was moving quickly now, angling back and forth as he'd done in the training session earlier. In the distance, over the sounds of lovesick frogs, she could hear Mollie calling for Emma, as well. Mollie had chosen to walk the street, in case Emma had chosen to follow it. She'd knock on doors, as well, to get the neighbors in on the search. Everyone was doing what needed to be done. She needed to focus on that.

"Watch your step." Alex pointed to a broken branch she'd been about to trip over. "I know you're worried, but keep your head in the game."

She nodded. She would focus, for Emma's sake.

They were on an old walking trail, one that Cassie had taken many times in her life. Hopefully Emma had stuck to it. She'd be easier to find if she was on the path. "Do you think he knows where she went?"

"Definitely. See how high he's carrying his tail? He does that when he's got the scent."

Alex's confidence gave her the strength to start calling again. "Emma! Can you hear me, Emma? If you can hear me, say something, sweetie."

She strained her ears until she thought they would bleed, but there was no response. So she called again and again. Every step, every minute took an eternity.

"He's leaving the trail. You'll need to stay closer now, single file."

The dog had no trouble negotiating the thick press of wax myrtles and slash pines, but it was slow going for Cassie and Alex. Had her daughter really pushed through this kind of brush? "I can't believe Emma would have climbed through all this."

"She might have if she thought the kitten did. Or she could be on the other side of it. Remember, Rex isn't limited to following her exact path. He's scenting the air for her. He's going to take the shortest route to where she is right now."

Rex's shortcut had her arms covered in scratches, but she kept moving forward. At least in the trees it wasn't quite as cold. They trudged through for several minutes. Then suddenly they were back on the walking path again. Rex was picking up speed, his zig-zags getting tighter. Could he be narrowing in on her? Frantic, she called again. "Emma! Emma, it's Mommy. Can you hear me?"

Again, Rex veered off into the brush, this time angling down an embankment toward a creek that ran through this part of the refuge. Sliding down after him, she and Alex tried to keep up. "Wait, do you hear something?" Alex asked.

She paused, finding it hard to hear anything over the pounding of her heart. At first, there was nothing, but then she heard a whimper. "Emma?" Rex barked, then whined. Letting go of the root she'd been grasping, she slid down the rest of the way on her bottom. Alex was right behind her, his flashlight joining hers as they scanned the area.

There. Rex was nosing something on the ground a few feet away from the creek bank. Was it Emma? Dear God, were they too late? A sob ripped through her as she ran. Falling on her knees, she pushed the dog aside. There, curled up in the roots of an old oak, was Emma, white and motionless.

* * *

"Don't move her!" If the girl had any serious injuries, movement could make them worse. Cassie flinched at his words, but didn't pick her daughter up. Instead, she lay down in the mud beside her, murmuring something to her.

"Mommy?"

The child's voice sounded weak, but coherent. Thank God. As Cassie continued to soothe the girl, he swung his pack off his back and rummaged for an emergency blanket and the Thermos Mrs. Marshall had given him. "Here, put this on her."

Cassie tucked the flimsy metallic sheet over Emma, but the girl kicked at it, pushing into a sitting position. "Careful, honey, we need to make sure you're okay. Does anything hurt?"

"No. But I can't find Trouble. I looked and looked, and then I couldn't find me, either. I think we both got losted. Can Rex find Trouble like he found me?"

"Your grandma already found Trouble," Alex said. "He's waiting back at the house for you. I bet he's real worried about you." He placed a disposable thermometer strip on her forehead as he spoke and was relieved to see she was cold, but not yet hypothermic. "You're sure nothing hurts?"

She shivered, but shook her head. "My tummy's hungry. I didn't get any dinner."

Cassie hugged the girl, holding her tight. He could see the emotion in her eyes, but her voice was calm and upbeat. "I'm sure Grandma saved you a plate, but first we have to get you back up there. Can you walk?"

"I think so. I walked a really long time, but then my legs got tired and I sat down to take a rest."

"How about I give you a ride instead?" Alex could get her back to the house and medical attention faster if he carried her.

She nodded.

"All right. Why don't you have some of this hot chocolate your grandma sent while I call everyone and tell them you're okay? Then we'll all go back to the house and warm up. Oh, and here, your grandpa thought you might like this to keep you company." He handed her the stuffed rabbit he'd used for a scent article. Delighted, she snuggled the worn toy and curled up closer to her mother.

Satisfied the situation was in hand, he radioed in their status, then called Cassie's parents with his cell phone. They promised to relay the good news to Mollie and alert the neighbors, leaving him able to focus on getting Emma out of the woods, literally.

The cocoa seemed to have put a bit more color in her cheeks, the hot drink raising her spirits along with her body temperature. "You ready to go?" he asked her.

"Yes, please. I want to see Trouble."

Alex shook his head at the girl's tenacity. "All right, I'm going to pick you up, and you just hold on and enjoy the ride." Cassie helped the girl stand. Then he scooped Emma into his arms. She weighed nearly nothing, and he once again was reminded of what a close call she'd had.

Cassie led the way, using her flashlight to illuminate the path for both of them. This time, they stayed on the trail, trading the longer distance for easier going. Every so often, Cassie would lay a hand on Emma, as if to reassure herself the girl was safe. He didn't blame her. He was still shaken, and it wasn't his kid. Rex seemed to be the only one unaffected by the ordeal. He was enjoying the nighttime hike, sniffing trees and marking his territory. Just being a dog.

Cassie was watching him as well. "He gets free vet care for life. And anything else he wants. He's amazing."

"I think he wanted to find her as much as we did. He adores her."

"There they are!" Mollie's voice had Emma scrambling to get down. He tightened his grip. "Hold on there, sweetie, we're almost there."

They met up with Cassie's parents, Mollie and a paramedic team in the backyard.

"Is she okay?"

"She's fine, Dad, but you shouldn't be out here. You're not supposed to be doing stairs yet."

"Right here is exactly where I should be," her father replied gruffly, then planted a kiss on his granddaughter's head.

Cassie rolled her eyes, but Alex didn't blame the man. He must have been out of his mind not being able to help with the search.

"Just be careful going back up, okay?" Cassie asked.

"I will. You just get that girl inside and warmed up. I'll take my time, now that she's safe."

"You can all take your time," Alex said. "She's going to get checked out by the paramedics before anything else."

Emma spoke from his arms, still wrapped in the shiny emergency blanket. "What's a purple-medic?"

Cassie pointed to the waiting medic team. "These are paramedics. They're kind of like doctors, but they come to you instead of you having to go to Dr. Hall's office. They just want to give you a quick check-up."

Emma's eyes were wide, but she nodded. By the time Alex made it across the yard and up the steps, she was chatting about kittens with the medical team, winning them over with her charm. Inside, she proudly showed off a few new scratches, which turned out to be the extent of her injuries. Her body temperature was rising, as well, and the paramedics left her with a few neon bandages and instructions to drink lots of fluids and get a good night's sleep.

Once the paramedics were gone, everyone sat down to a late supper in the cozy country kitchen. Even Rex got his own plate of chicken stew. Emma cleaned her plate, but was rubbing her eyes by the end of the meal.

"I think I'd better get her home and into her bed," Cassie said, standing to clear her plate.

"Leave the dishes on the table. I'll get those later," Mrs. Marshall insisted. "And you don't have to go anywhere. You're welcome to spend the night here."

Cassie gave a weary smile. "I appreciate that. But honestly, I think we both need our own beds more than anything right now."

"I'll drive them home." Alex wasn't going to be satisfied until Emma was home, safe and sound. "And Mollie can bring you your car tomorrow sometime. The clinic is closed on Sundays, right?"

"Yes, but—"

"That's a great idea. You just give me a call tomorrow when you're ready for me to come over," Mollie gave her friend a hug, then left with Cassie's keys in her hand.

Alex said his own goodbyes, then escorted Cassie and Emma to the car. Mollie had left Emma's booster seat on the front porch, and he installed it in the backseat of his personal SUV, thankful he hadn't driven the department-issued vehicle today—there would have been nowhere for Emma to sit. "Your chariot awaits."

Giggling, the little girl let him buckle her in, her laughter a balm after the panic of the evening. For such a tiny thing, she stirred up big feelings, ones he didn't have a clue how to handle.

Chapter 10

The drive home was a complete blur for Cassie. All she could think about was how close she'd come to losing her little girl. She tried to do all the right things, to live her life as carefully as possible, and yet she'd almost lost her daughter. Over and over in her mind, she saw Rex lying beside Emma on the cold ground. What if they hadn't gotten to her as soon as they had? What if Rex hadn't been trained so well? What if Alex had never moved to Paradise?

"We're here. I'll get Emma if you'll get the door."

Digging in her purse, she remembered Mollie had her keys. No matter. She kept an extra in a green ceramic frog by the front door. Retrieving it, she ignored Alex's raised eyebrow and opened the door for him.

"Remind me to discuss home security with you later," he whispered, carrying a sleeping Emma cradled in his arms.

She rolled her eyes, but knew he was right. One more thing to fix, to be responsible about. "Her room's down here." Keeping the lights off, she led him to the end of the short hall and into her daughter's pink-and-white room. Watching Alex gently lower Emma into her bed, as if he'd done it a thousand times, took her breath away. This simple moment was the kind of thing other families took for granted. Turning her back, she dug through the small white dresser for a nightgown. "I'll get her changed and be right out." She needed a minute to collect her thoughts, and she couldn't do that with him standing so close.

Once he left, she changed Emma out of the dirty clothes and into the clean nightgown. The exhausted girl never even stirred. Tucking the covers over her, she kissed her now warm forehead.

Alex was waiting in the living room, inspecting the various photos hanging on the walls. "She looks just like you did as a kid."

"Thanks. I think so, too. Listen, about tonight—"

"You don't have to say anything."

"Yes, I do. Emma means everything to me. If you hadn't been there, if we hadn't found her…" Her throat constricted, the sobs she'd been holding back finally breaking through.

Alex pulled her into his arms. "Hey, don't cry. I was there, and we did find her. She's going to be fine."

She sniffled. "What she's going to be is grounded for the rest of her life." With her head resting on his chest, she could feel his deep chuckle as well as hear it. "You think I'm kidding. I probably have a head of gray hair now."

He stroked her hair gently, caressing her. "Still looks as beautiful as ever," he whispered against her ear. Shivers of awareness danced across her skin, waking desires long buried. "I thought I was going to lose it out there. I don't know how you held it together."

"I had you." And that was the truth, she realized. He'd been there for her, giving her strength, making her stronger than she was on her own. Even now, she could feel the power radiating off him. Just once, she wanted to feel the full force of him.

Rising up on her toes, she looked at him, gave him a chance to pull away. When he didn't retreat, she pushed forward, taking his mouth with her own. He hesitated, then gave in with a moan, running his hands down her body, then back up again to tangle in her hair. He smelled like hot chocolate and pine trees and felt like heaven. Maybe this was wrong, but every fiber in her body was screaming for more.

She ran her hands up under his shirt, reveling in the hard planes of his body. Needing to see him, she tugged at the fabric, and he released her just long enough to strip it off. Panting, he rested his forehead on hers. "Are you sure this is what you want? Maybe I should go."

This was her out. Her chance to stop this madness and play it safe, by the book, the way she always did.

Screw that. Playing it safe hadn't kept her daughter from being lost or her dad from being injured. And it was one night. One night to break all the rules and just let herself feel. She deserved that. She needed that.

"Please, stay."

Alex had never been so turned on in his life. He'd tried to do the right thing; he'd given her a chance to kick him out. But no way was he strong enough to leave while she begged him to stay, not when she was tearing off his clothes and kissing him as if he was the last man on earth. He'd seen her fragile and upset; he'd seen her patient and gentle. Now he was seeing her passion, and it was more than he could take.

The most primal part of his brain wanted to take her right there on the living room floor. But with Emma in the house, that wasn't an option. Lifting Cassie, he carried her to the hallway. "Which room?" he managed to grunt as she rubbed against him.

"First door," she said in between nibbles on his neck.

He somehow made it to the bed, where they stripped each other in record time, barely stopping long enough for him to grab a condom from his wallet. Then Cassie was pulling him down on top of her, arching up to meet him. He tried to take things slowly, but she sped him on, urging him with her body to give more until they came together in one final moment of ecstasy.

Rolling, he pulled her against him while he tried to catch his breath. He could feel every heartbeat clear down to his toes, and instead of feeling spent, he felt more alive than he ever had before.

They shouldn't have done this, but he was glad they had. In fact, he didn't want to leave; he wanted to do it all over again. But he only had the one condom. Grabbing a tissue from the box on the nightstand, he went to dispose of it and froze.

"Um, Cassie?"

"Mmm-hmm?"

He tossed the offending latex in the trash and looked her in the eye. "The condom broke."

"Cassie, I'm so sorry. I've never had this happen before."

She had. Once. And the evidence was sleeping in the room at the end of the hall. Alex reached out to brush her hair out of her face, and she jumped as if he'd burned her. She couldn't think when he was touching her. Pacing, she tried to comprehend what had just happened. Five years without sex, and this happens the first time she lets herself feel something? "Can you sit down so we can talk about this?" His voice was soothing, the way you might talk to a scared animal or child. But it didn't help.

"No, I'm trying to think. I pace when I think."

"Well, then, can you at least put some clothes on? Because I'm trying to think, too, and you're a bit distracting right now."

"What?"

He gestured at her still-naked body.

"Oh, yeah. Sorry." Turning her back, she grabbed a robe from the hook on the back of the door.

"No need to apologize, I was enjoying the view. We moved too quickly for me to get a good look before. You're gorgeous, you know."

"Thanks, but not helpful."

He sprawled out on the bed, making no move to cover his own nudity. Not that he should; his body was beyond impressive in every way. But unlike him, she was too worked up to be distracted by anything, even him.

"Is the timing…well…right? Do we need to be worried?"

She tried to do the math in her head. "I don't know. I need to get my phone." She crept out to the living room as quietly as possible. The last thing she needed right now was to wake up Emma. Her phone was in her purse in the middle of the floor. She took it and Alex's discarded shirt back to the bedroom, then pulled up her calendar app. "I think we're safe." She set the phone down and collapsed on the edge of the bed. She was going to be on edge until she got her period, no matter what the calendar said.

"I meant what I said. I've never had anything like this happen before. So you don't have to worry as far as diseases go. I'm healthy."

Her laugh was brittle. "Yeah, I'm healthy, too." If you didn't count the stress-induced heart attack she'd just almost had.

He put an arm around her shoulder, and she let herself lean against him. "So, are we good?"

She swallowed hard. "Yeah."

"Good enough to go again?" he teased, his hand stroking up and down her back.

She ignored the way her body reacted even through the thick robe and stood up. "I don't think that's a good idea."

He ran a hand through his sex-rumpled hair. "I know. I guess I should go, then."

"Probably." She tossed him his shirt and left him to dress.

She was waiting at the door when he came out.

"Thank you again for finding Emma. And, well, everything."

He leaned down and planted a chaste kiss on her lips, igniting a slow burn that worked its way south. "Thank you for an amazing night. Sleep well."

She closed the door after him and leaned against the cool wood, hoping to douse the heat he'd raised. Sleep? He'd saved her daughter, rocked her world and then scared her to death in the space of one evening. She'd experienced more emotion tonight than she had in years.

Of course, he had no way of knowing that. He didn't have kids, didn't want kids, so although he'd been a rock tonight, he couldn't know how she'd felt. As for the sex, she very much doubted that was an unusual occurrence. He could have his pick of women in Paradise and probably did. He'd been too much of a gentleman to say so, but she knew a one-night stand when she saw one.

She still couldn't believe she'd attacked him like that. Her only excuse was the lingering trauma of nearly losing Emma. Her emotional control had been stretched too thin for too long, and he'd been around when it finally snapped. He'd been convenient, and she'd been overwhelmed. That was all.

Any other emotion she thought she felt could be chalked up to the drama of the night. She wasn't looking for a man, and he definitely wasn't looking for a family.

So why was she crying?

Chapter 11

The smell of coffee and frying bacon greeted Alex as he stepped into his mother's town house. She'd heard about the search last night and had called to invite him for breakfast. Mom's cooking or a bowl of cold cereal? He'd been half out the door before hanging up the phone.

"I'm in the kitchen," his mom called from the direction of all the good smells. "Make sure you wipe your feet."

Busted, he backed up a step and carefully wiped his shoes on the mat. All these years, and he still couldn't get away with anything when it came to her. Once he was sure he wouldn't track in any dirt, he found her standing over the stove. She set down her wooden spoon to give him a hug, then stopped and gave him a long, hard look. "So, who is she?"

"What are you talking about?"

"You tell me." She waved the spoon as she talked. "You've got that look on your face, the same look you had when you mooned over Rebecca Stutz in the sixth grade. And every girl since." She poured him a cup of coffee and handed it to him. "So, who is she? Is it that pretty animal doctor?"

He nearly choked on a mouthful of coffee. "How do you know about her?"

"What, you think you're the only one who can put a few clues together? Everyone knows. This is a small town, *mi hijo*. There are no secrets. So tell me about her."

"Sounds like you already know everything." She raised an eyebrow, and he capitulated. "She's great. Beautiful, smart, fun—"

"But?"

"But she has a daughter."

"And you don't like her little girl?" His mother's tone warned him he was on shaky ground. She'd been a single mother herself for many years.

"No, that's not it. Emma's a great kid. I really like her."

"So what's the problem? Is this doctor lady not a good mother?"

"Her name's Cassie. And she's a fantastic mother. She was beside herself last night when Emma was lost. She tries so hard to do the right thing by her girl. You'd really like her." She would, he realized. They were both strong women who'd made the best out of the hands they were dealt.

"But getting involved means I'd be involved with the daughter, too. And if the relationship progressed, I'd have to step into a role I can't fill. I don't have the first clue about how to be a father." He sat down on a stool and stared at the floor. "She deserves better."

"Please. There is no better. You are a good man, and you'll be a good husband and father someday. Not like—"

"But what if I am like him?" He stood, nearly knocking over the stool. "What if I'm exactly like him? I'm sure he didn't think that he'd turn out the way he did, that he'd put his own selfishness ahead of his family, but that's how it ended up. I'm used to being on my own, not having anyone to answer to. What if I can't change? What if I try, and then years from now, I can't handle it and I ruin their lives?"

His mother drew herself up and gave him the same look she'd given him when he brought home a bad grade in elementary school. "If you want something badly enough, you'll make it work. You always have. You've never been afraid of hard work, and a relationship is work like any other. It's all about putting in the time and effort. But only you know if it's worth it to you."

His mother's words made a kind of sense, but acid still boiled in his belly. She was his *mami*—of course she thought the best of him. If she was wrong, he'd be hurting innocent people.

Not that he'd been thinking about that last night. He hadn't been thinking at all. The minute Cassie had pressed her lips to his, he'd been working off pure instinct. Normally he trusted his instincts, but could he now?

His mother passed him a plate with bacon and eggs and put a tray of *mallorcas*, a sugar-topped pastry, on the table. The comforting smell awakened his appetite, and he dug in, chewing as he thought. There was no reason he had to make a decision right now. For all he knew, Cassie wasn't even interested in anything long-term.

"You think too much."

"What?" What kind of comment was that?

"You. You're thinking about everything that can go wrong from now until the day you die when you haven't even been on a date yet."

His face heated, and he shoved more food in his mouth, trying to avoid his mother's gaze.

"What? You've been out with her already?"

Damn. He swallowed carefully. "No, not exactly. But last night we spent some time together after all the excitement with Emma."

His mother narrowed her eyes at him. "I'm not going to ask because I don't think I want to know. But all the more reason you should take her out, do something nice. Behave like a gentleman."

"Yes, *Mami*."

"Now finish up so you can give me a ride to Mass. If we hurry, you'll have time for confession first."

This was why he usually avoided his mother's house on Sunday mornings. But darn it if the food wasn't worth it.

"Thanks for bringing me my car." Cassie swung into the driver's seat as Mollie scooted across to the passenger side. Emma was already buckled in in the back.

"No big deal. But I have to say, I'm surprised you're

up so early. I thought you and Emma would sleep in after last night."

Cassie rubbed her eyes. "Yeah, I thought so, too. But she was up at the crack of dawn, just like always. So since we were up, I figured we might as well be productive. We can pick up the rest of the decorations for the dance and be back in time for a nap. Hopefully."

"And you're okay with Emma going back to your parents' house so soon?"

"Honestly, Mom and Dad are as traumatized as anyone. They won't take their eyes off her for a minute. And seeing her bright-eyed and bushy-tailed will make them feel a bit better. We rushed out of there pretty quickly last night. Besides, taking Emma shopping for party supplies is like taking an alcoholic shopping for booze. She'd want to buy everything in sight."

"Whatever you say, boss."

They dropped Emma off with her grandparents, who were, as expected, eager to see she hadn't suffered any ill effects from her adventure the night before. And it seemed Emma wasn't the only one who'd gotten up with the sun. Cassie's father had already been to the hardware store and was installing small sensors on all the doors.

"These will alert us every time the door is opened and they'll keep buzzing if the door isn't shut all the way. She won't slip out unnoticed again."

Touched, she gave him a hard hug. "Thanks, Daddy."

He returned the hug, then spoke around the nail he had clenched in his teeth. "I've got another set of these for your house. Thought I'd drop by and install them when I'm done here."

"I'd love that. Thank you."

"Got to take care of my girls. Now, you and Mollie go shopping and don't worry about things here. You deserve a bit of fun."

Cassie turned away before her father could see her blush. She'd certainly had her share of fun last night, but she wasn't about to tell her father that. "Okay, I'll see you later. Bye."

She walked as quickly as she could to the car, then pulled out of the drive. As soon as they were on the road, heading to town, Mollie started in on her.

"So spill it. What happened with Deputy Sexy-Pants last night?"

She coughed, trying not to laugh. "What makes you think anything happened?"

Mollie rolled her eyes. "Because you know better than to wake me up this early just to go shopping. So there must be something you're dying to tell. So tell me everything, and include lots of detail."

She couldn't stop the grin she felt splitting her face. "You mean, besides sleeping with him?"

"What?" Mollie shrieked. "You had sex with him? Last night? I thought you'd maybe made out, a good-night kiss, that kind of thing."

"Well, we did that, too."

"Who cares about that now? Go back to the sleeping together part. Is he as gorgeous naked as I think he is?"

She thought of his hard, tanned body and nodded. "Oh, yeah."

"So does this mean you guys are dating, or what?"

"I don't know. I don't think so. I mean, we didn't discuss it. Things got a bit complicated, and then he left."

"Huh? I mean, it's been a while since I've engaged in that particular activity, but I don't remember it being very complicated."

Cassie eased into a parking space behind the stationery and party goods store. Turning off the car, she stared out the window. "The condom broke."

"Are you kidding me?"

She covered her face with her hands. "I know. I still can't believe it. One minute I'm coming on to him, and the next I'm pacing the room, panicking that I'm pregnant."

"Well, are you?"

"I don't think so. I'm pretty sure the timing wasn't right."

"Wait, did you say you came on to him?"

"I totally did. I didn't even know I had it in me, but hell, Mollie. I've spent so long trying to do everything right, and bad stuff still happens. I figured I might as well do something I wanted to do for a change. So I went for it."

"Well, good for you. I mean, not for the whole birth-control fiasco, but still, it's nice to know you still have some life in you. But what are you going to do now?"

"I have absolutely no idea."

"Well, I do. We're going to shop. I don't mean just party stuff. This kind of news calls for at least a new pair of shoes, if not a whole new outfit. Actually..." she said, tapping her fingers on the door handle. "We can look for a new dress for you to wear to the dance. Something that will knock his socks off. When I'm through with you, he won't know what hit him."

Cassie sipped carefully at her hot tea and eyed the pile of bags and packages on the coffee shop chair beside her. Had she really bought all of that? They'd probably still have been shopping if she hadn't distracted Mollie with the promise of caffeine and baked goods. She wiggled the shoe box out of the stack and snuck a peek under the lid again. "I'm going to break my neck walking in these."

Mollie set down her café con leche and broke open a chocolate-filled croissant. "No, but Alex might, tripping over his tongue when he sees you."

The sharp-heeled shoes were higher than any others Cassie owned, but they were incredibly sexy. As was the dress Mollie had talked her into. And the lingerie that was so barely there she'd blushed when the checkout girl rang it up, much to Mollie's amusement. She didn't even know why she'd bought it. She wasn't planning on a repeat of last night—was she?

"So when do you think you'll see him again?"

"I honestly don't know. I guess at the dance, if not before."

"That's almost two weeks from now. You've got to see him before that! You should call him."

"And say what, exactly? 'Thanks for the most passionate night of my life. Were you interested in having coffee sometime?'"

"Most passionate night? You cannot let this guy get

away. If you won't do it for yourself, do it for all of us who barely remember what a good man is like."

"You really think I should go for it?" She wanted to believe that he *was* a good man, but she'd been wrong before. Really, really wrong.

Mollie straightened in her chair, a devilish look in her eye. "I definitely do. And I take it back. You don't have to call him."

"What? Why not?"

"Because he just walked in."

She turned, and sure enough, there he was. Heart pounding, she ate him up with her eyes. He was wearing snug jeans and a black T-shirt, the uniform of bad boys everywhere. But he was one of the good guys. He'd proved that to her, over and over. So why was she so scared?

"Hey, Alex, over here." Mollie waved him over with all the subtlety of a Great Dane. She wasn't afraid of anything.

"Hey, Mollie." His gaze shifted to Cassie. "Hello, Cassie. How are you?"

"I'm good." Good? That was her version of witty conversation?

He smiled, that long, slow smile that made his eyes crinkle just a bit and brought out his dimples. "I'm good, too. Great, actually, now that I've seen you. I was going to call you when I got home, but this is even better."

Mollie pulled out a chair for him. "Have a seat."

"Well, I was going to get some coffee—"

"I'll get it. My treat. You and Cassie sit and chat."

As if realizing he had no choice in the matter, he sat

down and watched Mollie dart to the counter to place an order. "So she knows, huh?"

Cassie chewed her lip. "Well."

He placed a hand on hers where it rested on the table. "I'm not mad. In fact, I might be a bit flattered."

"Flattered?" That was much better than angry.

"Well, I figure, if you thought it was awful, you might be too embarrassed to share."

His thumb was tracing little patterns across her skin, short-circuiting her brain. Mollie saved her from responding by plunking down a coffee cup next to their joined hands.

"Well, aren't you two cute."

Cassie smacked her with her free hand.

"What? You are. Anyway, you two enjoy. I'm going to run over to the library and pick up some books I reserved. Whenever you're done, you can just pick me up over there. Bye-bye." She breezed out with a wink, bumping the pile of bags as she went.

Alex grabbed them, but not before several of them spilled their contents to the floor. Of course, the lingerie box had ended up on top, the store name emblazoned on the lid for anyone to see. He tapped a finger on it. "So, doing some shopping, I see."

Her face was on fire. She might actually die of embarrassment right here in the town coffee shop.

He grinned, then put everything back in the bags. "Sorry, but you're driving me crazy here."

"I am?" She was?

"Yeah." His deep voice sent flickers of awareness down her spine. "But I also know that we kind of got things out of order, and I'd like to make up for that, if I can."

"Out of order?" Had she messed something up last night? It had been so long since she'd had sex, maybe she'd done something wrong.

"Yeah, I realized that we haven't actually been out on a date. And I'd very much like to take you out and get to know you a bit. What do you think?"

"What about Emma?" Damn it, she hadn't meant to blurt that out. "I mean, does it bother you that I have a child?"

His face turned serious, and he ran a hand through his hair. "I'll be honest. If you'd asked me that a month ago, I would have said yes. But Emma's a great kid. Of course, it probably helps that she's out of the diaper stage. Anyway, what I'm trying to say is, I'm not willing to walk away from whatever's happening between us. I don't think I can."

Alex waited, his heart pounding, for Cassie to say something, anything. He'd taken a chance; now it was up to her. He couldn't take it back now—and he didn't want to take it back. But if she wasn't willing to try, there was nothing he could do.

"What did you have in mind? As far as a date, I mean."

He let out the breath he'd been holding and resisted the urge to kiss her. He'd said he wanted to take things slowly, and he meant it. At least, he did when he wasn't actually this close to her, smelling the mango-scented body lotion she wore. Reeling in his libido, he focused on her question. "I was thinking dinner, Friday night. How does that sound?"

She nodded. "I'll get someone to watch Emma."

"I'll pick you up at seven?"

"That sounds perfect." She gathered up her packages and stood. "I really should get going, but I guess I'll see you Friday."

"You can count on it." He got the door for her, then took his coffee and strolled back to his car. Grabbing one of the *mallorcas* out of the bag on the front seat, he munched it while sipping the strong brew. Rex raised his head hopefully. "Sorry, buddy, these are for people only." The big dog sighed and lay back down on his blanket, content to snooze through their shift. At least one of them would be caught up on sleep.

Not that he was complaining. Every moment spent with Cassie last night had been amazing. He only wished they'd had more time together. Once with her was definitely not enough. He'd lain awake the rest of the night, his body unwilling to calm down. He hadn't felt this worked up since he was a teenager. And seeing those lingerie boxes hadn't helped.

Cassie in lingerie wasn't something he should be thinking about if he wanted to keep his promise about starting over and moving more slowly. Jumping into the deep end had made his hormones happy, but that kind of plan wasn't fair to Cassie or her daughter. He was venturing into unknown territory, so slow and steady was the way to go. Until he knew he could make things work, he needed to keep himself under control.

Checking traffic, he pulled out onto the street carefully. Sunday afternoon was a busy time for downtown Paradise, with the after-church crowd hitting the shops and restaurants before heading home. Families of various sizes strolled up and down the sidewalks, giving him a good view of what his future might look like if he and Cassie ended up together.

Watching a man with a toddler on his shoulders, he wondered if his own father had ever done anything like that. He certainly didn't remember any father-son outings. All of his memories were of disappointments and broken promises. He'd die before he'd put Emma through that kind of pain.

But for the first time, he found himself wondering what it would be like to be one of the good fathers. To have someone look up to him, want to be like him. Would he be strengthened by that kind of love? Or would he feel stifled by the responsibility, the way his father had? Being a parent meant being there all the time, forever. He'd never even managed to keep a plant alive for more than a month, let alone commit to a human for the long haul. Maybe he didn't have what it took. But the way he felt about Cassie, and Emma, made him wish he did. Maybe that was enough for a first step.

For now, he needed to keep his mind on work. He was due in for a staff briefing at the top of the hour, and the chief deputy had asked to speak to him afterward. Luckily the Paradise Isle substation was only a mile away from the café. He was able to park, change and make it to the conference room with time to spare. The meeting itself was uneventful, mostly covering the new forms the county had started requiring and a reminder about the free bike helmet program now in place. Deputies were to keep a few in their vehicles to hand out if they saw a child violating the helmet law. Alex had already handed out several since he'd started the job. He'd rather hand out helmets than tickets any day.

Meetings like this used to bore the heck out of him. He'd never seen a need to sit around talking about things when he could be out actually doing something. But lately he'd found himself looking forward to the briefings. The information he gained made him more effective when he was out on patrol, and he liked having a view into the big picture. Funny how a bit of time and experience could change your perspective. Maybe there was hope for him yet.

Chapter 12

Cassie stripped off her dress and threw it on the bed with the other five she'd tried and discarded. A knock at the door had her scrambling for her robe. "I'm coming." With her luck, Alex was here early, and would find her half-naked with no babysitter. Holding the terrycloth together, she peered through the peephole.

It was Mollie, thank heavens. Turning the lock, she let her in.

"I got your message and came right over." She eyed Cassie's ugly orange robe. "And none too soon. Shouldn't you be dressed by now?"

"Yes, and I would be, but Mom canceling kind of threw off my schedule."

"Is she okay?"

"She will be. It's just strep throat. But she's contagious until she's been on the antibiotics a few days, so—"

"So I'm here to save the day. No problem. Emma's easy. You're the difficult one. Have you even picked out what you're going to wear?"

She thought of her torn-apart closet and winced. "Not exactly."

"And when is he picking you up?"

She checked the clock. "Any minute."

"Well, I'm hardly one to give fashion advice, but I'm pretty sure anything would look better than that robe."

She had a solid point. "Emma's—"

"Emma's handled. I'll make her some dinner, and then we'll watch movies and drink hot chocolate. Don't worry about her. Just go take that thing off before your Prince Charming shows up and thinks you've turned into a pumpkin."

Mollie always did have a way with words. Retreating into the bedroom, she heard Emma's squealed greeting for her favorite babysitter. Gratified that her daughter would have a good night, she braved the closet again. It would help if she knew where they were going to eat, but Alex hadn't said when he'd left her a message confirming the date, and she hadn't had a chance to call and ask. More to the point, her stomach had clenched up in nervous knots every time she thought about picking up the phone to call him. Which was ridiculous; she wasn't an awkward teenager anymore. There was no reason to be nervous about a simple date.

And no reason to be so worked up over what to wear. Telling herself to stop acting like a lovesick schoolgirl, she chose a simple but attractive sweater and a black pencil skirt. A pair of strappy black heels that she'd purchased on a whim last year finished the outfit.

She'd just finished her makeup when Mollie poked her head in the room. "He's here. And he's gorgeous.

If you don't hurry up, I'm going to go out with him myself."

"I'll be right out." Luckily her hair didn't require much work. A quick brushing and she was as ready as she was going to get.

In the living room, she found Alex sitting on the floor, coloring with Emma. Relaxed, lounging in her living room with her daughter, he looked like a dream come true. What would it be like to have this kind of scene every night?

Whoa. Tonight was about dinner, not happily-ever-after. She was going to scare him off before they got out the door. "Sorry you had to wait."

He looked up and grinned. "No problem. Emma was an excellent hostess. She even gave me first pick of the coloring books."

Those dimples were going to be the death of her. "I'm happy to hear it."

Mollie came in, licking a wooden spoon. "Mac and cheese is ready, so I'm going to steal my dinner date away from you folks."

Emma jumped up, nearly knocking over the crayons in her excitement for her favorite meal. "Bye, Mom. Bye, Deputy Alex." Whizzing past, she raced into the kitchen.

"Well, I guess she's okay with you leaving, huh?"

Cassie shrugged. "I guess so. Although a kiss good-bye might have been nice." She grabbed her purse and checked that she had her cell phone and keys. "So where are we going?"

"Actually, that's up to you."

"Um, okay."

"You have two options. If you're up for it, I'd love to make you dinner at my house. I picked up some food and wine, and I am fairly certain I won't set the house on fire. But if you'd be more comfortable, we could go out. I've got reservations at Isle Bistro, just in case."

He cooked? She wanted to say yes to that, but could she trust herself to be alone with him? The restaurant was a safer choice, but it would be loud and crowded on a Friday night. Not exactly the best atmosphere to get to know each other.

"If you do let me cook for you, I want to be clear—it's just dinner. I'm not trying to trick you into anything else."

She believed him. That he'd thought to give her another option showed he wasn't trying to manipulate her into something. Besides, she was dying to see what he could do in the kitchen—no guy had ever made her a meal before. "You're really going to cook?"

"Absolutely."

"Well, let's go, then."

Yelling a goodbye to Mollie and Emma, she followed him out to his car, where he held the door and offered a hand to help her climb up. Ignoring the thrill of awareness that his touch sparked, she settled into the SUV. How was she going to survive an entire evening with him if just the touch of his hand got her all worked up? And why did he have to smell so good?

"Are you okay over there?"

She realized she was gripping the seatbelt like a lifeline and relaxed her hands. "Fine."

"You know, I meant what I said. I'm not trying to seduce you or anything. I don't want you to be worried about my intentions for tonight."

"No, I trust you." And she did. She was the one she didn't trust.

Alex parked in front of his apartment. He'd chosen a ground-floor unit that had a small yard in a newer building just a block off Main Street. He'd barely opened the door before Rex barreled into him. Spotting Cassie, the big dog darted off, returning to drop a rather damp tennis ball at her feet. "Sorry, big guy, but I don't think you're supposed to play ball in the house."

"Definitely not. He knocked over a lamp the last time."

She gave the disappointed dog a scratch. "Can I help you in the kitchen?"

"No need. I already made the salad, and everything else is going right on the grill."

"The grill. I should have known. Somehow I couldn't picture you standing over a hot stove."

"Grilling counts as cooking." At least he hoped it did, because she was right—he wasn't much use in the kitchen otherwise.

"I suppose it does. Besides, I'm too hungry to argue."

He was hungry, too, but not the way she meant. He'd been trying not to stare since he picked her up. She was sexier in her ladylike skirt and sweater than any bikini-clad beach bunny. Tearing his eyes away before his body betrayed the direction of his thoughts, he opened the refrigerator and found the platters he'd made up earlier.

"Can I help carry something out, at least?" She'd followed him into the tiny kitchen, unaware of the effect she had on him.

"You could bring the wine. It's on the counter by the stove." Hefting the trays of meat, he let her open the door to the patio. "While the grill heats up, I'll get the table ready. You just sit and relax."

Inside, he found the plates and silverware, and a stack of cloth napkins he didn't remember buying. Stacking everything up, he grabbed the salad bowl with his free hand and headed back outside.

He'd expected Cassie to be sitting at the table sipping her wine. Instead, she was out in the yard, playing tug of war with Rex. She'd kicked off her shoes and was barefoot, laughing in the grass. And she was beautiful.

She saw him and paused. "I hope you don't mind. He really wanted to play."

Mind? He couldn't think of anything he wanted more than to see her laughing and happy like she was right now. "Of course not. Have fun. I'll let you know when the food's ready."

Loading up the grill, he watched her play in the moonlight. He'd never met anyone like her. She was dedicated and driven, and if he hadn't looked closely, it would have been easy to think that's all she was. But he'd seen the softer side, the playful side that he had a feeling she didn't often let show. He admired how seriously she took her work and family responsibilities, but everyone needed some downtime. He had a feeling she didn't allow herself nearly enough of it.

He was just turning off the grill when she came back and collapsed into a chair.

"I hope you worked up an appetite out there. The food's ready."

Reaching for the wine glass he'd filled for her, she took a sip. "Perfect. I'll just go wash up."

"Past the living room, first door on the right."

"Thanks."

He had the food on the table when she returned. "Wow, that looks amazing."

"So do you."

She blushed at the simple compliment. He got the feeling she wasn't in the habit of hearing them. Obviously, she'd had at least one prior relationship, but maybe she wasn't as experienced as he'd thought. One more reason to back up and slow down. And maybe do some damage control while he was at it. "Listen, about the other night. I want to apologize."

She looked up, eyes wide. "Apologize?"

He rubbed the back of his neck. "Yes, apologize. I shouldn't have taken advantage of the situation. You were vulnerable, and I should have realized that."

She crossed her arms against her chest, and her chin jutted up. "You know, I'm a grown woman, and I make my own decisions. I don't need you to look out for me."

"No, I didn't mean it that way. But I also don't want to be a reason you look back and regret anything."

She paused, her fork midway to her mouth. "Do you regret it?"

"Absolutely not."

Her face relaxed. "Good. Me, either."

Time to change the subject. "It was good to see Emma so happy today, after everything."

Cassie swallowed and nodded. "She's bounced back like nothing ever happened. Out of all of us, I'm pretty sure she's the least traumatized."

"She's a lucky girl to have so many people who care about her."

"She does have that. My parents are nuts about her, obviously. And Jillian and Mollie both help out when I need them to. They're great friends, and Emma's really comfortable with them."

"What about her father. Does he spend much time with her?"

Her lips pressed together in a hard line.

"I'm sorry. If that was too personal a question..."

"No, it's fine. I'm actually surprised you hadn't heard the whole sad story already."

"I'm new in town, remember?"

"True, but once people find out you're interested in me, it will come up. Trust me."

"Well, if that's the case, it's probably better I hear it from you."

Cassie folded and then refolded her napkin, finally setting it down next to her plate. "I met Tony right after I graduated from veterinary school. I'd spent the last months—years, really—working my butt off, and I thought I'd earned a bit of fun. So I went with some girlfriends on a gambling cruise, one of those boats that goes out into international waters for a few hours."

He nodded. "A booze cruise."

"Yeah, basically. Tony was there with some buddies and we kind of hooked up. He was older and a first mate on a yacht docked in Port Canaveral. He was fun and so completely different from anyone I knew. Later he took me dancing, and to clubs, all the things I'd missed out on holed up in my room with my books." Picking up her glass, she drained the last of the crisp wine. "I thought he loved me. Even so, we were careful, except for the first time. But you know what they say. It only takes once." At the tightening in his jaw, she said a silent prayer that history wasn't going to repeat itself. "Anyway, when I found out I was pregnant, I still thought everything would be okay. I was about to start work at the clinic, he had a decent job, and we'd have our own little family." Looking back it was hard to believe she'd ever been that naive. "As I'm sure you can imagine, he had a very different reaction."

"Was he angry?"

"Not exactly. He just said he needed some time to think about it. That was about five years ago. I haven't seen him since."

"What? What happened to him?"

She shrugged and started stacking the plates. "Last I heard, he was in the Bahamas. He had some friends who worked boats down there. Honestly, I haven't tried too hard to track him down. Let sleeping dogs lie and all that."

Alex took the plates from her hand, setting them back down with a *thunk*. "But what about child support? Even if he doesn't want to stick around, he could still be sending money."

"The money isn't worth it. If I tracked him down, made him pay, he might fight me on custody. As far as I'm concerned, he lost out on that chance when he left, and I'm not going to let him come back and screw up her life. I've seen what that does to kids—having dads who come and go, breaking promises, forgetting birthdays. I'm not going to put Emma through that, not over money. Having no father must be better than having one who doesn't really care."

Chapter 13

Alex thought about all the times his dad had left him waiting, all the baseball games he'd been too drunk to remember, the school award ceremonies he didn't bother to show up for. Alex's heart had been broken more times than he could remember, and he had the emotional scars to prove it. "You're right. Nothing's worse than waiting for a parent who never shows up."

She sniffed and nodded. "So you see why I have to be careful. I can't mess up like that again."

His head spun. "Wait, what? How is this your fault? He's the one who ran out. That's all on him."

"But I let it happen. I went out with him. I believed him. I went to bed with him. If I'd been smarter—"

"Stop it." He took her by the shoulders. "You were young, and maybe you made a mistake. Guess what? Everyone makes mistakes. The difference is, you did everything you could to make things right. You've been an amazing parent to that little girl, and that's what counts. He could have done the same. Hell, even if he didn't want to stick around, he could have at least made an effort to help support you and the baby financially." He looked her in the eyes. "Don't blame yourself for his failings."

He wanted to kiss her until she believed what he was saying. He wanted it so much that he let go and took a step back. So this was why she'd looked so upset when Jillian and Mrs. Rosenberg had been talking about proud fathers handing out cigars. This Tony person certainly hadn't stuck around to celebrate or do anything else, for that matter. Angry at a man he'd never met, he worked to calm himself. Getting upset wasn't going to help anyone, least of all Cassie.

Calling Rex over, he stroked the dog's soft fur, feeling the tension seep away. "Your Tony sounds a lot like my dad. Lots of fun, but not someone you can count on when things get tough. The difference is, my father stuck around, at least for a while. He'd hold down a job, pay a few bills, buy a few groceries, then get fired for coming in drunk or not showing up at all. Even when he was working, he was more likely to spend his paycheck on drugs than pay the rent. We moved around a lot until my sister was old enough for school and Mom could get a job. Things got better when she stopped relying on him for anything."

"Oh, Alex, I'm so sorry. That had to be so hard."

"It wasn't great. By the time I was in middle school, he was pretty bad off. He went from using to selling and got busted."

"He's in jail?"

"I don't know. Probably. He's been in and out so

many times, he probably has a cell named after him. I stopped keeping track years ago."

"Is he why you volunteered for the mentor program?"

"I guess, yeah. I know what it's like to grow up without a man around to look up to. And I know how easy it is to head in the wrong direction. I had a teacher who took an interest in me, got me thinking about college instead of easy money. Otherwise, I could have ended up just like my old man."

Cassie came over to where he stood and wrapped her arms around his waist. Tipping her head back, she met his gaze. "But you didn't. You're hardworking, dedicated and caring."

"You forgot sexy."

Her eyes twinkled up at him. "That goes without saying."

This time he was the one to initiate the kiss, capturing her mouth the way he'd wanted to all night. Her lips were warm, her tongue hot as she opened for him. Pulling her against him, he forced himself to go slowly, to draw every second of enjoyment out of this. It would be so easy to pull up her skirt and take her right there on the patio. The little moans she made told him she wouldn't tell him no. But he'd made a promise. Holding himself in check, he gentled the kiss, smoothing her hair with his hands to soothe himself as much as her. Sensing the shift, she pulled away and looked up at him, questioning.

"If we don't stop now, I'm not going to be able to stop." Just watching her, with her lips swollen and her cheeks flushed, made him want to pick her up and cart her off to his room. But after what she'd been through with her ex, that wasn't an option. He needed to prove to her he wasn't going to turn and run when the going got tough. Hell, he needed to prove it to himself, too. Until then, he had to keep things from getting too intense too fast. And sex with Cassie was nothing if not intense.

She swallowed, understanding showing in her eyes. "So, now what?"

"How about a drive before I take you home?" At the mention of a drive, Rex came bounding over, nearly tap dancing in his excitement.

Cassie laughed. "Rex certainly thinks it's a good idea. And I do, too. A drive would be nice."

He took the dishes into the house, leaving them in the sink for later. At the front door, Rex waited impatiently, his leash in his mouth. Alex never should have taught him that trick. "You know, I don't have to bring the dog along. He'll be fine here."

"Oh, bring him. I'm sure he's used to going everywhere with you."

Outnumbered, he snapped the leash on Rex. "Fine, you can come. But she gets to ride shotgun."

"Mommy, I'm bored." Emma's pouting had started within minutes of her arrival at the clinic and was giving Cassie an epic headache.

"Honey, I'm sorry, but we can't go home yet. I've got a patient coming in later, and I have to finish up some paperwork."

"Then I wanna go to Grandma's house like I always do."

Cassie sighed. Emma was usually so good, but today she was really out of sorts. Her dad had what was hopefully his final visit with the orthopedist today, and her mom had wanted to be there to ask some questions. Once her father was back at work, Cassie could spend more time with Emma in the afternoons, but until then Emma was just going to have to cope. They all were.

"Do you have any puppies or kittens for me to play with today?"

"Honey, I already told you we don't. I know. Why don't we go up front and get some paper and crayons, and you can color for a while?"

"I guess." Emma started down the hall, scuffing her feet. It really was pretty boring at the clinic today. Normally there were clients in and out who would show Emma some attention or pets to play with. Today was slower than normal, and even Cassie felt a bit restless. The weather outside wasn't helping, either. Today was the first day of really warm weather and everyone had a bit of spring fever.

"Mommy! Come look. Rex is here!"

Rex? He didn't have an appointment; she'd just checked the schedule a few minutes ago. Coming around the corner, she saw Mollie tossing Rex a treat, the phone at her ear, and Alex leaning on the counter, looking exactly like a man in uniform should look.

"Is Rex okay?"

"He's fine, just a bit bored. I thought we'd stop in and pick up a few of those dental treats you told me about and pay a visit to a pretty lady." He looked down at Emma and smiled. "Seems we got a two-for-one deal on that."

Relieved there was nothing wrong, she ran a hand through her hair, trying to smooth it. It was always a mess by this time of day. "How have you been?" It had been a few days since their dinner, and she had missed him more than she'd expected. Not that she thought he'd been avoiding her, but they both had busy schedules that didn't seem to overlap much.

"I'm good. Better now that I've seen you. I hope you're ready for the dance this weekend?"

She felt her cheeks warm. "Definitely."

"That's good because I'm looking forward to dancing with a particular volunteer."

Emma looked up from playing with Rex, her eyes wide. "Are you taking Mommy and me to the dance?"

"Oh, no, honey, Alex didn't mean—"

"I'd be honored to escort you and your mother to the dance." He winked at Cassie. "In fact, that's really why I stopped by. To formally invite you to be my dates."

"Yes!" Emma pumped her little fist. "I told Mommy you were going to be our valentine."

Alex raised his eyebrows. "Is that right?"

"Uh-huh." Features falling, she scuffed the toe of her shoe across the tiled floor. "I wish the dance was right now. Then I'd have something to do."

"I'm afraid it's been rather slow here this afternoon," Cassie explained. "It's not much fun for a little girl."

Alex scratched his chin. "Well, maybe I could help out with that a bit. I'm not on duty for another hour. Think I could convince you two to take a break and get some ice cream with me? On a sunny day like this, it's practically against the law to stay cooped up inside."

"Can we, Mom? Can we? You don't want to break the law, do you, Mom?" Emma was practically vibrating in excitement.

"How can I turn down an offer like that? Let me grab my phone in case there's an emergency, and we'll go."

Heading back to her office, she realized she was nearly as excited as Emma. Not over the ice cream, but just from seeing Alex. Whenever she was around him her senses were heightened and her mood lifted. He made her feel good, happy with herself and her life. Just his presence, and his smiles at her daughter, were enough to have her walking on air. It was as if he was the final piece to a puzzle she'd been trying to figure out all her life. Scary, but exhilarating, too. And unlike her previous relationship, this time she would take her time and just enjoy things as they happened.

Grabbing the phone, she stuck it in her pocket and rejoined Emma and Alex. "Mollie, want me to bring you back something?"

The petite receptionist nodded at Alex. "If you run into another one of him, that would be perfect. Otherwise, a strawberry milkshake would be great."

Cassie rolled her eyes. "I'll do my best. Call me if you need me."

"Will do, boss. Have fun."

They walked outside into the kind of weather that made Florida famous. Blue skies, puffy white clouds and enough sunshine to remember that soon enough it would be summer again. The Sugar Cone was a couple of blocks down near the middle of town, an easy walk on such a nice day. She and Alex strolled hand in hand, Rex heeling beside them while Emma skipped ahead. Soon enough they were in front of the old-fashioned ice-cream parlor.

Cassie looked down at the dog; he wouldn't be allowed inside. "If you know what you want, I'll get it for you so you can stay out here with Rex."

"Two scoops of rocky road in a waffle cone. And thanks."

She nodded and followed Emma, helping her with the heavy glass door. "Do you know what you want?"

Emma pressed her face to the glass-fronted case, examining her choices. "Chocolate chip, please. In a cone."

Cassie joined her, scanning the brightly colored options. "I think I'll have mango. In a bowl, so I don't drip all over my work clothes."

"A good choice." Woody, the owner of the shop, started scooping. "Anything else?"

"Actually, yes. I need a double scoop of rocky road in a waffle cone and a strawberry milkshake, please."

"Coming right up."

Outside, they sat at one of the sidewalk tables, silent except for the occasional woof from Rex when someone he knew passed by.

"I swear, I think that dog knows more people on the island than I do," Cassie remarked after yet another person stopped to pet him.

"He's my secret weapon. I use him to get people to like me."

"Is that so?"

"Hey, it worked on you, didn't it?"

Watching him, sitting next to her daughter, eating ice cream together, she could only nod. She liked him, all right, more than she knew how to handle.

Getting into his patrol vehicle, Alex wondered how long it had been since he'd had such a simple, pleasant afternoon. A year ago, he never would have believed that watching a little girl eat ice cream would be life-changing. But watching her smile as she licked up the last bit of ice cream had made him realize that as much as he'd missed out on having a father, his father had missed out, too. Whatever demons drove him had cost him the joy of seeing his children grow up.

Alex headed away from town toward the beach road, the vastness of the horizon a counterpoint to the new view he'd stumbled upon. He'd always thought that his father had chosen adventure over the mundane, that the drab ordinariness of family life just couldn't live up to the lure of the streets. But these past few weeks with Cassie and Emma had been anything but ordinary. Being around them made everyday things better, more intense, more exciting. There was nothing boring about the way a child interacted with the world. If anything, Emma gave him a chance to see the world through new eyes, to find the fun in things that had become commonplace.

He'd worried that he couldn't be a family man because of his adrenaline-junkie ways. But the highs and lows of the past few weeks had been more intense than any he'd had on the force.

So why did men like his father and Cassie's ex leave? What made them give up what should have been the best part of their lives? The only thing he could think of was fear. The night Emma had been lost, he'd thought he might die himself. Loving a child was like having your heart out there walking around in the world, where anything could happen. From skinned knees to broken hearts, there were so many ways she could be hurt and only so much he could do to protect her. But surely the good times, the Christmas mornings and Father's Day brunches, made up for that, right?

His feelings for Cassie were just as intense. She made him want to be better than he was, to be the kind of man she deserved. She'd been through so much; just hearing about the way her ex had treated her made him sick inside. She deserved better. Emma deserved better. They deserved a man who would be there; instead, Cassie'd had to make do on her own, all while worrying that the loser might show up and demand custody one day.

Not that that seemed likely. In Alex's experience, men who abandoned their families weren't likely to show up years later, wanting to play house. Besides, wouldn't he be responsible for all that back child support? That would be a tidy sum by now, and more than enough incentive to stay lost rather than start coughing up money. Not that playing the odds was enough to calm Cassie's mind. She would have that fear hanging over her head as long as he was out there.

Alex would like nothing better than to go back in

time and handle the deadbeat, man to man. He hated that the creep could still upset Cassie, and selfishly, he didn't want anything standing in the way of them building a family together.

A family. Was that really what he wanted? Pulling over, he let the car and his mind idle. Images of Cassie flashed through his head. Her gentleness with the orphaned kitten, her strength when Emma was lost, her passion and fire when they were alone together. Meeting her had changed everything, and he never wanted to go back.

He wanted to be there when she had a bad day, to find ways to make her smile or share in the laughter of a bad joke. And he wanted to be there for Emma, too. That little girl had wrapped him around her little finger the first time he saw her, and there was no pretending he didn't love her. Hell, he loved both of them.

He wanted both of them in his life, and damn it, he was going to make that happen. He'd never failed to accomplish anything he'd set his mind to and wasn't going to start now. He just needed to convince Cassie that it could work, that he could make things better for her, not worse. He needed to convince her that he was worth the risk and help her let go of the past and all the pain that had gone with it.

And he had a pretty good idea of how to start that process. He just needed to make a few phone calls to the right people.

Pulling out his personal phone, he located the number he needed and dialed.

"Ramsey, Rodriguez and Cates. How may I direct your call?"

"Ms. Cates, please. Tell her it's Alex Santiago." Now to hope that the time they'd spent working together when she was with the district attorney's office had earned him a favor. Kris Cates had a reputation for being harder than the criminals she put away, but like him, she had a soft spot for kids who'd gotten a bad rap. If he could get her to listen, she'd help.

"Alex?"

"Kris, I've got a problem, and I think you might be able to help."

Chapter 14

"So are you excited about tonight?" Jillian took her lunch out of the break room microwave and stirred the spicy gumbo.

Stomach turning at the sharp smell, Cassie just nodded. Suddenly the tuna sandwich she'd packed didn't seem so appetizing.

"Are you okay? You look a bit pale."

"Just a little bit queasy. Nerves about tonight, I guess." She forced a smile and reached for a package of crackers to have with her water. Maybe the saltines would settle her stomach. Jillian had taken to stashing them around the clinic in an attempt to conquer her morning sickness.

"Oh—my—God." She stared at the package still in her hand, trembling.

Jillian's mouth dropped open as she looked at the crackers and made the connection. "No, you don't think? I mean, could you be?"

"I didn't think so. I can't be, right? I mean, what are the odds? This is just nerves. That's all."

"Well, are you sleeping with him?"

Cassie's cool cheeks heated. "Yes, but just the one time. We decided to slow things down."

"It only takes once. You know that."

She did know, only too well. Her stomach twisted, remembering. "No way. I can't be pregnant. Alex is still getting used to the idea of Emma, and she's older. Not in diapers is what he said." Head whirling, she clutched her stomach. "Oh, God, I think I'm going to be sick."

Racing for the bathroom, she made it just in time to empty what little was in her stomach. Flashes of morning sickness with Emma came racing back, bringing on another round of retching. Behind her, the door opened a crack.

"Are you okay? Can I get you anything?"

"Um, no, I don't think so, unless you have a pregnancy test handy." Straightening up, she moved to the sink. Luckily she kept a toothbrush there for days she had garlic for lunch. Brushing her teeth and splashing some water on her face helped, but the only thing that would make her feel really better would be knowing she wasn't pregnant.

Not that she hadn't dreamed of giving Emma a sibling one day. But not like this. Not now, when she and Alex were just getting started. If he'd been cautious before, he'd be petrified now. And who could blame him?

Mollie crowded in behind Jillian. "Hey, what's going on? Why's everyone in the bathroom?"

"Cassie threw up."

So much for keeping this on the down-low. "I'm fine.

I must have eaten something that didn't agree with me, that's all."

"But you didn't eat anything," Jillian protested. "You started to open those saltines I brought in, but you didn't eat any yet."

"Wait, she wanted your saltines? And she's throwing up?" Mollie turned back to Cassie, eyes wide. "Oh, my God, are you pregnant?"

"No." Having intuitive friends was really a pain sometimes.

"Maybe," Jillian countered. "You did sleep with him. You need to take a test. I have some at the inn. I can run home and get one."

"Wouldn't it be faster for me to just run to the drugstore?" Mollie asked. "If anyone asks, I'll tell them it's for a dog or something."

"You can't use them on dogs," Jillian pointed out.

"I know that, but they don't."

Cassie felt her lips twitch. Even with her world crashing down, her friends could still make her smile. "Fine. Mollie, take some cash from my purse and go get a test. And maybe some ginger ale for my stomach. All this crazy talk about pregnancy is making it worse. Then once you both see that it's negative, we can move on with our day."

Two lines. That couldn't be right. Maybe they'd changed the tests since she'd taken that one five years ago. With shaking hands, she grabbed the box back out of the trash and read the instructions again. And again. Deflating like a balloon, she slid down the wall, landing in a pile on the floor. She was pregnant. And just like before, she was going to have to figure things out on her own. At least this time she knew what to expect. She wouldn't be scared by Braxton Hicks or looking up the symptoms of colic online at 3:00 a.m. She knew how to take care of a baby. What she didn't know was how to tell Alex.

She needed to do it now before he started getting any more pie-in-the-sky ideas about a relationship with her. She grimaced. If she'd wanted a surefire way to scare him off, she'd found it. Breaking the news on a second date should pretty much guarantee there wouldn't be a third, not after he had made such a big deal about wanting to slow things down. Having a baby together was pretty much the opposite of that.

But before telling him, she had to face her friends. From her spot on the floor, she called them. "You can come in."

Both women squeezed into the tiny room. Jillian went to Cassie, but Mollie dove for the test on the sink. Holding it up, she squinted, then passed it to Jillian. "You're pregnant. You must know how to read these things."

Jillian took one look and started crying. "Oh, my goodness, you're pregnant—we're going to be pregnant together!" Taking the Kleenex a bewildered Mollie handed her, she blew her nose. "I'm sorry, honey. I know you're more upset than excited. But really, it's going to be wonderful. Just think, our babies will grow up together."

Okay, so maybe she wasn't alone this time. She'd

have her friends; that meant something. And it would be fun to be pregnant together; she'd never had a mom friend before. Sniffling, she took the tissues from Jillian. "Look what you did. Now I'm crying."

Mollie looked from one crying woman to the other. "Hell, if this is contagious, I'm getting out of here."

Laughing through her tears, Cassie shook her head. "Trust me. That's not how it happens." Sobering, she stood up, pulling Jillian with her. "Seriously, though, what am I going to do?"

"For starters," Mollie said, "we're all going to get out of this bathroom. This is getting weird. Then, Jillian's going to put the Closed sign up—you planned on closing early anyway because of the dance—and cancel whatever appointments are left. Then we can all go have some ice cream or a pedicure or whatever it is girls are supposed to do when bonding. We'll figure out everything else together."

Jillian nodded, tears forming again. "She's right. No matter what happens with Alex, you and that baby are going to be loved to pieces."

Looking from one woman to the other, Cassie had to smile. Her luck with men might be lousy, but she sure knew how to pick her friends.

Alex nailed the last board in the makeshift bandstand into place. In a few hours, this place would be transformed, and it felt good to know he'd played a part. Smiling, he pictured himself dancing with Cassie in front of the bandstand later tonight. He couldn't wait to get his hands on her, even if it was in the middle of a crowded room.

"What're you grinning about?" Nic wiped the sweat off his face with the bottom of his T-shirt. "We've been working like dogs for hours, and you're grinning like a fool."

"No. I'm not. I'm just picturing what it's all going to look like when it's done."

Nic smiled knowingly. "You're picturing Cassie all dressed up in something slinky. That's what you're thinking about."

"Hey, watch it."

Nic held his hands up. "No harm meant. Seems like you're pretty serious about her, huh?"

Alex dusted his hands on his jeans, then met the other man's gaze. "I think so, yeah. I don't know that she's ready for anything serious, but I'm hoping I can convince her."

"And you're okay with her having a kid? Not every guy wants to take on a family all at once like that."

"I'm more than okay with it. I thought I wouldn't be. My dad wasn't exactly father of the year, and I just didn't want to even get into the whole family thing. But Emma's great. Kids are great. Heck, I don't have to convince you. You're having one of your own soon."

Nic took a swig from a bottle of water, swallowing hard. "Yeah, it's kind of terrifying, but in a good way, you know? I mean, there are so many ways to screw up, but still, I can't wait to have a son to teach things to, do things with, you know?"

"Wait, it's a boy? You found out already?"

Nic grimaced. "Uh, yeah. But can you pretend you didn't hear that? Jillian wants to wait a bit before we tell people, so she can do a big announcement or something. She'll kill me if she finds out I told you."

"Hey, no problem, man. I don't want to get you in any trouble. In fact, I'd appreciate it if you didn't say anything about my intentions with Cassie. I don't want to scare her off by moving too fast."

"Intentions? What exactly are you thinking here? Marriage?"

"I know it sounds crazy, but yeah, eventually. I think it will take some time to get her to trust me, but I'm in this for the long haul." Just saying it made him feel as if he'd won the lottery—how much better would the real thing be?

"Congrats, man." Nic slapped him on the back and handed him an unopened bottle of water. "Here's to new beginnings."

"I'll drink to that."

Taking a deep drink, he realized Nic was becoming a real friend. He'd made a few buddies in the department since moving here, but it was a different kind of friendship. He relied on them to watch his back, but he couldn't see talking to them about his relationship problems or anything like that. That was likely his own fault; after what had happened in Miami, he'd kept to himself, afraid to let his guard down. Maybe it was time to work on that, too. After all, he'd told himself Paradise was going to be a fresh start, the place where he put down some roots. Cassie was part of that, but if he was going to build a life here, he'd need to put in the effort and meet people halfway.

"You going to stand there looking dreamy-eyed all day or get some work done? We've still got to hang the lights and set up the tables."

"Yeah, I'm going to help, but let's hurry, okay? I want to swing by the florist before I pick up Cassie and Emma." He was going to make sure tonight was a night they'd never forget.

Chapter 15

Cassie nervously twisted her hair around a finger, checking her image in the mirror. Did she look pregnant? Would everyone be able to tell? Would Alex be able to tell?

"You look fine." Mollie took her hand and led her away from the mirror. "Better than fine. You look amazing. Alex is going to flip when he sees you. If he's not in love with you already, he will be when he sees you in that dress."

"I don't think a dress is going to do any such thing." Although she did look good in it. The red material clung to her curves, draping nearly to the floor. The neckline showed just a hint of cleavage, but the back was cut away nearly to her waist, and a slit exposed her thigh every time she took a step. If seduction was a dress, it would be this dress. Too bad it would go to waste tonight. Seduction was what had gotten her into this predicament.

"Where's Emma? She's usually in here underfoot when I'm getting dressed."

"She's making up another batch of Valentine's Day cards in the kitchen. Don't worry. I told her, no glue, glitter or paint."

"Thank you." It had taken forever to get Emma to choose a dress; if she ruined it, they would never get her in another one.

"So, are you going to tell her about the new baby?"

Cassie checked to be sure the bedroom door was still closed. "Not yet. I'll have to eventually, especially if the morning sickness keeps up. But I want to talk to Alex first. I need to figure out where things stand before she starts asking a zillion questions."

"So you're definitely going to keep it?"

"Absolutely." There was no doubt in her mind about that. She'd had her crying fit this afternoon, but her maternal instincts were already kicking in. "It's going to be hard, but I've done the single mom thing before, and I can do it again. Besides, this time I have you guys to help."

"You know, it might not be like that, not this time. Alex isn't Tony. He's not going to take off. He's too responsible for that."

"Maybe. It would be nice if he was part of this baby's life. But I'm not going to count on it." She'd been burned before. And selfishly she dreaded the idea of working out a visitation schedule. She'd heard horror stories about ugly custody battles and didn't want to fight over a baby as if it was a prized toy instead of a family member. Of course, given Alex's feelings on children, it might not come to that.

Mollie tugged at the hemline of her dress. "Well, I'll

be there for moral support if you need it. Although I'm not sure how long I'm going to last. Why couldn't we have had a casual fundraiser, like a fish fry or something? I could wear shorts to a fish fry."

"You look gorgeous. And you're going to be too busy fighting off eligible men to even think about what you're wearing."

Mollie rolled her eyes. "I doubt it. Besides, I'm going to be hanging out with Emma so you and Alex can have your talk. Unless you aren't going to tell him tonight? You could always wait a bit before you say anything."

"No, I have to tell him before he starts getting any more ideas about us. No use putting off the inevitable. Besides, once Emma knows, everyone in town will know. She can't keep a secret for more than a millisecond."

"I see your point."

A knock at the front door ended the conversation and sent Cassie's pulse skyrocketing.

"Want me to get it?"

Cassie nodded. "Please." Taking a few deep breaths, she reminded herself that everything would be okay. Alex might be angry, but she could handle that. She just needed to get through the night; then she'd worry about everything else.

Forcing herself into the living room, her heart jumped at the sight of him. He always looked good, but wow, could he rock a tux. He would have fit right in on a red carpet somewhere in Hollywood. For a moment, she let herself pretend that nothing had changed, that they were just two people having a romantic evening. Maybe she could wait just a little longer before she ruined it all.

But the longer she held on, the harder it would be to let him go. Better to do it and get it over with. But not here—she'd wait until they'd finished with their duties at the dance. The kids were counting on everyone to make the dance a success, and her personal problems shouldn't stand in the way of that.

Alex turned and saw her standing in the hallway. "You look amazing. I'm going to be the envy of the island tonight with you on my arm."

"And me," Emma added, twirling to show off her dress.

Kneeling, Alex slipped a tiny corsage over her wrist. "Of course. In fact, I think you'll be the prettiest one there."

Enchanted, Emma examined the flowers while Alex crossed over to Cassie. "I got one for you, too. Here, let me." She held still while he pinned a tasteful white orchid spray to her dress. Could he feel how hard her heart was beating? The scent of his cologne teased her, making her want to forget everything and just bury her head against his chest.

"Are you okay?" he asked, a concerned frown on his face. "You seem awfully quiet."

"She's just worried about getting there on time, that's all," Mollie interjected. "In fact, we really should be going. Mrs. Rosenberg will have a fit if we're late."

"She's right." Cassie nodded, grateful for her friend's quick thinking. "Let's hit the road." The sooner they left, the sooner the whole night would be over, and she could start finding a way forward.

Alex carefully buckled Emma's car seat into the backseat of his SUV, then helped the little girl climb in.

Emma sat up straight as he adjusted the straps, then surprised him with a kiss on the cheek. "Thank you for being my valentine."

Swallowing past the lump in his throat, he smiled. "No, thank you." He'd always considered himself a tough, masculine kind of man, but he was no match for a four-year-old in a party dress. Cassie had already let herself into the car and was ready to go, so he climbed in and started the engine. Mollie was going to follow in her own car. "So, which one of you do I get to dance with first?"

"Me! Pick me," Emma called from the back.

"All right, you got it. But you have to let me dance with your mommy, too."

"I know that. She's your valentine, too, so you have to dance with her."

Cassie just nodded while looking out the window. She'd been awfully quiet since he picked her up. Was she worried about the event? Or had he done something wrong?

"Hey, everything okay?" he asked in a low voice, mindful of Emma in the back.

"Hmm? Oh, sure, everything's fine. I just have a lot on my mind."

"Mommy didn't feel good earlier. She had a tummy ache. I heard Mollie say so."

So much for keeping the conversation private. "Are you sick? You don't have to go if you aren't feeling well. I can explain to everyone."

"No, I'm fine. Just a minor case of nerves, or maybe something I ate. I'm fine now. Besides, Emma would be heartbroken."

"I could still take Emma—"

"I said I'm fine."

Taken aback by her sharp tone, he let it drop. Maybe she didn't trust him to take Emma by himself, which kind of stung. Or maybe she really was fine, although her color seemed a bit off. Either way, he was going to keep a close eye on her tonight. If she started feeling bad, he'd insist on taking her home.

She was quiet the rest of the way to the Sandpiper, but Emma kept up a constant chatter to fill the gap. It seemed she was most looking forward to the cupcakes and seeing Mrs. Rosenberg, whom for some reason she adored. He was half in awe, half terrified of the woman himself.

Soon enough he was pulling into the packed parking lot. Not spotting any open spaces, he idled for a minute. "Why don't you ladies get out here, and I'll go find a spot on the street."

Once his passengers were safely on their way, he circled back out and found a parking spot a block away. It seemed most of the town had come out early to be sure everything was ready. Luckily the kids were coming by bus, so they wouldn't have to walk too far. Hiking back, he wondered if expanding the parking lot was in Nic's renovation plans.

Up at the main entrance, the streamers he'd helped hang were blowing gently in the wind, illuminated by twinkling white lights. Mrs. Rosenberg stood sentry at the front door, decked out in a fluorescent-pink sequined dress and a corsage the size of a dinner plate. Waving her clipboard, she flagged him down. "I need you to help fill the coolers with ice. And then after that, the ladies in the kitchen will need some help carrying the food trays out."

"Yes, ma'am." He hoped she didn't keep him running all night; he had a few dances to claim.

As if reading his mind, she winked at him. "And then go find Cassie and her girl. Enjoy yourself. You've earned it."

Letting out a breath, he thanked her and made a beeline for the kitchen before she thought of any other projects for him to do. On his way he passed Jillian, looking radiant and starting to show. "You look beautiful. Nic's a lucky man."

She blushed and put a hand on her belly. "Thank you. I'm afraid I feel a bit oversize at the moment. My scrubs at work are a lot more forgiving than evening wear."

"Like I said, beautiful." And he meant it. He thought of how Cassie must have looked carrying Emma and was sorry he'd missed it. Maybe someday they'd have a child of their own. That thought would have terrified him a few months ago. Now it just seemed the natural way of things. They'd date, get to know each other better, and down the road, who knew? The future was wide-open.

He'd moved ten bags of ice and carried out more

baked goods than he'd seen in a lifetime before he was able to look for Cassie. He checked the lobby, which seemed to be the gathering spot for the island's senior set, then moved to the back porch. Parents and children sat eating cake at tables covered in pink-and-white tablecloths. Winding his way through them, he was stopped every few feet by people he'd met while volunteering or out on the job. It struck him that he'd made more friends in his short time in Paradise than he had in a lifetime in Miami. Not because the people in Paradise were so much different, but because he was different. He'd grown up protecting himself from being let down, but what he'd really done was isolate himself. For whatever reason, being forced to start over had helped him get past that.

"Deputy Alex, come see!"

Emma was at a smaller, child-size table set up on the part of the patio that wrapped around the side of the building. Covering the table were markers, paper and various odds and ends. Several other children were huddled around the table with her, studiously working on what must be some kind of Valentine's Day craft. "What did you make?"

"It's a Valentine's Day spider! See, it's red and has candy stuck in its web instead of flies."

Trying not to laugh, he picked up the paper. "Wow, that's really creative."

"Thank you. Now can we dance? I've been waiting forever."

"Absolutely. I promised, didn't I? And I always keep my promises."

* * *

Cassie watched Alex and Emma walk onto the make-shift dance floor and felt another piece of her heart break. Emma looked so happy, gazing up at Alex as if he was the father she'd never had. How would she take it when she found out there was going to be a baby that really was Alex's? Would she be jealous if he turned his attention from her to the baby? Or worse, if Alex wasn't willing or able to be there for this child, would it shatter the dreams Emma had built up about what a father was?

Cassie would have given anything to fix this for her little girl, but it was out of her hands. Once Alex knew, it was up to him. And he'd been perfectly honest with her about his issues around fatherhood. He'd asked to take things slow, and she was throwing them both into the fast lane.

Jillian stepped up beside her and followed her gaze. "You know, you might be wrong about him. That doesn't look like a man who is afraid of children. In fact, he looks pretty smitten with your little girl."

"I'm sure he likes Emma, but—"

"Cassie, Alex isn't Tony. You need to stop expecting him to act like Tony. Give him a chance. Go talk to him." She gave Cassie a little push. "And if you need me, I'll be over at the refreshment table, loading up on key lime pie. Just look for the lady eating for two. Now stop standing here staring and go get your man."

Not having any better ideas, Cassie started down the stairs toward Alex and Emma. Spotting her, Alex waved. "Honey, I think it's your mommy's turn for a dance. Why don't you go find some of those cupcakes you were talking about?"

Energized at the thought of the treats, she darted off in a blur of pink lace.

Alex shook his head. "Where does she get her energy?"

"Well, I think it helps that she still gets an afternoon nap."

He chuckled. "I'll have to try that sometime. How about you? Are you feeling any better?"

She nodded, not wanting to open that can of worms just yet. "Didn't you promise me a dance?" One dance couldn't hurt, right? And he looked so good in his tuxedo, she just couldn't resist. She'd be strong later; right now she just wanted to lean into him and let the music carry her away. Taking his hand, she let him lead her onto the floor and pull her close enough to melt against him.

"Have I told you how beautiful you look in that dress?"

She shook her head, not trusting her voice.

"Well, you do. You're absolutely stunning. Of course, you always are."

In a few months, he might not think so. Soon she'd be too big around for anyone to consider her stunning. Choking back her sob, she forced herself to try to enjoy the moment.

"I've been thinking." Alex's deep voice resonated through her body. "I know I said I want to take things slowly, but I think you should know how I'm feeling. The truth is, I'm crazy about you."

Looking up, she kept her voice in check. "And what about kids? You said you weren't sure you'd ever be ready for them."

"I know, but the more I'm around Emma, the more I'm crazy about her, too. And it's not like you're talking about a houseful of kids. It's just Emma, and she's wonderful, like her mother."

Wonderful. Except in about nine months, it wouldn't be just Emma anymore. Screwing up her courage, she stopped dancing. "Listen, Alex, we need to talk."

"I thought that's what we were doing." Confusion filled his eyes.

"Oh, there you are, Alex." Mrs. Rosenberg appeared at the edge of the dance floor. "I'm afraid I must pull you away for just a moment. We need someone strong enough to move some crates in the kitchen, and I can't find anyone else."

Cassie stepped back, dropping her arms from his shoulders. "Go. I should go check on Emma, anyway."

Hesitantly he walked away, leaving her alone on the dance floor.

"Hey, there's my girl. Did you save a dance for your old man?" Her father smiled, and she felt tears prick her eyes.

"Sure, Dad." Placing her hand in his, she let him lead her slowly around the floor. He was still a bit stiff, but he did remarkably well, given that he'd stopped using the cane only a few days ago. Soon he'd be back at the office, a godsend, considering the circumstances. Her parents had given her so much support when she'd had

Emma, and they would again. That was one thing to be grateful for.

"What's going on, sweetie? Are you crying?" He offered her a freshly starched handkerchief from his suit pocket.

Hastily wiping the tears away, she smiled. "I was just thinking how lucky I am to have you and Mom." It was the truth; she did have the best parents. She just hated to disappoint them again.

"Well, I'm not sure what brought that on, but thank you. We're pretty proud of you, too. But speaking of your mother, I'd better go rest this leg before she catches me down here and makes a scene."

Giving him a quick squeeze, she smiled and watched him limp up the stairs to the patio, where, sure enough, her mother was watching, concern on her face. Her parents had that rare kind of love usually found only in romance novels and love songs. She'd always assumed she'd have that kind of relationship one day, but so far she hadn't even managed a long-term boyfriend, let alone a successful marriage.

Heading for the back of the inn, she tried to smile and be polite to everyone, while inside all she wanted was to go home and curl up in her bed until morning. But first she needed to tell Alex about the pregnancy. She'd never be able to sleep otherwise. She found him in the kitchen, holding Emma up to the sink so she could wash her hands. Such a simple thing and a reminder of what might have been.

"Hi, Mommy. I ate two cupcakes!"

"That she did, although how much she ate versus how

much was on her hands, I'm not sure. I figured we'd better get her cleaned up before she got chocolate all over her pretty dress." He set Emma down and handed her a paper towel.

"Thanks. I appreciate it."

"Can I go play with the other kids now? Miss Jillian said there were going to be games on the side porch."

"Sure. I'll come watch in a little bit."

Once Emma was out of earshot, she turned back to Alex, her hands clenched in front of her.

"We need to talk."

Chapter 16

Alex carefully finished drying his hands, taking the time to fold the dishtowel he'd used and hang it back up on its hook. He was in no hurry to hear what Cassie was about to say; the look on her face made it clear this wasn't good news. Besides, he'd dated enough women to know that "we need to talk" was relationship speak for "I want to break up." He should have realized something was off when she was so quiet earlier. But he'd been so caught up in how he was feeling, he hadn't stopped to think if she was in the same place.

No, he'd just come out and told her that he was crazy about her, basically said he loved her, and then left her standing there while he played pack mule for Mrs. Rosenberg. Not exactly the most romantic way to handle things. He must have scared her, read the signals wrong.

"If this is about what I said earlier, if I came on too strong—"

"No, it's not that." She looked over her shoulder nervously. "I'd rather talk somewhere more private, if that's okay."

This was definitely not good. But he needed to hear what she had to say before he could come up with an argument, so he just shrugged. "Sure. Nic and Jillian are outside supervising the games. We could use their office."

She didn't say anything, just went down the short hallway that led to the private suite of rooms separate from the public side of the inn. A small, comfortably-furnished office doubled as a sitting room and had a thick oak door that Cassie closed behind them. "You might want to sit down."

"I'm fine, thanks." He'd stand on his own two feet and handle this like a man.

"Well, when Emma said I wasn't feeling well, that was partly right."

"Wait, are you sick? Is it something serious?" Words like *cancer* and *multiple sclerosis* cluttered his head.

She managed a sad smile. "No, I'm not sick, not really. But there is something serious going on." She twisted her hands, her knuckles turning white. "You remember our night together after Emma was lost?"

"Of course I do. It was the most amazing night of my life." What on earth did this have to do with her feeling sick? Unless… But she'd said the timing wasn't right. That couldn't be it. "You're not saying you're pregnant, are you?"

"I'm sorry." Her voice cracked, but she kept her head up and her shoulders straight. There was fear in her eyes, but strength as well. "I just found out today. I didn't know how to tell you, or if I should tell you—"

"If you should tell me?" Voice rising, he tried to keep his temper in check. "How could you even consider not telling me?" Another thought intruded. "Are you even sure? You said you didn't think it was the right time."

"Do you think I'd be having this conversation with you if I wasn't sure? Do you want to see the test with the two lines?" Her eyes narrowed. "Or are you questioning if it's yours?"

Was he? No, not really. They'd never said they were exclusive, but he didn't think she was the type to be dating multiple men. Which meant, if she was right, all his doubts about becoming a father didn't matter. He was going to be one, ready or not.

Sweat pooled along his back as the full impact of what she was saying hit him. He opened his mouth, then closed it again, not wanting to say the wrong thing. Finally, realizing he hadn't answered her question, he shook his head. "No, I believe you. I just don't know what I'm supposed to say. I don't know what to do."

Silent tears marked her face. "Well, the good news is that you don't have to do a damned thing. I've done this on my own before, and I'll do it again."

"Cassie, no, I didn't mean that. Of course I'm willing to do whatever I need to—"

She threw her hands up, determination written on her face. "No, stop right there. I don't want my baby to have a father who's there just because he thinks he's supposed to be. You made it very clear how you felt about fatherhood and having kids. I'm not asking you for anything. I just thought you should know before anything more happened between us. Now, if you'll excuse me, I'm feeling tired and I'd like to go home."

He ran a hand through his hair, too confused to argue. "Fine, I'll go get the car."

"Don't. I think it's better if I have Mollie drive Emma and me home." She was openly crying now. He wanted to go to her, to comfort her, but she would surely push him away. So he just stood there, helpless, while the woman he loved walked out the door.

Half blinded by tears and emotion, Cassie nearly ran Jillian over on her way down the hall. "Oh, my God, I'm sorry, Jillian. Are you okay?"

"I'm fine." She reached out and steadied herself against Cassie, assessing her friend. "More to the point, are you okay?"

Cassie sniffed and rubbed at her eyes. "Not really, but I will be. I just need to get home and have some space to figure things out."

Jillian's eyes filled with sympathy. "So you told him?"

"I did. And he was shocked, and confused, and doesn't know what he wants to do. Which is a luxury he gets to have, being a man. I, however, know what I need to do. I need to get my child and get home, and then start rearranging my entire life to accommodate a baby that *is* coming, like it or not."

Jillian's jaw dropped open. "He didn't say you shouldn't keep the baby?"

"No, nothing like that." Thank goodness. That might

have really sent her over the edge. "He just really didn't have much to say at all."

"Well, he probably needs some time to process everything. Even Nic was a bit overwhelmed when I broke the news to him."

"The difference is, Nic wanted a baby. You two were actively trying, so you knew he would come around. Alex and I were definitely not trying. He once said fatherhood wasn't even on his radar. So I don't think I'll hold my breath."

"I don't know if he's lying to you or to himself, but something isn't right here. I've seen him with Emma. He adores her. And don't forget, he was the first one to sign up for the new mentor program. And he's spent hours of his personal time helping to make this dance a success so that those kids get what they need. He even came and helped make those silly heart decorations, remember? Does that sound like a guy who shirks commitment? I'm telling you, you need to give him a chance. Don't you remember how upset you were when you found out today? And you had Mollie and me there with you to support you. So maybe just give him some time, okay?"

That all sounded logical, but in her experience men seldom were logical in this kind of situation. Still, she'd at least think about what Jillian had said. "Fine, he can have time. Nine months, in fact. But for now, please, I just want to go home and go to bed."

"Why don't you go wash your face and freshen up a bit? I'll find Emma and Mollie and meet you out front in a few minutes."

"Thanks."

In the bathroom, she scrubbed off her ruined mascara and tried to finger comb her hair into some semblance of normalcy. No need to scare Emma—not that her rambunctious daughter was likely to notice after all the excitement. Thankfully it was a clear shot to the front door from here, so she wasn't likely to run into many guests. Taking a deep breath, she checked that the coast was clear and made it outside without seeing anyone. Emma and Mollie were already waiting on the stairs, looking through the party favors in Emma's goody bag.

"Hi, guys, ready to go?"

"Do we have to go already?" Emma protested with a yawn.

"Yes, sleepyhead. It's way past your bedtime, and mine, too."

"Then why isn't Deputy Alex taking us home? He brought us here. Shouldn't he drive us back?"

"He wanted to, but he has to stay and help clean up," Mollie said brightly. "That's why I'm taking you home. I don't like to clean up."

"Me, either." Emma let herself be buckled in without any more protests or questions and a few minutes later was softly snoring.

"Thank you for the ride, and everything."

"Hey, that's what friends are for. That, and babysitting. All I ask is first dibs on baby snuggles."

A baby. She was going to have a baby. She'd been so busy freaking out about it she hadn't let herself think about the good parts. First smiles and the smell of baby powder, things she'd treasured with Emma and was going to get to do all over again. Her heart might be broken, but a baby was a pretty amazing thing. She needed to remember that and focus on the good things to come.

At the house, she gave Mollie a hard hug. "Keep reminding me about the baby snuggles, okay?"

"Anytime. Now go to bed and get some sleep. You look like hell."

Mollie's smile tempered her words, and anyway, she was right. Exhaustion didn't begin to describe the level of tired Cassie was at right now. Lifting Emma out of the seat, she managed to carry the sleeping girl inside without waking her. Helping her use the potty and change her into a nightgown was a little trickier, but soon she was tucked into bed, looking too sweet to be real. On impulse, Cassie bent down and gave her an extra kiss, saying a silent prayer that no matter what happened, they'd all come out of this stronger and happier. Because no matter how her heart hurt, her children were counting on her.

Alex stacked the last of the folding chairs, leaving the Sandpiper's wide, whitewashed porch looking oddly deserted after the chaos of the evening. Since Cassie's big announcement, he'd been on autopilot, mindlessly moving from task to task. Stacking chairs, taking down decorations, sweeping floors; those were things he knew how to do. How to handle the situation with Cassie? He didn't have a clue. Obviously, considering she'd left in tears.

He still didn't know what to think, let alone what to do. So he grabbed the chairs and carried them to the storage building. As long as there was still work to be done, he could avoid everything else. Maybe that would give his shell-shocked brain time to start working again.

He was on his way back when Nic stepped out from the darkness, walking Murphy on a long leash. "I'm surprised you're still here. Jillian told me what happened with Cassie."

"What happened is, I let my hormones override my common sense. It's not like I'm a dumb teenager. I know how to use protection. I let her down, and now she's furious with me."

Nic stared at him. "That's what you got from your talk with her? That she's mad at you for getting her pregnant?"

"Well, yeah. Hell, I'm mad at myself. But I'm not the one who has to go through the whole labor and delivery thing."

Nic shook his head. "You, my friend, are an idiot. She's not angry—she's terrified."

"She sure seemed angry."

"Well, maybe she was looking for some support from you. Some kind of solidarity, given the situation."

He thought back. He hadn't really offered any support; he'd been too busy asking questions. Questions that, in retrospect, made him sound like a jerk. "Right. Man, I messed up. She must hate me. First, the condom broke. Then, when she tells me she's pregnant, all I can do is ask stupid questions."

Nic chuckled and slapped him on the back. "I think that's a pretty normal male reaction. But you've got to move past that. She's going to need you."

Cassie was so strong, it was hard to imagine her needing anyone, but Nic was right. She was carrying Alex's child, and that meant she was going to have to accept his involvement in her life, no matter how upset she was with him. She was carrying his child, and that gave him rights.

His child. *Dios mío*, he was going to be a father. Knees buckling, he leaned against a tree and tried to breathe normally. He'd sort of come to grips with the idea of someday, maybe, being a stepfather to Emma. But that was far in the future; this was happening now. Or sometime in the next nine months, anyway. Besides, Emma was older. Babies were different; they had floppy heads and you could break them if you held them wrong. And they couldn't tell you what they needed—they just cried. How on earth was he supposed to know how to take care of a baby?

"It's scary stuff, huh?" Nic asked, grinning.

How could he just stand there with that stupid look on his face? "Scary? It's terrifying. I'm not qualified for this."

"None of us are, my friend. But you'll learn. Look at it like a new assignment. You'll study up, maybe do some on-the-job training, and whatever you don't learn ahead of time, you'll figure out as you go. At least Cassie's done this before. Jillian and I are both rookies. Now, that's frightening."

Despite himself, Alex smiled. He did have a veteran partner—if she was still interested in being his partner. That he might have permanently ruined his chances with Cassie was more frightening than the idea of becoming a father. Which meant he needed to fix things. The baby, he'd figure that out. But letting Cassie go was unthinkable.

Pushing himself up from the tree, he broke into a jog toward his car.

"Hey, what are you going to do?"

"Whatever it takes."

Chapter 17

The coffee and stress of the past several hours were wearing a hole in his stomach, but Alex wasn't ready to quit yet. Night shifts were nothing new, and although he preferred footwork to computer searches, he wasn't going to complain. He'd spent the night reaching out to contacts down south, working his way along a web of information. Thankfully, many of them kept the same odd hours he did and worked quickly and discreetly. A few minutes ago, he'd found what he thought was his target, and now all he could do was wait. If his information was right he'd know soon.

Too keyed up to sleep, he checked a few sports stats and then, feeling foolish, found himself searching for baby-care websites. Close to an hour later, he had a half-page of notes in front of him and more questions than when he started. It seemed he'd underestimated the number of ways one could injure or maim a baby. Everything from what position they slept in to when they had their first bite of food seemed to be imbued with the potential for danger. And that was just in the first year of life. What the websites didn't say was that there would be bullies and book reports and bad dates, and no way to protect them from it all. How could he ever have thought parenting would be boring?

And before that even started, there was the pregnancy to get through, and after that the birth itself. He hadn't been brave enough to watch any of the birth videos he'd come across, but he'd read enough to freak himself out. Of course, Cassie was the one dealing with that, but he didn't intend for her to face it alone.

He couldn't carry the baby for those nine months, but he could try to make Cassie's life easier, handle what could be handled. Which was why he'd been on his laptop all night when he should have been sleeping. If he could track down Cassie's ex, find out where he was, if he was coming back and what his intentions toward Emma were, maybe he could ease some of the burden she'd carried for the past five years.

Of course, there was the chance he would stir something up and make more trouble. That's why he hadn't followed up yet on the information his lawyer friend had sent over. He hadn't wanted to risk making things worse. But the stakes were different now. If he was ever going to have a chance at a real family with Cassie, he needed to know where he stood, and so did she. Always looking over her shoulder was keeping her from looking ahead, and they'd never be able to plan a future together that way. And if he was going to be in Emma's life, he needed to know everything he could about her, and that meant knowing about the man who had fathered her.

Getting up to refill his coffee mug, he nearly tripped over Rex. The big dog had sensed something was up and had been at his side all night. "You need to go out?" Rex thumped his tail and rose, stretching leisurely the way only animals and small children seem to do. He let the dog out and then filled his mug with the overheated dregs from the pot. If he hadn't heard anything by the time he finished this cup, he'd try to get some sleep.

As if on cue, his email alert chimed. Straddling his chair, he clicked on the newest message and quickly scanned the text. Got him! It seemed Tony Williams was now a first mate aboard a sport-fishing boat in the Bahamas. Alex's contact over there said the boat was operating out of Nassau, less than two hours away by plane. He could shower, drop Rex off, catch a flight out of Orlando and be there by lunchtime. And after that? It was anyone's guess.

Cassie woke at dawn to a kitten purring in her ear. Pushing the little gray monster away did no good; the kitten was relentless when it came to food. Her eyes shut, she tried to ignore the cat climbing onto her chest, his sharp nails pricking her skin as he kneaded her with his front paws. She didn't want to wake up. As long as she was asleep, she didn't have to think about Alex, or the baby, or the million other things demanding immediate attention. At least the clinic was closed. She'd anticipated spending her Saturday recuperating after a late night at the dance. That she'd be dealing with morning sickness and a broken heart had never occurred to her.

Sensing she was awake, Trouble began meowing.

Not a quiet, demure mew, but a full-blown meow that made it sound as if he was in danger of actually starving to death. Giving up, she lifted him off her and sat up, petting the cat to keep him quiet. She could really use a few minutes of quiet before Emma woke up. "Keep the volume down, and I'll feed you, okay?"

She pulled on her robe and shuffled into the kitchen, the kitten darting between her legs and generally being a nuisance. He was really lucky he was cute. Putting the kettle to boil, she opened a small can of cat food and dumped it into a saucer on the floor. Delighted, the roly-poly critter pounced, nearly upsetting the dish. Grinning at his antics despite herself, she leaned on the counter and waited for the water to boil.

Once she'd made her tea, she eased open the sliding door and settled into her favorite chair on the patio. The hot mug warmed her hands, and she tucked her feet up under her robe against the early morning chill. Dew clung to the leaves of her orchids, and in the distance, a woodpecker was drilling for his breakfast. This was her happy place, her personal oasis from the bustle of everyday life. Right now she had half a dozen different plants in bloom, and on the breeze there was the first hint of the season's orange blossoms.

Alex had never been out here, never seen this little corner of her world. There were a million little things about each other they didn't know. But when she was with him, that hadn't mattered. They'd shared the important things, the things that made them who they were. She knew about his father and his fears for his own future. And he knew about Tony, and the accident, and the pressure she was under. She'd thought that had been enough.

"Mommy, where are you?"

"I'm on the patio, sweetie."

Emma's face peeked around the door, her eyes still glassy from sleep. "It's cold out there."

"Then I guess I'd better come in, hadn't I?" Getting up, she took a last look at her flowers, then scooped Emma into her arms and carried her to the kitchen. Setting her on a stool, she rinsed her mug in the sink. "So, what should we do for breakfast today?"

"We should have pancakes and bacon. I love bacon."

Cassie's stomach flip-flopped. Bacon didn't sound so good to her right now. Actually, cooking suddenly sounded like more trouble than it was worth. "What if we go out for breakfast instead? We could pick up some muffins and then take them over to the Sandpiper and have a picnic in the yard. How does that sound?"

Emma pumped her little fist. "Yes! Muffins and juice?"

She ruffled the little girl's strawberry-blond curls, so like her own. Would this new baby look like her or like Alex? "Yes, juice, too." In fact, juice and plain toast sounded like the perfect breakfast to settle her queasy stomach. "We'll go as soon as you're dressed and ready."

The lure of blueberry muffins had Emma dressed in record time. Cassie didn't take much longer, not bothering to do more than walk through a quick shower and throw on jeans and a T-shirt. She really needed to spend the day doing laundry and catching up on housework, but she was as eager to get out of the house as Emma. Some fresh air and time with Jillian would help clear the fog from her head. Then she could focus and start working on a plan.

Emma kept up a one-sided conversation about last night's festivities as they drove to and from the bakery, stopping only when they pulled into the gravel lot of the Sandpiper. "Can we have our picnic now, right away?"

Cassie freed Emma from her seat and grabbed the bakery box full of muffins. "Let's go up and say hello to Miss Jillian and Mr. Nic and see if they want some muffins. Then you and Murphy can have a picnic together."

Not bothering to reply, Emma tore off toward the front door. Following more slowly, Cassie was just turning off the path when not one, but two dogs came running up. "Hey, Rex, what are you doing here?" Stalling, she stopped and petted both dogs. She wasn't ready to face Alex yet. She was barely able to face herself. But Emma was expecting a picnic, which meant there was no going back.

Squaring her shoulders, she followed the path up to the inn, where Emma was waiting on the stairs for her. "Did you see, Mom? Rex is here, so he can come to the picnic with Murphy."

"So it seems." Unless she was lucky and Alex was just leaving. Why would he be here, anyway, and so early in the morning? Pounding up the stairs to the front door, she held the door for Emma and her four-legged buddies. Not finding anyone at the front desk, she headed back to the kitchen, where Jillian was mixing up some kind of batter at the counter.

"Are you making pancakes?" Emma stood on her toes, trying to see into the bowl.

"I sure am. With blueberries in them. Do you want some?"

"Yes, please." Emma nodded, eyes wide. "I wanted pancakes, but Mommy took us to get muffins instead. Now I can have muffins and pancakes on my picnic."

Familiar with Emma's little adventures Jillian didn't bat an eye. "Then I'll make sure to pack some up for you. Just don't let Murphy eat them."

"Or Rex," Emma added.

Jillian stirred harder, not looking up from the bowl. "Right, or Rex. Listen, Emma, why don't you take a muffin out to the yard, and then I'll bring you some pancakes when they're ready?"

"Okay." Emma carefully extracted an oversize muffin from the bakery box, then headed out the open back door, Rex and Murphy at her side.

"So, why is Rex here, Jillian? And where's Alex?"

Jillian wiped her hands, coming over to sit next to Cassie at the old oak table that dominated the kitchen. "We're dog sitting. But listen, it's not what you think."

What? Where the heck was Alex that he couldn't take Rex with him? They went everywhere together. "What do you mean? Is he having some kind of work done on his apartment or something?" That would make sense.

Absently rubbing her growing belly, Jillian sighed. "No. He had to go out of town and wasn't sure how long he'd be gone, so he asked us to take care of Rex for him."

Cassie's stomach dropped. It was just like with Tony. She broke the news, and he left town the next day. It was happening all over again. Clutching the table, she felt the little bit of juice she'd managed to get down curdle in her stomach.

"No, Cassie, it isn't like that. He's not running away. He said he had some business to take care of, that's all. He's coming back." She scooted closer and grabbed Cassie's hand, squeezing it in reassurance. "Listen, you have to be logical. Even if he wasn't in love with you—and I know he is—his job, his apartment and his mom are all here. He's not going to just walk away from all that, right?"

Breathing carefully, Cassie worked to calm herself. Jillian was right. He had to come back. Alex had responsibilities here that he wouldn't abandon in the middle of the night. He had an apartment full of stuff and a job that expected him. Of course, he could be out looking for a new job and a new apartment. Just because he was coming back didn't mean he was planning to stay. "Did he say anything about what he was doing, or where he was going?"

"No, he didn't. He said he couldn't say anything yet. But Cassie, you're going to make yourself crazy if you keep imagining the worst. Alex is a good man, and you know it. You've got to give him some slack, give him a chance to prove himself to you."

Could she do that? Could she put aside her trust issues and hope for the best? Or would she just be setting herself up for even more heartbreak?

Alex's flight landed right on time, setting down on a small runway in what seemed like the middle of the ocean. Grabbing his carry-on bag from the overhead compartment, he made his way off the surprisingly small plane and stood in line at the customs checkpoint. Traveling from Florida to the Bahamas was commonplace, and the whole procedure took only a few minutes. Outside, he entered the first car in a line of waiting taxis and instructed the driver to take him to the Harbor Bay Marina.

His sources had indicated the charter boat Tony was working on operated out of that marina. The charter company's website said it specialized in half-day trips, morning and evening, which meant it should be docked for the next hour or so between sessions. That should be plenty of time to have a one-on-one chat with the deadbeat dad. He didn't want to waste more time on this guy than he had to.

Paying the driver with American dollars wasn't a problem, since Bahamian dollars were pegged to the American dollar, so both were equal in value and accepted everywhere in the small country. Finding the right boat was a bit more difficult. His information didn't include the slip number. He did have the boat's name, though, and hopefully someone would be able to point him in the right direction. Otherwise, he'd have to wander around hoping to find it, and with hundreds of vessels docked in the marina, it could be back out on the open ocean long before he finished his search.

Turning slowly, Alex scanned the marina in an attempt to get his bearings. Five long wooden docks stretched out into the turquoise water where boats of different sizes and shapes were docked. Set back from the water was a cluster of buildings. There was what looked to be a restaurant with indoor and outdoor seating, a store selling tourist-style clothing, and another, smaller shop that looked to be more of a bait and tackle store. He headed for that one, assuming that a fishing charter would at least occasionally need to buy supplies from there.

A buzzing fluorescent bulb and large open windows lighted the store. Narrow aisles offered a dizzying array of equipment, some of which he knew to be top-of-the-line. Striding toward the back of the store, he noted that it seemed clean and well kept, despite the lingering smell of salt and fish. At the rear counter he found an elderly man with dark, weathered skin and close-cropped silver hair playing solitaire.

"Need some bait?" he asked while slapping down cards.

"No, but I could use some help. I'm looking for a boat, the *Marlin's Lair.* Do you know where I could find it?"

"You looking to charter a trip?"

"Something like that."

The old man's bushy eyebrows narrowed. "Maybe you could explain why you're lookin' and then maybe I can tell you where to look."

Deciding honesty would work better than a lie, Alex nodded. "I'm looking for someone. Do you know a Tony Williams?"

"I do." His tone implied he wasn't happy about the fact.

Sensing an ally, Alex laid it out for him. "He's got a little girl. She's four and has never met him, never gotten any support from him. Her mama seems to think that's for the best, and the look on your face tells me she's right. If that's the case, I'm here to find out if he's willing to keep staying away and put it in writing. If he's not, then I need to know that, too."

The shopkeeper's gaze was sharp and assessing. "I'm thinking the girl and her mama mean something to you, yes?"

Alex swallowed hard. "They mean everything to me."

"I thought so." He smiled and shuffled his cards while he talked. "If Tony's working today, and with that one you never know, he'll be at slip fifty-six. He's blond, kind of skinny, probably looks hungover."

Grateful for the help and the silent vote of confidence, Alex said goodbye and walked back out into the blazing sunlight. Even in mid-February, the temperature was nearing eighty degrees, although the ocean breeze kept it from feeling too warm. Making his way down the seawall, he kept his eyes on the slip numbers. The second long dock held slips fifty to one hundred, and a few spots down he could see a fishing boat matching the description of the *Marlin's Lair*.

Shading his eyes, he watched for signs of anyone on board as he walked down the rough wooden planks toward the boat. No one was in sight, but there was a radio blaring from somewhere below deck. Now what? Go aboard and see what happened, or wait for someone to come out? Time wasn't his friend, but boarding a strange ship unannounced probably wasn't the smartest move.

Movement near the bow of the boat caught his eye.

Someone was coming around from the far side, a rag and cleaner in his hands. He was tall and lanky with sun-bleached hair falling in his eyes. He fit the description, but was it Tony? Only one way to tell.

"Tony Williams?"

"Yeah, I'm Tony."

"Mind if I come aboard?" Not waiting for an answer, he stepped onto the deck.

Setting down the rag in his hand, Tony flipped the hair out of his eyes and squinted at Alex. "Do I know you?"

"No, but we do have a mutual acquaintance. I'm a friend of Cassie Marshall's."

Shock and then panic flashed across the man's face. "What the hell? I haven't even talked to her since—"

"Since you found out she was pregnant?" Alex stepped in closer and caught the familiar scent of old booze and desperation. He'd smelled that same ugly combination on his father more times than he could count. Pity mixed with the anger already churning in his gut. The guy had abandoned his daughter, and for what? To drink and party his way into an early grave?

As Tony shuffled backward, his eyes darted back and forth, no doubt looking for an escape route. "What, you looking to run away again? You seem to be pretty good at that. What I want to know is, are you going to stay lost? Or does Cassie need to get her lawyer working on Plan B?"

"Plan B? What the hell is that?"

Alex smiled, his thumbs in his belt loops. "It's where

she adds up all the child support you owe, and you start paying it."

"You gotta be kidding me. Listen, I was young. I couldn't take care of a kid—"

"You were older than Cassie, and she still had to do it. Without you. And she'll keep doing it without you, but she's worried you're going to show up one day and decide to play daddy dearest."

"What? What the hell would I do that for? I haven't bothered her yet, have I?"

Bothered? How about hadn't paid child support, helped out, or made any effort to bond with his daughter? "I guess she thought you might want to get to know your daughter at some point."

Tony shook his head. "She doesn't need a guy like me screwing up her life. And I don't have a lot of time, you know, for stuff like that. I'm fine just doing my own thing, and they can do theirs."

"I can see that, but legally, it doesn't work that way."

"What do you mean?"

"What I mean is, in the eyes of the law, you're her father."

"No, man, I'm telling you. I'm not cut out for the father thing, you know?"

"Unless you sign away your rights, it doesn't matter if you're cut out for it or not."

"Wait, I can sign something, and that's it? I don't have to pay anything or do anything?"

"If that's what you want. It would mean you agree you have no more rights as her father. No custody, nothing."

Tony's face blanched. "Custody? I don't even know

where I'm going to be staying half the time. I don't want any kind of custody. You tell Cassie to give me the papers and I'll sign them. I just want to be left alone."

Chapter 18

Cassie tucked Emma into her bed, smoothing sheets that would inevitably end up tossed on the floor by the morning. "I was thinking we might go by Grandma and Grandpa's tomorrow after church. Would you like that?"

Emma nodded and snuggled farther down under the covers. "That will be fun."

Fun for Emma. Not so much for Cassie. Having to tell them she was pregnant again wasn't on her top-ten list of ways to have a good time. But it had to be done. Her father was scheduled to come back to work on Monday and it wouldn't take him long to figure it out, considering she couldn't take X-rays while she was pregnant. And she'd need to be a little more careful of lifting, as well. With her dad not fully up to par and both her and Jillian pregnant, things were going to get interesting pretty quickly; in fact, they'd probably have to hire some extra help. Nothing about any of this was going to be simple, but then, nothing ever was.

Except her love for Emma. Leaning down, she

pressed a kiss to Emma's forehead, smelling the baby shampoo she still used. "Good night, baby. Sleep tight."

"Night, Mommy," Emma mumbled, her eyes already closed. After spending a good portion of the day at the Sandpiper playing with the dogs, her little girl was worn out. Someday they'd get their own dog, but not now with a baby on the way. Housebreaking a puppy and changing diapers with only a four-year-old to help didn't sound like a very good plan.

Leaving Emma to sleep, she wandered the house, feeling lost. Laundry was piling up in the hampers, the dishwasher was ready to be emptied and there were bills to pay. All the normal things she'd neglected this weekend needed to be done, and she didn't have the energy or motivation for any of it. But avoidance wasn't a valid strategy, not even for housework. Grabbing a basket, she started with the laundry. Her scrubs and Emma's school clothes went into the washer, then the fancy smelling detergent she splurged on. Everyone said the generic stuff worked just as well, but when your job entailed blood and bodily fluids, it was nice to know your clothes smelled pretty.

She'd just closed the lid and turned the machine on when she heard a knock at the door. It was half past eight; who on earth would be stopping by on a Saturday evening? Mollie, maybe; she sometimes came by when she needed help with her college chemistry class. But usually she called first. More curious than concerned, Cassie set the basket on top of the washer and went to look.

More knocking had her gritting her teeth. Whoever

it was, they had better not wake up Emma. She normally was a sound sleeper, but still, there was no need to pound like that. Throwing open the door, she started to say so, and froze. Alex. Now, that was unexpected.

He looked like hell with bloodshot eyes and wrinkled clothes and somehow still made her knees weak. "Can I come in?"

Wordlessly, she let him pass, closing the door behind him. She wanted to go to him. It would feel so good to just lean into him, let him carry some of the worries that weighed her down. Instead she stood her ground, hands on hips, and waited.

"How are you? Are you feeling okay?"

Damn it. Staying strong was hard enough without him being all nice. "I'm fine. I have to admit, I was surprised to see Rex at Jillian's today. I wasn't sure what I was expecting from you after last night, but you leaving town wasn't it. Although, given my limited experience, maybe I should have."

Alex winced as if she'd dealt him a physical blow. "I'm so sorry. I thought I'd be back before you even knew I was gone."

"No, it's fine. You needed some space or something." At least he came back.

Fiddling with the manila envelope in his hands, he took a step toward her. "Actually, I just had something I had to take care of. Something that involves you and Emma." He handed her the envelope. "I had an attorney friend of mine draw these up. I hope that's okay. She's good. I trust her."

An attorney? Was he filing for custody already?

She took the paperwork, hating that her hands shook. "Maybe I should just have my lawyer look this over later."

"I'd really like you to read it, please. It's important."

Giving in, she sank onto the couch, tucking her feet up under her. In front of her, Alex paced with the nervous energy of someone who had passed exhaustion hours ago. Whatever this was, he seemed to have put a heck of a lot of effort into getting it. Unfastening the little metal clasp, she slid out the stack of papers inside. Most of it was a jumble of legalese, but the purpose of the forms was clear. At the top, printed in bold letters, were the words Petition for Termination of Parental Rights. Tears blurred her vision, obscuring the rest of the document, not that she needed to see more. He was abandoning this baby, just like her ex had abandoned Emma. With more class, maybe, but in the end, the result was the same.

"You didn't waste much time, did you?"

"When something needs to be done, I do it. I thought you'd be grateful to have things wrapped up, finally."

Finally? It had been only one day. He'd found out she was pregnant and found a lawyer to write up papers to rid himself of the problem in one day. And on a weekend, no less. He couldn't even wait until Monday, when the offices would be open. No, he went God knows where to track down someone who could do it on a Saturday. So much for giving him the benefit of the doubt or thinking he was too responsible to walk out on his own child. She should have been listening to his words, not her heart. He'd told her he wasn't ready to be a father and now he wanted to put it in writing.

Shoving up from the couch, she threw the papers down, resisting the petty urge to stomp on them. "You can take your damn papers, Alex. I'm not signing anything."

"What?" Alex stood amid the papers scattered on the floor and tried to figure out when the woman he loved had completely lost her mind. Her face was flushed with anger and if looks could kill, he'd need his Kevlar vest. Was she upset that he'd gotten involved in her private life? Or had she been wanting her ex to come back, after all? "I thought this was what you wanted."

Her eyes grew wider as she stared at him, tears streaming down her face. "What? Why would you think I wanted this?"

"Well, when we talked about Emma and her father, you said you worried he'd come back one day—"

"So you decided to make sure I never had to worry about that with you?" She stomped off to the kitchen and he followed at a cautious distance. Knives were in the kitchen, after all. She'd filled the kettle and set it on the stove before her words penetrated his brain.

"Wait, what? What do you mean, worry about it with me? What does this have to do with us?"

She slammed her mug down so hard, he half expected it to crack in her hand. "Signing away your rights to this baby has everything to do with us. How on earth can you think otherwise?"

His rights? "I'm not signing anything away."

Exasperated, she pointed back at the living room. "Then why did you get the papers drawn up? Are you just messing with me? Because it's not funny."

His sleep-deprived brain finally started to make the connection. "You think the papers are about our baby?"

"Who else would they be for?"

Rounding the counter, he put his hands on her shoulders, steadying her. "Tony signed those, not me. I tracked him down, and he's willing to give up his rights, permanently."

Cassie went boneless under his hands, nearly collapsing. Propping her up, he led her to a stool at the counter before letting her go to turn off the now-screeching kettle.

"You found Tony? When? How?" Blinking rapidly, she stared at him. "And more than that, why? Why would you do that?"

"One thing at a time." He poured the water into her mug and added a tea bag from the canister on the counter. Pushing it toward her, he sat down on the other stool. "I started looking for him a little while ago. I have some contacts down south, private investigators and such, and I thought they might be able to track him down. And I talked to a woman I know from the district attorney's office in Miami. She works for a private practice now and has a reputation for protecting kids. I wanted to find out what the options were—she's the one who drew up the legal forms. When you told me you were pregnant I decided to push forward."

Emma swallowed hard. "Don't you think you should have discussed this with me first?"

"Maybe. Probably. But at first I didn't know where he was. And then, last night—well, you weren't in the mood to discuss things. Besides, I didn't want to get your hopes up if I couldn't find him. But I did find him, working on a boat in the Bahamas. He's been there ever since he left, probably afraid that if he came back to the States, you'd make him pay child support."

"So that's where you were today? You flew to the Bahamas?"

He nodded.

She rubbed at her eyes, exhaustion showing on her face. She didn't look as if she'd slept much more than he had. "We can talk about it tomorrow," he said, "if you're too tired—"

"No. I want to know the whole story. What did you say to him? What did he say? What does he want?"

"I told him I knew you and his daughter, and you deserved to know if he was coming back. I also reminded him that he owed quite a bit of child support. As for what he wants, he just wants to be left alone. He has no interest in custody or anything else and said to tell you he'd sign whatever he has to sign."

"So that's it? He signed the papers and he's out of our lives for good?"

"Basically, yeah. I mean, the judge has to approve it, but given the circumstances it shouldn't be a problem."

"I know I should say thank you, but I can't even wrap my head around this yet. And the dumb thing is, part of me is sad. Not because I want to see him," she added quickly. "But it sucks that he couldn't pull it together enough to be there for her, that he doesn't even want to know her or anything."

"That's not dumb at all. It is sad, but from where I sit, he's the one missing out." He placed his hand on hers, stroking her soft skin with this thumb. "No man in his right mind could walk away from you and Emma."

Cassie's pulse pounded in her ears. Was he trying to say he wasn't going to walk away? This was way too much information way too fast, and she couldn't think straight with him touching her. Pulling her hand away, she stood up and headed for the patio. Maybe some fresh air would help her clear her mind so she could make sense of everything.

Behind her, she heard Alex let out a low whistle as he stepped outside. "This is amazing."

Smiling, she sat down on her favorite chair. "It is pretty wonderful, isn't it?"

"It's like something out of a magazine. You could charge admission."

She gave a mock shudder at the thought. "I don't think so. This is where I come to get away from everything. No tourists allowed."

"Well, then, I'm honored to be allowed into the inner sanctuary."

"You should be," she said with a grin. It was crazy how easy he was to be around. After all the stress of the day and the shock of his news, she should have been a basket case. But being near him somehow helped put her mind at ease. Which *was* crazy, considering most of her stress could be traced back to him.

"Are you okay? I know this was what you wanted, but like you said, it's still a big deal."

"I'll be okay. But I have to know. What made you decide to get involved? Why go to all this trouble?"

He pulled a chair over, the metal legs scraping across the concrete. As he sat down, his brown eyes shone with an intensity she hadn't seen before. "I didn't decide to get involved. I already am involved. Up to my eyebrows. But I knew you couldn't move forward—we couldn't move forward—if you were constantly looking over your shoulder, waiting for your past to show up and ruin things. I wanted to give us a fresh start."

"Us?"

He leaned closer, taking both of her hands in his. "Yes, us. You, me, Emma…and the baby. Our baby. Whatever happens, I'm not running away. I'm not your ex, and I'm not my father."

"But…" Her brain stuttered and stalled. "I thought you didn't want children. You said you were scared—"

"I am scared. Hell, I'm terrified." He grinned and squeezed her hands. "But just because something is scary doesn't mean I'm going to turn tail and run. I've faced down drug dealers and gang bangers. I think I can handle an unarmed baby."

"Really?"

"Really. I admit the idea of being a father frightens me. But you know what frightens me more?"

She shook her head, emotion a lump in her throat.

"Losing my chance with you."

"You still want to be with me?" Maybe she'd heard

wrong, misunderstood. She'd been doing a lot of that lately.

"If you'll have me." His voice was rough but sensual, like the ocean during a storm. Goose bumps dotted her arms as if he was already touching her.

"You're sure?" she whispered, afraid of breaking the spell if she spoke too loudly or moved too quickly.

Alex's words, on the other hand, were loud and clear. "I've never been more sure of anything in my life." He drew her into his lap, settling her against the hard planes of his body. "I'm not saying it's going to be easy. I don't know how it's all going to work, but I know that I want to try."

Curling into him, she let herself feel all the things she'd been denying. He was there, he wasn't leaving and he felt so very good pressed against her in the dark. Turning her head toward him, she looked for something in his eyes to tell her this was a mistake. But all she saw were sincerity, trust and a longing that matched her own. He'd made no promises for the future, but his pledge to try meant more than any declaration of love could. Honesty was what she needed, not pretty words.

"Would it be okay if I kiss you now? I've been dying to since our dance last night." His breath tickled her ear as he spoke, sending little sparks up and down her spine.

In answer, she reached up and brought his lips down hard on hers, kissing him with all the pent-up fear and hope and worry and love that had tangled her up in knots. He met her intensity with his own heat and passion. Everything she didn't know how to say, she said with her lips against his, her body molding against him.

Only when she was afraid she might actually explode with need did she pull away, panting in his arms.

"Wow." His eyes had gone nearly black under the starlight, and she could feel his heart pounding through his chest. "If leaving town for the day results in that kind of treatment, I'm going to be gone a whole lot."

She smacked him on the arm. "Not funny."

He winced. "I suppose not. Chalk it up to my lack of sleep. I'm running on empty, and as good as that kiss was, I should get myself home before I'm too tired to drive."

He was leaving already? She'd pictured something much more…well…intimate happening. "You could stay."

"I can't. I called Nic when I landed and told him I'd be by soon to pick up Rex. Besides, there's Emma. I don't want our first conversation about us to be when she wakes up and finds me in your bed. That's not fair to her."

She sighed. "You're right. I don't want that, either. You just make me so crazy, I can't think straight."

"Good." He kissed the tip of her nose. "I love that you're just as affected as I am. Now, you're going to have to get out of my lap or I'm never going to be able to make myself go."

Sliding out of his lap, she could feel exactly how much he wanted to stay. "When will I see you again?"

"Is tomorrow soon enough?"

Alex watched Cassie's face turn serious. "Actually, we have plans tomorrow."

"Oh." Maybe he'd read her wrong and she was still mad?

"No, don't be upset. I do want to see you, but we are going to my parents' house tomorrow after church." She laid a hand on her still-flat belly. "I need to tell them about the baby."

"Tomorrow?" Heck, he'd just found out himself; he'd thought he would have a little time to get used to the idea before they started telling people. Not that he was ashamed, but he would have liked to have a plan, and ideally a ring, before that news got out.

Cassie grimaced. "I know. I'm not wild about everyone finding out, either. But my dad's coming back to work on Monday, and I won't be able to hide it. There are safety issues, with radiation and anesthesia and such."

He hadn't even thought of that. He'd been so wrapped up in his own baggage, he hadn't even considered how she would juggle the pregnancy with her career. "Is it safe for you to keep working? Because if it's about the money, I can—"

"Don't worry. I'll be safe. I just have to take a few extra precautions. Which means I have to tell my dad now, and he can't keep a secret from my mom to save his life, so I might as well tell both of them at once. I'm not exactly looking forward to it, but it is what it is. They need to know. Might as well get it over with."

"Then I'll go with you." This was as much his doing as hers, and if she was brave enough to face her parents, the least he could do was be there to support her.

"What? No, you don't have to do that."

"I know I don't have to, but I want to. I should be

there for you. And your parents need to know that I'm going to be a part of this baby's life, and yours, if you let me. After Tony, I think I may have my work cut out for me."

She grinned. "They already love you. After you found Emma...trust me, liking you isn't a problem. I'm the one that they'll be disappointed in. Again."

"You've got to be kidding me. How could anyone be disappointed in you? You've raised an amazing little girl on your own and made an impressive career for yourself. I can't imagine they are anything but impressed by you."

Shadows clouded her eyes, but she nodded. "Maybe. We'll see, I guess. But are you sure you want to do this?"

Did he want to? Not exactly. But she needed to do this, so he needed to be there. They were a team now, whether she realized it or not. "I'll be there. Just tell me when and where."

"We'll go after the ten o'clock service, if that's all right. Emma doesn't want to miss Sunday school."

"I'll be there. I already arranged to have the rest of the weekend off."

"Well, okay, then." She looked at the door, then at him, as if trying to find another reason for him to stay. A feeling he shared, but couldn't give in to. But if he had his way, there wouldn't be too many more late-night goodbyes.

"Good night, Cassie." He gave her a soft, lingering kiss that only reminded him how much he wanted to stay. Still tasting her, he pressed a hand to her belly.

"Good night, baby. Don't give your mama too hard a time, okay?"

Cassie bit her lip, tears shining in her eyes. He hated that she was so surprised by the smallest bit of affection from him. Knowing how hurt she'd been made him want to go right back to the Bahamas and feed Tony to the sharks. Giving her one last quick kiss on the forehead, he let himself out while he still could.

Outside the stars were shining as if they'd been polished, each a bright pinprick of light against the dark island sky. Getting in the truck, he wondered again at the circumstances that had brought him here. If his partner hadn't screwed up, if he and his fellow officers hadn't betrayed him, if the Palmetto County sheriff's office hadn't had an opening at just the right time, he might never have come to Paradise, never met Cassie or Emma. Now, driving through the quiet streets on the way to pick up his dog, he couldn't imagine living anywhere else.

Paradise had given him a place to lick his wounds, to start over. But the island was more than a temporary sanctuary; it had become a real home. Maybe part of that was meeting Cassie; it was hard to say. Both the woman and the place had seduced him, and he had no intentions of letting go of either one.

At the Sandpiper, he walked quietly up the stairs and through the front door. The front desk was vacant, but lying in front of the fireplace in the main lobby were Rex and Murphy, both passed out. In a similar state, Nic was sprawled on one of the loveseats, eyes closed and an open book on his chest. The dogs noticed Alex first. Rex stretched like a cat, then rolled over for a belly rub. "Wow, I'm gone all day and you don't even bother to get up and say hello?"

A rumble from the couch drew his attention back to Nic, who was now sitting up and rubbing his eyes. "So, how did it go? Did you find him?"

"I did. I even got a bit of help from a local. It seems he's not very well liked down there."

"Imagine that." Nic stood and stretched. "So, what did he say?"

"He signed away his rights. He'd do anything to avoid paying all the child support he owes. You know, he didn't even ask about Emma. Didn't want to know how she's doing or see a picture. Nothing." At least Alex's old man had tried. He'd cared, but it just hadn't been enough. "If nothing else, I can understand now why Cassie was so sure Emma was better off without him."

Nic nodded and walked to the kitchen, snagging a couple of sodas from the fridge and handing one to Alex. "How did Cassie take the news?"

"Not well at first. She saw the papers and thought I was giving up my rights to our baby."

"Oh, wow. Way to mess that up."

"No kidding. But once I explained, everything was fine. Better than fine." He smiled, thinking of that amazing kiss on the patio.

"Hot damn, good for you. So, when's the wedding?"

Alex coughed, spewing soda down the front of his shirt. Nic laughed and handed him a towel.

"Don't tell me you haven't thought about it. Remember, I proposed to Jillian not long ago, so I know the signs."

No point in pretending. "Fine, yes, I'm thinking about it. But I don't know if she's ready yet. I want things to be right."

"Dude, she's in love with you and she's pregnant with your child. What else are you waiting for?"

Chapter 19

Nic's words haunted him. Tossing and turning all night, he asked himself this: What was he waiting for? He loved her. He was certain of that. And he wanted them to be a family. Fatherhood hadn't been the plan, but if he was going to do it, he wanted to do it right. Part-time wasn't enough, not after all the time he'd missed out on with his own father. He wanted to be there when Cassie felt the first kicks, to rub her feet when they hurt or buy her ice cream when she craved it. And most of all, he wanted to make love to her every night and wake up to her soft body against his each morning.

Which was why he was up and knocking on his mother's door at what felt like the break of dawn. Scratching at his two-day beard, he waited for the door to open. Hopefully he'd caught her before she left for Mass.

"Alex?" His mother's worried face appeared at the open door. "What are you doing here so early? Is everything okay?"

"It's fine, Mama. I just needed to talk to you about something."

Relaxing, she accepted a hug and shooed him toward the kitchen. "There's coffee ready, and I'll make us some breakfast while you tell me what's so important."

"Just coffee, please. I'm not hungry."

She pinned him with a hard stare. "Not hungry? Are you sick?"

"No, Mama, I'm not sick. I'm fine, in fact. I promise."

She scrutinized him as if looking for some sign of illness before turning away to pour the coffee. "This is about your animal-doctor friend, then, yes?"

How did she always know? He accepted the cup of strong, rich coffee and took a sip, waiting for her to sit at the table with him. Instead, she stood over him, watching with the same sharp gaze that had intimidated him as a child. This time, however, he wasn't confessing some childish sin.

"So? What is it that has you so tied up in knots you can't even eat your mama's cooking? Did you mess things up with her? Because if you did, you need to face up to it and make it right."

There was no way to say this, other than just to say it. "She's pregnant, Mama."

His mother narrowed her lips, considering. "And are you the father?"

"Yes, ma'am." He was in for it now; he'd sat through enough lectures as a teenager to know her feelings about premarital sex and unintended pregnancies.

"Oh, Alex." Tears filled her eyes as she smiled. "A baby? I'm going to be a grandmother?"

Stunned, he nodded as she fanned her eyes. Wasn't she supposed to be yelling at him? "I thought you'd be upset. Because of what the Church says and—"

"The Church says babies are a blessing. And that's what this baby will be. Anything else is water under the bridge."

The knotted muscles in his shoulders released a bit. He hadn't quite realized how worried he'd been about her reaction until now. "Thank you for being so supportive. It means a lot."

She smacked his shoulder, tears still slipping down her face. "Don't be silly. I'm your mama. Now, are you ready for breakfast, or is there more?"

"Well, there is one other thing." He grinned. "I wanted to ask about Grandma's ring. I'm going to ask Cassie to marry me."

His mother wrapped her arms around him, nearly smothering him in her enthusiasm. "Mom, you're choking me."

She gave a final squeeze, then stood up, smiling as if he'd won the Nobel Prize and the World Series all on the same day. "A wedding and a baby. The ladies at the senior center are going to be so jealous."

"You're going to have to hold off on bragging for now. She hasn't said yes yet. And she doesn't want to tell people about the pregnancy right away, I don't think. We haven't even told her parents yet. I'm meeting her over there for lunch."

Her face fell a bit, but she nodded. "Then I'll wait. Oh, let me go get you the ring."

He finished his coffee while she rummaged in her bedroom. Who'd have thought his strict, super-religious mother would have reacted so well? He knew he was doing the right thing, but it was nice to know he had her support.

"Here you are. Your grandfather gave it to your grandmother, and she gave it to me. Now you will give it to Cassie." She placed the small plain box on the table in front of him. Opening it, he found the ring as he remembered it—a brilliant round diamond resting in an antique setting. Hand-wrought scrollwork covered the elegant platinum band, and inside was inscribed the word *Forever*. He could buy a new ring, but somehow he thought Cassie would appreciate the significance of a family heirloom.

"Thank you. It's beautiful. She has to say yes now."

"She'll say yes because she loves you. I was trying not to pry, but I saw you at the Sandpiper the other night on the dance floor. She looked at you the way a woman looks at the man she loves."

"I hope so." He didn't know what he'd do if she said no. Which was why he wasn't going to ask until he'd had time to prove himself to her. He couldn't risk rushing her and pushing her away.

"Remember, don't say anything. We'll tell her parents today about the baby, but then she needs some time. I'm not going to rush her, so you're just going to have to be patient."

"I won't say a thing. Now go get cleaned up before you go over there. You look like something the cat dragged in."

"Gee, thanks." Between her and Nic, his ego was taking a beating. "You sure know how to flatter a guy."

She waved her finger at him. "You don't need flattery. You need a shower and a shave. Maybe a haircut, too. I can get my scissors—"

"No, no, that's okay. I'll take care of it." He put the ring in his pocket and gave her a hug goodbye. He was grateful for her support, but right now the woman he needed to see was Cassie.

Cassie bowed her head for the closing prayer, adding her "Amen" to those of the congregation. Once the organ belted out the final hymn, she made her way up the aisle to the main doors, dodging the line of people waiting to shake hands with the priest. Normally she would join the throngs that stood around chatting after the service, but today she was too keyed up.

Emma was just finishing up her snack when Cassie got to her classroom to pick her up. Her craft for the week, an angel with glittery wings, was drying on the table next to her. "Hey, sweetie, time to go to Grandma and Grandpa's house."

Emma sucked the last of her juice from the little cardboard box and nodded. After saying her goodbyes she walked out with Cassie, clutching her masterpiece, as if it were made of jewels instead of glue and glitter. "Can I give my angel to Grandma?"

"Sure, honey. I bet she'd like that." Loading her into the car seat, Cassie was careful not touch the glue on

Emma's still-wet creation. "Oh, and Deputy Alex is going to be there, too. Is that okay?"

The little girl's eyes lit up. "Yay! Is he going to bring Rex, too?"

"I don't know. Maybe." Starting the car, she headed toward her parents' home on the outskirts of town. Butterflies flew a serpentine pattern in her stomach as she got closer, a combination of nerves, anticipation and hormones. Rolling her window down helped. The rush of fresh salt air settled her stomach and cleared her head, leaving just the excitement of seeing Alex again. She needed to know that what happened last night wasn't a dream. It had seemed real last night, but in the light of day it was hard to believe.

Turning into the driveway, she spotted Alex's SUV parked by the house. He was early—maybe he was as eager to see her as she was to see him. Pulse thrumming, she let Emma out of the car and headed up the walk. They were still a few feet from the house when a loud bark announced their presence.

"Rex is here!" Emma broke into a run, her paper project fluttering in her hand.

"Hey, there." Alex opened the front door and watched Emma fly by him to look for her furry friend. "I guess I know which of us she really wanted to see." He smiled at Cassie, his dimples doing dangerous things to her heart.

"Sorry. Don't take it personally."

"I won't." He leaned down and gave her a quick kiss, then took hold of her hand. "I missed you."

Her cheeks heated. "I missed you, too. I was afraid I'd dreamed last night."

He lowered his voice so only she could hear. "Honey, if last night had been a dream, it would have ended with us in bed, not with me leaving to pick up my dog."

Every nerve ending flared. How was she going to get through today with that thought tormenting her?

"Cassie, there you are. Come on back. Alex was helping me man the grill."

Startled, she tried to drop Alex's hand, but he kept a firm grip.

"I don't want to hide, Cassie. Especially given the circumstances. Unless you have some reason you don't want people to know about us?"

"No, it's not that. I'm just...surprised, I guess. I'm not used to thinking of us as, well, an *us*." He'd said he wanted to make things work, to be with her, but what did that mean, really? One minute she was rude to him, the next he saved her daughter, and now they were having a kid together. Where in all of that did holding hands fit in?

Apparently not as prone to overthinking as she was, Alex pulled her along with him to the back patio. At the far end, sweet-smelling smoke wafted from the grill. Down on the grass, Emma was playing some kind of elaborate game with Rex involving a half dozen tennis balls and a soccer net.

Her father turned from cooking the food when they came out, his eyes widening a fraction when he saw them holding hands. Looking from one to the other, he raised an eyebrow. "Elizabeth, why don't you come out here and join us?"

Her mother stepped out onto the patio, wearing a striped apron over her jeans and blouse. "What is it, David? I'm not done with the coleslaw yet."

He reached into his wallet and pulled out a ten-dollar bill. "I just wanted to pay up on our little bet."

"Bet?" Cassie glared at her father. "What bet?"

Her mother took the money and tucked it into her apron pocket. "Your father was being hardheaded and wouldn't listen when I told him you two were falling for each other." She shrugged. "Anyone could see it."

Cassie's mouth dropped open. They'd bet on her love life?

"Sorry I cost you a bet, sir," Alex said with a grin.

"No worries. You making my daughter happy is worth more than all the money in the world. Just take good care of her."

Alex cleared his throat and squared his shoulders. "I fully intend to, sir. Her and the baby."

"Excuse me?" Her father's shocked tone matched the look on her mother's face. "Baby?"

Stepping forward, Cassie met his gaze head-on. "I'm pregnant, Daddy. I'm sorry."

"Sorry. What do you mean, sorry?" Her mother waved away the apology. "You've always said you wanted a sibling for Emma someday. And we've always wanted more grandchildren, haven't we, David?"

At her mother's heated look, he quickly capitulated. "Of course we have. I was just surprised a bit, that's all. You two haven't known each other that long and—"

"And nothing, David Andrew Marshall. Love has its own timing, doesn't it, honey?" She held out her arms and Cassie accepted the hug, her eyes filling. "Now, when is this little bundle of joy going to make an appearance? We have so much to plan—a baby shower, your registry—"

"A wedding," Alex said.

"What did you say?" Cassie asked. She couldn't have heard that right. Except her parents looked as stunned as she felt.

"A wedding." He moved directly in front of Cassie, his gaze never wavering from hers. "I was planning to ask you later, when things calmed down." He shrugged. "It kind of slipped out."

"It slipped out? What on earth is that supposed to mean?" She heard the hysteria in her voice, but didn't particularly care. What did he expect with an announcement like that?

He ran a hand through his hair and took a deep breath. "It means that I messed up and got everything out of order, again." He turned to Cassie's father. "Sir, I'd planned to talk to you and Mrs. Marshall and ask for your blessing. Heck, I wanted to talk to Emma, too, and feel her out on the idea."

"And when was all this supposed to happen?" Cassie asked. Everything was happening so fast. Just last night she'd thought he was running out on her; now he wanted to marry her?

"Not for a while. I thought you needed some time

to adjust to the idea of us being together, to learn to trust me."

"I do trust you. I know I haven't acted like it, but I do."

"Well, then, maybe it's better this way. I know it's fast, but Cassie, I don't want to wait. I know what I want, and I want you."

Dumbfounded, she watched him pull a small box out of his pocket and get down on one knee.

Behind him, Emma climbed up the steps to come lean against Cassie's side. "What's he doing, Mommy? Did he fall down?"

Alex smiled at her. "I did fall, for you and your mommy. In fact, I'm head over heels in love with both of you."

Emma tilted her head, looking for injuries. "Are you going to be okay?"

"Well, that depends."

Heart thumping wildly, Cassie let him take her hand. Everything was happening in slow motion; even the birds seemed to have stopped chirping. "Cassie Marshall, you've already filled my heart and changed my life. I don't want to ever give that up. Please, will you marry me?"

"Mommy, say yes," Emma said in a stage whisper, her eyes like saucers.

Cassie hugged the little girl and whispered back, "I don't know. You think he might make an okay daddy?"

Emma nodded. "The best, and he'll bring Rex, too!"

Laughing, Cassie looked back down at Alex. "In that case, yes, Alex Santiago, I'll marry you." She winked at Emma. "But you have to bring Rex with you."

Chapter 20

Cassie pulled the last pin from her hair and breathed a sigh of relief. The fancy updo her mother had talked her into had turned out gorgeous, but she felt more herself with her curls loose around her shoulders. Across the room, Alex watched, his eyes smoky with desire. Sprawled on the bed, his bow tie long gone and his tuxedo shirt open at the neck, he was the sexiest man she'd ever seen. And as of a few hours ago, he was her husband.

She'd wanted a small, quiet ceremony, but between her mother and Alex's mom, who was possibly the sweetest woman on the planet, she'd been outvoted. Almost half the island had ended up in attendance. At least she'd gotten her way with the location. They'd been married in her parents' backyard, only a month after Alex had proposed. Tomorrow, they'd be leaving for their honeymoon, a trip to Puerto Rico to meet some of Alex's relatives. But tonight Emma was with her grandparents, and she and Alex were finally alone.

"Think you could help me take off my dress?"

"I thought you'd never ask." In an instant, he was behind her. But before he had a single button undone, there was a knock at the door.

"Don't answer it."

"I have to. It could be my mom—something could be wrong with Emma. I'll be right back, I promise." She started for the front door, the silken skirt of her dress swishing as she walked.

Alex followed, padding barefoot down the hall. "Whoever it is, they had better be quick."

Silently agreeing, Cassie opened the door, then nearly slammed it shut again. Heart pounding, she stared at the man on the doorstep.

Behind her, Alex stiffened. "Who is it?"

Cassie opened the door the rest of the way, making room for Alex to stand beside her. "Jack Campbell, the man I told you about from the accident." Her voice shook, but she stood tall. She was not going to let him frighten her.

Alex stepped forward, positioning himself in front of Cassie. "You shouldn't be here, Jack."

Swallowing, Jack nodded, taking in Cassie's wedding dress and Alex's tux. "I'm sorry, I didn't realize... Well, I mean, I'd heard Dr. Marshall was getting married, but I didn't know it was today."

"Well, it was, and you're interrupting our wedding night. So if you would just go—"

"I will. I just need to say something to the doc first." He peered around Alex to make eye contact with Cassie. "I just wanted to tell you I'm sorry—"

"Jack, I don't think now is the time—" Alex moved to close the door.

"No, it's okay." She'd spent too long thinking about this; she didn't want to bring it into her new life with Alex. "Let him have his say." Maybe then she could put it behind her.

Jack twisted his hands together. "I came to say I'm sorry about the accident. I'd been drinking that night. Hell, I drank every night. But I'm not drinking anymore—I'm in a program now. One of those twelve-step programs. And one of the steps is to admit my mistakes and try to make things right where I can. I admitted everything to the department, and they put me on a leave of absence." His voice cracked and his shoulders started to shake. "I can't fix what happened to you and your dad, but I'm going to make sure I don't hurt anyone else. I promise you that."

Cassie listened, waiting for the familiar surge of anger she felt whenever she even thought of Jack Campbell. She'd spent months convincing herself she hated him. Here he was, and all she felt was pity. "Thank you, Jack. That means a lot to me."

Alex wrapped an arm around her in support. "Stick with it, man. You have a family that needs you."

"I know, and I'm going to do right by them. Anyway, I'll leave you folks alone now. Oh, and congratulations." Backing down the walk, he grabbed an old bicycle and hopped on. Watching him ride off, she felt free. His confession had given her permission to move on.

"Are you okay?" Alex closed the door, checking that it was locked securely.

"I'm better than okay." She pressed her body against his, feeling the hard muscles of his chest against her breasts. "Now, are you going to make this marriage official or what?"

She barely had the words out before Alex stilled her lips with a kiss. Hungry for her, he teased at her lips, needing to taste her. She moaned into his mouth, pulling at his clothes. Without ending the kiss, he stripped his clothes off, giving her busy hands access to his body. Gritting his teeth against the throbbing need to take her, he pulled back.

"Let me undress you." Slowly, one by one, he undid the long line of pearl buttons, teasing himself with each peek at the skin beneath. As the last one gave way, the dress slid to the floor in a puddle of silk and lace. Dear Lord, she was completely nude underneath. "If I'd known you weren't wearing anything under this, I don't think I would have made it through the ceremony."

She turned, smiling, and his heart skipped a beat. This beautiful, sexy woman was his wife. The soft swell of her belly was his child. "Cassie..."

She came to him, pulling his head down to hers for a soft but sensual kiss. He couldn't wait any longer; she felt too good and he needed her too badly. Sweeping her up into his arms, he carried her down the hall to her bed—their bed now. Afraid of hurting her or the baby, he eased her down on top of him, letting her take control. The first time they'd made love, it had been frantic and out of control. This time, there was no rush, no fumbling, just her body and his, skin to skin and soul to soul until they melted together in a single moment of pure pleasure.